IRRESISTIBLE

BELLA MOXIE

*S*avina's steps faltered at the sound of a glass breaking.

"On your knees, lass." A male voice reached her in the brothel's back hallway, muffled but harsh.

She forced herself to keep moving, but her breaths were shallow and quick and her belly twisted with fear.

Men's boisterous laughter and answering high-pitched squeals and giggles grew louder with every step Savina took toward the brothel's parlor.

Madame Bernadette would be waiting for her.

One foot in front of the other, she left the relative safety of the dark alley behind as she walked further into this den of sin and vice.

"Savina, wait!" The hushed cry brought her to a stop. "Savina!" Her sister hissed from the doorway leading into the alley.

She whipped around and glared at Margot. "What are you doing here?"

Margot's dark eyes were wide with anguish as she rushed

forward. "Don't do this." She clung to her arm, and Savina didn't have the heart to shake her off.

She could have. Easily. Her sister was only one year younger, but she was far smaller thanks to years of sickness that had left her frail and slender.

Would Margot have been this frail if they'd never been forced out of their childhood home? Likely not. She'd no doubt be hale and healthy, a pink-cheeked brunette beauty thanks to doctors and hearty meals.

Savina felt an all-too familiar pang of regret before she harshly shoved it away.

She'd learned long ago that wondering what might have been was a fruitless endeavor. What mattered was surviving this moment, here and now.

And right now, Margot's pleading eyes were too big in her pale face—a vivid reminder of why Savina had to do what needed to be done.

"We'll find another way," Margot's voice pitched with panic.

"Like what?" She kept her tone soft, but her grip was firm as she removed Margot's hand from her arm.

"We'll...we'll go to Mr. Capp again." Margot's voice continued to rise in desperation.

Savina's heart gave a painful lurch. She might be dreading what was to come, and her pride shrieked at the idea of selling her body to some lecherous old brute just so she and her sister could eat.

But her own horror was nothing compared to seeing her sister's despair.

It was moments like these when Savina was nearly overcome with the urge to give in to her fury. The injustice of their situation. The hideousness of what she'd already done and would do again just to keep her sister alive...

Dipping her head, Savina forced down this swell of impotent rage. It had no place here. It never did any good.

Fighting their current reality was just as useless as wondering what might have been.

Once her hands were steady, she unclenched her fists and reached out to cup her sister's cheek. Margot's heart-shaped face tipped up, and Savina's heart swelled with affection at the sight of her sister's big brown eyes and delicate features.

Her skin had always been pale as snow which was why their father had dubbed her his little snow angel when they were little.

But now that ivory skin was too pale, a fact made more worrisome thanks to the dark shadows beneath her eyes.

Margot looked far too delicate for a place like this. Because she was. She was too delicate for Vestry Lane, and far too good.

This squalid stretch of dark alleyways and dirt-covered lanes didn't deserve an angel like Margot. "Hush, little snow angel." She'd hoped to tease a smile from her sister with the use of her old nickname. But it only served to make Margot's lower lip quiver as she gazed up at Savina.

Savina who, despite their lack of age difference, had been the one to take care of them both ever since their stepmother had banished them to this depraved rookery more than five years ago.

It had been Savina who'd begged and borrowed and, yes, *stole* for their supper. They'd both done their best to get the odd job and make their way, but with Margot's weak lungs, the most taxing of tasks fell to Savina.

Like this one.

"I'll talk to Mr. Capp," Margot said, her voice thin and hushed.

But she already knew it would do no good. Savina had

burnt that bridge well and good. Which was why it was up to her to find a new way for them to survive.

"He likes me," Margot insisted. "And surely he needs us—"

"He doesn't."

Margot flinched at her sister's hard tone. But it was the truth. It'd been nearly two years since Mr. Capp had hired Savina to work as a servant in his tavern. Two years of emptying chamber pots and cleaning up vomit and doing her very best to avoid the wandering hands and the vile men who'd corner her in the dark shadows.

It'd been two years of walking to work with a quivering belly, terrified of what awaited her. But at the end of the day she'd get her pittance, along with the dirty laundry which she'd brought home to Margot, who'd earned what she could by washing other people's filth off their clothing.

But the older Savina got, the harder it was to hide the swell of her bosom and the curve of her bottom. It wasn't just the customers who noticed. It was Mr. Capp himself.

And while Savina had done things in the past that she tried her best not to remember, this was one thing she hadn't been able to inflict upon herself.

Maybe if she'd had time to think.

Maybe if he hadn't caught her so unawares in that dark alley. Perhaps she could have reasoned her way out of it.

Yes, she knew she could have endured it for her sister's sake. Just as she'd endure it today. But he'd caught her by surprise, and his pawing hands and sour breath had been too much too quickly and…

Blast. What did it matter now? There was no turning back time to undo what she'd done.

And there was no chance in hell that he'd ever forgive her or her sister for the fact that one well-placed knee to his groin had left the tavern owner doubled over, moaning in pain.

He'd threatened to kill her as she'd run. And truly, the threat hadn't scared her, even though she knew he was capable of it.

A swift death was nothing to fear in Vestry Lane.

But Mr. Capp had done something worse. He'd taken away her measly income, and Margot's too, leaving them to face a long, slow, miserable death by starvation.

But no. Not anymore.

Not when she was still alive and capable of doing whatever needed to be done to ensure her sister's safety.

Savina straightened. "Sweetheart, I need you to go back home—"

"No!"

Savina forced her smile. Out of the corner of her eye she could see one of Madame Bernadette's burly guards edging toward them from the back exit.

No, it wasn't a guard. She breathed out a sigh of relief. It was King. A good kid, a couple years younger than she and Margot, but larger and stronger, with far more experience in surviving on the streets.

He was the first friend they'd found in Vestry Lane, and likely the only reason they'd survived those first few years.

It was he who'd taught Savina to defend herself the way she had. He would've doubled over laughing if he'd seen the way she'd laid old Capp out on the piss-covered cobblestones.

She was grateful to see him now, because it was hard enough to face the task ahead and she'd never see it through if Margot didn't walk away. "Go, Margot. I need you to go."

"But you shouldn't have to do this, you can't—"

"I can and I will." Savina's voice grew with more confidence than she felt. Truthfully, her stomach churned and her legs trembled at the thought of what was to come. But she'd survive it.

And these days, surviving was all that mattered.

"Go on." Savina pointed down the alley. "Go. Before Madame Bernadette sees you and gets ideas."

The very thought made Savina shudder, and she dropped her hands to Margot's shoulders to give her a push.

"I'll do it for you." Margot's voice grew sharp and loud. "You've sacrificed too much already. Savina, please, you—"

"King," Savina cut her sister off, turning to the lad with the handsome face and the eyes that were far too wise for one so young. "Take my sister home."

"No." Margot's eyes welled with tears. "Don't do this for me. We'll find another way."

King gave Savina a nod as he took Margot by the shoulders. "Come on then, Snow. You're only making it harder on her."

Savina swallowed and turned away. King was right.

She was dreading having her body used, and most likely abused, by some stranger looking to satisfy his urges, but seeing Margot's anguish on her behalf only made her own emotions rebel against the hard vise she'd clamped over them.

She took a moment to steady her breathing...and that was how Madame Bernadette came to find her.

Better known as Bernie to those who lived in Vestry Lane, the woman was famed for her garish wigs and painted face. The owner of this godforsaken den of sin, she was one of few who had coin to spare and enough food to keep her satisfied...and she had the full bosom and rounded hips to show for it.

"What's taking you so long, princess?" Bernie sneered. "Your man's waiting for his whore."

2

*S*avina's lip curled in disgust as the other woman's cloying perfume wrapped around her.

"Don't tell me you're thinking of backing out," the old madam taunted. Her eyes held a glint of malicious triumph.

For years now she'd been telling Savina that she was too proud for her own good. That one day she'd end up on her back in her brothel just like all the other whores.

Savina swallowed hard and set her features into a mask. Tears stung the back of her eyes and made her throat ache, but she wouldn't allow Bernie to see that.

It was bad enough that Bernie had been proven right.

Never, Savina had said so many times over the years. *I'll never be one of your whores. That will* never *happen.*

Her own words came back to taunt her now. Perhaps it was inevitable. Maybe she'd been a fool to think she could avoid this outcome. Savina blinked and bit the inside of her lip until it bled to keep tears at bay.

But Madame Bernadette laughed knowingly. "Now, now, love. It ain't that bad. I got you a better deal than most, didn't I?"

Savina's nostrils flared, her lips quivering. But this woman was her employer now. This woman owned her body.

But not my mind, not my heart, and most definitely not my soul.

She'd do what she had to do to keep Margot fed and healthy, and she'd do it without regret. But she wouldn't let this woman or this wretched place get the best of her.

She faced Mrs. Bernadette with arched brows. "What are we waiting for? Let's not be late for our customer."

The old woman's eyes lit with amusement and she cracked a smile. "You sure are an uncommon one, aren't ya? Just as high and mighty now as you were back in the day." Bernie's laugh was nothing short of a cackle. "When are ye gonna learn that you ain't no well-bred young lady, but a common guttersnipe just like everyone else."

A well-bred young lady.

The air rushed from her lungs. That was exactly what she'd been. But no one in Vestry Lane knew that, and Savina had to remind herself that this old crone was referring to those first years in Vestry Lane when she was still a child.

Back then she'd been young and sheltered and hadn't known how to act like anything *but* a young lady.

Oh, how the whores and drunkards had laughed at the two little girls, with their pretty, frilly dresses and their elegant manners.

Where's your mama, child? A lecherous old coot had leered down at them as they'd begged for food outside a tavern not far from here.

Margot had started to cry.

She's dead, sir, Savina had said. *But our Papa's just in there.* She'd nodded to the tavern. *He'll be out to collect us any moment now.*

Margot had cried harder as the drunkard stumbled off, no doubt in search of easier prey.

Papa's never coming back, Margot had whispered.

Savina had wrapped an arm around her sister's shoulders and held her tight. Their father had passed away only a month before. They both knew he wasn't coming back.

But it was one thing to know a fact, and another to fully understand it.

Savina suspected that was the moment she and Margot had fully grasped how alone they truly were in this world. That they had no one to rely on but each other.

It was the thought of Margot that had Savina's chin notching up as she tossed her long blonde curls over her shoulder in a manner so haughty she knew it would rile the old hag. "Well? Are you going to take me to him or shall I find him on my own?"

Bernie smirked."Good thing for me the fella who requested you is a right mean one. He won't stand for your airs, mark my word."

Bernie's sneer turned Savina's stomach, bile burning the back of her throat at what awaited her in Bernie's notorious back rooms. "No doubt this gent's got a firm hand. He'll put you in your place at long last, pet."

The fella who requested you...

"He requested me?"

Bernie shrugged as she led the way, past the drawing room and through a back hallway that smelled of opium and ale.

"Real particular, this one," Bernie muttered. "Wanted a young plaything. Pretty. Fair hair. Only the best for this bloke."

Savina's breathing grew shallow as they turned a corner toward the private rooms.

The hallway was narrow and dark, and the smell of ale gave way to the scent of sex and tobacco.

From somewhere down the hall came the sound of moaning, a woman's cries muffled.

Bernie kept talking, all about how this gentleman might look fearsome but had the money to get whatever he wanted. Already paid upfront for the honor of taking her maidenhead. "He's one of them wicked types, I suppose." Bernie's smile was cruel. "Likes to be the one to break in a new colt. I know the type well. Nothing gives them more pleasure than dominating a young, spirited thing like you." Bernie cackled. "Mark my words, princess. He'll put you in your place."

With each new step, Savina's fear grew. And it had little to do with Bernie's talk of this man's firm hand.

She'd been beaten often enough by employers and angry drunks that she didn't fear the back of a man's hand. It was what he'd do when he had her alone. The places he'd touch her. The liberties he'd take…

A shudder rippled through her but she didn't stop walking even as the hallway grew dimmer and they headed up a narrow flight of stairs.

Much as she didn't want to have her first job for Bernie take place in that drawing room, in front of a crowd, the idea of a private room scared her half to death.

She'd heard from the whores that the drapes of Bernie's private rooms were made of thick velvet, the bedding of the finest quality…and the doors secured with heavy locks.

Through the thin walls, Savina could hear the sound of grunts and the bed banging against the wall.

But as they drew further into the brothel, an occasional clink of coins told its own story, one that spoke of extravagant pleasure bought at a high cost.

Only wealthy merchants and high-born lords could afford these private rooms. And if they were coming to this part of town to have their desires indulged, it meant their desires were the sort to be kept secret.

She ordered her feet to keep plodding ahead when all she wanted to do was turn and flee. She itched to run to the hovel she and Margot shared with three others, take her sister and their meager belongings and go.

But where?

Her mouth went dry as they reached a new landing, and a fresh wave of sounds hit her. Not as loud and raucous as the first floor common room, but these sounds were all the worse for being muffled.

She heard a whimper, a cry, the undeniable sound of flesh on flesh…

A loud shriek made her jerk, and Bernie tipped her head back with a laugh at her expense.

"Oh yes, I've learned how to read clients, love, and this one is as dark as they come." She eyed Savina from head to toe. "I can hardly wait to see your uppity little arse when he's done with you." She leaned in close and Savina's nose wrinkled at the sour smell of her breath. "You won't be able to walk by the time he's had his fill."

Savina would normally have a response. But her mouth went dry as fear slid through her veins like ice.

Uppity. Her mind latched onto that word. Madame Bernadette wasn't the only one to call her that, and she'd come to hate the term. It reminded her too much of those first months in Vestry Lane.

Look at the uppity little misses, a nasty bully had said that very first night after they'd been unceremoniously dumped in this alley. The lad had caught them hiding in what he claimed was his doorway.

Only hours earlier Savina and Margot had received the shock of their lives. More devastating, even than the news of their father's unexpected death, was the startle that came with being woken by their stepmother's cool hands dragging them out of their beds.

Servants they didn't recognize gripped their arms so forcefully they were left with bruises. The nameless, expressionless men had followed their stepmother's orders, dragging them with mouths muffled out into the cold night.

They'd only released them when they were in the dark carriage and their stepmother leaned in after them. *Consider yourselves fortunate I let you live.*

Her beautiful face was serene as ever but her tone was as sharp as a knife's edge.

Savina had felt a world of confusion at the emptiness in the woman's eyes. At the coldness that bordered on hatred. *If you dare to darken my doorstep again, I won't give you the same courtesy twice.*

She'd slammed the carriage door in their faces after her parting words.

And that had been the beginning of Savina's living nightmare.

So yes, she and Margot had been deemed uppity and high in the instep that very first night, and they couldn't seem to shake it. Savina supposed some of those manners they'd been taught as children couldn't be untaught, and it made them stand out no matter how hard they'd tried to fit in.

They were fortunate when they'd found King and a handful of other urchins who were just as desperate as they'd been. They'd banded together the best they could, and had somehow managed to survive.

But as Savina and Margot grew older, there was no hiding the fact that they were women, and no matter how hard he and his crew tried, King couldn't save them from every man who looked at them and saw prey.

Savina stopped in front of the closed door Bernie

gestured to, bitterness and bile rising up inside her in equal measure.

Maybe this had been her inevitable fate from the moment she'd been tossed in that carriage. Because this was what became of women in the rookery.

Uppity or not.

"You waiting for an invitation, love?" Bernie sneered. She opened the door, her fingers cold as ice as she grabbed Savina by the upper arm and shoved her inside.

The door slammed shut behind her.

For a moment Savina was blind. The room dark, much darker than the hallway and common room had been, and as her eyes adjusted to the dim light, she thought perhaps there was a mistake.

She was alone. There didn't seem to be anyone in here.

Until…

"You're even prettier than I was told." The low growl came from the shadows to her right, and Savina jumped back in surprise. The voice held a hint of an accent she couldn't quite place.

"Skittish, eh? I suppose that's to be expected."

Her jaw clamped shut. She wasn't a coward…usually.

Blast, she needed her courage now more than ever, but it'd scattered in the wind the moment he stepped out of the shadows, so large.

So dark.

He was backlit by the candlelight flickering behind him so she could hardly make out his features.

Dread pooled in her belly and a flare of panic surged through her veins making her limbs tremble despite her commands to be calm.

Men like him love to break uppity little girls like you.

She squelched the shiver that made her belly quiver and

tensed every muscle into submission. She would *not* show fear. Not in front of this man.

Not in front of *any* man.

He could hurt her physically, but she would not let him break her.

She would never let him inside where it counted.

"Quiet, too," he murmured. "That's good."

She held her breath as he moved, but he didn't lunge straight for her. Instead, he seemed to unfurl from the shadows, growing ever taller and broader as his form melded with shadows and he slowly paced around her like a predatory cat sniffing out its prey.

As he grew near, she caught a whiff of sandalwood and leather, a rich, spicy aroma.

She couldn't make out much of his face, just glimpses of hard angles and deep-set eyes. But she could feel his gaze on her. What was more, she could feel his power like a palpable force in the room. It was in the quiet command of his tone and the easy confidence with which he moved his tall frame.

This was a man used to being in control. A man who no doubt preferred women he could control as well. He stalked behind her before surprising her by moving away, toward what she could now see was a bed, a candle flickering on the nightstand beside it. "Your owner says you're a biddable little thing—"

"She's not my owner." The words came out far softer than she'd intended. But with his every step out of the shadows and into the soft glow of the candle on the nightstand, he seemed to grow larger. Broader.

She saw the cut of his jaw now, and the straight line of his nose, and the deep furrow of his brow. When he reached the bed, he turned to face her, and there was no hint of kindness to lighten the darkness of his eyes, no hint of a smile to soften the grim hardness of his face.

A formidable man, to be sure. And handsome, she supposed, for an older man.

She could make out the lines near his eyes and on his forehead now, and a hint of gray at his temples where a scar cut down his right cheek.

He was older, but there was nothing even remotely feeble about this man. If anything, he seemed more terrifying now than he had when she'd entered. Her heart was pounding so harshly she could hear nothing but its thud in her ears.

But she forced herself to stand still. She would not run.

She would never cower.

The silence stretched, and the man's gaze never wavered from her. She felt him taking her in, all too aware that she was in the glow of another candle by the door. He could see all of her, while he was hidden in shadows.

His gaze raked over her, and when he finally spoke, her whole body seemed to jerk with awareness. "Take off your clothes. Now."

3

$\mathcal{P}$rince Edmund Halifax was doomed.

Surely there was no salvation for a man like him.

And yet, he continued to watch, mesmerized by this sweet young beauty, her movements jerky and her gaze filled with fear despite her attempts to appear unaffected.

His breathing grew ragged and a fire burned inside him, fueled by his own self-hatred and an undeniable reaction to her beauty.

He hated himself beyond measure. But that didn't stop his cock from growing impossibly hard or his lungs from filling with fire as this searing heat scorched him from the inside out.

God, she was stunning. Not just beautiful, no. She was a work of art.

And she's mine.

He stiffened at the unbidden thought. She was his responsibility. But she was not his. Not like that.

Not in the way his body wished to claim her as his own.

But the word *mine* still clung to his thoughts. It worked its way through his body as surely as blood pumped through his veins.

And all the while he watched her like a hawk. He drank in her beauty, taking in the sweet planes of her face, the angle of her jaw, and the courage written in every curve of her body.

It wasn't until her fingers fumbled with the fastening at her neckline that he came to his senses.

It was that small hint of fear that jolted him back to sanity.

Christ. What was he doing?

"I'm not going to ravish you, love." His voice was still too gruff, raw with hunger and little more than a growl.

Love. Where the fuck had that come from?

Her hands stilled.

Don't stop. He bit off the harsh command before it could escape. But just barely. His hands reached blindly for the edge of the bed, for something to hold onto lest he give in to this overwhelming urge to reach for her.

No. He wouldn't reach for her...not right away.

His loins stirred, tension coiling as his mind's eye filled with the fantasy of what he'd do. He wouldn't reach for her. Not at first.

First he'd have her start what he'd started. He'd watch her strip off those grubby, torn clothes that were an insult to her beauty, and he'd savor the sight of every sweet inch of flesh. He'd no doubt lose control before she got far and then he'd take over, tearing away that flimsy linen so he could feast on the sight of those lush breasts that he could see only the rounded tops of now. Then he'd tear that blasted dress in two to see her soft belly and her long legs, and...

Bloody hell, he was the devil himself for thinking about what he'd see between her thighs. Of the sweet, tight cunny he knew deep down in his gut was made for him and him alone.

His gaze lifted and he found himself once more staring into her eyes. His chest ached as he noted the tension in her shoulders and caught the hint of fear in the tightness around her eyes.

"I'm not here to hurt you," he said.

Her gaze grew shuttered.

Oh she tried so hard to hide that fear, and he suspected that was what truly took her from pretty to breathtaking.

So brave yet sensitive, so strong yet so vulnerable. He'd never seen anything like it in his life, and his heart pounded furiously with reverence and awe.

She made him want to drop to his knees at her feet, to worship her like a queen even as he fought the urge to scoop her into his arms and take her someplace he could have her all to himself.

Like a bloody devil, he found himself fighting the urge to do just that.

Steal her for himself.

Her eyes were wide with thick lashes that brushed against impossibly high cheekbones every time her lids fluttered in surprise. Her lips were so lush they looked swollen, as if she'd just been kissed.

A possessive anger shot through him hot and fierce, followed by a rage that filled him so completely he nearly forgot himself entirely. "Have you been with another man?"

He would kill any man who touched her. Then he'd tear that brothel owner limb from limb.

The moment he'd discovered where Savina was he'd made it clear that she had to remain untouched.

But what if he'd been too late?

Savina gaped at him, those swollen lips parting. "P-pardon?"

He ran a hand over his face, forcing a deep inhale. This wasn't why he was here. There was no time to waste.

"You requested a virgin," she said softly, as if reminding him.

No, he'd requested *her*. And he'd hoped like hell she was still a virgin when he'd described his ideal whore for that wretched excuse of a lady who owned this place.

Have men been forced on you? Did they hurt you? Am I too late to save you from that hell?

Of course he was too late. He was years too late.

He didn't know where to begin and she spoke before he could, her voice little more than a whisper but filled with such strength it made his chest tighten with an odd sort of pride. "You are my first...customer."

Relief left him in a ragged exhale. "Very well."

"Do I..." She wet her lips, her gaze darting about. "Do you still want me to..." Her fingers hovered.

Do you want me to strip for you? That's what she meant.

And yes. Fuck yes. There was nothing he wanted more right now than to see her fully. Every inch of her. He wanted to see her and taste her and then claim her as his own.

A shriek came from another room and he caught the girl's flinch.

Bloody hell. He wanted to do all those things, but not here. Not now.

And if he had any speck of honor and gentility, he'd never give in to his obsessive urges. But even as he thought it, his gaze caught on the sight of her fingers hovering over her clothes, like some sort of untutored seductress sent from hell. His very own siren...

"Undress," he barked, harsher than intended. "Those rags are filthy."

Her lips pressed together as she bent her head and resumed her task. This time he had the good sense to turn away from her.

He reached for the fabric on the bed, the gown he'd

brought with him. He tossed it in her direction. "When you're done, put this on."

There was silence, and then..."

"I...I don't..."

He heard her confusion, and hated himself for frightening her. He should have told her straight away that he wouldn't touch her.

"I don't understand." Her voice was level but he heard the quiver of confusion and fear underneath her bravado.

He glanced over his shoulder and...mistake.

This was a mistake.

She'd done as he asked and she now stood in nothing but her underthings. Fucking hell. His imagination was wretchedly incompetent. He understood that now.

Look away.

The command went unheeded as he drank her in from those elegantly arched brows, down to her pointed chin, her slender shoulders, the creamy, tantalizing curve of her breasts, and lower. All the way down to her stocking-clad toes, his eyes soaked in the sight like he was a starving man and she his feast.

But she wasn't.

She could never be.

And while he knew this logically, right now this fact seemed to be the most crushing disappointment he could imagine. To be this close to perfection and unable to do more than steal a glimpse.

And she *was* perfect. She'd grown up to be a beauty beyond compare. She was a goddess even in these tattered rags that passed for underthings. She ought to be adorned in the finest of silks and lace.

And she will be.

He finally tore his gaze away, focusing on dragging in

ragged breaths and relaxing the muscles that had bunched and tightened.

His hard shaft there was no cure for. Nothing short of burying himself between her thighs would ease this ache.

He shook off the thought.

He had to get her away from here. That was what mattered. Everything else was merely a distraction.

"You wish for me to don this gown?" Her voice was laced with confusion.

"Yes."

"But…why?"

He turned back to face her then, and the sight of her half-clothed and expectant—waiting for him to touch her. To taste her lips…

Desire ripped through him like fire, and he found himself barking at her as he fought to control it. "Just put it on, little girl."

Her lips parted and her throat worked, but she didn't flinch or show any hint of being hurt by his harsh tone.

His hands tightened into fists. He hadn't meant to snap. But the 'little girl' was for his benefit, not hers. It was a reminder of who this was and why she wasn't his to touch.

No matter how tempting. She might be a fully grown adult now, but she was still decades younger than him.

She held his gaze a moment longer, and then, pressing her lips together in a thin line, she held up the high-quality gown…and dropped it at her feet.

Admiration and intrigue did nothing to squelch this hot surge of lust he felt in her presence. If anything, it made reason harder to latch onto. His tone grew harder, darker. "You think to defy me?"

It was a tone that made grown men quake on the battle-field but she merely straightened her shoulders and lifted her chin.

Impertinent little imp.

His chest swelled with that feeling again. Something like pride. Which was irrational, obviously. He'd had no part in her raising, and she was nothing to him but a responsibility.

A reminder of a duty he'd failed to uphold.

But try as he might to remember that, the way she held herself went beyond appealing. She was temptation itself, as if crafted solely to appeal to his desires.

His cock ached for attention, and the sound of fucking going on in the next room didn't help matters. It filled his head with images of all the ways he'd take her. All the ways he'd make her scream his name…

"For fuck's sake," he muttered, glancing away.

"If you want to bed me, then bed me," she said, her tone hard and nearly convincing with its bravery. "I don't want any part of this…game of yours."

He didn't miss the way fear flashed in her eyes, and her fear stirred his anger.

Not at her, but *for* her. On her behalf. There was no justice in a world where this young lady had to fight her own battles. He strode toward her. "I told you I would not ravish you," he clipped. "And I meant it."

Confusion flickered in the depths of those brilliant blue eyes. "Then what…" She paused to swallow. "What do you mean to do to me?"

He reached a hand out and his gut twisted in anger when she flinched.

Someone had struck this girl. Or perhaps more than one person had taken a hand to her.

If he ever found out who he'd ensure they died a slow and painful death.

And that had nothing to do with the promise he'd made to her father all those years ago; it was a vow he made to himself right here and now.

He touched her cheek as gently as he could. Which wasn't all that gentle, really. He was a large man, with big hands and calloused fingers from years of riding and working alongside his men on the front lines.

Her gaze was cloudy with confusion when it met his. "What are you about?" she whispered. "What is this game?"

His heart faltered. "It's no game, love."

He ought to explain what brought him here and the plan he had for her when she walked out that door.

But the problem was…

His plan was shite.

He couldn't tell her everything he'd intended when he'd come here. All that had changed now. One touch of her skin and he knew with utter certainty that he'd been mistaken.

He couldn't go through with it.

But he still had to take her from this wretched place. And he would find a way to get them both what they deserved.

Revenge.

Her brows drew down, her lower lip trembling slightly as she waited for him to give her a command or, at the very least, explain himself.

But he needed to reassess his strategy. To look at the battlefield and gauge the best course of action.

Which meant…he needed time. He'd spent too long leading entire battalions to know that strategy was everything, and it couldn't be rushed.

And so he hesitated a beat too long.

Long enough for her to wet her lips again, calling his attention to that sweet little mouth of hers. "Then you don't want…" She hesitated, her brows drawing down. "You don't want *me*?"

Oh bloody hell. The air rushed from his lungs as his blood surged toward his loins.

You don't want me?

24

He'd never wanted anyone or anything more.

He didn't say that, of course, but whatever she saw in his eyes must have been answer enough because he heard her breath catch as she stumbled back a step.

"Easy, child," he murmured.

Her head snapped up, her eyes flashing. "I'm no child."

His lips twitched with an unfamiliar urge to laugh.

"Do not laugh at me," she snapped.

"My apologies." He continued to fight his smile. "But it's rather amusing to hear you claim you're no child while sounding like a petulant little brat."

Her brows pinched together quickly, her gaze burning hot and indignant.

"Stand down, little one," he murmured. In truth, he was mesmerized by that fiery glare.

Lord, but she'd be a sight to behold in the throes of passion.

"Little one, child, little girl," she sneered, her tone still petulant as she recited the names he'd used.

She'd left out 'love.'

"What do you want with me if you think me such a child?" Her brow arched in an excellent attempt to appear unfazed.

You are no child, he wanted to say. In truth, there was nothing childlike about her, despite her age. She couldn't be much more than twenty, but she'd seen too much, he supposed. Been through too many hardships to still be an innocent.

But he couldn't explain that he had to see her as Leopold's child if he stood any chance of keeping his hands to himself.

She was his friend's daughter—even if she was no longer a child.

"I'm here to help you," he said slowly. "I came here as…as a friend."

She backed up a step, and he could see her guard rising as she eyed him warily. "I don't have any friends." Before he could respond, she added, "I don't want any, either."

"Perhaps your sister does," he shot back.

Her eyes narrowed. "I don't have a sister."

He tsked, and her cheeks flushed with anger. Or perhaps embarrassment at having been caught lying.

"We both know that Margot is your sister—"

"How do you know about Margot?" Her eyes flashed again, that temper of hers flaring in an unexpectedly heart-warming display of protectiveness. "What do you want with her?"

He held his hands up, hoping to calm her.

"If you think you can buy me with gowns...or that I'll let you near my sister because you speak kindly and—"

"How many times do I have to tell you I am not here to have my way with you? Or your sister, for that matter. I'm here as a friend—"

"I don't have friends, I—"

"As a friend of your father's." He spoke over her protest, and watched with some amusement as her eyes widened in shock.

"My father?"

He despised the wariness in her eyes. Hated even more the people who'd put it there—her stepmother most of all.

"My father is dead," she whispered.

His heart ached. For her. For the friend he'd long since lost. But mostly with regret for all the years that had passed since his death.

Years when he could only imagine all that she'd endured.

"I was his friend in childhood." He kept his voice quiet.

She had the air of a spooked animal, ready to claw and fight as if he'd backed her into a corner. It had come about the moment he'd mentioned her sister, and had worsened with talk of her father…

He had a suspicion that one wrong word about her family or her past, and she'd bolt into the hallway and out of his life for good, regardless of the fact that she was still half-naked.

"Your father was Leopold Flint, the Baron of Galinore, and he was the only child of—"

"How do you know who I am?" Her voice was a hiss as she glanced fearfully toward the door.

"I told you, I was his friend."

"I don't believe you."

He took a deep breath. "I met your father at school when we were young and we'd kept up our friendship long after. We became as good as brothers during the short time we were both in the military. We fought together at the Battle of—"

"Why are you here?" she interjected. "Why now?"

"Because…" There was so much he could tell her. So many mistakes. So many lies. So many regrets. But her gaze was expectant, her skin growing paler by the second. "Because I could not find you until now."

That was the long and the short of it, he supposed. It was all that mattered. "I wasn't there for you and Margot when you needed me," he continued. "But I am here now. And I want to help you."

She backed further away from him.

She needed space. Her eyes were darting around the room, eyeing him, the gown still lying in a heap on the floor, the door…

"She'll kill us." The words tumbled out of her mouth, fast and erratic.

It didn't seem as though she'd meant to say it aloud. She pressed her lips together after it escaped. But he heard it.

And hiding his murderous rage was nearly as difficult as

hiding the fact that being this close to her was the worst sort of torture he'd ever endured.

Which was saying something, considering he'd been a prisoner of war. He was half blind with lust despite all his self-recriminations and commands to ignore the way her breasts heaved as her breathing grew shallow.

Christ. The girl was in shock and all he could do was ogle her bosom.

Do better, Edmund.

He cleared his throat, his mind searching for a way to ease her fear.

"Chess," he said abruptly.

Her brows hitched. "Pardon?"

"Your father and I shared a love of the game."

She blinked once and then again. "Chess," she repeated.

He felt like a fool. "Yes. It's a, uh…a game played on a board—"

"I know what chess is. You…you played chess with him… at our house?"

"No." He tipped his head as he considered. "Well, not often. The last time I came to your house you were a child."

Her eyes narrowed a bit. "But I'm not any longer?"

"No." His voice came out raspy. "No, you're not any longer."

She seemed slightly appeased by that, and once more he felt a twinge of unfamiliar amusement. How incredible that after all she'd been through, this woman still had her pride.

"We played a long game." After a huff of amusement, he murmured, "It seems long games are my forte."

"What do you mean a long game?" she demanded.

"I mean, we exchanged letters over the years, and in each we'd make our move." A smile tugged at his lips at the memory that felt like it came from another lifetime.

Perhaps it had. So much had happened since then, it

hardly seemed like a real memory, but something he'd heard from a storybook.

Her lips parted and her eyes grew soft. "Are you…are you…" Her breath caught and then she let it out in a shudder. "Are you a prince?"

He did smile then, at the wonder in her voice. "Yes."

"From Prussia," she whispered.

He tipped his head.

"Prince Edmund," she murmured.

Something shifted in his chest. A tug of bittersweet satisfaction that she remembered him…or at least, remembered his name.

"We were never allowed to touch that chess board. The only time my father ever shouted at me was when I moved a bishop and nearly ruined your entire game."

Her lips curved up in a little smile that he knew wasn't for him. But it was so soft and sweet, it had him fighting a smile of his own.

"He was a good man." His voice came out gruff and croaky.

"He was."

"I'm sorry it has taken me so long to find you, Savina. I've only just discovered your whereabouts. I got here as quickly as I could."

She regarded him steadily. The wariness had faded, but he could not read whatever it was she was thinking as she studied him.

"I will get you out of here." He nodded toward the gown.

For the love of God, cover yourself. He swallowed the desperate plea. But he wasn't sure how much torture he could handle.

"I'll take you and Margot back to Mayfair, back to the life where you belong."

That had his thoughts darting back to his original plan. But now…

No.

There was no way. The thought of any other man touching her was abhorrent. He would not stand for it here, and he wouldn't allow it in good society either.

So what will you do with her then? Keep her for yourself?

He shook off the thought—the temptation. He'd figure all that out later. Once she was safe and away from this wretched whorehouse. "Just as soon as you fetch Margot, we'll be on our way."

She held his gaze for a long moment, clearly lost in thought. And then with a blink she seemed to come to her senses as she drew in a deep breath.

"No."

4

---

*S*avina's heart tripped and faltered at the flash of irritation in his eyes.

No. That was it. One word, but it settled between them like a rock, and the air seemed to ripple with an aftershock.

She'd offended him, that much was clear. He took a step forward, then another.

She tensed, and caught the way a muscle in his jaw ticked when she stiffened.

He stopped coming toward her, though. He stopped, still studying her like she was some riddle he couldn't decipher.

Which was good. It was better than how he'd been staring at her before.

She wasn't sure which was more disturbing—the hungry lust in his eyes when his gaze devoured her, or the way he'd insisted on treating her like some frightened, cowardly child.

She wasn't afraid.

Well...not of him.

But the thought of going back to society...

The thought of being anywhere near their stepmother...

Her stomach twisted at the memory of the one and only

time she and Margot had tried to return home. She'd held hopes of returning to Mayfair, to get help from their father's friends...or from anyone for that matter.

They hadn't heeded Lucinda's warning, and it had very nearly cost them their lives.

She shook her head now as Edmund took another step toward her.

Edmund. The Prussian prince her father used to speak so highly of. She still couldn't quite believe he was here. That this was him.

And that he was there to rescue her and Margot...?

Hope was a cruel little fiend, and she knew better than to trust that flicker of light.

She extinguished it quickly, letting her suspicions creep in, instead.

He was moving toward her still, slower now but with a determined look in his eyes. She forced her feet to stay put. She would not back away from him, and she wouldn't allow him to order her about like she was still a little girl.

She might be younger than him, but she hadn't had the luxury of innocence for far too long.

"No," he finally repeated, tasting the word as if he'd never heard it before.

He likely never had.

A nervous laugh started to rise up in her but she swallowed it down. She remembered her father telling her about this fearsome warrior, this commander of men...

No doubt he was not at all used to hearing the word 'no.' Not from his men.

And certainly not from a woman.

She swallowed thickly when he stopped so close she could smell the warm, spicy scent of his cologne as he towered over her. Tipping her head back to maintain his gaze, she tried to steady her heart.

It was no use.

She couldn't even pretend it was fear that had her belly fluttering and her lungs struggling to draw in air.

He was overwhelming, especially this close. So broad and well-built, and with an air of competence and confidence that made some part of her long to lean forward, to rest her weight against his chest and let him take care of her.

But there was that heat in his eyes that had her fighting the urge. It was a fire he tried to disguise, but she was no stranger to men's desires.

Unlike the drunken fools who were forever trying to grope her in the hallways and take liberties in the alley, however, this man's desire didn't turn her stomach.

Not in the least.

In fact, she felt an answering stir low in her belly that shocked her.

Was this what desire felt like?

His gaze dipped to her lips and her mind went blank. Only images filled her head. Vivid, visceral images of what it would feel like if he were to pull her into his arms. If that grim slash of a mouth were to cover hers...

"What are you thinking, little girl?" His voice was a low drawl and it held a hint of mockery.

She straightened. *Little girl.* A frown turned down the corners of her mouth, even though she knew she was giving him what he wanted. He'd said it as a taunt. He was trying to irritate her, and she couldn't say why.

His gaze moved over her face, down her neck, burning her skin everywhere it fell.

"Why would a woman who seems to be in full possession of her wits say no to my offer, hmm?" He reached a hand out and caught her chin, tilting it up so she was forced to meet his gaze. "Are you waiting for a better one, perhaps?"

Her nostrils flared as she tried to keep her temper in check.

"Are you wondering if the next man who comes to this room will make the same offer? Or perhaps you're curious to see what most men would do to that sweet body of yours."

A low sound escaped her. An embarrassing sound, halfway between a growl and a moan, as that prickly heat spread to her limbs and seemed to pool between her thighs.

"I'm not curious about what most men would do," she clipped. "Just you."

His eyes flared wide, and a second later his hand dropped as if she'd burnt him. She staggered back a step, nearly as shocked as he'd been by that comment.

It was true.

But that didn't change the fact that it was wrong. He was a stranger.

"You've learned how to play the coquette, I see." His expression was shuttered, the look in his eyes cold and hard. "The streets have taught you how to get what you want from a man, is that it?"

No hint of the warmth she'd seen when he'd told her of his friendship with her father. This was the military leader she'd heard about.

This... a fearful voice whispered, *this is a man who's not to be trifled with.*

And yet, that merely made her want to push even more. It made her want to see how far she could go before he snapped.

It made her ache between her thighs to think of what he'd do to her when he did.

"Isn't that what you want?" Her voice came out soft and almost husky, filled with a sensuality that took her by surprise. She hadn't even known she could sound like that.

She moved toward him, reveling in this newfound power

as she watched that coldness battle with a fire that matched the heat in her blood. "The way you're eyeing me now, my lord...I'd say you're the one who's going to get what he wants. Isn't that why you told me to undress for you? To go back to your home with you?"

God, what was wrong with her? That ache between her legs throbbed when his eyes flashed with anger. She held her breath when his hands clenched, and she found herself waiting for him to touch her...to take control of her...

He wanted to.

And heaven help her, she wanted him to reach for her, to grab her and hold her and—

"Your father would be ashamed," he growled.

Said so simply and yet it had the effect of a blow to her gut. No, it was worse than that. It was like a knife that sliced directly to her heart. She spun away from him before he could see just how much he'd hurt her.

A silence fell and wrapped around them, tense and unforgiving.

"I understand that you must be surrounded by men who want only what your body can offer." His words hit the air, low and rough.

"And you're trying to tell me you don't want that from me," she shot back over her shoulder, derision and disbelief poisoning every word.

He let out a huff. "I won't deny that you are an extraordinarily attractive woman, Savina. But if that was all I was interested in, we both know I could have had you the moment you entered this room."

She bit her lip as she considered that, and felt the warmth of his body as he came up close behind her. His voice was so low that it made her shiver.

"I could have refrained from telling you who I was," he

pointed out. "Instead of tossing you a fine gown, I could have watched you take off your clothes."

His hands came to rest gently on her shoulders, and her breath caught. Her breasts felt too heavy and they ached the same way her sex did. Her whole body felt this neediness that was new and confusing.

She leaned back into him, wanting more than the light touch of his hands on her shoulders. He didn't move his hands but he did dip his head so his breath fanned across her cheek with his next words. "I could have ordered you to touch yourself, or I could have forced you onto your knees…"

She shivered as his words conjured images in her mind's eye.

"I could have commanded you to lie on the bed, or perhaps I'd have been too eager for that. Maybe I would have just had you hitch up your skirts and bend over—"

"Stop." It came out weak and breathy, not at all the angry protest she'd meant it to be. "You're trying to embarrass me, but it won't work. You and father's other friends…you are the reason Margot and I are here. If I am a coquette, as you say…if I have no innocence left after surviving on these wretched streets, who do you suppose is to blame for that?"

She stopped, hating how her breasts heaved with emotions that were too heavy and too confusing to name. Hope warred with fear which battled with anger.

And beneath it all was this newfound sensation of longing that made her feel weaker and more vulnerable than she'd felt in years.

Christ, how she hated feeling weak.

He was quiet for so long, Savina began to think he wouldn't answer.

"You're right, of course." The grim resignation in his voice made her chest tighten. His hands shifted, turning her to face him.

This close she could well see the scar on his jawline and the crinkled corners of his eyes. "No amount of apologies will change what has been done." He stared down at her with such sincerity she felt tears clogging her throat. "But I am sorry, love. I am so sorry it took me so long to find you."

Her lips quivered, but she clenched her jaw and blinked hard and fast. She would not cry in front of this man...or *any* man.

She'd made that vow long ago.

"I was not there when you needed me," he said. "But I am here now. So come with me. If not for your sake, then for Margot's."

The words hit their target, no doubt as he'd planned. She'd do anything for her sister.

Which was precisely why she couldn't give in to that needy voice begging her to let this strong, powerful man solve all of her problems.

She drew in a deep breath. "Prince Edmund—"

"Just Edmund," he corrected. "Prince makes me sound like some sort of hero."

"And you're not?"

His lips twitched slightly, and the glint in his eyes was rueful. "I am not."

"Fine, then...Edmund." She wet her lips, trying to catch her breath. "Margot is the reason I must still refuse."

His brows lowered and...goodness.

She inhaled sharply. He was oddly striking when he stared at her like this—like he was a predator and she his prey.

It made her belly flutter and her heart pound...

It made her want to run just to see if he'd catch her.

"Surely Margot would be safer away from here," he started.

She shook her head, even as she wondered how much to confide. Did he know what Lucinda had done?

Was Lucinda still in Town?

Savina and Margot may have never left London, but they might as well have been living in another world these past five years.

If he knew Lucinda…

If he didn't believe her story or went to their stepmother to relay their claims…

She clamped her mouth shut. It was far too risky.

"What are you not telling me?" He shifted, crossing his arms and fixing her with a glare that made her feel rather like a disobedient child.

Or perhaps a naughty coquette.

There was that urge again—to push and taunt just to watch him lose control. To see that dark fire come to life in his eyes again...

"Savina," he said slowly. "I am not a patient man. Do not test me."

She pursed her lips, feigning a pout when really her mind was racing with how much she could admit to this man. "Margot is not well," she finally confessed.

This was true to some extent. Margot's health had recovered from her last illness, but she'd always been a frail child, and all these years of hard labor and squalid conditions had made her weaker still.

"What is wrong with her?" When she didn't immediately answer, he huffed in impatience. "Savina, surely her health would be much improved if she were to come to live with me. I could get her the best doctors and medicine and—"

"No!" It escaped before she could stop it. But all she could picture was Margot in society.

Margot coming face to face with Lucinda.

His eyes widened in surprise. "You're afraid."

It wasn't a question so she did not answer.

"She can not face the *ton* in her condition," she lied.

"I will ensure you are both welcomed as the daughter of a respected peer, the way you ought to be."

She narrowed her eyes, wishing she could read his mind to see just how much he knew about the reason they were here. About who had abandoned them to this life.

"I cannot claim to understand all that's been done to you." His expression grew somber. "But I mean to make it right."

She took a deep breath, trying not to be affected by those words. He made it sound so easy. For a moment she wondered if perhaps she'd died and awakened inside a fairy tale. One where handsome strangers arrived out of nowhere to save the desperate maiden.

It was a silly notion, made that much more ludicrous when she heard the shrieks coming from the couple in the next room.

She shuddered at the sound. Was that woman screaming in pleasure...or pain?

"If you are too afraid to face the ton—"

"I am not afraid," she snapped. At his arched brow, she added, "Not for my sake."

Indeed, even as she said it, a hot flood of anger shot through her. For years, she'd wished she could face Lucinda once more. Wished she could exact revenge...

She would have done it the last time they'd met three years ago but it had been impossible when Lucinda had a guard holding a knife to Margot's throat.

She straightened, a new idea taking hold. This man was offering her a chance to face Lucinda again. And perhaps this time she could do so without putting Margot at risk. "Send my sister away."

"Pardon?"

"Margot cannot face society in her state, and she needs to be somewhere with fresh air so she can recover."

He tipped his head, his eyes flashing with intelligence as he thought this through. "Do you not wish to go with her?"

"Do you wish for me to?"

His lips twitched and finally he admitted, "No. I'll confess, I have other plans for you."

"What plans?"

He shifted, and when his eyes dipped, she felt her heart leap everywhere his gaze fell. "That I cannot say just yet. Meeting you, I've...been forced to...reconsider."

She frowned. "Did I not live up to your expectations?"

A smile then. Small and secretive, but it took her breath away when it made his eyes crinkle and his gaze gleam. "On the contrary. You've exceeded them." His gaze flickered over her face as if drinking her in.

Savina wasn't sure anyone had ever looked at her this way. Like she was the only person in the world. The only one who mattered, at least. His gaze seemed to take in every last freckle and memorize every inch of her skin.

She knew for certain she'd never felt so...so seen.

It left her feeling oddly winded.

"That is the problem, you see," he added with another cryptic twist of his lips. "I was not anticipating....you."

Questions nagged at her. What was it he hadn't expected? What were his plans?

He stuck a hand out as if to shake her. "Do we have an agreement, then?" he asked. "I will make arrangements to ensure your sister is safely escorted to a property I own near Bristol. It is by the seaside with plenty of fresh air. There she will be under the best care, and you..."—he arched a brow—"You will join me. For my purposes."

That last part seemed to be added on as an afterthought

and the mystery in that promise made her shiver. But she slid her hand into his, because honestly...did she have any other choice?

His taunting had hit the mark earlier. It wasn't as though she had any other offers of help coming her way, and if Margot could be taken somewhere safe to recover...

His hand seemed to swallow hers in a grip that was firm and rough...surprisingly rough for a gentleman of such high standing, and his grip was so firm it made her wonder fleetingly if she should still run.

But Savina did not run. Ever.

And this man might have his secrets...and yes, perhaps she was right to fear him. But surely making a deal with this stranger was worthwhile if it meant she'd finally have her chance at revenge.

When he dropped her hand, he nodded toward the forgotten gown. "Now, if that's settled. Get dressed."

"Turn around first," she said.

With a sigh he did as he was told.

She watched his back warily as she bent over. For a little while there she'd forgotten just how naked she was, but she was keenly aware of it now as she slid the heavy gown over her, and ran her hands down a material so fine she nearly wept at all the memories it conjured.

"Could you help me?" She turned so he was faced with her back, and his hands deftly dressed her, an act so intimate it made her dizzy with that odd desire to let him take care of her.

But she wouldn't, of course.

She couldn't.

She turned to face him when he finished. "What will you tell Madame Bernadette?"

He chuckled. "What will she care what I do with you? I've paid for you, after all."

41

Of all the things he'd said and she'd done, for some reason that was what brought the heat of humiliation into her cheeks.

He'd *bought* her body.

How utterly shameful. She dipped her chin but he caught it.

"None of that, love," he said. "We have much work to do, and travel to arrange."

She nodded, throat tight at the warmth in his eyes.

"I will take care of you, Savina," he said. "You and Margot both."

She opened her mouth, meaning to say something sharp and witty. What came out was, "I don't trust you."

His crooked smile was rueful. "I don't care."

He brushed a thumb over her lower lip and the way his gaze darkened as he followed the movement made her heart thud wildly in her chest. "Perhaps you're right not to." After a thick silence, he dropped his hand and took a step back with a forced smile. "But you will in time, love. Mark my words."

5

*M*argot paced along the cobblestones that separated her squalid little home with Savina from the gaming hell beside it.

"You're gonna catch your cold out here, Snow." King was leaning against the brick wall of the gaming hell, along with two boys from his crew.

Snow. King had heard Savina teasingly refer to her as 'snow angel' enough times that it'd caught on. Which was nice in a way. A sort of regular reminder of those days before this rookery.

Without those reminders, memories of the years before they'd come to Vestry Lane might vanish into the wind.

Still, as she tightened her cloak as protection against cold March breeze and resumed her pacing, King's nickname irritated her. He was younger than her by two years, and yet somehow everyone still treated her like *she* was the child.

"You shouldn't have made me leave," she snipped.

King didn't argue. They'd been over this three times already. And even though he'd apologized the whole way from Bernie's to her home, he hadn't loosened his grip on her or even left her alone in the hour since.

He and his crew had been standing guard as if they were afraid Margot was going to storm into Bernie's and drag Savina out kicking and screaming.

Margot frowned. She had half a mind to.

Of course, Savina was taller and stronger, but even so…

For once, Margot wished she could be the strong one. It was bad enough that Savina had endured that dreadful tavern, day in and day out, to provide for her. But this…

What she was doing right now…

Margot's stomach turned at the thought of it. Truthfully, she didn't know much about what happened between a man and woman. She only knew the whispers and crass jokes she'd overheard.

But the thought of any man having his way with Savina in that debauched brothel was enough to make her sick to her stomach.

King walked over to her, hands in his pockets and a look of sympathy softening his sharp features. "Go inside, Margot. There's nothing you can do to help her."

She wanted to stay angry with her friend, but one look at the kindness in his gaze, and her resolve melted. That kindness was so at odds with his rough nature and tough reputation, it never failed to make her soften.

Besides, his presence out here was the only reason Margot felt safe enough to come out to stretch her legs. "There's no room to pace in there." She gestured toward the tenement housing behind her.

Even with the crooks and the drunkards on these streets, she preferred to be out here whenever she could. The cramped room she shared with Savina seemed to grow ever smaller the longer she was in there, until some days she thought she might start banging her fists on the mold-covered walls just to escape.

She drew in a deep breath and gave a little cough that had King scowling over at her.

She ignored her friend. He meant well, but it wasn't sickness that'd made her cough, just the overwhelming stench of piss and stale air that never seemed to leave this alley, not even when there was a chilly breeze like there was today.

"Go on," King said gruffly. "Get inside where it's warm." At her look of disbelief, he smirked and amended, "Where it's warm*er*."

Margot snickered. King's room was on the same floor as hers, and they often joked that it somehow managed to be colder inside than out during the winter.

At least outside she had the chance to sneak a glimpse of the sun during the day.

"C'mon, Snow," he urged, nudging her arm when she made no move to leave. "If you go inside, I can make sure your sister gets a proper escort home when she's...well, you know, when she's through."

Margot wrinkled her nose with a wave of revulsion over what was taking place just down the street. But King's point couldn't be ignored.

Savina had, no doubt, asked him to look after her. And the loyal King would never go back on his word.

But for once, it wasn't Margot who needed looking after. So, following another tense silence, she relented with a sigh. "All right, I'll go in, but please, King..."

He was nodding before she could finish, and gripping her by the shoulder to steer her inside. Despite the age difference, he'd outgrown her years ago. "I'll keep an eye out for her," he promised.

With one last sigh, she headed inside.

It felt like an age passed, when really it wasn't even an

hour, before Savina came bursting into their room, apologizing to the young mother who was urging her to shush as she'd just gotten the babes to sleep.

Margot stood stiffly in the center of the room, waiting as Savina whispered goodnight to the other woman and shut the door behind her with a soft *snick.*

"Are you all right?" Margot rushed to her. "Oh, sweet Savina, are you in pain? Was it awful? Are you—"

"Hush, Snow." Savina laughed.

She *laughed.*

Margot narrowed her eyes in confusion. She was well used to her sister hiding her pain and shame behind false laughter and brave smiles, but this...

This seemed genuine.

"Come. Sit with me." Savina held out her hand. Margot took it without thought, letting her sister pull her to the bed, where they sat on the edge. "You will never guess what has happened."

Margot's jaw was hanging open by the time Savina finished. "Prince Edmund?"

That was all she was capable of. Her mind was sluggish with disbelief.

"You remember Father talking about him, do you not?"

Margot nodded slowly. "I'd always thought he was imaginary. Like my friend, Greta."

They shared a smile at that and Savina patted her arm. "I know, dear. It's a lot to take in all at once."

"You say he wants to help us..." Margot's voice was thready and faint thanks to the tears that threatened. "It seems...almost too much to hope for..."

"My thoughts exactly." Savina's tone held an edge of mistrust.

But that wasn't what Margot felt. Only a heart-aching awe. This was it. The miracle she'd prayed for. She smiled as tears filled her eyes. "I knew someone would come for us," she gushed. "I knew Father's friends wouldn't abandon us forever."

Savina opened her mouth and then closed it. Margot was grateful her sister had kept her cynicism to herself. She knew full well that Savina didn't believe in miracles...and she didn't have any faith in the members of the *ton* who'd let them disappear without a trace.

"Did he say how he found us?" Margot asked.

Savina shook her head. "He didn't say and I did not ask. I was afraid..." She hesitated, fear flashing in her eyes.

There was only one person who brought that look in Savina's eyes—that mix of icy fear right alongside hot fury.

Their stepmother.

"You were afraid he'd tell her where we are," Margot guessed.

Savina shrugged. "I don't know how much he knows. If it's her word against ours..."

Margot nodded. "You were wise to stay quiet until we know more."

Savina arched a brow. "Until *I* know more."

"What do you mean?"

"I mean...I don't want you anywhere near Lucinda. Or that son of hers."

"Benedict? Surely he doesn't know what his mother did. He was always kind to us—"

"Margot."

Margot clamped her mouth shut. It always annoyed Savina when she made excuses for anyone in their former lives.

When Savina worked herself into a righteous fury on the topic, she used to say she'd destroy the lot of them. Every single member of the *ton*, whether they were innocent or guilty.

There were times Margot feared her sister truly would.

"Margot, listen to me, dearest." Savina reached for her hands. "I trust Edmund only so far as I have to. Whether I like it or not, we need his assistance to get out of this place."

Margot nodded. "But you don't trust him."

"I...I don't know who to trust." Savina's expression was terrifyingly vulnerable, but only for a moment. She squeezed Margot's hand. "Which is why I've asked Edmund to send you away."

"What?!" Margot reared back. "What do you mean?"

Savina's lips pinched in that way of hers. It was a look that said she was digging in her heels and there was no point in arguing.

Well, too bad. "I am not leaving you, sister."

"You must." Savina let her hand go so she could stand and pace the tiny room. "We both know that for some reason Lucinda has it in for you. She might not like me, but she sees you as a threat."

Margot winced. She wished she could argue the point, but there was truth to it. In the days after his death, Lucinda had cornered her more than once, asking her questions she did not understand in the midst of her grief. Shaking her violently when she couldn't answer.

And that night four years ago when starvation and desperation had driven them to defy her orders...

They'd been so desperate. Savina's plan had been to find their old housekeeper. She reasoned that Lucinda must have told some sort of lie about what had happened to them. If they could only let one of their former acquaintances know the truth then surely someone would help them.

But they'd been children when they'd left. They didn't have friends of their own, and had no notion of how to find their father's acquaintances. So they'd dared to go back to their home to find a servant who might speak on their behalf.

They never got that far.

That was the day they realized that Lucinda had spies everywhere and had been keeping tabs on them.

Lucinda had separated them. But Margot's captor had given her enough freedom that she'd heard what Lucinda said to Savina. She'd questioned her on what Margot had told her. What they knew.

And then she'd seemed to enjoy herself. Laughing as she asked Savina about how the little princess was faring in Vestry Lane. Asking if she'd had to spread her legs for coin yet.

The memory left Margot trembling. But it was what came next…

It was Lucinda's offer that was the real reason Savina was insisting she be sent away.

They'd never talked about it. Margot wasn't even sure Savina was aware that she knew the taunting proposal.

"I have no qualms with you, Savina," she'd said. "You're pretty enough that I could make a fortune off of you. I could marry you to a wealthy man and strengthen my position here in society and—"

"Never," Savina had spat.

"Never say never, dear," Lucinda had chided. "You must know by now what sort of evils lurk in Vestry Lane. You and your sister are helpless and too beautiful for your own good."

Savina had grown quiet.

Lucinda's voice was smug. "I'll make you an offer, darling. One that's good for tonight only. Stay here and we'll tell the world that you've been off visiting family this past year…"

"What about Margot?"

"Margot cannot stay." Lucinda's tone had turned cold.

"But don't you worry, I would not send her back to that cruel fate."

"What…what do you mean?"

Margot still shuddered at the fear in Savina's voice. The memory of Lucinda's answer just as horrifying now as it had been then.

"I'll end her quickly, dear. It will be painless and sweet, just as she deserves."

"You…you would murder her? Why?"

"So that you might live." Lucinda's tone had held a dreamy quality. "We cannot thrive with her under this roof. So my offer stands. You can stay here—alone—or go back to Vestry Lane together."

"Margot, do you hear me?" Savina's voice cut into her memories and Margot blinked her way back to the present.

"Sorry, I…what were you saying?"

Savina gave her a sympathetic smile and repeated herself. "You shall go to Bristol. It's near the sea, dearest. The sea. A half day's ride and you'll be able to walk in the sand. Just think of it."

Margot's heart bloomed with desire, even as her mind rebelled in fear.

Nothing gave her joy and peace like being in nature, surrounded by bird song with a sweet breeze on her face, long grass tickingling her skin and a vast sky above her.

And nothing gave her worriment like the idea of being separated from her sister.

"Edmund assures me you'll have a footman and driver, and when you get there you'll have a proper chaperone and—"

"And what will happen to you?" Margot asked, her voice high with fright.

"Edmund shall take me to his home—"

"How do we know we can trust this man?" Margot interrupted. It wasn't beyond her notice that Savina was referring to this man as Edmund.

Just Edmund.

As if they were already intimate acquaintances.

"I told you, I'll only trust him so far as I must—"

"Which means you don't trust him at all." Margot's finger shook as she rubbed her temples.

Savina hesitated. "If he was a friend of Father's—and I do believe he was—then… we… can."

Margot heard the uncertainty there, and her heart twisted with unease. "I don't want to go."

Savina gave her that look. A patronizing expression that made her appear a stern mother and not a sister only one year her senior.

Meanwhile, Margot sounded like a petulant child as she protested. "I will not go."

"You must. I will fix this for us, Snow." Savina tucked Margot's hair behind her ears, giving her an affectionate smile. "I will fix this so that you and I can be together again without fear. But the only way I can do that, is if I know you are safe somewhere far from here, where…"

"Where Lucinda can not touch me," Margot finished glumly, her shoulders deflating.

Savina met her gaze. "When all is set right, I will send for you and we can finally be free. Away from this place."

Margot's lips trembled. "I don't want to leave you."

Her voice held all the fear and sadness she'd been trying to hide just the way Savina always did.

But she'd never been as good at hiding her feelings, and after so many years of relying on one another and being each other's sole family, the thought of parting was breaking her heart. "I won't be able to bear it. I'll be so worried, Savina. You in society. What will Lucinda say? What will she do?"

"Well, I won't be alone. I'll have Edmund, and..." Savina faltered, her tone just as wary as Margot felt.

Neither of them truly trusted this stranger. And to place Savina's fate in his hands...?

"I cannot do this if I am worried about you," Savina continued. "I'm sorry, but you will only be a distraction. I need to know you are safe and well, dear sister. It shall take all my effort to win back what is truly ours. I don't want you anywhere near it."

Margot couldn't stop the tears, and soon they were holding each other close, murmuring assurances and consolation to each other as they talked of what the future might bring... until their small fire died out and they fell asleep on the bed.

Whoever this Edmund was, two days later, Margot was marveling at his efficiency.

"So you're really leaving us then," King said. He'd recently taken on a new crew member who was even bigger and broader than he, with a bent nose and shuttered eyes.

He was big and terrifying, which made him an excellent addition to the crew. But to Margot's mind, this boy they called Beast reminded her more of a beaten puppy than a fierce monster.

Which was why she gave him an embrace as well, along with all the other boys in King's crew. "We were lucky to have found you, King," Margot whispered against his cheek. He squeezed her back and she knew he was capable of no more than that. King would never let himself become emotional, which was probably why he released her so quickly.

She'd put off saying goodbye to him and Savina for as long as she could.

The driver and a blank-faced footman sat atop the carriage at the end of the alley. They'd been waiting patiently for their charge, and Margot felt guilty for delaying this journey.

"Where is this prince of yours?" she asked Savina. "Are you sure he'll come for you?"

Savina nodded. "I told him I wanted to say goodbye first. He's making my arrangements as we speak, I promise."

Margot's throat grew tight as she returned her sister's nod and then threw her arms around King again. "You're as good as a brother, King. We'd never have survived without you."

"Take care of yourself, Snow," King murmured as he patted her back.

Then it was time to say farewell to Savina, and King and his boys had the good grace to look the other way as Margot sobbed and even strong, brave, unflappable Savina gave in to a bout of tears.

"I will see you again soon," Savina promised.

"Just take care of yourself," Margot whispered, clinging to her sister's shoulders. "Don't take any chances, and don't do anything stupid."

"You know I cannot promise that," Savina joked as she pulled away.

Margot smiled through her tears. "I will see you soon?"

Savina nodded. "Of course you will."

Margot let the footman help her into the carriage, only to find a young maid waiting for her with a shy smile.

"Are you ready for the journey, miss?" the girl asked.

Margot let out a long breath, taking one last look at the wretched alley that had become her home. "I suppose I must be."

6

*S*avina had been waiting for years for her chance to escape the dreary misery that was this bleak rookery. And yet, now that her time had come, she found herself nervous to leave it behind.

She turned to King who waited beside her for Edmund's coach to arrive.

"You plan on telling me where you're off to, Savvy?" he asked.

Her lips quirked up at the nickname. Perhaps because he'd been given the task of naming himself as an orphan on the streets, King had a penchant for monikers. He'd taken to calling Margot by her childhood nickname and had deemed Savina 'Savvy' when he realized that she always had a plan when it came to her and Margot's survival.

"I'm not going far," she finally answered. "But it might as well be another world."

He arched his brow, but didn't pry. King respected the fact that Savina wasn't quick to share her plans with others. "Never thought I'd see the day you willingly parted with your sister."

She frowned. It had only been a matter of hours since Margot had left, but Savina already worried about her little sister.

"King, do you have any contacts near Bristol, by chance?"

His grin was quick and wicked. "My boys can get information from all over England. What do you need?"

"I need to know when my sister arrives safely in Bristol. And I need to find out that information from someone I trust." She held out the last of the coin Edmund had given her before they'd parted ways outside the brothel.

He'd been loathe to let her out of his sight, but she'd rightly pointed out that they both had arrangements to see to and plans to make.

King eyed the coins she held out for a long time before snatching it up. Pride was all well and good, and honorable intentions were nice indeed. But pride and nobility didn't put a roof over one's head, and it did nothing to fill one's belly.

She nodded toward the coins he clutched. "There'll be more of that soon enough."

He tipped his head, his gaze full of questions he didn't ask.

Where would she be getting this money? Who was this man they were trusting with their fates?

She was grateful she didn't have to explain. Doubts filled her mind and made her stomach churn. The longer she'd replayed what Edmund had said—and all that he hadn't said—the more worried she grew. What if she was trusting the wrong man?

She'd been so intent on not giving away her own hand that she hadn't asked the questions she should have. How *had* he found them after all these years? And how much did he know of why they'd come to be in Vestry Lane?

And, more importantly…what was his plan for them once they left?

King's low whistle had her glancing up to see a fine carriage heading their way.

"Don't see that sort in these parts every day," King murmured with a lopsided grin.

Savina drew in a deep breath. These doubts were too little too late. Perhaps she should have asked more questions, even if it meant exposing her own secrets…but there was nothing to do about it now.

She'd made her choice. And Margot was already on her way to a new life. Savina turned back to King as the carriage rolled to a stop. "Can I count on you, King?"

"You always can, Savvy. You know that." He tucked her money away, but his gaze never left hers. "You just want to know when Snow gets there safe, right?"

"I want to know that everything she has been promised actually comes to pass."

She listed off what awaits Margot, and King agreed once more to keep his ear to the ground.

"It might take me a little time, but I'll be in touch."

She nodded, letting out a shaky exhale. "As soon as I have an address, I will send word to you. You can contact me there."

He nodded, tipping his hat. "Good luck to you, Savvy."

She bit her lip, eyeing the dark alley that had been their home these past five years. "And to you, King."

Savina had wondered if Edmund would show up to escort her to this new home of hers, but only a footman greeted her, stepping down from beside the driver to hold the door open and let her in.

She wasn't disappointed, of course. Her need to see him again wasn't desperate. It was just that she had so many questions, that was all.

She gave King one last wave before the carriage took off.

To where? She didn't even know that. With a muttered oath, she looked out the window, helpless as a babe as this carriage took her wherever Edmund had instructed.

Whether she was placing her fate in the right hands remained to be seen, but she was far from helpless, she reminded herself as buildings and street corners rolled past outside the carriage window.

If her time in Vestry Lane had taught her anything, it was that. She could be more cunning and could endure more than she ever would have guessed.

If Edmund proved himself untrustworthy, she'd steal what she could and run away. She'd steal enough to make a new life for her and Margot.

And if he truly was a friend of her father's and could be trusted...

She leaned back in her seat and folded her hands in her lap.

Well, then she would stay in London long enough to get her revenge on Lucinda. And maybe, just maybe, claim what was rightfully theirs.

She didn't let herself go too far down that road. Hopes and dreams were fine for sheltered young ladies, but Savina couldn't afford such luxuries.

She'd been truthful when she'd told Edmund that her father had only shouted at her once and it had been about that silly chess game of theirs.

But the part she hadn't mentioned was what had happened after his shout.

He'd laughed at himself for overreacting, and then had knelt down beside her, holding up one of the pawns that had already been knocked out of the game.

Do you know what this is, my dear? This is a pawn. And this is a rook...

And that had been her very first lesson in the game of chess. The first of many as he'd used a different board and new pieces, so as not to disturb his ongoing battle with the foreign prince who'd been off in some faraway land.

Her father had taught her well, and those lessons had proven more worthwhile, during her time in Vestry Lane, than any lesson in etiquette or embroidery.

She knew that to succeed, it was necessary to have an end goal. But when it came to strategizing, it was best to focus on the next move at hand, and then wait to assess how the opponent responded.

One move at a time, he'd told her. *That's how you keep your prized piece protected. That's how you win in the end...*

And that was precisely how she'd deal with Lucinda.

The carriage came to a stop in a neighborhood that was clean and pleasant, but not the height of style. The street was lined with townhouses that were well-maintained but not lavish, by any means.

Her brows drew together as she considered the plain reddish-brown bricks that made up the home they'd stopped in front of. Was this where Edmund lived?

She hadn't expected him to take her to her father's home. While neither had mentioned Lucinda in their few conversations, he seemed to understand that Savina could not go there.

Was Lucinda still living in their old home?

What would she do if Savina arrived on her doorstep?

But no. She forced her hands to clasp together. This battle with Lucinda could not be rushed. She had to bide her time. Find out just how much Edmund knew, and what sort of lies Lucinda had been spreading.

She would confront her wicked stepmother, all right. But this time she'd do it when she was on firm footing and held power of her own.

Which meant…

She took a deep breath and eyed this simple townhome.

It meant trusting Edmund. For now, at least, he was her only ally, and whether he could be fully trusted or not, she had no other choice but to accept whatever help he offered.

The carriage door swung open and the footman offered his arm to help her out.

"Thank you," she murmured, as she stepped down.

Even in this decidedly middle class area, she felt like an oddity. She'd worn the gown that Edmund had given her. Which made her feel overdressed in Vestry Lane, but here made her feel a little more like she belonged.

Still, she was keenly aware of the dirt beneath her nails and the callouses on her hands. But at least she wasn't wearing her ragged old frock.

"This way, miss." The footman led her forward.

She hurried to keep up with him as he opened the front door and stepped aside for her to pass.

Savina stopped short just inside the entry and caught her breath as a wave of emotion hit her. The entry with its black and white tiled floor and vaulted ceiling were not opulent, but it was finer than anything she'd seen in years.

And clean. So very clean. The wood of the staircase bannister gleamed with polish and the walls were sparkling white.

If mold or mildew had ever dared to sneak into this space it had been swiftly wiped away.

The air smelled of lemons and some spice that made her mouth water. And then a kindly looking older woman was hurrying out of the back of the townhome, a bright smile on her face. "Good afternoon! You must be Miss Savina." The woman bustled about with an energy that seemed at odds with her short and plump figure. "I'm Mrs. Baker, your housekeeper. How do you do?"

"*My* housekeeper?" Savina uttered after murmuring a greeting in kind.

"Why, yes. Your uncle hired me to help look after you as you adjust to life in London society."

"I see," she said slowly. "So he told you then, that I..."

"That you've just returned from abroad," the house-keeper filled in cheerfully. "It must be quite overwhelming to be back in London after so much time at the boarding school."

Savina nodded, feeling like a nitwit. How had it not occurred to her that Edmund would have crafted some lie about her absence. And even more tall tales about what she was doing back here in London.

A surge of fear took hold. What had he told Lucinda?

Did she know that Savina was back?

Had she told him some lie about how Savina and Margot had come to be in such a low place?

Yes. Yes, of course she had. She'd no doubt crafted some story to make herself out to be the victim. Maybe she'd said they'd been kidnapped. Or they'd run away.

Her mind swirled with possibilities. It didn't truly matter, she supposed. What mattered was how much Edmund knew, and most importantly...what he believed.

If his allegiance was to Lucinda then she wouldn't be able to trust him at all.

"Come, dear, you must be tired and hungry," Mrs. Baker said. As she escorted her to a small dining room, she continued prattling on about how her maid was drawing her a bath and they'd have her clean and fresh just as soon as she'd finished eating.

The next two hours passed in a dreamlike blur as Savina allowed herself to get swept away by the housekeeper and two maids who fulfilled her every need before she could even ask.

By the time Edmund arrived, Savina was clean, clothed, and her belly was truly full for the first time in years.

Oh, how she hoped Margot was eating this well.

"Your uncle has arrived, miss," a maid announced.

Savina wasted no time hurrying down the steps to the townhome's small foyer, just in time to see Edmund closing the door behind him.

He looked up, and she halted. One foot on the step below her and her hand on the bannister, she froze.

It was him. It was the man she'd met the other night...and it wasn't.

He was the same, but different somehow. Maybe it was the light of day or the fact that he was dressed to the nines with his black hair slicked back as if showing off the silver that marked his temples and threaded through his dark hair.

Whatever it was, when his gaze met hers, her mind went blank.

All her questions about his connection to Lucinda and his plans for her and her sister faded into the background as her heart thudded and her hands shook with silly nerves.

His smile was small and a little crooked as he took her in from head to toe. "You look lovely, my dear."

Said with such a doting, paternal air, she was taken aback all over again.

She blinked, suddenly aware of the servants who bustled about. Ah, so this was the part he played today.

A doting uncle, of sorts.

She took a steadying breath as her wits returned. With slow steps this time, she joined him at the bottom of the staircase and gave him a curtsy that she hadn't used in five years.

He chuckled softly. "Well done."

Her lips tipped up in a tremulous smile. She'd meant to put on a brave front the next time she saw this man. But to her dismay, she found herself nervously awaiting his approval.

She pressed her lips together and lifted her chin in the hopes that he couldn't see through her facade.

Odd how it was easier to be brave dressed in rags in Madame Bernadette's vile whorehouse than it was standing here in an elegant foyer wearing a new gown.

She felt like she was an actress playing a part, when truly, this was who she was born to be.

A proper young lady.

So why did it feel so wrong?

"Well?" She finally broke the silence as she threw her hands out to the side in a decidedly ungraceful gesture.

His lips twitched, but then his gaze darkened and dipped, taking in the tight bodice of this new gown. Her skin warmed and she felt a hot wave of pleasure as she held her breath.

"I had a hunch you'd look spectacular in blue," he murmured.

Heat caught and spread, like kindling next to a flame. She looked down at herself, feeling the brush of silk and taffeta against her too-sensitive skin. "You chose the color?"

"I chose everything." His voice was so low none of the servants could have heard him, but she blushed all the same. The thought of him picking fabrics and giving instructions for the cut and fit of her gowns sent a lick of pleasure curling through her.

Her fingers trembled against the silk of her skirts. It felt oddly intimate.

She couldn't stop a flare of mischief–the same urge to tease and taunt that he'd brought out in her at the brothel. "Everything? Even the garments I'm wearing under this gown?"

His nostrils flared and his gaze darkened. "Everything. And I will ensure you never want for anything again."

Her blush deepened. Why? She couldn't say, and she refused to name this sweet warmth that made her chest feel too full too fast.

She'd seen hunger in his eyes at the brothel, but this was different.

There was desire in his gaze, yes. Undoubtedly. But it was tempered by something warm and tender. It was only remembering how little she knew of him, and his intentions, that had her keeping her distance rather than rushing to his side.

"Have you eaten?" he asked. "Have they been taking care of you?"

"Yes. Thank you, my lord," she murmured. Was that how one addressed a prince? She had no idea. Foreign princes were few and far between in Vestry Lane.

But his eyes flashed with approval at her soft tone and subservient demeanor, and that warmth inside her spread and grew as he moved closer and then paced in a circle around her as he'd done the other night at the brothel, making her feel like a captive on display for him.

His fingers brushed lightly over her back, and sifted through her long blonde waves which were thick and gleaming after her bath. When he stopped in front of her, his fingers lingered, brushing over her shoulder.

An innocent touch that burned her skin like a brand.

She swallowed hard, fear following in desire's wake. Even if this man proved to be a trusted ally—which was still very much in doubt—this effect he had on her was a danger she didn't know how to protect herself against.

The way his mere presence heightened her senses and made her heart race left her more vulnerable than a babe in the woods.

His gaze raked over her once more, and his voice was gruff when he spoke. "We'll have to polish you up a bit before you enter society, but I'd say you're off to an excellent start."

She arched a brow, all those questions she had rising to the surface. "An excellent start for what, exactly?"

7

---

evenge, he could have told her.

But he did not. For all her bravery, there was a fear and mistrust in her that made him hesitate.

Bloody hell, she was too tempting for her own good. Made all the more so by the fact that she seemed utterly unaware of her own allure.

He'd already dismissed his original plan for her, but now he even questioned the wisdom of bringing her into society at all. Every gentleman in the ton would be eyeing her, fantasizing about her….

And she is mine and mine alone.

His hands fisted. Fucking hell, he had to stop thinking that. It'd become a pervasive, obsessive thought from the moment he'd seen her the other night. A craving that only seemed to grow even when she was out of his sight.

And now that she was here within reach, it took all of his will not to take her in his arms and crush that luscious body to his.

But that look in her eyes kept him still, his hands at his sides.

He'd misjudged her the other night, that much was clear. With her hair gleaming in the candlelight and her eyes wide as she gazed up at him, he was achingly aware that despite her notched chin and her squared shoulders, she was terrified.

Of him?

He didn't think so.

But he couldn't blame her for not blindly trusting him. He'd told her blessedly little—about himself or his plans. And now, as he bought himself time by dismissing the servants, he tried to figure out how he could put her at ease.

"You have been ill-treated by everyone who ought to care for you," he said softly when they were alone in the town-home's drawing room. "I mean to right those wrongs."

Her lips quivered and her fingers twitched. Almost like she too was fighting the urge to reach out…

"Do you mean…" She wet her lips and his cock took notice. "Do you mean my stepmother?"

His white hot rage was impossible to deny. "Yes. Among others."

"So you will help me to…to get justice?" Her voice was soft and her eyes unreadable.

"I will."

"How did you find us? How did you know to look for us?" When he didn't immediately answer, she added, "Margot and I assumed that Lucinda spread a lie about us." She lifted a shoulder. "Told people we'd died or run away or—"

"That you were sent off to your father's distant family in France, and then to a finishing school abroad," he finished. "You were grieving, you see. And you could not bear to stay in that home."

"Ah." She nodded. "Yes, of course." She nibbled on her lower lip and…Christ. Did she have any notion what that did to him? Did she know what kind of torment it was to be this

68

close and not be able to claim her mouth and taste those lips and—

"Bloody hell," he muttered, turning away.

This was his best friend's daughter. A woman half his age.

He'd never fooled himself into thinking he was some sort of saint. Years of inflicting harm and ordering carnage on the battlefield had taught him he was no noble knight. But he'd never thought of himself as a wicked devil until this girl came into his life.

"How did you learn the truth?" she asked.

"At first, I regret to say that I believed her lies."

After a pause, she surprised him. He'd thought she'd be angry to hear it—just how thoroughly he'd failed her and Margot. But she pursed her lips with a nod. "Lucinda has always excelled at deception."

"Indeed. But keeping track of her lies…that is where she faltered."

There was more he could say. So much more.

But it would not help to rid her of the wariness he could still see lurking in her eyes.

And if she did not trust him, this new plan would never succeed.

He waited for more questions. When none came, he found himself wanting to tell her more. To tell her something to make her feel as though she could trust him.

"Your father wrote to me, you know."

Her head jerked back a bit. "Oh?"

"Not long before he died. He said…" He stopped, weighing his words. "He mentioned you and your sister. He told me that he'd remarried to provide you and your sister with a mother figure—"

"Please," she interrupted. Her throat worked as she swallowed. "Don't."

He nodded, his heart aching for the woman before him… and the girl she'd once been.

Leopold couldn't have known that he'd let evil into their lives. "He reminded me in that letter of the promise I'd made to him after your mother died. He was worried, you know, about the fact that you and Margot only had one parent left. And I… I vowed that I would look after his family if anything were to ever happen to him." He moved toward her. "I should have been there sooner. But my current business had me traveling the world. I didn't receive word of your father's passing until nearly a year after the event. And by then…"

She inhaled swiftly, her tone too brisk. "By then we were well gone. Yes, I remember that much." She cleared her throat. "And…Lucinda?"

"I found her living in your father's home." He shrugged. "I believed her when she'd said you were in good hands."

Something nagged at him.

The truth.

He'd known right from the start that she was manipulative; that she was playing her own game all along. He'd known it but he hadn't cared. Not enough, at least.

He hadn't realized until too late that Lucinda wasn't just another manipulative, greedy woman. That she was something so much worse.

Savina's gaze was curious. He could all but see the questions there.

"And now?" she asked. "Lucinda…"

"Still resides in your father's home," he clipped. "Which is why you are here. For now."

Her eyes narrowed slightly. *For now.* She'd heard the promise, that lie within those words. "If she knows I'm back—"

"She's not in Town at the moment," he cut her off. "The

Season has only just begun and she has not yet made her entrance into society."

It was hatred, plain and simple, that made her eyes glow and her cheeks flush. "I see."

He waited for more questions…about him. About her past. He turned, heading to the bottle of brandy that sat out on the mantle. How much could he tell her?

How much would she believe?

"What is your plan for me then?"

He turned around in surprise and found her watching him with a knowing little smile.

"Pardon?"

"I assume you have some plan for how to bring me into society." Her eyebrows arched in question.

He let himself register the fact that she was not grilling him about the past. That she seemed content, for now, to look toward the future.

She was putting her trust in him…at least a little. The thought was humbling. "I realize it's not much time, but in four days there is to be a ball. All the *ton* will be there. If you arrive and cause a minor sensation—"

"Then my stepmother cannot get rid of me without more questions than she can answer," Savina finished.

He stared at her for a long moment, taken aback by the jaded cynicism in her voice that seemed so at odds with her demure, docile expression. Not for the first time, he found himself marveling at the enigma before him. How was it that she seemed so innocent and yet so jaded? So brave and so fearful, so strong and so delicate.

The girl was a study in contradictions and it made him want to unravel her, and uncover every facet that made her who she was. The need to know her fears, to banish them from her life…

It was so overwhelming it drowned out all common sense.

His chest tightened at the thought of being the man who protected her when she was afraid and who took on her battles when she was in need and….

He shook his head and poured himself a glass. "You understand, precisely," he said. "I know it might not be ideal for you, after all you've been through, but announcing your arrival into society in such a public manner is likely the most advantageous—"

"I'll do it," she interrupted.

He arched a brow.

"I'll do it," she said again. "Whatever you need me to do to make my entrance a success, I will do it." Her eyes flashed with something mischievous and dark—a look he was beginning to equally adore and despise. "I am yours to command, my lord."

And there it was. The naughty little minx who came out to play when he least expected it.

She would drive him mad when all was said and done. She knew precisely how to be at once an innocent damsel and a seductive temptress.

She knew exactly the sort of game he liked to play…

With her. No one else. For all his years, he'd never experienced this draw before, nor entertained such delicious and dirty fantasies.

How did she know exactly how to push and when to pull? How did she know how to make him feel like a terrifying beast as well as a knight in bloody fucking armor?

He tossed back a swig of his drink, as if that might help to clear his head. Too late, though. All of his blood was surging to his loins, and all his mind was good for was conjuring up every which way he could fuck her in this room.

Bent over the back of that settee. Pounding into her in front of the fire.

His brilliant fucking mind had suddenly become incapable of doing anything but cataloguing all of the ways he could make his new ward come.

And there was no way she didn't know what she was doing to him. His manhood swelled against his breeches, as desire made every muscle in his body tighten. His gaze dipped to that sumptuous hint of cleavage and there...

Her nipples hardened under his watchful stare. That thin, soft silk he'd chosen left little to the imagination as her hard peaks pressed against the fabric and a flush stole up her neck.

His gaze lifted to meet hers, and the air hummed with this thick awareness.

Good God. His lungs worked hard to function. She felt it too.

He moved closer even as he told himself not to. "Mine to command, hmm?"

Her lips twitched with mirth and her eyes danced with that mischievous amusement. "Yes, my lord."

"What have I done to instill such obedience?" he murmured.

"You mistake me, sir." Her tone was laced with something tart and sweet at once. "I am never blindly obedient. But in this particular instance it seems our interests are aligned. And as you are more familiar with the ways of society, in this regard, I believe that you know best."

He let out a huff of amusement. It was impossible to say how much she understood of her own sultry power and how much she was experimenting—a clever young lady just starting to learn her power over men.

He had no issue with her experimenting with flirtation and seduction. Hell, he adored it.

But only if she played this game with him. No one else.

Something primal cut through his haze of lust. He caught her by the chin, and watched with fascination as her lips parted on a gasp and her eyes darkened with desire. "Are you playing the coquette again, pet?"

She wet her lips and her gaze grew intent as she watched his response. "I…I don't know," she admitted.

He narrowed his eyes, alarmed by the way his heart seemed to melt with that answer. Christ, she was adorable even when she drove him mad.

He leaned down close so she could see the fierce intensity that he felt. "You want to play, pet? That's fine by me. But don't let me see you toying with another man like this, or you'll see what it truly means to be under my command."

Her gaze was hungry. So bloody hungry.

Christ, how was he supposed to resist this temptation?

He brushed his thumb over her lower lip, adoring her little gasp.

"Do you understand?"

She pouted. And hell if he knew whether he wanted to laugh or shout.

She batted her lashes, that teasing glint in her eyes so clear he could practically hear her laughter. But her pupils were dilated and her lips parted. Good God, the girl was just as turned on as he was. "I understand that you'd have to discipline me, my lord," she breathed. "Is that right?"

He huffed again, amused and exasperated. "God save me from naughty, tempting young ladies."

Her lips twitched up as he dropped his hand from her chin. "Am I?"

"Naughty?" he shot back, tempering the word with a teasing tone that made her smile. "Absolutely."

"But am I…" She shifted, her gaze flickering with hints of vulnerability and bravery in a way that nearly cut him down at the knees. "Am I tempting?"

Bloody hell, but this woman had no idea. He leaned in, torturing himself by moving in close enough to feel her shallow breaths as she waited for his response.

"More tempting than a siren, and more powerful than a goddess," he murmured.

Her cheeks flushed with pleasure. "I don't feel terribly powerful."

He brought a hand up to touch her soft cheek. "But you are. I can see it in you. You are brave and strong—"

"Only because I've had to be."

It came out like an admission. A confession. And it made his heart ache.

God, this sweet thing would be the death of him.

He swallowed hard and moved back slightly, forcing his tone to be level. "In my experience, people show their true nature when put to the test. You have surely been tested, but you've risen from the ashes like a phoenix."

Her eyes glimmered with emotion and for a long moment they stayed like that, the moment filled with intimacy that was so bloody wrong.

And yet he couldn't drag himself away.

"Thank you," she whispered.

"No, thank you," he said. "For being strong enough to face your enemy."

"And she's…she's your enemy too, is she not?"

There was that wariness again, which he could hardly blame her for.

But it also reminded him that now was not the time to tell her everything. She didn't fully trust him, and she wouldn't understand.

"Edmund," she prompted.

"Your enemies are my enemies, love." His voice was low and rougher than intended. "Always."

It was the best he could do. The best he could offer.

For now, at least.

He took a step back and then another. "I've given strict orders for how you are to be prepared for the ball," he said, his tone far more his normal as he turned away from her. "I will see you in four days' time."

"But…" Her voice was high and confusion marred her pretty brow. "Where are you going? Isn't this…" She glanced around. "Isn't this your home?"

He smiled then, and it felt like his first genuine smile in a decade. "No, my dear. This is *your* home. Yours and your sister's, if she chooses to join you here."

"But…"

His smile grew as her voice trailed off. "Much as I'd love to live under the same roof with you, love…" He lied. It would be the worst form of torture. But his teasing words made her blush, and he adored the sight. "I fear it would not do well for your reputation to be living alone with a man twice your age with whom you are not related."

"Oh, I thought…" She wet her lips and this time when she blushed, he felt the heat of it in his loins.

Had she wanted to be under the same roof as him?

He turned away, cursing under his breath. It didn't matter if she felt this yearning or how strongly. It wasn't going to happen. Not now. Not ever.

"I'll see you in four days' time," he called and clipped out the door while fighting the urge to glance back.

8

*M*argot's expression must have been as bleak as the weather, because her maid, Betty, joined her at the window with a cheerful, "Don't fret, miss, we'll be back on the road and arriving in Bristol in no time, mark my words."

Margot summoned a wan smile. "You said the same thing yesterday."

"Aye, but this rain can't hold forever. And a day or two behind schedule won't change the fact that we'll have you in Bristol by the end of the week."

Margot couldn't help but laugh at that. She wished she shared Betty's sanguine attitude about this delay in plans. It wasn't as though she had anyone waiting for her in Bristol. Truthfully, she was a little frightened of what her life would be like when she arrived. The only thing to truly encourage her was the thought of the ocean breeze kissing her face as she strolled along the sand.

But that nervous tension only grew the more they were delayed by the onslaught of rain which had flooded the river they were meant to cross. All of this sitting inside, waiting in cramped quarters…

It made her itch to throw open the doors and run straight into the woods.

"Shall I tell the innkeeper to fetch you some stew?" Betty asked. "We've got to put some meat on those bones."

Margot smiled. "That would be lovely, thank you."

She cast one last look at the torrential downpour, offered up a prayer that her sister was faring well, and then went to join Betty and the others in the noisy tavern hall that made up the first floor of this roadside inn.

The footman and driver looked well in their cups. She couldn't blame them. There was little else to do but drink ale and play card games. She tried not to be too frustrated by this delay, but after so much time tucked away in tiny hovels, she couldn't bear being trapped inside any longer. Not now when true freedom was so close.

But then again, soon enough, she'd be in the nice, clean home, she'd been assured. Not far from the seaside.

She'd never seen the sea and could hardly imagine what it would be like. All that mattered though was that she could be outside without fear. Fresh air and wide open spaces, that was all she wanted.

She turned away from the window with a sigh. She'd have her fresh air soon…but not today. And in the meantime, she really shouldn't complain. For the first time in years she had a hot bath whenever she wished, and a bed to sleep in. Not to mention a seemingly never ending supply of decent food.

Betty and the driver had groused about this inn but, to Margot, this place made her feel like a queen .

There was only one available seat in the inn's tavern, so she sat at the end of a table that held a family with small children, along with some rough-looking men.

Margot watched the young mother eye the men warily

before inching her children down to the end of the table. But Margot didn't mind these men. They were a little dirty, perhaps, and they reeked of ale, but they nodded politely as she sat and then went back to telling one another tall tales of their time on the road.

Margot grinned when a servant set a bowl of stew before her with a thud. Bread came next, and Margot dug into her meal with vigor, just barely holding back a moan when she bit into the chewy, flaky crust of the fresh-baked bread.

"Hungry, love?"

Her eyes flew open and she swallowed hard when she realized those men were staring at her.

She cleared her throat and forced a smile, aware of Betty's gaze on her from where she sat with the friend she'd made. Together they were knitting in front of the fire, but Betty's expression was expectant, waiting to see if Margot needed her to intervene.

Margot laughed softly at the thought. Betty must think her a fine lady, indeed, to have the coach that Edmund had sent, and the gown he'd supplied for her—a little too large for her thin frame, but fine nonetheless— and the means to purchase rooms for them all. If the servant only knew the sort of men Margot was accustomed to dealing with, she'd faint on the spot.

To the men who were watching her, Margot smiled. "I was rather hungry, yes."

"You look like a strong wind would blow you away," the eldest one said. His face was covered in wrinkles and a gray beard, but his eyes were kind.

Eyes, Margot had learned, were what truly told one of a man's character. If one were to judge on looks alone….

Margot had seen more than her fair share of handsome dandies behaving with cruelty and depravity back in Vestry Lane.

"Here." The old man pushed a carafe of wine in her direction. "You need to get some pink in those cheeks."

She dipped her head in thanks. "Please, go on with your stories," she said when they continued to watch her. "I did not mean to interrupt when I joined you."

One of the younger men, who looked to be related to the old man with the same dark auburn hair, chuckled as he reached for his glass. "These stories aren't meant for young ladies. My father shouldn't scare a wee thing like you."

"Rufus here's telling tall tales to scare us folks who've never traveled this far outside the city," a third man said.

"This is my first time leaving London as well," she admitted. Turning to the old man, she smiled brighter. "Is there truly anything so frightening on these roads?"

"The roads? Maybe not." With a twinkle in his eye, he leaned forward, resting his elbows on the table. "It's the woods you have to be frightened of, love."

His son sighed with a shake of his head. "Don't listen to him, miss. You've nothing to worry about."

"Well," the third man cut in. "There *are* highwaymen out there. That's a fact."

"Oh aye," the old man agreed, with a brogue that made Margot smile. It reminded her of some of her favorite friends in Vestry Lane, like the maid, Molly, and Thomas, who helped her lug the laundry back to its rightful owners when it was too heavy to do on her own.

"There are highwaymen to be sure." Rufus's voice was a slow sing-song. He was building up the anticipation and Margot found herself leaning in expectantly just as the others did.

"And none more fearsome than the hooded woodsman," he went on in a hushed voice.

"Who's that?" the third man asked.

"A brutal beast of a man," Rufus growled, really getting into it now.

Margot bit her lip to hold back a smile at the way he talked. Like he was telling ghost stories to little children.

"It's said he lives alone in these woods. Some say he murdered his own family..."

Rufus's son gave a snort of disbelief.

"Go on and laugh if you dare." Rufus pointed at him. "But I've seen 'im with me own eyes, I have. Larger than a bear, and far more dangerous."

"Don't tell me he has claws," Margot murmured, which made the men laugh.

Even Rufus grinned. "Worse, love. The man wields an ax."

"An ax?" Betty's voice beside her made Margot jerk, but soon she shifted over so Betty could join. And as the old man continued, Margot noticed more and more of the eavesdroppers around them crowding in close.

"He'll take your money and your jewels, like any highwayman." Rufus's voice rose. He was obviously loving the attention. "But whether he'll let you live to tell the tale...that's another story."

"And yet everyone seems to have a tale about this hooded woodsman," Rufus's son murmured, with a wink for Margot that made her giggle.

"Oh, miss," Betty said. "'Tis nothing to laugh about. I've heard the stories myself, and from men who've never been known to lie."

"Is that so?" Margot's eyebrows rose.

"We've all heard the stories," one of the eavesdropper's said. "It's why I brought extra servants on this trip. This stretch of road has become a hunting ground, that's for sure."

"You make him sound like...like an animal." Margot laughed in an attempt to lighten the mood. "Surely he's just a man."

"No, miss." Rufus's voice was grave. "If he ever was a man, he ain't no longer. He's more beast than human, of that I'm certain."

"He don't hunt deer, is what they say. He makes his living on human flesh," one of the crowd called above the shocked murmurs.

"I heard he only eats the hearts and brains."

"I heard he turns the skin into clothing, just like you would an animal hide."

"He's all but legend," Rufus's son shot back. "Stop scaring the ladies."

"I'm not frightened," Margot insisted. And indeed, she wasn't.

At first…

For the next hour, she listened as tavern guests argued and laughed, weaving tales taller than the next. The hooded man who kept to the woods wasn't nearly as frightening, in her opinion, as the men who called themselves gentlemen that preyed on the weak and poor in her old neighborhood.

So she laughed along with Rufus's son as the stories grew wilder and soon morphed into another topic altogether as one guest after another shared horrific stories they'd heard about fellow travelers.

After a while, Margot excused herself to go to her room, relishing the silence, broken only by the occasional burst of loud laughter or music from the tavern below. The sounds kept her company as she pulled out the parchment the driver had purchased for her from the innkeeper.

She'd learned her letters from her father, though she'd been out of practice for so long, she wasn't sure her letter made any sense as she tried her best to recount her travels to Savina. Or maybe King?

Honestly, she didn't have an address for either, but pretending at least for a little while that someone would read her account made her feel less lonely. And putting it all into words made her head stop spinning and her anxiety abate.

By the time she slid into the warm, soft bed, she was quite at ease, and drifted off easily into a deep sleep.

That was when the nightmare began.

Half-man, half-beast, a hooded creature stole her away into the night. She sat up with a start, the room pitch black as she gasped for air.

With a sigh, she fell back against the pillows and shook her head in exasperation at her own silly nature.

She knew better than to fear fantastical monsters. Everyone knew they didn't exist, and the world was filled with evil far more real.

But no matter how many times she told herself she was being ridiculous, images from her nightmare kept her company until the sun finally rose in the east.

9

Four days into this new life, and Savina hardly recognized her own reflection in the mirror.

"You look beautiful, miss," her maid murmured with a shy smile as she stepped back to admire her handiwork.

Savina's own smile felt tremulous as she stared at the stranger in the mirror. "You've outdone yourself, Marie."

The girl's cheeks turned bright pink with pleasure before she dipped her head and hurried out.

Four days. Savina eyed her reflection. But already so much had changed. She could only hope that Margot was faring as well, particularly with her health. Savina lifted a gloved hand and touched her cheek.

Days of eating well and sleeping in a comfortable bed had improved her appearance drastically. Each day she'd gone outside with one of the maids, who hovered around her, and she'd soaked in the sunshine and fresh air.

It was almost impossible to believe that this home and her former were both within the same city.

And tonight, she'd finally be going out. Beyond just this

house and its garden, where Edmund had asked her stay—*for her own safety*, he'd said.

He hadn't expounded, and she'd stopped asking.

They'd found themselves caught in a sort of web. Not of lies, but of secrets. She believed him when he'd said that her allies were his. But she'd also noted every oddly worded phrase and every hole in his story.

He'd told her the truth. But not all of it. And with no one else to ask about what she'd missed these past five years, there was no one to give her more information on the lies that had been told...

No one to confirm Edmund's story or to explain what his agenda might be, and why he needed her here in London.

He had his own plans, that much she knew. But he was dreadfully sparse with the details, and that made it impossible not to fall victim to those suspicious voices in her head. The ones that reminded her that Lucinda had spies everywhere.

That she'd made the mistake once of underestimating her stepmother and had very nearly lost Margot as a result.

And so her tongue had swollen with fear every time she thought to ask after Lucinda or the details of how Edmund had found her and what he had planned.

And he, for his part, had been tightlipped about...well, everything.

He'd come to visit her every afternoon, but unlike that first day, he never touched her. He never said anything even close to improper. All he did was bark out orders to her and the servants, to ensure that she was primped and dressed and groomed and educated.

"You must be ready in time for the ball," he'd demanded.

"Ready for what?" She'd finally asked, only the day before.

His gaze had been cutting. Almost like he resented the fact that she'd dared to question him.

Her chin came up and he glanced away, his lips twitching.

"Ready to make your first appearance, of course," he'd mumbled.

And then, for the first time in days, she'd finally overcome her fears and blurted out the question she'd been holding inside. "What about Lucinda?"

There was so much packed into that one question. When would she face her? What would she do once she learned Savina was here?

How would they take back what was rightfully hers?

At his cold, unreadable stare, her heart had stuttered. His silence stretched too long, and every suspicion she'd battled these past few days had suddenly felt validated.

He was holding out on her. Maybe even lying.

"Your father's wife is no concern of yours," he'd finally said. "She cannot touch you now."

She'd opened her mouth to ask more questions, but with that he'd turned and left her.

Did he have any notion of the threats Lucinda had made? Could he possibly understand how dangerous she was and the sort of evil she was capable of?

A commotion came from downstairs.

It would be Edmund here to collect her for the ball.

She shook her head and pinched her cheeks before getting to her feet.

Right now, the past didn't matter. She'd gotten her answer, and that was enough. Lucinda was not his friend, and she wasn't in London.

Even now she couldn't decide how she felt about that. On one hand, she'd give anything for a chance at taking her revenge.

But on the other hand...

Well, Lucinda was still the monster from her nightmares.

And being here in this home and surrounded by servants and seamstresses, she felt wildly out of her depths.

She needed time to adapt, to plot and plan. First she had to get a lay of the land. See who her allies might be.

A smile tugged at her lips as she headed toward the staircase. She could hear Edmund's voice from the entryway below. So low and curt and commanding.

No doubt keeping the servants on their toes just as he did with her. Making her model her new gowns for him, and practice her curtsy and table manners until he was satisfied she would fit in with the other young ladies.

She paused at the top of the stairs, and when his gaze lifted and he spotted her, she was certain that time had come to a standstill.

Her hand slid along the bannister as she descended, and she was abnormally grateful for its support as his fiery, focused gaze left her breathless.

It had been days since she'd seen that fire in his eyes, and there was no denying its heat everywhere his gaze landed. From the lace that lined the decolletage to the trim waist with its pale blue silk, and down all the way to her slippers.

She still wasn't quite accustomed to such finery, but right here and now she was grateful for it. Pride bloomed within her at the warm approval in his gaze.

No, not just approval. That was hunger she saw there, and the sight was a blessed relief.

Why? She couldn't say, didn't wish to look too closely. All she knew was that the lack of it had left her feeling cold during his visits, and more alone than ever.

Her breath caught as he reached for her hand. Not for the first time, she found herself victim to his secrets. She knew so little of this man. He came and went, but she knew not where he ran off to or if he had a family of his own somewhere.

The thought never failed to leave her feeling queasy.

Surely he wouldn't have encouraged her flirting if he had a wife and children. Would he?

There were times she could have asked, of course, but it seemed as though they'd formed some odd sort of truce.

No questions asked, no lies or evasions in response.

It had been a tentative sort of truce, and now it struck her how cowardly she'd been. She knew blessedly little of this man who'd gifted her a second chance at her old life, and it was her own fault.

And now, as she slid her hand into his and felt the warmth of his body surround her, making her feel heat all over and a glow of something warm and light in her belly that wasn't desire...

Oh, all right, it wasn't *only* desire. It was something else, as well. A sort of understanding or...or a connection, perhaps.

Something she hadn't felt with anyone before. After years of being so guarded and defensive, the way he made her feel was as unfamiliar as the fine fabric of this gown and the elegance of this home.

It made her want to lean into him. To let him support her.

It made her want to trust him. *Are you married?*

Three simple words. How hard would it be to ask?

Heavens, she could have asked Mrs. Baker and spared herself this torture.

"You look lovely, Savina," he murmured. "You do your father proud indeed."

Her father. She blinked, coming back to her senses as a flicker of emotion swept over her.

Her father was why she was here. She owed it to him, and Margot, to get revenge. She lifted her chin, clearing her mind of the suspicions and doubts and questions that were really none of her concern.

All that mattered now was that Edmund was her ally. He'd brought her here, and while he might have his secrets, he'd undoubtedly been her father's friend. And wasn't that all she really needed to know?

"Are you ready to make your entrance?" he asked.

I'm ready. She nodded, but the words stuck in her throat. Wordlessly, she let him lead her out the door and to the waiting carriage. As they walked, he told her about the family who was hosting this ball, and the members of the *ton* who'd be in attendance.

"You ought to be prepared, of course, to answer questions about your stay on the continent," he said, making her trip over her own feet as she turned to stare at him.

For the past few days he'd studiously ignored all mention of Lucinda and the lies she'd spread. Now, he ignored her stare and helped her into the carriage.

"So, as far as the guests gathered tonight are concerned, you've just recently returned from finishing school in northern France," he said. "Before that you were staying with an aunt in Lyon. Feel free to be creative in your responses. Lord knows your stepmother was blessedly vague when it came to you and your sister's circumstances."

"And Lucinda…"

"Will have no choice but to go along with whatever you say." There was a hint of malice in his expression that was oddly comforting.

Whatever his dealings with Lucinda, and whatever tales she'd spun, it was clear that this man, at least, was no friend of hers.

"And she will not be here tonight," she confirmed.

He hesitated a moment too long and his gaze didn't quite meet hers. "I do not expect to see her." Before she could ask any more questions, he continued. "We will not stay long. Just long enough to make an appearance and let it be known that you have returned to take your rightful place in society."

The carriage rolled to a stop, and soon Savina was distracted by the sight outside the carriage window.

Candlelight glowed from every window in the large manor before her, and a crowd of well-dressed gentlemen and ladies crowded by the portes-cochère, awaiting entry.

Could Lucinda be in there?

I do not expect to see her. That was hardly a resounding no.

Savina exhaled sharply, hoping to relieve her nerves. It did not matter if she was. Lucinda could not hurt her now. Not when she had Prince Edmund for an ally.

"You have nothing to fear, Savina," he murmured softly. "Whatever happens this evening, you must know that I only have your best interests at heart."

She turned to meet his gaze, but found it shuttered and unreadable. His tone was gentle, though. Surprisingly so. "Shall we?"

She nodded.

He helped her out and together they walked toward the crush at the door. No one seemed to be paying them any mind.

"Never forget, love," Edmund whispered. "You belong here. This is your birthright."

"My birthright is more than balls and fancy gowns, Edmund." Her voice sounded absurdly mournful amidst all the laughter and chatter of the crowd ahead of them, and she forced a small smile to temper it. "But this is a good start."

His lips curved up in that crooked grin. There and gone in a flash before anyone else could see it. Her chest tightened and her grip on his arm did the same.

That grin was knowing and devilish and kind all at once.

And Savina had the odd thought that it was meant only for her. That she alone was allowed to see it.

It was a silly notion, but one that held as they entered together, bypassing the footman who might announce their entry and skirting the edges of the crowd instead.

"Tell me if this all gets to be too much," he ordered.

She gave a small nod. But in that moment, there was no room for fear in her heart for there was far too much to take in.

The ball was well underway and dancers filled the center of the ballroom when they entered. On either side there were countless clusters of gentlemen and ladies talking and laughing as they sipped from their glasses and fluttered their fans.

The noise alone was overwhelming. The quartet playing on the far side of the room was nearly drowned out by all the voices. A shriek of laughter gave Savina a jolt of alarm.

Edmund leaned down to speak to her. "You've nothing to fear here, child."

Child. The word had her lips clamping together and she glared up at him. "I am no child, Edmund."

There was that flicker of a smile again and…

Her lips parted. Had he done that on purpose?

"Ah, Your Highness, there you are," an older woman called as she approached. "How gracious of you to attend our humble fete."

Savina's brows arched at the obvious lie, and she watched with a mix of amusement and irritation as Edmund lifted the woman's gloved hand and bent over it.

She, meanwhile, had gone unnoticed by the hostess as the older woman with the too-bright smile simpered and fawned over the prince.

Don't get too excited, my darling…

The memory of her father's voice made her eyes sting unexpectedly. The memory seemed to have been jarred out of her as she watched the viscountess flutter her lashes at Edmund.

He might have a prince's title, but it means little, to be sure. He's the youngest son of a youngest son, and while his name holds sway, he has little power.

And power, Savina had known even back then...

Power was what all men truly craved.

Savina tilted her head to the side as she studied the viscountess, still unnoticed.

Women too, she supposed. Every lady in this room was no doubt scheming for more power through marriage and connections.

Savina's gaze roamed the crowd.

"May I present Miss Savina Flint eldest daughter of the Baron—"

He was cut off by the older woman's gasp.

Savina wasn't ignored now. Oh no. The woman was gaping at her with something akin to horror, it seemed. Her eyes were wide and her jaw flapped open. "Lord Galinor's daughter. Back at last. Why, how marvelous!"

ime seemed to distort for Savina after that. First the viscountess introduced one friend and then another.

Soon she was surrounded by a host of older women, a few elderly gentlemen, and one girl who looked to be even younger than Margot.

"I'll be back, my dear," Edmund murmured to her. "I must see to a matter…"

He didn't elaborate, and Savina refused to be a ninny. She could handle being alone in this crowd for a short time. While everyone had expressed astonishment at her arrival, no one had asked a single question about where she'd been or what had brought her back.

In fact, the lack of care in that regard made her burn just a little.

But then again, she hadn't recognized any of the names or titles that had been thrown at her. When the conversation grew too dull to bear, Savina sidled up next to the young girl.

"Miss Mane, was it not?"

She knew it was. The viscountess had hissed in her ear

when the pretty redhead had approached, ducking her head shyly as she'd been introduced.

"Her father is Mr. William Mane. Surely you've heard of the crass businessman."

At Savina's blank expression, she'd added with a sniff.

"He owns every gossip rag in all of England." Leaning in, the older woman had hardly bothered to lower her voice despite the fact that the sweet young girl was standing right beside them. "I wouldn't have invited them at all but for the fact that Mr. Mane has managed to secure an understanding between his daughter and Lord Yarrow."

Savina had nodded, as if any of these names meant anything to her. But now, as the redheaded girl smiled at her eagerly, she found herself wanting to learn more.

In this Miss Mane, she saw a fellow outsider, and right now that seemed more than enough to endear her as a friend.

"Are you enjoying yourself?" she asked the girl.

The girl's smile faltered. "Er...yes?"

Savina laughed. "Mmm. Sounds as if you're enjoying this ball as much as I am." She leaned over to whisper. "Which is to say, not at all."

The girl's giggle was sweet and reminded her so much of Margot that it made her heart ache.

Oh, how she hoped her sister was safe and content in Bristol. King's man was taking a blastedly long time returning with news.

"My father and I were so pleased to hear you've returned to London society, Miss Flint." It sounded so very polite, it might have been rehearsed.

Savina smiled. "How very proper."

"Pardon?"

"Oh, nothing, it's just..." She shook her head. "You seem awfully young to be coming to a party like this one."

The girl smiled again, and this time Savina caught the look in her eyes—a cynicism that belied her age. Perhaps she bore more of a resemblance to herself than to Margot…

"Not so young." With a pointed glance to a cluster of elderly gentlemen nearby, Miss Mane added, "I'm old enough to be married, after all." Her smile quivered. "Soon I will be attending these balls as Lady Yarrow."

Savina frowned over at the men. "Is your intended one of the men over there?"

The girl's sigh was so soft Savina nearly missed it. "Yes, Miss Flint—"

"It's Savina, please."

"Then I do hope you'll call me Vivian."

They shared a smile of understanding. Oh yes, this sweet girl would definitely be a friend.

Vivian leaned in and gestured with her fan. "My father you met, I believe…"

Savina nodded. The older man had an ingratiating smile that made her wary of him instantly.

"My fiancé is the lord he's speaking to just now."

Savina gaped in horror. "But…no."

"Yes."

"But he's ancient!" And that was being kind. The stooped man had thinning silver hair and a cane and— "Vivian, how old are you?"

The other girl's smile was a little sad, but mostly amused, it seemed, by Savina's reaction.

It was settled. Savina liked this girl immensely. She liked anyone who could laugh in the face of sadness.

"I shall be fifteen next month." She swallowed. "And that is when I shall marry."

"No. Surely not." Savina straightened, outraged on this girl's behalf. "That man is eighty years old if he's a day."

Vivian shushed her, but the effect was rather ruined by a giggle. "Sorry, it's just...you seem so horrified."

"That's because I am."

Vivian's answering giggle, made Savina like her even more. So young and sweet, and with her whole life ahead of her.

True, Savina might not be that much older in years, but in life experience she felt as though she'd lived several lifetimes.

However, just then, the look Vivian gave her made her seem far older than fifteen. "It's a good match. Or so I keep being told."

The last part was added under her breath. Savina turned to her. For the first time since they'd arrived, Savina very nearly forgot about the crowd around her and who she might meet while here.

She was well and truly focused on the girl beside her. "If you do not wish to marry him—"

"Oh no, please. It's all right. My father insists, you see, and...and I don't mind. He'll provide well for me, and..." She trailed off, no doubt at Savina's expression of disbelief. "And I'll have a family of my own."

The girl's expression grew so sweetly optimistic that Savina didn't have the heart to deny her this hope.

"I'm sure you are right," Savina said quietly. But before she could say any more, the air was cut through with a voice that Savina had grown used to hearing in her nightmares.

"Why, if it isn't my darling stepdaughter," the voice cooed. "Savina, my dear...."

Savina turned slowly, her heart hammering and her stomach sinking. Her gaze landed on Lucinda and when their eyes met, everything in Savina recoiled as if she'd been struck.

Lucinda looked the same. Exactly the same. Her dark eyes, the curve of her lips. That dark auburn hair that was piled upon her head like a crown. The woman was the same height as Savina now, but in her mind's eye, she was still taller, still more powerful.

No!

Savina snapped out of it, pushing aside that age-old fear and straightening to her full height just as Lucinda reached her.

She was a child no longer. She was a grown woman and she'd faced far more terrifying foes than Lucinda.

To her surprise, Lucinda caught her by the shoulders and drew her in for an airy kiss on both cheeks. "At last," Lucinda cried.

For their audience, of course.

Savina was well aware of the stares they were receiving. Stares Lucinda was actively trying to garner.

Savina's heart pounded furiously as her mind raced to catch up. Lucinda didn't seem in the least surprised to see her, and that...

That was a disappointment, Savina admitted to herself. She'd hoped to shock Lucinda. To revel in her fear.

But her stepmother was smiling at her with an outrageously false kindness.

"How good to see you, my dear," she said. And then, with a focused look that seemed to peer straight inside Savina, she added, "And where is your sister? I thought she'd be at your side, like always."

Savina's mouth opened but no sound came out. She'd practiced a hundred quips, had come up with a slew of insults for the day she finally faced Lucinda.

But somehow here, surrounded by Lucinda's ilk, and the center of attention amidst a gawking crowd of strangers...

She couldn't think of a single retort.

Instead, she found herself struggling to adapt as Lucinda continued to gush and prattle, turning some of her comments to the people surrounding them. "...doesn't she look just as beautiful as ever. So like her mother, is she not?"

It was a performance. All of it, a performance.

Just as she'd executed her role of doting stepmother back when Savina was little, she reprised the role now with obvious relish. Her eyes glittered with a knowing amusement when she caught Savina staring.

To Savina's relief, Edmund's tall form cut through the crowd to her left even as Vivian sidled closer on her other side. "Are you all right, Savina?"

Vivian was sweet, and apparently intuitive enough to sense that Savina was not delighted to see her stepmother.

Far from it.

But the sight of Edmund's scowling expression, the sneer that tugged at his lips as he took in the two of them talking, had relief pulsing in her veins. Her lungs started to expand as if she could fully breathe for the first time.

He was nearly to them now, and Savina's mind echoed the words *Ally. Friend. I am not alone.*

His gaze flickered to hers and his jaw tightened. She heard it again with a surge of relief.

This time I am not alone.

Lucinda followed her gaze, and to Savina's surprise, the other woman's face brightened at the sight of him approaching.

His scowl didn't seem to faze her in the slightest, let alone make her cower as Savina had hoped it might.

"Edmund, darling," she laughed, her tone light and high with welcome. "Come and join us, won't you?"

As if he wasn't doing just that.

Savina tried not to let her surprise show when Lucinda rested a hand on Edmund's arm in a possessive gesture.

They knew each other then. The fact that she'd called him Edmund proved they knew each other well.

Which wasn't a surprise, was it? She'd been married to his best friend. Of course they knew each other. He'd never said he didn't know her. It didn't make them friends.

And she knew full well he was not Lucinda's ally.

Your enemies are my enemies. Hadn't he told her that?

Savina bit the inside of her lip to try and focus. She must ignore the emotions that Lucinda's presence stirred and focus on the next move in the game that was laid out before her.

"Lucinda, you are looking well," Savina said.

Lucinda's brows arched at the use of her given name. But if she thought for one moment that Savina would use their father's title or, heaven forbid, call her Mother...

Ha! Anger was a blessed relief as she faced down the other woman.

At last.

Finally.

Lucinda pretended to lower her voice, but everyone around her could hear her murmur, "I wish I could say the same, dear, I really do. But my goodness, your overseas travel must have taken quite a toll on you..." She trailed off with a tsk as she eyed Savina from head to toe in ill-disguised dismay.

Savina burned with rage and embarrassment as a group of women behind her tittered behind their fans.

Her tongue itched to lash out. *You wretched woman. You vile beast.*

But that was not the game afoot. This was not the time for shouts and insults. If she wished to face Lucinda on her territory, she had to play by the ton's rules.

"Lucinda." Edmund spoke up, and Savina felt a flare of gratitude that he was there. "Come, my dear. It is her first outing."

Savina finally tore her gaze from Lucinda to stare at him. *My dear?*

His tone was arrogant and cool, and his gaze was so patronizing when it met Savina's, her anger ratcheted up and made her blood boil.

What was he doing?

Why was he talking to Lucinda like she was his friend and Savina was some inferior young upstart?

Lucinda looped her arm through Edmund's with a smile that made Savina feel sick with its clear satisfaction.

"I can hardly believe you found her, Edmund." Lucinda shook her head, her gaze bright with what one would assume was triumph. "My dear, darling stepdaughter." She clasped a hand to her chest, her voice carrying for all to hear. "When you ran away after finishing school, I began to lose hope."

Fury made Savina's head fuzzy. With one phrase, Lucinda had rewritten the tale of how Savina had come to be back in London like a deft poet.

And Savina was left gaping. Again. Blast it all, she was woefully out of place and ridiculously uninformed.

She shouldn't have come here tonight. She should have been more prepared.

Her gaze moved to Edmund as understanding began to dawn. He should have prepared her for this.

Lucinda expected her to be here, and it was Savina who'd been caught in a trap.

She quivered as that now familiar rage coursed through her like a tempest. And like a storm at sea, she was helpless in its wake.

Lucinda, meanwhile, kept talking, filling the air with some farfetched tale about how Savina had run away and been missing until 'dear Edmund' had found her.

Savina didn't have to glance around her to know that any good sentiments she might have incurred up until this point were dashed, now that she was made out to be a trouble-making runaway.

A scandal.

A hysterical laugh rose up in Savina, as she stared at Lucinda and then a grim Edmund.

Her hands tightened into fists and for one moment she fantasized about lunging forward and dealing with this cunning guttersnipe the way she would a thieving whore back in Vestry Lane.

The way King had taught her.

Her lips curved up into sneer and she physically ached to plant a facer right here and now. But a glance at Edmund's dark, burning gaze reminded her of where she was and why.

"All that matters is that I am here now," Savina managed to interject. "I was so very homesick, you know. I do wish you would have brought me back sooner."

She drew in a steadying breath, her voice high and breathy and youthful as she addressed Lucinda...and the crowd. "It has been so difficult to be away from you all."

Lucinda's jaw ticked, and her nostrils flared as sympathy for Savina spread through the gathered crowd.

Savina's smile felt infinitely more genuine as she reveled in this small victory.

But then Lucinda recovered, and with a smile for the sake of their audience, she said, "Yes, you're right. It has been too long." Her lips quivered with emotion. "For a little while there I'd feared we'd lost you forever, but..." She took an unsteady breath, and Savina was certain she could feel the sympathy of the crowd once more swinging back in Lucinda's favor. "But then my dear husband refused to give up his quest to find you."

Lucinda turned her smile up to...Edmund.

My dear husband.

Savina's mind went blank. She lost the ability to smile

completely and for a moment she thought she might lose consciousness as she dragged her eyes back to Edmund's face.

Husband.

He didn't meet her gaze. He was busy staring down at Lucinda. His...his wife?

No. No, that couldn't be true. But...

But...

She'd called him husband. And everyone around them, including Edmund, seemed to accept this as true.

She was distantly aware of Vivian's soft, sweet voice beside her whispering, "Are you all right?"

Was she? The thought was nearly laughable.

She stumbled back a step to get away from Lucinda's vindictive smile. It was a smile of supremacy. She knew she'd aimed true.

Savina couldn't stand it.

Lucinda turned her gaze up to Edmund, letting out a watery laugh. "You found her, sweet man. You found her."

Sarina's blood ran cold as Edmund returned her smile. "Yes, my dear. I found her...for you."

"But what of sweet Margot? Where is she?" Lucinda asked.

"She was not fit to return right away, I'm afraid. Her health has been somewhat of a concern. But I have ensured she has the best care possible." Edmund's attention was fully on Lucinda now, and a voice shrieked in her mind.

Rage, yes, but also...betrayal.

He'd found her for Lucinda.

He'd delivered her to the evil woman who'd ruined their lives, and now he'd do the same with Margot.

Her breathing came quick and shallow. She could not cry here. She could not rage and scream and lash out.

That inability made her chest feel too tight and her head swam with incoherent thoughts that raced in a loop.

"Not to worry, my dear. She is in need of some rest and recuperation. She will join us when she is well again," Edmund was saying.

"Oh, my Benedict will be so pleased to hear the news." Lucinda looked at the ladies around them. "You know he really was heartbroken when he'd heard the girls ran away from their school. Such a scandalous affair. " She looked to Savina with a saccharine smile. "It will take some effort to bounce back from this, my dear, but we shall all do our best."

Savina's skin went hot and cold at once, it seemed.

Like no time had passed at all, she felt herself helpless in the face of Lucinda's conniving ways.

And the worst part was, she'd come here of her own volition. She'd left relative safety and had sent her sister off on her own, and all because...

Her desperate gaze darted back to Edmund.

All because she'd been foolish enough to think she could trust this man.

Savina didn't bother with excuses. She waved off Vivian's concern as she turned on her heel...and ran.

11

*E*dmund's lungs hitched at the pain he saw in Savina's eyes just before she'd turned away, fighting her way through the crowd.

He started to give chase but Lucinda's fingers dug into his arm like claws. "Now, now, my dear. Let's avoid causing another scene for poor Savina, hmm?"

Her voice was a coo that made his stomach churn as he turned to look at her.

Beautiful.

Perfection, that was what Leopold had said in his letter after he'd married.

No one could replace my dearly departed Eloise, but my new bride, Edmund...she is kindness itself, and will be such a good influence on the girls...

She is perfection.

There's no such thing as perfection, old chum. That's what he'd said in jest in his response.

Lord, if only he'd known then how horrid Leopold's choice of wife could be.

She batted her lashes up at him. "Darling, why do you

look so distressed?"

The smugness in her eyes was in direct opposition to the affection in her voice.

"Not distressed, my dear," he said. "Merely surprised, that's all."

"But surely I was the one who ought to be shocked." Her eyes glittered with malice. "I assume you did not tell me you were bringing my darling stepdaughter to the ball tonight because you meant to surprise me." She patted his arm with her free hand. "Such a doting husband you are."

His jaw clenched tight.

Her voice lowered further, and while her smile never faltered, her tone turned cold as ice. "Did you think you could sneak her into society without me knowing, dearest?"

When he didn't answer, she turned a wistful gaze toward a departing Savina, casting herself as the very picture of a concerned mother figure. "Or perhaps this was your idea of a joke." She glanced up at him, her eyes hard. "If so, it was a cruel one, don't you think?"

Cruel. Yes, that was what it had been. He tugged his arm free, leaning down. "What matters is that she's back. Everyone knows it. And there's nothing you can do about that."

Her smile fell, her nostrils flared, but she didn't try to stop him this time as he followed in Savina's wake.

The crowds parted more easily for him than they had for Savina, but all the while he dodged and sideskirted his way through the daunting crush of onlookers and gossips, he cursed himself for how the evening had played out.

It was his fault. All of it.

Lucinda had more spies in her network then he'd given her credit, and in underestimating her, he may very well have driven Savina away for good.

Alarm flared. All this searching and planning and

plotting…

He couldn't lose Savina now.

"Savina," he called when he reached the long, dark hallway leading to the hosts' private quarters and caught sight of her skirts whipping around a corner.

She didn't slow down, or even glance his way.

All he'd managed to do was startle a pair of lovers who had stolen away into the shadows. The woman squeaked in alarm as he ran in their direction, but he paid them no mind.

The blasted girl was going to ruin her reputation before they'd even begun to restore it.

"Savina, stop!" Edmund overtook her just as she rounded another corner, into a pitch-black hallway, and without thinking he caught her to him, crushing her back to his chest as he buried his face in her neck, heedless of the way she fought and railed like an alley cat.

"Stop it," he snapped, his voice a low growl in her ear.

Lifting her into his arms, he carried her into the nearest room. Only moonlight gave some semblance of where they were, and he stopped just inside, shutting the door behind him. "Do you want to undo all my work, is that it, princess?"

The sound she made was more of a snarl than anything he'd ever heard.

"Bloody hell. Calm down."

She only fought harder, but his arms were tight around her waist, and all her fighting managed to accomplish was pushing that sweetly rounded bottom of hers against his groin. He shifted to get a better hold of her and now his hands were splayed across her ribcage, so close to the underside of her breasts, it took all of his will not to let them slide up a little further, to touch the bosom that had been driving him mad from the moment he'd seen her atop the staircase, a vision in silk and lace…and just enough tantalizing cleavage showing to bring a man to his knees.

When her heel came back and connected with his shin, he let out a grunt and moved forward toward a desk that was illuminated by the moon's glow.

He didn't stop until he had her trapped against the hard wooden surface. She let out a gasp.

"Control yourself, or I will have to take control for you."

Her head came back to press against his shoulder as she tried to wriggle her way free.

All she did was cause him excruciating pain as that lithe body of hers writhed against his. His cock was hard as a rock, and he knew she felt it whenever she ground her bottom back against him.

His grip on her tightened. "Stop that."

"Or what?" This time she rolled her hips in a deliberate move meant to torture.

His body reacted instinctively, giving in to temptation as slid a hand up and cupped her right breast. He squeezed the soft, warm flesh, hidden only by that thin slip of fabric.

Her sharp intake made his cock throb.

"You like that, princess?"

She shook her head, but she didn't speak. Instead, her back arched as she pressed against his hand. He could feel the hard nub of her nipple against his palm, though the fabric, and the sound that escaped her was a soft moan.

It was more than he could bear. Nearly a week he'd been so close to her he could smell her intoxicating scent and feel the warmth of her skin. He'd been aching to have her from the very start, and now she was here in his arms…and she was moaning like a needy little angel.

Shifting slightly, he nudged one of his knees between her thighs to part them, and this time when she rocked her arse up and back, his swollen cock fitted perfectly between her thighs.

She stilled.

He...

Oh Christ save his soul—he ground his hard cock against her bottom.

Her breathing grew harsh and shallow but she made no move to stop him or pull away. The thick materials of her gown and his breeches were between them, but his muscles bunched and tensed as heat flooded his loins and made thinking nigh impossible.

He forced himself to still. To breathe. His hand still cupped her breast, and he told himself to move it. To back away.

But just before he could, she shocked him by rubbing her bottom against him again. Softly, almost tentatively. And while one of her hands stayed planted on top of the desk, the other came up to cover his hand which rested on her breast. She arched slightly and his hand on her waist tightened as he fought the urge to take what she offered.

To pull down that bodice until her perfect tits spilled over. To hitch up her skirts and feel that soft wet heat between her thighs and...

His mind stopped and his chest grew painfully tight when she moaned as if...as if she was dreaming of the same satisfaction.

She turned her head to the side, and her breath fanned over his jaw. "Is this how you take control...*stepfather?*"

The word was as good as a shock of ice water dumped over his head. He jerked back slightly, and Savina took advantage of that little space between them to turn and face him head on.

He was still close enough, though, to see the desire there in her eyes. Even in the moonlight, he could see the flush in her cheeks and the way her lips were parted as she struggled to catch her breath.

She wasn't unaffected.

And she hated him for that.

He understood this just as he understood that what she was really upset about wasn't him touching her.

"You're her husband." Her face twisted with revulsion. "You took me away from that place, and I trusted you. I let…" With a soft groan she covered her eyes.

His heart slammed against his ribcage at the sight of her agony.

"I let you take Margot away." Her hand dropped and her eyes flashed with anger and desperation. "What have you done with her? Where is she?"

"Your sister is safe and well," he assured her.

"I don't believe you."

"I got word from my driver that they've been waylaid by weather and are spending some time at a roadside inn, but he expects they'll be in Bristol by week's end."

She blinked rapidly. "Why would I believe that? Why would a trust a word you say when—"

"When I'm married to the guttersnipe who ruined your life?"

"So you know, then. You know what she did—"

"I know enough." He heaved a sigh and let out another breath.

"And I know nothing," she bit out.

Hell. He couldn't blame her for hating him. Couldn't even argue with that mistrust that was in her eyes. He'd meant to tell her…

He knew he'd have to tell her. "I couldn't risk telling you my relationship with Lucinda."

Her lips parted, her eyes wide with disbelief and censor.

A muscle ticked in his jaw. He wasn't used to having to explain himself. Not to anyone. But he owed her this much, at least. "You barely trusted me as it was, and I couldn't risk you running from me—"

"Liar." She spit the word in his face. "You lied to me from the start."

"I didn't tell you the whole truth," he admitted. "But I did not lie about who I am or my intentions for you."

"So you planned this then?" Her eyes sparked with rage. "You planned to bring me back here just so she could humiliate me—"

"No!" He gripped her arms, pulling her close. "Savina, no. I was going to tell you. After you were introduced. She wasn't supposed to be here tonight, and I planned to tell you my connection to her just as soon as—"

"You're a liar." Her face hardened, her eyes dark as the night in the dimly lit room. "Why should I believe anything you say?"

God, how he hated the pain in her voice. She tried, yet failed, to cover it with anger. When she pulled away, out of his reach, he didn't stop her. It would be best for everyone if she stayed far away from him.

These past few days had been torture enough. Anytime he was alone in the same house with her, he'd done everything in his power to keep her at arms' length.

And now here, tonight...

He scrubbed a hand over his face before turning to face her.

She was still backing away from him. Slowly. Warily.

His chest ached to see that wariness.

"How could you marry that woman knowing what she'd done—"

"I did it for you. For your sister." There was truth there... if not the whole of it.

"Ha! Five years we survived in that hellhole, doing things you couldn't even imagine to keep ourselves fed and warm." Her voice was ragged, and her hands clenched into fists. "I'd never have come with you if I'd known—"

"Precisely."

His one word sliced through her tirade and left her gaping.

He moved toward her, clamping down on the heat that surged with every inch he drew closer. "Would you have come with me if I'd told you who I was?"

Her brows drew down. "Of course not."

"I knew you did not trust me. And with good reason, I'd add." He took one more step and was oddly heartened when she didn't back away from him. "I understood that you would not trust me at all if you knew I'd married that woman."

"And you were right. I don't."

He scrubbed a hand over his face, striving for patience. But between Lucinda's barbs and the state of torturous arousal he was in every time Savina was near…

His patience was limited.

"I cannot believe you sprang this trap on me." Her breasts heaved as she struggled to contain her emotions. He tried not to notice.

But hell if he could forget the way she'd felt in his arms. The way she'd responded so quickly and with such passion.

If he were a lesser man he suspected he could have her here and now, in this dark room. He could kiss her and touch her in ways sure to make her tremble until she willingly hitched up that gown and parted her legs and—

"Fuck." He turned away from her with a growl. If this plan was ever to succeed, he had to stop thinking of her like she was a woman.

Like she was *his* woman.

She wasn't, and she could never be.

"Yes, I imagine that didn't work out at all the way you'd planned." Her tone was taunting.

He shot her a dark look. "What do you know of my plans?"

"Blessedly little."

"Just as I know little of yours," he quipped. For a long moment they stared at one another and he was grateful she didn't try to protest. "There is nothing meek or biddable about you, love, and don't think I believe for a moment that you didn't come back to society without a plan of your own."

She shifted, her lips pouting.

God how he wanted to crush her to him and nip at her lips until she sighed in submission.

"My only plan was to see her," she said at last, her voice quiet.

"Only see her?" He didn't try to hide his disbelief.

"To start. I wanted to learn as much as I could about her. To watch her. To find her weakness." She tipped her head to the side and even in this dark lighting, he could feel her gaze on him, studying him. "I made the mistake once before, you see, of confronting Lucinda unprepared."

He didn't respond, but something in his demeanor gave him away.

She arched a brow. "Ah, so that part you do not know."

He gritted his jaw. Blast. He was not used to being kept in the dark. Well, not by anyone but Lucinda, of course. And he and his fair, repulsive bride had made an art out of their secrets and manipulations.

A muscle in his jaw ticked as he eyed Savina, a pale, incandescent beauty in the moonlight.

A treasure. And his best friend's daughter.

A young lady who ought to have known nothing of the darker side of life. She ought to have been raised with a dozen nursemaids, and governesses, and footmen all willing and able to do her bidding.

And instead she was alone in the dark with a man she didn't trust.

A man who perhaps…she *shouldn't* trust.

He pushed aside the thought.

"So you see, I learned the hard way that to do battle with a woman like Lucinda requires patience and cunning." Her brows drew down in a glare. "And yet you ruined any chance of that with your lies."

"I did not know she'd be here tonight. She wasn't supposed to be in town, but—"

"I don't believe you. You've done nothing but lie."

"I never lied about being your ally."

She stared at him for a long moment, searching his features like maybe she could read his secrets there.

"Then why?" Her voice held a note of pleading that nearly undid him. This young lady held herself together so well, kept her chin so high, but her vulnerability slipped out when she forgot to keep up her guard.

"I told you," he said slowly. "You never would have come with me if I'd—"

"Yes, yes." She waved aside his words. "But you could have told me after. You could have given me some warning."

The look of betrayal couldn't even be hidden by the shadows, and he felt his chest split in two. He never wanted to see that look in her eyes again.

Especially not when she was gazing up at him. "You could have warned me before I'd walked in here tonight."

"I did not know," he said slowly. Admitting it was painful to his pride.

Her brows knit in confusion. "You didn't know that bitch was your wife?"

A huff of surprised laughter escaped him. "No. Of course not. I meant…" He sighed. "I'd hoped to shock her, not you."

She held his gaze steadily.

"She wasn't supposed to be in town tonight. I'd hoped you could make your entrance into society first. Spread stories about your time abroad and how happy you are to be back..." He waved a dismissive hand. "I was hoping to catch her off guard before her return."

"But she knew." Her nostrils flared. "She knew what to expect, and I was the one caught off guard."

He flinched because...yes. That was indeed what happened.

"You're not sorry," she said.

He paused, considering his response. "I did not mean to hurt you tonight, Savina. In the end, I do care about you and Margot, and getting you both what you deserve."

"But?" she said. There was that taunting tone again as she crossed her arms over her chest. "Come now, Edmund. We both know I am not the child you wish I might be. I stopped being a child a long time ago thanks to her."

"I know." His voice was gruffer than intended. But for chrissakes, he was painfully, brutally, achingly aware of her maturity.

That was the problem.

"For all your friendship to my father, I cannot imagine you brought me here solely to look after my interests or Margot's," she continued. Her eyes were narrowed, her gaze much too clever and insightful. "You had an ulterior motive. I want to know what it is."

His lips twitched up at the corners, something deep down in his chest lightening at that stubborn tone and her demanding ways.

A little minx, if he'd ever met one.

"I do want to help you, Savina. I did not lie about that."

She narrowed her eyes even further, and could have sworn he saw her mind working. "But you want to hurt Lucinda more."

He blinked in surprise. And he hesitated just a moment too long.

"Ah, I see," she said.

The disappointment in her tone made his muscles tense and he had to fight the urge to reach out for her. To end this conversation.

But here in the dim moonlight, he felt more seen than he'd ever been in his life. She looked at him and saw straight through him.

Right to the dastardly, clever bastard he'd always been. The one her father had been much too good for. The man who always had an agenda.

Even now.

Even with her.

Savina crossed her arms as she assessed him, her gaze filled with censure. "You want to help us because we are your friend's daughters, but more than anything you want to win whatever game you're playing with your *wife*."

Her lips curved into a sneer at that word, and he couldn't blame her. The word wife had come to turn his stomach.

"Why? Did she cuckold you?" Her sneer turned to a smirk. "Or did she lie and deceive like you did to me?"

A muscle in his jaw ticked once more. "Don't compare me to her, love."

She looked like she might argue, but she kept silent.

"I'm on your side," he said.

She made a sound of disbelief. "I'm on my own. Like always."

"No. Not anymore." He moved closer and this time he gave in to the temptation to touch her. He cupped her cheek as gently as he was able. "I have a history of my own with Lucinda, it's true. But it's not what you think. She did not have an affair."

Her eyes flashed with an emotion he couldn't name. "So she's a faithful little wife to you then, is she?"

He nearly laughed aloud as that dark emotion in her eyes took on a shape he knew well. It was the same emotion he felt every time he thought of another man coming anywhere near Savina. "Don't tell me you're jealous, love."

She scowled.

He smiled. It was a crooked, wicked grin that only highlighted his scar and would no doubt frighten most gently bred ladies.

But if anything, it seemed to put her at ease.

"Lucinda and I have a marriage in name only," he said. "It has always only been a business arrangement."

Her gaze turned searching again. She wanted to believe that. His heart gave a sharp kick at the thought.

"I don't trust you." Her words sliced through the thick tension between them.

He dropped his hand from her cheek but held her gaze. "And I don't expect you to."

Surprise and maybe even disappointment flickered across her features.

"You've been treated too badly by so many," he added. "I know that your trust will not be easily gained. But I swear to you, on your father's grave, that I will help you and your sister. That has always been part of my plan."

"Just not the entirety of it," she snapped, speaking aloud what he'd left unsaid.

He didn't argue. "Our goals align, Savina. That is all that matters."

"Is it?" She flinched ever so slightly before she seemed to catch herself. Then her gaze grew shuttered and her eyes dropped. "I suppose it is."

"Then, princess…" He waited until she lifted her eyes to meet his gaze. "Do we have an understanding?"

12

Our goals align, Savina...

      Edmund's words still rang in her ears as he hurried her into a waiting carriage. How he'd managed to arrange for his carriage to meet them and slip her out through a servants' entrance was still a marvel.

The man had taken control of the situation with a firm hand and a tone that brooked no arguments.

Just as he'd taken command of her.

Her body still ached, her gown too tight where it stretched over her tight nipples, her bottom wriggling against the seat of the carriage as she recalled the feel of his hard member pressing between her thighs.

Control yourself, or I will have to take control for you.

As the carriage rattled beneath her, she was all too aware of Edmund's gaze upon her. Watching her like she might jump out of the moving vehicle at any moment in some act of rebellion.

And truthfully, some part of her wished she could, if only to escape his burning gaze, which seemed to see every part of her.

His low voice cut the heavy silence. "I will escort you to your home and return to make your excuses."

Her jaw clenched. So many aspects of that one simple comment set the fire of rage burning once more in her belly.

Rage and...something else she dared not name, but which seemed to be intertwined with her fury.

She turned to look out the window, but the night cast the cobblestone streets in darkness and all she saw was the shifting outlines of townhomes.

"My home," she muttered. "Now I see why I couldn't come to stay with you, I suppose." When he made no response, she turned to face him. "Tell me. Did you take my father's home in addition to his wife?"

The tick of a muscle in his jaw was the only sign that he'd heard her. "Don't be a child, Savina."

A blow for a blow. But this time her mind went back to the way he'd felt pressed against her. He'd taken control, yes, but there'd been no doubt in her mind that he'd had no control over his body's reaction to her.

Satisfaction slid through her at the knowledge that he'd been just as affected as she. And she had been affected, there was no doubt about that.

Even now, she found her gaze sliding down to rest on his mouth. A cruel, harsh gash of a mouth that was undoubtedly accustomed to issuing orders and being obeyed.

And yet, she couldn't help but wonder if it would soften with a kiss. If that firm touch he'd used to fondle her breast would gentle in a moment of tenderness.

Her throat swelled even as her belly tightened with a nervous flutter of anticipation.

"Where has your mind gone, pet?" His voice was a low rumble that sent a shiver down her spine.

She glanced away quickly, but not quickly enough. He

must know what she'd been thinking, and she was grateful for the darkness that hid the blush in her cheeks.

It was the novelty of it, that was all. That was the only reason for this odd curiosity and the stirring of urges that made her feel hungry and needy.

She'd been touched by one other man, and it hadn't felt anything like what she'd experienced tonight. She'd assumed that was how it always felt when a man pawed at a woman. That the slick, oily dread and the stomach-turning revulsion were what she'd always feel with a man.

Oh certainly, she'd heard some women in Vestry Lane giggle and squeal and whisper lewd comments about the pleasures they experienced with their lovers. But truly, Savina had thought it an act.

A display of eagerness for the men in their lives, to ensure their paying customers returned.

She shut her eyes for a moment, ridding her mind of the image of what it would be like to lie in Edmund's bed, to part her legs for him...of Edmund's broad chest and firm arms trapping her, holding her down as he growled out dirty commands and....

Her inhale was a gasp that split the silence as good as a knife.

"Tonight was too much for you." Edmund's tone was achingly gruff. Not quite gentle, but far less harsh and distant than she'd grown accustomed these past few days.

Suddenly he was right back to being the man she'd met during their first encounter—that mysterious, surprising man she'd come face to face with in a brothel.

Not her father's friend. Not her stepmother's husband. Just...Edmund.

"You should have warned me," she said, just as quietly.

He didn't answer, but the lack of a protest seemed to be an admission of its own.

"Now she's gotten the best of me." The words tasted as bitter as they felt. "All this time of waiting for revenge and—"

"And you will have it," he finished.

His tone was so certain, she blinked in surprise.

"I admit," he said slowly. "Tonight's encounter was not ideal. I underestimated the extent of her resources. She caught me off guard."

His voice was stiff, as was his posture.

"I take it that doesn't happen often," she murmured.

His huff of laughter made her belly flutter anew. She swallowed hard. This man had betrayed her trust. He'd let Lucinda win...this round at least.

She straightened. But the battle was not over yet.

She found herself thinking of her father's chess board. Lucinda might have caught a pawn, but now Savina was in a better position than she'd been before.

After all, the initial encounter was over and done. That satisfaction faltered when she recalled the way it had ended. "She cast me as the runaway daughter. I'll be a scandal."

He grunted in agreement. "There's an upside to being a scandal, you know." His gaze met hers. "So long as you know how to play it to your advantage."

She gave him an appraising look. Her thoughts spun off in multiple directions at once as she realized what he meant. If she wasn't expected to abide by traditional societal conventions, then that changed things, did it not?

Ideas began to form, mere wisps and threads, but enough to give her hope.

If she wasn't bound by societies' rules, well then...that was all the more freedom for her, now wasn't it?

Edmund's brows drew down. "I don't like that look of mischief, Savina. Whatever ideas you're forming, drop them right here and now. I will ensure that you and Margot receive what is rightfully yours, but I will not have you endangering yourself in the process."

"A little late to be worried about my welfare, don't you think?"

He leaned forward. "Lucinda will pay for what she's done to you, but she will be taken down by me, do you understand?"

Her earlier anger bubbled up in her chest and she tried her best to swallow it down. She needed this man.

Her mind drifted to Margot.

They both needed Edmund's help. And whether Savina liked it or not, she'd already placed her trust in him by letting him handle Margot's arrangements.

Her belly fluttered with nerves. How she hoped she had not made a mistake for which her sister would have to pay.

The silence grew thick again, and as they approached the townhome, she found she hated this plan. "Don't go back there," she said before she could stop herself.

The thought of Lucinda smiling so smugly at Edward, of her wrapping her hands around his arm and squeezing tight.

The thought had a dark, slithering snake coiling in her belly.

"I must," he said.

For the first time since she'd met him, he sounded...tired. Possibly weary.

"I need to make your excuses and try to temper whatever gossip Lucinda has started about you."

"And then?"

He met her gaze evenly, waiting for her to explain.

"After the ball," she said slowly, surprised by how calm she sounded given the tumult inside her. "Will you return to my father's home with Lucinda?"

When he didn't answer, that dark poison in her gut spread to her limbs.

"Just the two of you, I suppose," her tone turned taunting. "So cozy. What a lovely image."

His eyes snapped with anger but he didn't take the bait. "Not just the two of us. Benedict will have returned with her."

"Aw, little Benny." Her voice dripped with disdain.

She'd only met him as a child a handful of times and had liked him little even then. He'd been spoiled and coddled, and both girls had ceased to exist in their stepmother's eyes whenever he was around.

It should have come as no surprise that he would be back in her claws now that he was grown.

Was he still under her persuasion?

Was he still that spoiled and entitled little brat?

The carriage stopped and she knew better than to ask Edmund for any information he wasn't readily willing to give. And up until this evening that had been detrimental indeed.

But now...

Well, now that she'd made her entrance into society and Lucinda knew she was here, there was no reason she ought to be a prisoner in her own home, was there?

True, she might not have succeeded in making many acquaintances this evening, but...

She thought of the sweet, young Vivian who'd been kind to her when everyone else merely whispered about her and cast her curious stares.

Vivian, whose father was said to be the man behind the gossip rags.

Perhaps she'd come away with one friend. And one well-connected friend was all she needed in order to learn about the other players in this game.

Her lips were curved up in a smug little smile by the time

the driver opened the door for her and Edmund bid her a good night.

Perhaps this evening hadn't been such a loss after all.

She held Edmund's gaze through the carriage window as it rolled away, taking him back to the ball.

Back to his wife.

Her gut twisted with anger and shame. She'd placed her trust in that man too quickly and had been burnt for it.

The housekeeper met her with a brilliant smile and Savina let a maid bustle about her, getting her out of the glorious gown and unpinning her elegant coiffure.

All the while her mind was whirling.

It was no good now to moan about the mistakes she'd made. All she could do was keep her eyes on the next move in this game of chess.

And Savina had her next mark in mind.

Benedict.

Little Benny. His mama's pride and joy.

He was Lucinda's weakness, and what luck that he was here in town. She bid her maid goodnight but sat for a long while in front of the vanity, regarding her reflection as she plotted out the first step in her new plan.

First thing in the morning, she'd send a note to young Vivian and see what sort of knowledge she could glean. Particularly about what had become of Lucinda's precious Benedict.

When at last her candle flickered, nearly extinguished, she blew it out and headed to her bed.

She'd missed Margot ever since she'd put her in that carriage and sent her on her way. But tonight…

Tonight Savina felt more alone than ever. The servants answered to a man she hardly knew. And the only person she could call friend in this part of town was a girl more powerless than even she and Margot.

Our goals align, Savina.

She stared up at the canopy above her bed, only just visible in the darkness.

Edmund could not be considered a friend. And now she knew better than to trust him.

Once more she thought of Margot.

With a shaky sigh she nibbled on her lip. She knew better than to trust Edmund...any more than she already had.

But Margot's safety was in his hands. The deed was done.

"Oh Snow, I hope I haven't made a mistake in trusting him with your safekeeping." The whisper sounded loud in the darkness.

Loud...and silly.

She turned onto her side with a huff.

It was paranoia talking, that was all. Margot was probably already in Bristol, safe and well. She'd no doubt get a letter from Snow or a message from King telling her so.

Fear still niggled.

Margot *was* safe...wasn't she?

13

*R*ain still spattered the windows of the inn, but the driver assured Margot that the passage was now clear.

And thank heavens for that.

Margot wasn't certain she could survive another day cooped up inside.

"Are you certain you'll be all right?" Her maid hovered at her shoulder.

She turned to face Betty, smiling at the concern she saw there. "I promise. I'll be fine."

The driver and footman accompanying her were as good as friends after spending so much time under one roof. She had nothing to fear there.

And as soon as she arrived in Bristol—the driver informed her—she'd be greeted by a houseful of servants, lady's maids included.

"Your sister needs you," Margot added, patting the young woman's arm in assurance. "Sick with a baby on the way and four little ones to tend to, she is far more in need of your two hands than I am." She smiled. "I will be fine for the remainder of this journey. And rest assured, Prince Edmund will not be made to believe you abandoned me."

The maid pursed her lips but didn't argue.

"We should be there by nightfall, barring any further mishaps," Margot continued.

She sounded more confident than she felt. The storms had ebbed, and the men sent to scout out the roads had told them that the bridge was clear, but looking out at the gloomy, gray sky did little to reassure her that their journey would be smooth.

"If you're certain, miss," Betty finally said.

Margot smiled. "Of course I am."

The maid gave her quick curtsey before walking away, no doubt to make her own arrangements back home to care for her sister.

And Margot was left alone.

Not for long, though. Soon enough, the driver came to fetch her and help her into the carriage.

But once inside, she felt that isolation again... and had far too much time to think. And stew.

By nightfall she would be in Bristol, and in a new home. But for how long? And when would Savina join her?

And—the worry that had been nagging at her for days now—could they really trust this man who claimed to be their father's friend?

"Do we have any other choice?" she murmured.

The empty carriage seemed to mock her with its answering silence.

When her thoughts turned to Savina, and her worries turned to fear for her sister's safety, she knew she had to think about something else. Anything other than the uncertainty that lay before her and whom she'd left behind.

She nearly wept with relief when the carriage halted for a brief reprieve at an inn far smaller and more rustic than the one where they'd stayed in for days. Still, it was a blessing to Margot to step outside into the gray afternoon and feel solid ground beneath her feet.

Her stomach still felt the rock and roil of the carriage, which had tossed her this way and that with every turn in the road.

When the driver and footman told her they were ready to continue, they must have seen some of her weariness because the driver gave her an understanding smile.

"The roads should be all right now, miss. Safe enough to continue. We should still reach Bristol by nightfall... as long as we have smooth passage through the woods."

She narrowed her eyes at the slight hesitation in his voice, wariness stealing over her. "Why would we not have smooth passage?"

The men shared an awkward smile. "Nothing for you to worry about, miss." The footman gave her an unconvincing smile.

"Just stories," the driver added.

And all at once she remembered.

She nearly laughed out loud. Surely these grown men weren't truly afraid of this beast who supposedly haunted the woods.

Feasting on human flesh? She gave a little huff of amusement. Really, how silly. It might have given her a nightmare or two, but surely these men weren't honestly frightened by such tales.

But she saw the men casting dubious glances in every direction as they headed back to the carriage.

"You're not..." A nervous laugh escaped. "You're not truly worried about that hooded hunter, are you?"

The driver didn't look amused. "The village folk around these parts might have spun the stories into a tall tale, but there's no doubt that these woods aren't safe for travelers."

"Do you mean..." She hesitated with one foot on the carriage step. "There really is a hooded huntsman in these woods?"

The footman cut in before the driver could. "Nothing for you to worry about, miss. We take every precaution against highwaymen and the like."

She nodded and returned his small smile. Highwaymen she didn't find so terrifying. She hadn't spent five years in Vestry Lane without running into her fair share of pickpockets and thieves.

She sighed at the memory of King and his crew. Some of her dearest friends were pickpockets and thieves...and worse.

No, it wasn't the mention of highwaymen that had her shoulders tensing as the carriage set off into the thick overgrowth of the woods.

It was the 'and the like' that the driver had mentioned.

With nothing to focus on but the sight of trees moving by the window she found herself remembering every gory detail of those tall tales the townsfolk had regaled her with back at the inn.

A monster who hunted in the woods, just waiting for innocent travelers to pass through...

More beast than man, he lived on human flesh.

She shivered at the thought even as she mocked herself for falling for it.

Still, the dark woods seemed to grow ever darker as the trees grew thicker, blocking out what little sun was visible on this dreary day. And when thunder cracked and the rain started to pour in earnest once more, Margot gripped the edge of her seat.

The carriage rocked and swayed, then suddenly picked up pace with a swiftness that had her gasping. It swayed violently and she screamed as she toppled out of her seat, the carriage tipping as one of the back wheels gave way with a loud snap.

The world tumbled around her as she was tossed from one end to the other, and for a moment all she knew was pain as her elbows and knees banged against hard surfaces. The carriage overturned and she could no longer tell up from down.

The door popped open and she tumbled out, thrown off the road and landing with a forceful thud on the ground.

A piercing pain shot through her face as it smashed against a rock and hot blood poured from her nose, down her breast and across her dress.

For a moment, all she could hear was the sound of her own panting breaths and her pulse racing in her ears. The air in her weak lungs grew thin and raspy, her vision blurring. She blinked a few times, pulling the world into focus...

She nearly wished she hadn't. The sight before her made her eyes widen in panic.

Arrows were flying, and the sound of pistol fire echoed in the woods. But what made her heart plummet was the sight of the footman lying in the road with an arrow in his heart while the driver scampered away.

"No, wait!" she screamed. "Don't leave me!"

He continued to run while Margot fought for air, screaming once more and she covered her head and cowered into a ball.

Run, Margot! Run! You must move!

Savina's voice rang in her head.

Go, Margot! Run!

The urgent cries broke through her panic, sending her into action. Scrambling to her feet, Margot ran, but she could hear hoof beats behind her.

She risked a glance over her shoulder and whimpered at the sight of a man gaining on her.

Large and broad, his hood was pulled down too low for her to see anything but a bearded jaw and a fearsome glower as he urged his horse on...

He was heading straight for her.

She let out a terrified scream and tried to run faster, but her lungs were burning and the uneven ground seemed determined to foil her escape. Her foot hit a dip and she felt her ankle give, twisting painfully as she tripped and fell down the hill.

Tumbling with whimpers and cries, she slapped at the ground, trying to slow her descent until she came to an ungraceful stop at the bottom of the hill.

The rain pelted her skin as she lay there, puffing and in pain.

Her heart raced so wildly she thought it might leap straight out of her chest.

She was alone. In these strange woods.

And that man...

She sat up straight as she heard the horse and its rider racing down the hillside.

Don't just lay there, she heard Savina shout. *Run!*

But her ankle shrieked with pain when she tried to stand and her head spun and throbbed with the movement. The masked man pulled his horse to an abrupt stop and jumped down, swinging his crossbow over his back. And that was when she saw it, the gleaming metal ax at his side.

Fear held her captive just as surely as that glower.

This is the huntsman.

Every ridiculous and terrifying tale came to the forefront of her mind as he drew closer and closer until he hovered over her, so large and broad, he blocked the rain from hitting her body.

He shifted, reaching down toward her.

She screamed and tried to scramble away but her traitorous body was frozen in terror, and her head and ankle throbbed in such searing pain that spots danced in front of her eyes.

Her rasping breaths grew weaker still.

And then the world was lost as she fell into a pit of black oblivion.

14

*S*avina hovered in the doorway of her new friend's drawing room, her enthusiasm for her plan waning with Vivian's ever-growing delight.

"Do come in," Vivian gushed. "Oh, I am so glad you've come."

Savina took a few steps inside the quiet, dark room. "I hope it's all right that I've arrived unannounced."

"I'm delighted to have a visitor." Vivian beamed. And indeed, her green eyes were lit with excitement.

"Your father won't mind?" Savina asked as she untied the bonnet her maid had so neatly perched atop her head.

"Why would he mind?" the younger girl asked.

Savina lifted a shoulder. "Oh, I don't know. Perhaps because I ran off last night in a way that likely caused tongues to wag."

Vivian's expression shifted and her smile held a hint of sympathy. "I wouldn't worry about that. Your stepfather explained to everyone that you hadn't been feeling well since your long journey."

Stepfather. The word made her insides tighten and that fury returned so quickly it made her breath catch.

Liar. She'd never forgive him for withholding that information, for putting her at such a disadvantage during her first reunion with Lucinda.

Of course...

She toyed with the edge of her gloves as snippets of their conversation came back to her, as it had all night and all morning until she'd fled for Vivian's as much to avoid her own thoughts as to retrieve information.

He'd made one point that she still could not refute. If she'd known he was Lucinda's new husband, she would never have trusted him. Not enough to let him look after her and Margot, at least. Of that she was well aware.

But he could have told her eventually. He should have told her before last night.

"...and the rest of the evening was quite uneventful," Vivian was saying.

Savina lifted her head with a sharp inhale. She'd come all this way to avoid thoughts of Edmund, and if she gave in to those them now, they'd lead to one particular memory that she couldn't erase from her mind no matter how hard she tried.

The feel of him pressed against her...the way he'd held her and touched her and the sound of his voice so close to her ear...

She swallowed hard against a surge of heat that nearly made her lose her footing.

Lord, she'd never forgive herself for the way she'd responded to him.

She'd lost her senses entirely. She'd forgotten her own pride and her righteous anger, and all because he'd taken control of her body...

She still wasn't sure how he'd done it. Many men had

pawed at her over the years. One she'd even allowed to do...more.

She shook off the thought. That experience was so at odds with the way Edmund had made her feel, it couldn't be compared.

Edmund had made her weak and needy, but powerful at the same time because he seemed to crave her as much as she'd craved him.

Her whole body had felt like it was reaching for something. Like it was missing something vital. Something that only he could provide.

"I do hope you're feeling better today," Vivian said gently.

Savina smiled, forcing her mind back to the present. "I am. Thank you. But you won't be in trouble with your father for spending time with a scandal like me, will you?"

Vivian's loud laughter faded when she realized Savina was serious. "Oh. Dear me." She tipped her head to the side, her expression curious.

Once again, Savina felt a pang of longing for Margot. Her sister would be fast friends with Vivian—they shared the same sort of gentle nature along with a kindness that could so easily be used against them.

"You do know who my father is, do you not?" Vivian grinned. "He is a newspaperman. He makes a living off other people's scandals and their gossip."

"Then I supposed I am most welcome," Savina deadpanned.

Vivian laughed again. "Indeed." She held her hands out in a helpless gesture. "I rather fear he'd be *too* delighted if he learns you came to visit. He'd be all too eager to hear what you have to say."

Savina's shock must have been written on her features because Vivian shook her head, her smile gentle once more.

"Have no fear, Savina. I am not so feeble that I cannot keep secrets. Whatever you say here today remains between us."

Savina exhaled loudly. "Oh, that is reassuring. And the same holds true with me, you know." She bit her lip, considering her words. "I do not claim to know you well, and lord knows we haven't known each other for long, but you're the only kind creature I've met in London and I hope that you'll consider me a friend."

Vivian's eyes welled with happy tears. "You have no idea how much I'd like that."

"It is settled then," Savina said as Vivian rang for tea.

Once they were settled, Vivian turned to her with a frankness that was rather alarming. "Now then, why don't you tell me what it is you need from me."

Savina wished she could say 'nothing at all!' but the girl was much too clever for lies. "It's information I need. You see, I have been away for many years and..."

Vivian's gaze grew sharp. "And you need to get a lay of the land."

"Precisely." Savina nodded.

Vivian glanced around as if to ensure they were alone, then leaned in with a hushed voice. "Well, then you have come to the right place. Who do you wish to know about?"

Savina's fingers twisted together. "I want to know all that has happened while I was away, but most particularly any rumors concerning my stepmother, my new stepfather—" The word caused a sneer that she had to take a breath to dispel. "And, of course..." She leaned forward as well. "Anything you can tell me about Lucinda's son, Benedict."

Vivian pursed her lips and nodded. "Of course." A hint of a mischievous smile lit her pretty eyes. "The question is... where shall I begin?"

By the time Savina left her new friend behind, she was full to the brim of gossip. She'd come to the right place, of course. Savina suspected few young ladies were as tapped into the rumor mill as the daughter of a man who owned the city's largest gossip rags.

Her steps felt lighter as she descended from the hired hack and made her way home.

No, to Edmund's home.

Any bond she might have been tempted to feel for her father's friend had been nothing but an illusion. Silly optimism on her part. But no more.

From here on out, she was done being the docile little lamb who followed his orders.

She let herself into the townhome, not waiting for any of Edmund's servants to assist her with her hat and gloves. On a table in the drawing room she found a letter waiting for her.

She unsealed it and recognized the nearly illegible scrawl immediately. It was from King, and after reading his short missive hungrily she sighed with relief.

He'd confirmed what Edmund had told her about Margot having been delayed. Or she had been, as of two days before, when one of King's men had heard news of her.

So. At least Edmund hadn't lied about that.

Her heart was lighter knowing that Margot was either still safely tucked away in an inn, under the protection of her traveling companions, or—hopefully—already arrived in Bristol and settling into her new home.

"Welcome home, miss," the housekeeper greeted when she came upon Savina still clutching King's note. "Shall I tell Cook to start preparing dinner?"

Savina straightened. The older woman had been so kind to her, but there was always a sort of divide between them.

At first for Savina it had been the uncomfortable awareness of the fact that she was supposed to be the mistress of this home when she knew nothing of what it meant to be such a thing.

Between that and not knowing how much the older woman knew of her circumstances, Savina had felt the divide between them keenly. But now there was suspicion between them as well. Savina eyed the other woman wondering how long she'd worked for Edmund.

"No need, Mrs. Baker," she said. "But thank you."

She was *his* servant, not hers. That was the issue. Edmund was the one paying Mrs. Baker's wages, after all, and it was to him she'd be loyal.

Savina's skin crawled at the thought that any of these kind servants would spy on her and report back to Edmund. She hated to even think it. And yet, she knew she'd have to be on her guard.

"You're not hungry?" The older woman's face was a picture of maternal concern.

Savina hesitated. Oh, how she wished she could trust that this woman would keep her secrets. But Savina had learned a long time ago that the key to survival was not trusting anyone.

And if she'd had any doubt, Edmund's betrayal was just another reminder. She couldn't trust anyone. Not in this town, at least.

"I'm going out." She smiled in the face of the other woman's confused frown, ignoring the unspoken questions. "Tell Millie I'd like her to help me dress, won't you? And tell Charles I'll be needing the carriage."

Mrs. Baker's lips parted, and Savina could all but see the questions that lingered there. But when Savina continued to meet her gaze evenly, offering no details nor explanation, the older woman merely nodded as she dipped her head in acknowledgment. "Very well, miss."

15

*I*mpatience made Edmund irritable.

He'd rather be anywhere but here. But after last night's disastrous attempt to surprise his wife with the appearance of her long lost stepdaughter, he couldn't take any chances.

He certainly couldn't leave her alone at a society event to spread whatever lies she'd concocted this time.

He'd known from the start that his wife was a liar. But just how adept she was, how devious and clever, and how manipulative...

Well, he discovered new depths every day.

Who said marriage didn't come with surprises?

"Isn't that right, darling?" Lucinda cocked her head to the side to smile up at him as the baroness hosting tonight's soiree beamed expectantly.

"Mmm," he murmured.

The conversation didn't concern Savina or her sister, and as such he'd paid it little mind.

He was a man known for his singular focus—one didn't

build a trading route to rival the East India Company without that sort of dogged determination.

But when it came to Savina, this focus was something more. He couldn't stop thinking of her.

He hadn't stopped thinking of her since the moment she'd walked into that brothel room.

And tonight...thoughts of her nearly drove him mad.

What was she doing? What was she thinking? Most of all, what was she planning?

He had no doubt she was up to something. And he couldn't even blame her.

He'd asked her to trust him, and then he'd proven he couldn't be trusted.

A weaker woman might have wept or hidden away. But Savina wasn't a coward, and she wasn't one to hide.

Not when there was a fight to be had.

His lungs hitched at the memory of the fire in her eyes. A flicker of wariness had followed the mischief in its wake.

She was up to something. But what?

Lucinda placed a hand on his arm as she prattled on to their hostess about how happy they were to have her precious Benedict home with them again.

Benedict, meanwhile, could be heard laughing from the far side of the room. The charming young gentleman was regaling their host with some tale about his most recent trip abroad.

Fair-haired and as handsome as his mother was beautiful, the man was little more than a boy. A child.

Dull and dutiful, and utterly lacking his mother's ambition...and her cruelty. Which was precisely why Edmund had thought to match him with one of Leopold's girls.

Savina, he'd assumed, would be the obvious choice.

Lucinda would hate it, and it would restore to the girls the fortunes and places in society that they'd lost. They'd once more be back in their father's home, and have every comfort.

It had seemed an obvious answer to the problem that was his dear friend's long lost daughters. A simple solution and he could say he'd done his duty to Leopold.

But the moment he'd seen Savina he'd realized what a foolish idea that had been.

She wasn't some faceless, unknown woman to be married off to a simpleton. She was intelligent, fierce, bold, and strikingly beautiful. She was…

Mine.

A muscle near his eye began to tick, making his vision grow fuzzy with possessive rage as if Benedict, or some other man, might even now be plotting to steal her away.

He forced his fists to unclench at his sides. Savina was safe, at the home he'd bought for her, surrounded by servants he trusted to take care of her.

She was under his care and his control…if not currently in his sights.

"And what about your daughter?" their hostess asked.

The sudden tension in Lucinda's grip on his arm was the only sign that having Savina referred to as her daughter rankled.

"I'm afraid my stepdaughter already caused gossip at last night's function," Lucinda said. Her laughter was knowing, with a hint of indulgence.

Such a kind and understanding stepmother. That was what her laughter said. It was the same condescending tone she'd used the night before.

Tension crept into Edmund's muscles.

He wasn't sure he'd ever forget the tearful betrayal in Savina's eyes the night before.

He'd thought it was best to withhold information. He'd

needed her to enter society first. It was all part of his larger strategy to make his wife pay, but...

But had it been worth it to lose her trust?

He never did get his answer. Because just then the hostess spoke up again in surprise. "And yet you still allowed her to join you here tonight. How gracious you are, my dear," the baroness said to Lucinda.

He felt Lucinda go still beside him. As one, they turned toward the drawing room door. And then...

There she was.

The air rushed out of him at the unexpected sight of Savina posing in the doorway, a smile on her lips.

Gorgeous, was his first thought. The second was the word he'd been hearing since he'd first set eyes on her.

Mine.

Her golden hair was styled in a simple yet elegant updo, adorned with a few delicate flowers that matched her pale pink gown. Her dress was made of fine silk that hugged her curves, with a low-cut neckline that revealed porcelain skin. Her eyes were bright with excitement as she entered the room and looked around her for...

What? That made him tense even further because...what was she looking for?

Or...who?

What was her plan in coming here tonight? Because she did have one, that much he understood. He'd underestimated her from the start.

The girl was clever. And she was here for a reason.

But what? He did not know.

And that was a problem.

"Did you invite her, Edmund?" Lucinda's sharp tone had him blinking down at his wife.

Her delicate features were pinched in irritation that she couldn't quite hide behind her docile smile.

Satisfaction warmed him. So this was a surprise to her as well. That was something, he supposed.

When he didn't answer, her nostrils flared in anger. "Just like you sought her out in the first place, I'd imagine. How did you find her, hmm?"

He stared at her for a moment.

Interesting. She'd shown more of her hand than she'd meant with that comment. She hadn't spoken a word to him in private the night before. They'd parted ways the moment they'd returned home. To Leopold's home, as he still thought of it.

To Savina's home.

"Nonsense." He met her gaze evenly. "*She* found *me*."

Her chin jerked back in surprise as her eyes narrowed warily.

She wasn't certain if she believed him.

Well. No one had ever claimed his wife was stupid.

Cruel, undoubtedly. Selfish to the point of being heartless?

Of course.

But she wasn't dimwitted and she knew better than to reveal the truth now when she had no notion of how much he actually knew of Savina's situation.

She fluttered her fan instead. "She reached out to you?"

They were both studiously ignoring the whispered gossip among the crowd behind them. It was all about Savina and her sudden appearance.

"Mmm," he murmured. "It seems she'd come upon some difficult times and wished to return home." He watched her carefully waiting for any sign of guilt or, heaven forbid...a conscience. "She wasn't certain if she'd be welcomed, and so she sought me out."

At Lucinda's searching stare, he added, "I was her father's dearest friend, if you'll recall. It seemed she remembered my

147

name, and of course it's not so difficult to find someone when one knows where to look."

He'd spoken so mildly that she blinked in confusion.

Satisfaction rippled through him at the small win.

Had he meant more by that? That was what her flicker of confusion seemed to say.

Yes. Indeed he had. If she'd given him the slightest clue as to where to look, he'd have saved Savina and her sister long ago.

Regret lanced through him and he tore his gaze away from Lucinda's searching stare to seek out Savina.

He didn't have to look far. She was the center of attention, and by all appearances, she reveled in it.

"Thank you so much for having me," she said sweetly to their host who'd hurried over to greet her.

The older man bent over her hand, and Edmund's lips twisted in sneer.

He was far too close to Savina, his attentions too excessive.

Mine.

Edmund stepped toward Savina, but she was already walking away, and Edmund found himself in the embarrassing role of pursuer. Like a lovesick pup he found himself chasing her through the clusters of guests, as she headed directly toward...

A roar of rage nearly escaped because all at once he understood why she had come.

For *whom* she was here.

Benedict.

16

*B*enedict was easy to find.

Savina's confidence wavered slightly under all the stares, but she reminded herself of what Edmund had said only the night before.

There were advantages to being a scandal.

Besides, this crowd had nothing on the sort of foul brutes she'd dealt with these past five years. There was nothing they could do to her that was worse than what she'd already experienced.

There were perks to being stronger and more resilient than anyone realized.

The thought made her lips tip up at the corners. She wasn't the frightened young child Lucinda had driven away.

And it was Lucinda's own cruelty that had made her the formidable foe she intended to be.

There was something rather fitting about that.

She narrowed her eyes on Benedict, who seemed to be one of few in this opulent drawing room who hadn't marked her arrival.

He was deep in conversation with a pair of dandies, but

Savina put on her most dazzling smile and stepped up next to them.

The two men looked away from Benedict, their expressions suddenly curling into appreciative grins as they appraised her from head to toe.

Savina ignored them completely and turned to Benedict instead, standing so close to her stepbrother she came just short of touching him, allowing just enough space between them for propriety's sake, before curtsying deeply.

"Good evening, my lord."

She'd spent the entirety of her time since leaving Vivian's, planning out just how she'd greet the man who was, she now knew, on the hunt for a wife.

Oh yes, her time with Vivian had been very helpful indeed.

"Pardon me for intruding," she continued. "But I couldn't help but notice you from across the room."

She tilted her head back to meet his eyes, his gaze landing on hers like a punch of awareness that sent a shockwave through Savina's whole body.

It wasn't lust she felt. This wasn't the sort of dark, intoxicating rush she experienced whenever Edmund's gaze devoured her.

This felt more like triumph. It felt like winning. For once, she held the power, even if that power was merely sexual in nature.

But if she played her cards right, soon it would be more.

How would Lucinda feel when she realized her precious little son was falling for her wretched stepdaughter?

"My goodness," Benedict breathed.

That's when she realized, it wasn't just attraction she saw in those golden brown eyes, it was recognition too.

"My name is Savina," she continued softly.

"Savina!" His eyes went wide as his suspicions were confirmed.

His warm gaze filled with surprise and...delight.

Any fears she might have had regarding Benedict's role in his mother's plans, or even any awareness of what she'd done to them as children, melted in the face of his warm welcome.

"How wonderful to see you." He ignored his curious friends just as she did. "I'd heard that you were back in Town, but I hardly believed it."

"It's been so long, I wasn't certain you'd remember me," she admitted. The shy smile felt only a little awkward, and it grew more natural with his every reassuring gesture.

"Of course I do." He turned so fully, he had his back to his friends now, and they had the good grace to walk away and leave them in peace.

"I remember you and Margot so fondly." His gaze grew soft. "I was so sad to learn that you'd chosen to visit with family abroad rather than stay in your home after your father's passing."

It shouldn't come as a surprise any longer. What she hadn't learned from Edmund, Vivian had supplied.

She knew full well the lies her stepmother had been telling about her these past years.

And yet, her heart gave a harsh tug at the thought of all these people, aware of her existence and yet not caring enough to check up on them. "Yes, well," she managed through a tight throat. "I'm back now..."

"And Margot?" His brows arched hopefully.

"She's not in Town at the moment but I hope she'll be joining me soon."

"Oh, that is wonderful to hear," he gushed.

His gaze fell on something or someone over her shoulder and his smile froze before falling flat.

Savina knew who she'd find before she turned. She'd felt

his approach and was aware of his proximity as surely as if he'd wrapped his arms around her from behind.

"Oh, er...have you..." Benedict stammered beside her. "Are you acquainted with my stepfather?"

Edmund loomed over her, the creases around his eyes and mouth more pronounced than ever as he glared down at her.

A slow smile spread across her lips when she caught the fury in his eyes. She understood it without him saying a word.

She'd disobeyed his orders.

She'd gone behind his back and taken action on her own.

She lifted her chin and cocked a brow.

He still thought she was his to guide and control, and maybe in a way she was—he was her only source of money and the sole reason she had a roof over her head, after all.

But Savina wasn't about to be owned by anyone ever again.

It had taken her far too long to have this sort of power over her own fate, and she intended to enjoy every single moment of it.

Her blood grew warm and heat pooled low in her belly as he placed a firm hand against her back.

His gaze held hers captive as he spoke to Benedict. "Excuse us for a moment, won't you?"

17

The little brat smirked up at him.

Edmund's pulse hammered as he eyed how close she was to Benedict, as he noted the protective way Benedict had shifted.

"I'd like to have a word in private, Savina," Edmund clipped.

One corner of her mouth hitched up. Her smirk was mocking, but now a dimple flashed, a hint of sweet innocence inside those lush lips that spoke of a woman who knew exactly how much power she wielded.

Benedict spoke to her softly. "If you'd rather I join you..."

Edmund swung his glare in the direction of the spoiled young man before him. He was more a stranger than a son after so many years off at school and then traveling with friends.

But his glare now reminded Benedict who held the power here.

And it certainly wasn't little Benny.

"It's all right, Benedict," Savina murmured. When she cast

her gaze in Benedict's direction, the smirk was gone and she looked for all the world like a helpless, vulnerable young lady.

But when she lifted a hand and brought it to rest on Benedict's upper arm, he caught the way she squeezed it, the way his lips parted and his eyes grew dazed as he stared down at her angelic beauty.

The little minx. He had half a mind to take her over his knee right then and there.

The thought made his cock stir. No, not here. When he took this little hellcat over his knee it would be in private.

No one but him would set eyes on her slender thighs or her rounded arse. That would be for him and him alone.

He reached for her arm, aghast at his own thoughts. When had he decided that he would make her his?

When had this obsession gotten so out of his control?

He didn't know, but when she paid no mind to his hand on her arm, he knew with certainty that he'd be teaching her who she belonged to.

She was his—and it was well past time she knew what that meant.

Savina leaned in toward Benedict and whispered something in his ear that made him laugh, a hint of pink tingeing his ears.

For the love of Christ...

"Now, Savina," he growled as he tugged her elbow.

Her lower lip jutted out ever so slightly and he had the urge to lean down and nip at it just to hear her gasp.

Bloody hell. He was in a crowded drawing room filled with society's elite, and all he could do was stand here helplessly watching his ward flirt with another as he fantasized about claiming her for himself.

"Don't be angry, stepfather," she said in a singsong voice

meant to taunt. She dropped her hand from Benedict's arm, but he still gazed at her in adoration.

Fuck. That was fast. The girl had barely fluttered her lashes and she already had the boy exactly where she wanted him.

If he hadn't changed his plan the moment he'd met her, he would have been pleased. But as it was...

"Be a good girl and do as I say," he snarled softly.

Her lips parted and her eyes darkened with awareness.

Her calling him stepfather. Him ordering her to be his good girl.

It was the game they'd been playing from the start, with rules they both seemed to understand.

It was a push and a pull. A tug of control, a show of power. He leaned down close to whisper in her ear. "Don't make me show you what happens to naughty little girls who don't obey their guardians."

Her breathing hitched and a moment later she'd settled a hand on his arm. "Very well. Perhaps this is a lecture best heard in private." She turned to Benedict. "Do save a dance for me, won't you?"

Edmund barely heard his response. He was too busy watching Lucinda, who was glaring at Savina from across the room.

"Oh look," Savina said, all sweet innocence as he led her a few paces away. "It seems Lucinda isn't pleased at all about my reunion with Benedict."

"Careful, little one," he said under his breath.

The look of pure hatred on Lucinda's face was enough to make Edmund's blood run cold.

Lucinda seemed to have only one weakness, and Savina had just gone after it.

His protective instincts overshadowed all else and he tugged Savina further away.

"Go home," he muttered.

"But Stepfather—"

"Don't call me that."

"I just got here," she continued as if he hadn't interrupted.

"What do you think you're doing with Benedict?"

She kept her smile sweet. "Don't tell me you couldn't figure it out, Your Highness?"

A muscle in his jaw ticked. She was intentionally trying to anger him.

Her cheeks flushed pink as she smiled.

Bloody hell, she was thoroughly enjoying this. And he might have enjoyed Lucinda's anger too...

If he didn't despise seeing Savina flirt with another man.

The fact that it was Benedict grated his nerves. The boy was a child. An entitled, useless one at that.

But as he gazed down at her high cheekbones, her eyes so bright with passion, he couldn't lie to himself.

He'd have been just as furious to watch her flirt with any other man.

Because she's mine.

"Ah, I see you haven't learned your lesson." Lucinda's voice cut into their silent staring contest.

Savina turned to the older woman with a pleasant smile. "My lesson?"

"Indeed, you've been away too long, my dear," Lucinda said smoothly. "You really ought to take some instruction in deportment, familiarize yourself with the expectations of the *ton* before you embarrass yourself again."

"No need," Savina said breezily, before Lucinda had even finished. With a dramatic sigh, Savina glanced over at Benedict with feigned adoration. "Your son has been kind enough to offer his assistance as I transition back to...my old life."

A tension fell between the three of them. Edmund was

torn between wanting to watch and applaud as Savina stood up for herself ...

And resisting the urge to toss her over his shoulder so he could carry her far away from these people who could hurt her.

Blast. Why hadn't he sent her to Bristol with her sister?

He'd known from the start that he couldn't live with watching her marry Benedict just so he could get revenge on Lucinda.

He'd known his plan was shite, and yet he'd still brought her back here to this—the enemy's territory. Why? Why hadn't he just sent her away? Given her and Margot money and sent them somewhere safe to hide until he ousted Lucinda from their father's home—and his life—once and for all.

In the end, Edmund could neither intervene nor stand by and watch, because the tense conversation was interrupted by the host. "Your Highness, won't you lead the way to the dining room?"

The friction disappeared with a start.

"Wonderful. Dinner sounds lovely." Savina smiled sweetly. And then she proceeded to claim his arm. Leaving Lucinda to follow behind them.

"Naughty girl," he muttered under his breath, a smile tugging at his lips and his tone teasing.

It was alarming how quickly his anger faded when that gloved hand was on his arm and her smile aimed up at him.

She batted her eyelashes, her air just as teasing as his, as she murmured back. "And you love it."

He wanted to argue, wanted to deny it, but he simply couldn't.

He didn't take his eyes off her as they walked into the dining room and took their seats at the long table.

Blessedly, the hostess had seated husbands and wives on separate ends of the table to ensure more conversations amongst those less well acquainted, and so the battle between Lucinda and Savina was put to the wayside.

"You'll sit here," he commanded his ward, dragging a chair next to his as a footman scrambled to accommodate his last minute seating request.

His wicked little Savina looked too amused by far as she settled in beside him. "Tell me, Edmund. Are you really so fascinated by my conversational skills...or do you just wish to keep an eye on me?"

He gave a grunt of amusement and when he leaned in to respond, he caught a whiff of her scent. His heart gave a lusty thump, the blood in his veins turning to liquid fire.

Desire seemed to pulse between them, erasing whatever clever comeback he'd had in store. And so he answered honestly. "Perhaps a little of both."

She smiled, but he caught the flicker of confusion in her eyes as she studied him. He noted the way her breasts rose and fell when she leaned into him.

She felt it too. He'd known that from the start. Even in the brothel, terrified and mutinous, he'd seen the way her nipples had hardened and her pupils had dilated.

He reached a hand out, stealing a touch of the bare skin on her upper arm as he leaned in closer still. "I assume you're in no position to be naughty sitting next to me, so for the remainder of dinner, I'd love nothing more than to converse with you."

He was struck by how true this was.

These past days, he'd done his utmost to keep distance between them. But tonight, after seeing the way she was with Benedict...

For the next couple of hours, at least. They weren't alone. They were in the relative safety of a crowd.

Unlike at her home, no matter how much he might itch to snag her by the waist and drag her into his lap...he couldn't give in to that temptation here.

He was safe...relatively speaking.

Her gaze flickered, as if trying to read him like a book. He let her.

For once, he let her.

Her gaze dipped. "Very well."

He felt an odd sort of tenderness tightening his chest. Affection mixed with desire until he felt drunk with it. He reached for his wine in the hopes it would sober him.

"It's been an age since I've had a proper dinner," she admitted quietly as the first course was brought out by footmen.

His head snapped to the right. "Haven't they been feeding you properly at the townhome? I'll—"

"No," she said quickly, and then started to laugh at his anger. "No, nothing like that. Cook feeds me so well it's a wonder I fit into these fine gowns you've gifted me."

She glanced over at him almost...shyly. And his heart responded with a swift kick to his ribs.

"Thank you for the gowns, by the way. And the cook and the food and..." She reached for her own wine, and her hand trembled slightly. "I'm not sure I ever did thank you for that. For all of it."

He let out his first real exhale since they'd parted the night before.

He knew she was still angry with him. The small bit of trust she'd had in him was no doubt doused for good. But right here and now, she was speaking to him again, and almost as a friend.

"Think nothing of it," he murmured. "It's the least I could do."

She didn't argue. Likely because she knew he was right.

"What I'd meant was, I haven't had proper company for dinner," she finished. "I've forgotten what it's like..."

He watched her as she gazed at the jovial crowd around them.

"How does it make you feel?" The words came out unbidden, curiosity having gotten the best of him as he tried to interpret every flicker of emotion passing through her eyes.

She turned to him with a smile that reached straight inside of him and twisted his heart. "Lonely."

His brows hitched slightly and she laughed.

"I know that makes no sense. But it's one thing to be stranded out in the cold. It's a whole other matter to be out in the cold looking in on a family having a warm, cozy meal by the fire." Her smile was bittersweet. "I suppose that makes no sense to you."

His chest tightened again and his heart hammered like it was trying to sound a gong. "It does," he said gruffly.

"But..." she reached for a thick slice of bread and shot him a mischievous little smile that made him fantasize about all the ways he might tease out that smile...in his bed.

Which led to thoughts of how she'd look writhing beneath him, her legs wrapped around him, her inner muscles tightening around his shaft as he buried himself inside her, showing her in no uncertain terms that she belonged to him.

"For tonight, however," she continued on, blithely unaware of the turn his thoughts had taken. "For tonight, I'm going to simply enjoy being inside, out of the cold...and at the party."

He raised his glass with a small smile. "I think I can help with that."

He caught a nosy glance from the hostess who was no doubt eavesdropping and so he spoke e a little louder as he addressed Savina. "Tell me, what do you most want to see while you're staying in London?"

Her eyes glimmered with amusement. "Well, I've heard the Vauxhall Gardens are not to be missed," she started.

The delicious aromas of food filled the air as more dishes were brought out, and he found himself charmed by Savina's growing delight as she threw herself into talking and laughing, as if she truly had no other care in the world.

The dinner was a feast, with all sorts of dishes that were both familiar and foreign to Savina's taste buds.

Edmund would never have believed how much he enjoyed her delight. But truly, watching her savor a new taste was better than experiencing it himself.

"What?" she asked with a laugh when she caught him staring at her lips transfixed.

"You're so expressive." He could not keep the awe from his voice. "You're...fascinating."

She dipped her head, but not before he caught her blush.

Bloody hell. Her blushes were more dangerous to him than her wildest attempts at flirting.

Coy women he'd dealt with most of his life. But Savina's particular mix of worldly and innocent was like a rare delicacy. A delicious blend that kept him on his toes, as he never knew what she'd say or do next.

One moment she was flirting with him, the next she was blushing like a girl who'd never left the nursery.

Lord but his aching chest and his throbbing cock were in a constant battle over which he wanted more—to throw her on her back and fuck her until she screamed his name...

Or to hide her someplace safe where she could be protected from everything.

Including himself.

"You look serious all of a sudden." She lowered her brows in what he assumed was an imitation of him.

His lips twitched with amusement.

"What were you thinking of just now?"

What sounds you'd make the first time I bury my head between your thighs and taste your sweet cunny.

He could only imagine how much she'd blush if he were to speak that truth.

"I was thinking of unexplored places." He couldn't quite keep from dipping into a growl as his muscles tightened with desire.

"Have you done much exploring?"

"Mmm. But I imagine you have not."

"No, but I should like to."

He wondered if she had any idea what he was really speaking of. Her guileless eyes said no, but the husky tone of her voice, the way her gaze dipped to his lips...

Once more he was mesmerized by her many facets.

"I should like to hear you speak of it," she finished, her voice breathless and her gaze bright with emotions he couldn't name.

Forcing aside his lewd and lascivious fantasies, he focused on that bright gleam in her eyes. He put all his attention on trying to coax out that dimpled smile that was so genuine and pure he knew without a doubt he'd do anything to protect it.

Anything to protect her.

She'd survived so much thanks to her strength and her determination, but he'd do whatever it took to keep her from having to face any more injuries.

Edmund kept her entertained for the next hour with stories of his travels, and how different the culture and cuisine was compared to England.

"Thank you," she said quietly when dinner came to an end and the men began to leave for cigars and brandy.

"For what?" he asked.

"Your stories. For making me laugh. For making me feel like I'm not alone for the first time since Margot left."

"You miss her."

She nodded. "I do. But..." She glanced down the table toward Lucinda with a sigh. "I'm happy to know that wherever she is tonight...she is safe."

18

---

*M*argot woke with a start.

The first thing she became aware of was the sound of a crackling fire, then the soft patter of rain outside registered, eliciting blurry memories that she was struggling to make sense of.

The pain came a heartbeat later. The incessant pounding in her skull, the throbbing of her ankle, all mixed with the duller ache and sting of scrapes and bruises.

She struggled to sit up, the dark room coming into focus as her eyes adjusted to the glow of the firelight.

Her heart leapt when she realized she'd been placed on a bed, her gown still wet.

Memories flooded her once more, and with a little whimper the last sight before she'd lost consciousness came into focus.

The hooded beast stalking toward her.

Was that where she was? In the man's lair?

Her eyes darted across to the fire, the warmth of the hearth contradicting the chilling images of a beast so feral he ate human flesh.

Human flesh.

Her breath hitched, her heart galloping as she recalled every horrific tale told at the inn. The men's raucous laughter echoed in her mind. She'd been so cavalier, dismissing the rumors with a smile of her own. And yet—

A scraping sound from the corner made her stomach clench. She sat upright with a gasp, which soon became a whimper as the sudden movement had a fiery ache splitting her head in two. She pressed cold fingers against her temples and squeezed her eyes shut for a moment.

As the pain began to ease, she peered into the darkest corner in time to see the hulking shape move forward. Backlit by the fire, she made out his large frame and strong, bearded jaw.

He was a beast, big and broad and towering over her like a bear.

"Please don't eat me." The words spurted out in a rushed panic, her chest heaving as he jerked to a stop.

That's when the sound of her voice registered. The words pulled her from her waking nightmare and she instantly wished she'd held her foolish tongue.

She couldn't make out his expression, but the huntsman continued to stare, his unreadable glare making her feel small and vulnerable.

"I..." Her voice trailed off as fear held her throat in a tight grip. Her mind scrambled, and she latched onto her first concern. "What has become of my travel companions?"

He shifted with a grunt and she scrambled backward, her hands becoming lost in a thick blanket as terror urged her to put more distance between them.

"Please," she whispered. "Are they... well?" He grunted again and her eyebrows furrowed. "My footman?" She looked around the small space as if he might magically pop out from under the bed.

The huntsman gave a throaty growl, his voice a deep rumble when he spoke. "Dead."

Her inside froze for a terrifying moment, ragged breaths punching out of her when she suddenly remembered the poor footman's body, splayed on the ground with...

"An arrow." Her gaze jumped to the beast, the words choking her. "You killed him."

"He was firing a pistol at me."

"And the-the driver?"

"Ran like a coward." His derisive tone said it all, but Margot was too busy breathing a sigh of relief.

Thank goodness her maid had not accompanied her as well. She hated to think what would have become of sweet Betty.

A shudder raced through her and she wrapped her arms around herself, trying to control the shakes that had started in her belly and were now jerking her limbs as well.

The silence was as thick as molasses, covering her in an uncomfortable, sticky sensation. And just as she had as a child when she'd woken with nightmares, she found herself babbling in a bid to end the uneasy taciturnity.

"Hopefully the driver made it back to the inn. And at least my maid wasn't with us. That's a blessing, is it not? Perhaps she would have escaped as well, but one never knows." Her breathing grew shallow. "Arrows were flying every which way. One could have so easily landed in her heart too. Not that you would kill an innocent woman. She would not have been firing a pistol at you. Of this, I am certain." The words were tumbling out so fast and shaky, but she couldn't seem to stop them.

What was she doing? She was talking to this man... this killer... who'd attacked them, as if he were any other man and not one with the ability to end her life with a quick snap of her neck.

She glanced at his large hands. So broad with thick fingers that could wrap around her throat with ease.

She swallowed hard. "Are you...do you..."

She could all but hear Savina's laughing voice in her ears. *Shush, Snow. You'll wake the dead with all your chatter. Be still, child.*

But she had to ask one final thing before sealing her lips for good. Through chattering teeth she managed, "D-do you mean t-to hurt me?"

His answer was a silent step toward her.

She went rigid as his shadow covered her. He was a wolf stalking his prey and she shrunk away from him, trembling as she instinctively tried to protect herself.

It was a fool's hope.

The size of him. He could do whatever he wished with her.

He stopped a foot away and crouched down.

She could make out his features now. His face was half-shadowed by the fire, but he was huge and broad and solid. A beast.

Fear leapt in her chest as he lifted a hand and cupped her cheek.

She leaned away from his calloused touch. "Please, you must let me go."

"Why?" His voice was husky and deep—a throaty growl the likes of which she'd never heard before.

She blinked at the simple answer. "Because...because you must."

His hand dropped from her face and the room was bathed in silence once more. The only sound was her erratic breathing as she struggled to control her shaky limbs and raging heart.

Was he going to kill her?

Ravage her?

Make her his slave?

"Why you're doing this?" she finally whispered.

His dark gaze assessed her before he muttered, "Because you were in the wrong place at the wrong time."

Her brow wrinkled in confusion. What did he mean by that?

"You did not need to kidnap. If you don't want me, let me go."

Jerking to his feet, he huffed out a growl, raking his fingers through his unkempt, shoulder-length hair. "You should have stayed away."

"I was not trespassing," she whispered, her voice growing in strength. "I was simply taking the road to Bristol. We did nothing wrong. And you... you..." She let out a desperate whine picturing the footman lying dead on the road. "Are you the hooded huntsman they speak of?"

He turned his back to her, and for the first time since he'd approached, she let out a shaky exhale, closing her eyes against the wave of exhaustion threatening to consume her. Everything seemed to hurt and pound as tears made her throat ache.

He glanced over his shoulder, glowering down at her. "Stay."

It was an easy command to follow, she supposed. Her body was shaking so hard, she didn't think she could move anyway.

She focused on the sound of his heavy steps as he walked into the shadows on the far side of this small stone...cottage? Her gaze whipped around as she took it in.

Yes, it was a humble cottage with what looked to be a thatched roof and two open doorways. One, no doubt, led to another room, while the other outside... to freedom.

How far was she from a road?

The wind howled outside and Margot shivered.

Think, Margot. What would Savina do?

Savina would run. No doubt about it. Tears stung her eyes at the thought of her brave sister.

Where was she now? Had she encountered Lucinda yet?

Part of her wished she was there with her, even though she knew full well she'd be of no help.

She wasn't the brave one. Never had been.

But now...

She looked around her.

Now she'd have to be, wouldn't she? Panic threatened to devour her as she realized the full extent of her dire situation.

The footman was dead, the driver gone. Her maid was no doubt back in London by now. And no one else had any idea where she was.

Although people were expecting her in Bristol. Prince Edmund's staff were waiting for her arrival.

How long would it take them to realize she had been stolen away by this beast?

Would Savina ever know what became of her if she disappeared forever?

She would be heartbroken, indubitably filled with guilt for sending her sister away.

It was that thought which had Margot's trembling body inching toward the edge of the bed. But the moment she tried to set her foot down, her ankle shrieked in pain.

The huntsman turned at her gasp, his eyes narrowed and fixed on her until she once more scooted back, huddling in the corner.

How could she escape when she couldn't even stand?

Add to that fact the wetness of her gown, which seemed to be soaking into her bones until she was frozen all the way through. Escape was futile in her shivering, helpless state.

And the beast well knew it.

Obviously convinced she wasn't going anywhere, he turned again and went back to his task.

Stay, he'd commanded.

She didn't have much choice, did she?

Her heart was still tripping and clattering in her chest, so she tried to think logically as a way to counter her wayward emotions. Perhaps he wouldn't hurt her. After all, he hadn't yet, and he could have. She'd been helpless in his care for who knew how long. She was helpless right now, yet rather than wrapping his thick, beefy hands around her throat, he'd gently touched her cheek.

What did that mean?

She didn't fool herself into thinking he was a hero. Her mind filled with the image of the fallen footman and she shuddered as her belly twisted with nausea.

No, this huntsman was no knight in shining armor. But perhaps...perhaps he wasn't as much of a cruel beast as the townsfolk believed. Did he seem disappointed that he'd had to kill the footman? And he'd let the driver run free, had he not?

Hope made her chest lighten... for all of a moment.

"Take off your gown and under garments." His low voice came from the corner, and her mind went blank as her heart leapt into her throat. Terror pulsed through her in sickening waves.

Oh Lord, please save me.

Clutching her gown tightly to her chest, she gasped when a large swath of fabric landed in a heap beside her. "What's this?"

No answer.

"What do you want for me?"

No answer.

Margo quaked, her fingers shaking so badly she could do nothing but clutch the top edge of her gown.

Her gown which was still soaking wet. Her undergarments which had plastered themselves to her skin.

"Strip," he ordered. "Then put that on."

Margo glanced over at the material beside her. She reached for it, surprised by how soft the linen was. It was worn and thin.

It was…a shirt.

It was *his* shirt.

His back was still to her, but for how long she did not know. The thought of him turning to find her half dressed made her shudder from head to toe. With clumsy fingers she reached for the material and found the opening.

"Don't turn around." The moment she said it she realized how ridiculous she sounded. As if she had any control over what he did or how he moved.

She scrambled to unfasten her gown but her fingers were clumsy and the gown clung to her wet skin. It took several attempts before she could peel the bodice down.

Casting furtive glances in his direction, she quickly threw the shirt over her head. Then she rid herself of the gown and peeled off her undergarments. They landed on the floor with a thud. Only then did he turn. Without looking at her, he reached for the gown and spread it over a chair she hadn't seen before. It was close to the fire and would warm her gown and dry it.

Hope battled against fear as he spread out the rest of her things. Would a man set on hurting or killing her really take the time to dry out her sodden clothing?

The thought gave her a surge of courage. "Why are you doing this?"

No answer.

Irritation flared. "Please. Please, just tell me anything. Why am I here?" After a pause, she continued. "Did you attack us for money? Did you get what you were after?"

The silence stretched taut as he moved about, ignoring her.

When she couldn't take it any longer, she began to babble like a fool again. "Please. Please, sir, do not hurt me. I don't know what you want, but if I can get it for you I will. I don't have any money—"

She stopped talking abruptly when he whipped around to face her with a growl. But if she thought he was going to start speaking, she was sorely mistaken.

He stalked toward her, and she whimpered as she tried to back away. She was all too aware of how flimsy this shirt was. How there was nothing but this scrap of fabric hiding her breasts and her womanhood.

The shirt was large enough to cover her thighs, but the rest of her legs were unbearably exposed.

She clutched the shirt around her as if it could save her.

With his every step in her direction, her muscles tensed and ached with foreboding.

Would he touch her?

Would he...take her? Ravage her in this stone cottage where her cries for help would go unheeded?

Fear made her whimper and scramble backward in the bed. But there was nowhere for her to go. She was already pressed up against a stone wall, and it was cold and hard against her back.

He kept coming until he was looming over her.

Beast.

It was all she could think.

Although he had yet to confirm it, this was undoubtedly the brutal highwayman she'd heard about.

His closeness made her shiver, but this near she could make out more of his features.

His hair was dark, a lock falling into his eyes, which were the color of bluebells—the small flowers that used to flourish in her childhood home. She would pick them in bunches, skipping through the grass to deliver them to Savina and—

She swallowed, focusing back on this beast, taking in his dark, thick beard and full lips, which were set in a line just as grim as his gaze.

His eyes dipped, and she felt his stare everywhere they landed, making her skin heat and her belly tighten with something a little like anticipation.

She swallowed hard.

When he moved closer still, a whimper escaped and she crossed her arms over herself. She was alone. With a man.

In his bed.

His gaze fell to her lips. They trembled under his scrutiny, before he lifted his eyes to meet hers.

"No crying." It was a command, blunt and terrifying.

She sniffed, her voice catching as she repeated him. "No crying."

He crouched at the side of the bed and suddenly he was at eye level with her.

She held her breath, but he seemed to freeze as well, and so they were locked in a moment of tense silence as they regarded one another. He seemed to be studying her the way she'd studied him.

"What are you doing?" she finally breathed.

He didn't answer. Of course he didn't. But when he reached for her she let out a squeak of alarm as she instinctively pulled away.

His brow furrowed. Then his movements were far rougher as he reached for her again, this time not letting her jerk away as he grasped her leg.

His hands were rough and calloused, the knuckles bloodied and scraped. They were strong hands, ones that spoke of hard work and toil.

Margo's heart pounded wildly in her chest as she looked

down at the sight before her. His thick fingers wrapped easily around her thin calf.

No man had ever touched her like this, and his sun-kissed skin looked dark against the pale milkiness of hers.

Despite the callouses, his touch was warm and gentle. The sudden and unexpected intimacy of it left her winded.

And she remained breathless as she watched his hands move lower, his thumb brushing the sensitive skin of her ankle like a lover's caress.

She blinked rapidly at the thought, finally gasping in air as she realized where her mind had gone.

What would she know of a lover's caress?

She'd never been touched by a man before. Let alone a lover.

Did all men's touches make a woman feel like this? Warm and overly sensitive, like her skin was attuned to every shift in the air as goosebumps rose wherever his fingers lingered.

His gaze lifted from beneath his lowered brows, the look in his eyes dark and...and hungry.

To her surprise it wasn't fear she felt in response to that look, but something else. Something heavy in her belly that seemed to settle between her thighs, making her ache in a way she didn't understand.

When his fingers found the swollen ankle, she bit her lip but couldn't hide the tears that sprang to her eyes at the stabbing pain his light touch evoked.

"Not broken," he murmured as he came to stand. He jabbed a finger in her direction. "Stay."

Her lower lip jutted out as she muttered, "I'm not a dog."

She might have been mistaken, but she thought she saw his lips twitch. He turned his back to her before she could be certain.

"Am I your..." She swallowed and tried again, mesmerized

by the sight of his muscles working beneath the fabric of his shirt as he tended to the fire. "Am I your prisoner?"

He glanced over his shoulder but his face was hidden in shadow.

His only response was a grunt. Not exactly eloquent, but it was enough.

Yes, the grunt said.

She was a prisoner.

She was *his* prisoner.

19

---

*S*avina was enjoying her evening so thoroughly, she nearly forgot about Benedict, Lucinda, and everyone else who had joined them for dinner. But as the meal came to an end, she noticed the others at the table glancing at her with curiosity, wonder or disapproval— depending on who it was.

But none of that mattered for those few hours as she indulged in good food and surprisingly witty conversation.

"What is it?" Edmund said when he caught her gaze lingering too long after their dessert was taken away.

"I just..."

I forgot how lovely it could be. I've been so blastedly alone...

No. She couldn't admit to any of that. Her smile was wry as she lifted a shoulder. "I hadn't expected you to be such a charming dinner companion, that's all."

His lips twitched. "We hardly met under normal circumstances," he finally said. "I'm afraid you've seen the worst of me."

"I wouldn't say that."

"Then what would you say?" There was amusement in his voice, but a genuine curiosity as well.

She weighed her next words carefully. "I think...we both have more on our minds than trying to win one another's good favor."

His gaze met hers, and once more she saw that clever mind at work. Knew without a doubt that they were thinking about the same topic.

"It would please me if we could be on the same side." His voice was gruff, his gaze unreadable.

"I would like the same," she admitted. "But that would require a level of trust that we do not have between us."

The flare of his nostrils was the only sign that her words had hit their mark.

If there was a lack of trust here, it was his fault, and he well knew it

He shifted until he was facing her, and with this new proximity, her heart began to gallop even as she told herself it was silly.

This man was nothing but a pawn in her plans, just as she'd been a mere player in whatever game he was conducting with Lucinda. They were useful to one another, perhaps, but that was the extent of their connection.

"I kept things from you, yes. But I had my reasons." His voice was a low, gravelly whisper, nearly drowned out by the rising voices around them.

Dinner was coming to a finish, the wine bottles clearly nearing their ends as well.

A loud whoop of laughter came from their right but neither Savina nor Edmund broke eye contact to turn and look.

Finally, Savina blinked. "Was that meant to be an apology?"

"No." His response was terse and Savina felt an unexpected laugh bubble up at the horror that tinged his voice.

"No," she repeated, not trying to hide her teasing. "I imagine apologies do not come easily for a prince."

A muscle in his jaw ticked, but she caught a hint of amusement in his gaze as well.

"I suppose a prince is raised to believe he can do no wrong—"

"On the contrary," he interrupted. "I know full well of my wrongs." His gaze grew dark and bitter. "I will never forgive myself for my failure to do right by your father." He leaned in close and she caught a hint of the scent that was so uniquely Edmund. "For my failure to do right by you."

The air was sucked from her lungs at the sincerity in his tone.

He wasn't groveling. He wasn't apologizing. Just stating a fact...

He would never forgive himself.

Her throat felt too tight. But before she could respond, he pulled back and glanced around the table as if only now remembering they were not alone. His next words were brusque. "You must leave."

"Pardon?" She blinked in surprise as he pushed away from the table, ready to join the others who were making their way back to the parlor.

"I'll make our excuses," he said.

"Our...what?" She glanced down the table toward Lucinda and Benedict. But then Edmund gripped her elbow and tugged so she was forced to come with him or make a scene. "Why must we leave?"

He stopped short in the hallway and spun to face her. "Because I know why you came here..."

They both grew silent when Benedict followed after

179

them, hesitating with an ingratiating smile when he found them in conversation.

"Oh you do, do you?" she murmured as she returned Benedict's smile.

Edmund's brows lowered and he tugged her into the next room. A music room that was empty of guests. "It won't work, Savina."

She cocked her head to the side. "What won't?"

His exasperated exhale told her she was fooling no one. "Lucinda will never allow her son to marry you."

Savina's lips curved up in a smile, even as years of hatred boiled up inside of her. She couldn't hide the bitterness in her voice. "What if she has no choice but to allow it."

The look in his eyes made her freeze. Everything in her went cold at the disdain and...and disappointment.

"You'd go that far, would you? You'd seduce a man just to trap him?"

Savina's smile faltered. She tried to swallow down a wave of...what? What was this sensation?

It twisted in her gut and made her chest too tight.

"I told you from the start, I'd do whatever it took to ensure that Margot is safe, and our futures secure. How else do you suppose I could get back what is rightfully mine?"

That muscle in his jaw jumped and she caught her breath when he leaned forward to growl, "You could let me take care of it. Trust me—"

"Ha! Trust you? I thought I already made it clear that you shall never have my trust."

His gaze burned into hers. "Even if you don't trust me, you need me."

That rankled, more than she wanted to admit.

"Or perhaps it's Benedict I need." Her tone was a childish sing-song.

His breathing was sharp and ragged, and Savina was

suddenly and acutely aware of the lack of space between them.

She could feel the heat radiating from his body, a stark contrast to the chilly words they'd shared. His scent was intoxicating and she found herself inhaling deeply as if she needed him for air. He was so close—too close—that she could feel his breaths on her face.

The tension crackled between them, a mix of anger and sexual energy that made Savina's heart thud furiously.

The moment felt like it stretched on forever until finally he reached out and grabbed her hand.

His touch was fire against her skin, sending sparks up her arm as his fingers intertwined with hers. She expected him to pull away, but instead he stepped closer until there was no space left between them at all. She could feel every inch of his body pressed against hers, from his rough fingertips to the hard planes of his chest beneath her palms.

He wrapped an arm around her waist, and she just barely swallowed a moan as she felt the hard jab of his manhood against her belly.

He was so tall and broad, he blocked out everything else. She was surrounded by him, his scent, his warmth, his hardness...

Her fingers itched to reach out for him as her lungs labored to breathe him in. And that heat that she'd only ever felt around him flooded through her so thick and hot, it made her legs tremble.

She had to squeeze her thighs together to alleviate the ache, and all the while she felt his searching gaze, so insistent that she finally caved to it, letting her head fall back so she could meet his gaze.

The moment their eyes locked, she knew her mistake.

His hunger was on full display, and she had no doubt he saw it mirrored back to him.

But even as she told herself to pull away, her traitorous body leaned into his until her aching breasts were crushed against his hard chest.

She whimpered as her nipples hardened and chafed against her too-tight bodice.

Fire drowned out every other emotion in his gaze, but with a curse he stepped away. "Not here."

Before she could ask what he meant by that, he dragged her out into the now crowded parlor. She remained mutely furious as he made their apologies and excuses for having to leave early.

The overbearing brute kept a firm grip on her and gave her no room to protest. All she could do was sputter in silent outrage at his highhandedness.

Her fury was so great, she was only dimly aware of Lucinda's smug smirk and Benedict's crestfallen frown as Edmund hurried her out the front door.

Anger pounded in her temples, but she kept her mouth clenched shut until they were locked away in his carriage.

"How dare you drag me away like I'm some naughty child?"

He caught her chin in his firm grip and leaned down so close she found herself hoping he'd claim a kiss.

"Trust me, darling, if you want to know how I punish naughty young ladies, it would be my pleasure to show you."

She pulled back with a gasp, hating her body's instant response. "What would you do?"

The whisper slipped out before she could stop it, and there was no use denying the plea in it.

Whatever he had in mind, she wanted it. The grip of his fingers on his chin, the low rumble of his voice... it made her want to lean into him. It made her ache in ways she didn't understand and didn't want to control.

It made her want to close her eyes and...and let go.

It made her want to trust.

But she couldn't trust him. She wouldn't. Not with her future, at least. Her mind knew that well. But her body still clamored for her to curl up in his lap, to let him hold her and stroke her and show her what it could be like...

For once, she wanted someone else to be in control. But not just anyone.

Him. Only him.

Why was that?

She frowned up at him, more confused than ever by this craving he brought out in her. And that was when she saw it. He was ... tortured.

He didn't want to feel this pull any more than she did.

And just like that, she felt the power sliding back into her hands. Moving across the carriage, she gave into this overwhelming urge. She settled herself into his lap, trying not to be affected by the feel of his hard shaft digging into that soft space between her thighs.

Trying...and failing.

Her breath left her with a gasp.

"What are you doing, Savina?" His voice sounded just as tortured as his expression. She leaned in closer, toying with his cravat as a new sort of energy ebbed her earlier anger...

Though it didn't dissipate entirely. Oh no, whatever this strange concoction was that made her blood feel hot and her skin too raw, it was fueled by her anger, and it seemed to feed on her need for revenge.

Thoughts of Lucinda and Benedict were far from her mind, though. This sense of revenge was for this man alone. This man who'd dared to tease her with hope. Who she'd secretly thought she might be able to trust...

How dare he make her think she wasn't alone in this world?

Her breasts felt heavy as she leaned in close. There was

that need again. That overwhelming desire to push and pull and prod until he lost control.

That would be his punishment.

This was a man who valued control and power over all else.

And tonight he'd made it perfectly clear just how she could make him lose that.

"What do you think you're doing, Savina?" he asked again, his whole body stiff as she snuggled into his chest, running a hand over the hard muscles of his chest.

"I'd think that was obvious." She let her lips find his earlobe as she whispered in his ear. "I want to hear more about how you punish naughty wards."

A groan escaped him and the primal sound of his lust made her sex grow so wet, she moaned in turn.

His fingers gripped her hips so hard she knew she'd have bruises.

And she *loved* it.

When she felt his manhood swell beneath her bottom, she pulled back so she could see his expression as she wiggled in his lap.

He ground his teeth together. "Savina...what are you doing to me?"

She wet her lips, all the anger and fear, gratitude and betrayal she'd felt toward this man mixing with this overwhelming desire until she forgot that anything existed outside of this carriage. "I'm seeing what it would take," she whispered, her voice coming out in short gasps of pleasure as she spread her thighs just enough so his hard ridge could press against her sex.

"What it would take for what?" he grunted.

Her smile was wicked as she leaned in once more to whisper in his ear. "How far must I go before you take me over your knee, stepfather?"

20

Savina's words took ahold of Edmund and refused to let go. The warmth of her body against his felt like a drug, every movement driving him closer and closer to the edge.

He wanted her. He'd known that from the moment he'd seen her. But what was more, he ached for what she was offering. Control. Power. The right to own her—or at least her body...

Her pleasure.

Oh, he knew full well what she was up to. She thought she held the reins, but one look into her bright, feverish eyes, and he saw what she couldn't possibly know she was asking for.

Relief from all the burdens she bore.

Escape from the anger and bitterness.

And someone to show her how to fulfill this yearning that he knew she felt just as keenly as he did.

"A spanking, hmm?" He turned his head to nuzzle her ear, inhaling her delicious scent. "Is that what you want, love? A little pain to match the ache between your thighs?"

She pulled back with a gasp so sweet and innocent, he didn't know whether to laugh or groan.

"Such a saucy little minx, and yet you don't know what this is, do you? You don't know how to find satisfaction when that sweet little body of yours is begging for my touch."

Her moan was answer enough, and then she was wriggling in his arms once more, torturing his hard cock as she tried to get more friction.

"It may be a spanking you deserve, my sweet, but right about now I'd say you need to be petted." He ran his hand up from her hip to her breasts and cupped one deliciously rounded mound. "Are you wet for me, sweetheart?"

She pulled back a bit, her gaze dazed and tinged with confusion.

He gave in at last, bending over her to touch his lips to hers gently.

Just a taste, that was all.

But one taste and he knew...

Oh Christ, how he understood now. Hunger rippled through him at the feel of her soft, sweet lips beneath his own, parting and molding to his like they'd been made for his kiss. And he truly understood then...

One taste would never be enough.

He pulled back with a start, staring at her in shock as desire coursed through his veins.

He caught the scent of her hair, and let his fingers tangle in its softness as he tried with all his might not to succumb to this intoxication.

No, it had gone beyond that. This was no mere attraction. No infatuation from which he could one day hope to recover.

It never had been. This obsession had always been more, right from the start. She'd been his from the moment he'd seen her, and there was no fighting it.

His hand still buried in her hair, he let his thumb slide over the silken skin of her jaw, the hard edge of her cheekbone. Her lips parted on a sigh and her eyelids fluttered shut. There was a look of relief in her expression. Of bliss.

And that was just from a simple touch.

Bloody hell. He could have her. He could have all of her. Right here and now in the carriage, and she wouldn't refuse.

No, she'd beg for it, his naughty little temptress. His sweet, saucy minx.

He stilled, forcing his lungs to work and his hands to cease their explorations. *Think.* For the love of God, he needed to think.

If he let himself take control over Savina...

If he gave in to this need that they shared…

Well then, there would be no denying it. He'd be making love to a woman who was under his protection.

And Christ, what sort of devil would that make him?

The carriage rolled to a stop before he could decide.

Moments later he was gently lifting her out of his lap, and helping her out of the carriage.

His body rebelled, hating him for denying them this.

Savina seemed surprised when he began to follow her to the townhome door.

"We're not through here, little one," he murmured.

The endearment was meant to be a reminder to himself about who she was, about why she was off limits. And perhaps it would have been effective if his tone hadn't warmed to something he hardly recognized, revealing a tenderness he couldn't hide.

She turned away, leading them inside, and only showing a mild irritation when he went ahead and dismissed her servants for the night.

When they were alone in the small but comfortable

drawing room, he turned to see that she was standing in front of the fire, her back to him.

The silence was far from companionable, and Edmund wished he could reach for her and pull her back into his arms.

But that wasn't what he was here for.

Still, he noted the tension in her shoulders, the stiffness in her spine. He cleared his throat and forced his mind back on task rather than go to her.

He was here because she'd overstepped, he reminded himself.

He was here to stop her from pursuing whatever foolish plan she had in mind.

"You need to stay away from Benedict, Savina."

"He's my stepbrother," she protested. "Why shouldn't I speak with him?"

He just barely held back a sigh. "Feigning ignorance is an insult to us both."

Her shoulders went back further.

Blasted woman and her pride.

"You may be clothing me and feeding me, but who I speak with is none of your concern. He's kind—"

"He's a puppet," he snapped.

"I found him quite charming, actually. He has certainly grown into a handsome man over the years."

Handsome.

Edmund tensed. He knew what she was doing, but even knowing this did nothing to stop the wild possessive rage that flared to life in a heartbeat.

"And he seemed quite pleased to see me as well," she continued.

Edmund growled and she whipped around to look at him.

She arched a brow, her eyes filled with defiance.

That look only fueled that fire. The thought of any other man touching her was unbearable, but a spineless wastrel like Benedict?

"Never," he snapped, his hands clenching into fists. "Benedict shall never be your suitor."

No man will court you. No man will touch you.

No one but me.

He struggled to keep those thoughts to himself. He had no right to stake such a claim.

At some point she'd marry. That was what she deserved, did she not? A life of her own. A family of her own…

The thought of Savina with a babe in her arms nearly cut him down at his knees. His heart felt like it had been pierced by an arrow.

She should have that, yes. A family and a future and…

Bloody hell. She ought to have it with some other man. But it wasn't just the thought of Benedict at her side that made him want to howl with rage. It was any man. Any man but him.

"I must marry," she said, as if reading his thoughts. "That's what young ladies do, is it not? So why not the man who is to inherit my father's estate?"

He caught a flicker of pain in her eyes and that made his fury feel wild.

Her pain made him come undone.

"If I must marry, why not him?" she said again, her tone growing sharper and higher as emotions clouded her bright eyes. "Why not take Lucinda's precious son as my own?"

He'd thought it himself. It was the logical move in his plan to take back what Lucinda had taken from his friend. Marry one of Leopold's daughters to the new heir and move along with his plans for his own vengeance against his wicked wife.

His hands clenched at his sides as Savina glowered at him.

"Well?" she demanded. "Don't tell me you don't see the wisdom in it. Surely you've thought it too."

He had. That had been the plan right up until she'd stepped foot into that bloody brothel.

He supposed that was what made this anger so unbearable. He hated himself in that moment for ever having considered it.

"I could seduce him easily," she continued, her tone so jaded and bitter he could hardly bear it. "You saw how he was with me tonight. I could seduce him, get caught, and then he'd be forced to marry me. And his mother would have to allow it."

Her words were coming quicker now, like she was trying to convince herself as well as him.

He strode toward her before he could stop himself, gripping her shoulders too roughly. "I did not save you from becoming a lady of the night just to watch you whore yourself out to—"

Her slap made a cracking sound that cut the air like thunder.

Pain shot through him, but it was nothing compared to his regret when he saw the anguish in her eyes.

"Savina," he started. "I didn't mean to say that you are—"

"A whore?" She spit out the word like it was poison. "Why not? That's what I was when you found me."

His heart gave a sharp tug when her eyes welled with tears. "Savina, no…"

"I already was." Her voice was hard, but her lips quivered. "I was a whore, Edmund. That's what she made me."

The words cut like a knife.

"Savina." He reached out for her, but stopped just short of touching her.

She was holding herself together with pride—her chin up and her eyes wet with tears, but none spilling over.

Understanding dawned. He'd thought he'd gotten to her in time, before she'd had to resort to selling her body…

Rage made his lungs falter and his muscles tighten convulsively. For all the world he couldn't say if the rage he felt was for the men who'd touched her, for his wretched wife who'd driven her to it…or himself for not saving her in time. "I thought…" For the first time in his life, he struggled for words. "That is, Madame Bernadette told me you were an innocent still…"

"It wasn't at her brothel." Savina turned her head away. "It was only once. One man."

"I will kill him," he growled.

Either she didn't hear his low vow or she knew it for the idle threat it was. How would he ever find the scoundrel who dared to touch his Savina?

"I gave away my innocence for a loaf of bread." Her voice was so soft, it sounded like she was talking to herself. Then she turned to him, and there was no denying the pain in her eyes. "I let him…" She trailed off with a swallow. "So Margot and I wouldn't starve."

He hated the wariness in her eyes. Like she was waiting for him to judge her. Or maybe she was judging herself for her actions…

A sick rage coursed through him. But she didn't need his anger now. It was too little too late.

"So you see, I already am a whore," she continued.

"No." He reached for her before he could stop himself, tugging her into his arms. "Never say such a thing."

Her gaze was hard when she lifted her chin to meet his stare, but her chin wobbled and her lips quivered.

She might as well have taken a knife to his chest. The pride, the hurt, the anger, and her fear…

All so pure and so palpable in this woman who was too young to have known such horror.

He touched her cheek as gently as he was able. "Never call yourself any such thing."

"Why not?" She lifted a brow, challenge in her eyes. "Is it not true? I sold myself. I sold my body—"

"To save your sister," he finished. "To save yourself. You did what you had to in order to survive and to keep your sister safe. That is courage, Savina, and any man who's ever fought on a battlefield would tell you the same."

Her eyes welled with tears but she pressed her lips together in a hard line.

He cupped her chin in his hand so she couldn't look away. "Sometimes good people must do horrible things for the right reasons."

She exhaled shakily and tugged her chin from his hands. "Why does it sound like you're speaking from experience?"

His lips quirked. "Because I am, of course. I have blood on my hands, Savina. My enemies and my friends who I failed to protect. What's more...I have to live with the fact that I failed you and your sister. I failed your father."

She couldn't stop the tears now, and his lungs burned at the sight of them.

"We were never *your* responsibility," she muttered.

He could argue. He wanted to argue. But that would only serve to appease his own guilt. And besides, he knew precisely what she meant.

He hadn't been the guardian in charge of them all those years ago.

Lucinda had been.

Bitterness filled his gut and made his blood run hot. How he wished they could have one conversation that didn't harken back to that vile witch.

"That's what this is about then." He stated the obvious. "Flirting with Benedict. This plan to trap him into marriage."

"Don't tell me you hadn't thought of it." She cut him with

a glance so sharp he was certain she could read his mind. "If you truly did bring me back to society so I might take my rightful place, you must have made that connection yourself."

He ground his teeth together, furious with himself for ever having thought it. But of course he had. It was perfect.

Benedict was nothing if not maneuverable. He was so easily manipulated, he would have been married off to Savina before he knew what was happening...and before Lucinda could intervene.

But now...

"No," he barked. "I will not have it. There are other ways. Ways that do not involve you demeaning yourself in such a manner."

Ways that don't involve Benedict's hands on you. Or any other man's...

He snagged her by the waist, pulling her close until their chests rose and fell against each other, and her exhales caressed his neck. His voice was little more than a rumble and he spoke through a clenched jaw. "You will never be his, do you hear me?"

"Why not? Do you have another plan?" Her tone turned taunting. "If so, I am listening, I assure you."

He hesitated. Of course he had a plan. He always had a plan. But he couldn't share his suspicions just yet. There were too many variables and...

And he hesitated too long.

"As I thought," she muttered, pushing against his chest.

He tightened his hold on your, irritation tingeing his voice. "Savina, you must understand. You cannot be so reckless—"

"Understand?" Fire flashed in her eyes.

Oddly that show of temper was a relief after witnessing her tears.

"You think I do not understand what's at stake?" She

pushed against him again, and this time he let her take a step back, though he didn't release her entirely.

Her fingers clutched at his jacket as she glared up at him.

"You think I do not know how important this is?" Her breathing grew short and ragged. "You completely ruined my plan tonight."

"I ruined nothing. That man—"

All of a sudden a choked sob came out of her mouth and she turned away from him with heaving shoulders.

For a moment he was paralyzed, more affected by her tears than he could stand. "Savina, I—"

"I must have my revenge." Her voice was low and guttural, full of such pain, he tried to pull her back into the safety of his arms, but she pushed him away. "I cannot stand the sight of that woman and her son, so proper and perfect. It may be wrong to use him, but I have been wronged." Her voice pitched and when she turned he saw that she was crying in earnest. "I have been wronged, Edmund!"

Her face was pale, streaked with tears, and filled with unbearable anguish.

"We did not run away, surely you know this. She banished us, treated us like street rats. Threatened to kill us if we ever came back."

His gut coiled, fury coursing through him. He knew as much from his investigating, but hearing her say it was another matter entirely.

"We lived on the streets, slept under bridges. The things I had to do in order to survive..."

She bent forward, sobs racking her body.

He wrapped his arms around her, pulling her against his chest. This time when she tried to pull away, he would not let go. Not until she was crushed against him.

His Savina.

His to care for. His to cherish.

His for the keeping.

"Hush, love," he murmured as he stroked her back, trying to absorb her pain and take away her horrors.

But he couldn't do that. All he could do was help her to get her revenge.

"You have been wronged, my angel," he murmured as he crushed her to him, his shirt growing wet from her tears. "You've been wronged, and I swear to you, I will not rest until you have your vengeance."

Her sniffles nearly broke his heart. "If I seduce Benedict—"

"You will do no such thing." He pushed her away, just far enough that he could see her eyes. He swiped a thumb over her cheeks to wipe away her tears. "You will not lower yourself in such a way, do you hear me?"

"I told you already—"

"I don't care about your past, Savina. I care about your future. About giving you the chance to be the sort of lady your father would be proud of."

That had her breath hitching and her eyes widened so sweetly he couldn't resist from swiping his thumb again, this time over her full lower lip.

"And you think you can help me to have that future?"

"I know I can. And I will." He leaned down closer until his nose grazed hers and their breaths mingled. "I will give you the life you deserve, Savina. Or I will die trying."

21

---

*S*avina didn't know who moved first.

One moment they were locked together in a tense silence that seemed to stretch for an eternity, so close they breathed the same air.

The next, his mouth crushed hers in a bruising kiss that had her forgetting her past and the future. Everything but this moment and the feel of his hot, wet mouth claiming hers.

His tongue parted her lips, and he thrust inside her with such authority and command, she moaned into his open mouth. Her head tilted back as she gave him even more access.

She was vulnerable. So painfully vulnerable, her breasts pressed against him and her neck arched.

So vulnerable and yet...she had no fear.

None. And none of the disgust she'd grown so accustomed to, either.

Oh no, this warm sensation spreading from her belly to her limbs and settling between her thighs had nothing to do with disgust.

Her hips arched and she squirmed in his arms. She couldn't get close enough. His mouth devoured hers in a hungry kiss that stole her breath and seemed to sear her like a brand, but it still wasn't enough.

Her nails dug into the fabric of his jacket as their bodies melded together. She looped her arms around his neck and clung to him, desperate to maintain the connection and get closer still.

She gasped between his ardent kisses, fire coursing through her veins. His lips moved from her mouth to her jawline, lingering in all the right places. Eliciting a trail of blissful sighs in its wake. He set her body ablaze when he caught her throat with an open mouthed kiss, then followed it up with purposeful sucking and biting that left no room for doubt—this man was hungry for her.

He was hard, everywhere; she could feel the bulge of his arousal against her belly as one hand descended firmly to grip her hips and draw her lower half even closer.

"Edmund," she moaned, "What are you doing to me?"

"It's all right, love," he growled, his voice low and gravelly, "This is what passion should feel like. This is the way your body should respond when the desire is shared."

Her mind was sluggish and foggy, too intent on memorizing every sensation to make sense of the actual words. Focusing instead on the soothing rumble of his voice. The way it made her feel protected.

Cherished.

"I shouldn't be doing this," he muttered.

That much she heard and for a moment panic took hold.

Her fingers clawed against the cloth of his jacket as his arms wrapped around her so tightly he brought her up off her feet. Dangling in his arms like a doll, she looped her arms around his neck and held him the way he held her.

Like she'd never let go.

"Don't stop," she whimpered. "Please, don't stop."

The needy sensation in her core grew worse by the second. It was the sweetest torture she'd ever known. It was delicious fire and it burned her to the bone.

"I won't. I can't," he admitted. "Just...I have to make you come. Let me make you come."

Make you come...

The words were meaningless to her, but she heard the agony in his voice that was a perfect match for her own.

"Yes." Whatever it was he wanted to do to her... "Yes."

She gasped for air as his lips moved from her mouth to her jawline, and down until his open mouth was savoring her throat, sucking and biting her as she strained against him, her body flush against his, and her breasts crushed to his chest.

He was as hard as stone. His thighs. His chest. His lips. His hands. Even his fingers were hard and merciless as he gripped her, pressing her closer so she could feel the granite bulge of his erection, flush against her sex.

Her hips rocked forward, and with a growl, he molded a hand to her bottom and squeezed so hard she cried out.

"That's my girl," he growled into her open mouth. "Scream for me."

Using both hands now, he lifted her bottom, urging her legs apart to wrap around his waist. The thick skirts of her gown were still between them, but feeling his hard body between her thighs made her incoherent with need.

She ached so badly down there, and she had no idea what to do to relieve the throbbing. She moaned and whimpered as she pressed against him, rocking her hips helplessly. She was rewarded with another long, hot, open-mouthed kiss.

"I know what you need, love. I'll give you exactly what you need to make the ache go away."

"Yes, yes, please."

He released her bottom and she whimpered. She needed that hard contact again. She tightened her thighs around his waist and rocked her hips trying to get more friction, more hard contact.

He brought his hand back down with a smack to her bottom, and her head fell back with a cry. The spanking was too gentle, padded by her gown, and the moan that escaped was high and needy.

She needed more. More of everything. More of that delicious friction between her thighs, more of that sweet pain. She wanted to lose herself in sensations, and frustration rippled through her at everything that kept them apart.

"More," she pleaded. "I want more."

He chuckled against her neck, but the sound was dark with lust. "That was for flirting with another man," he said as he massaged her bottom where he'd spanked her. "You shouldn't have done that, you know."

She was trembling in his arms, writhing and wriggling as she shamelessly rocked her hips against the hard shaft that teased her. "Yes," she panted. "I was naughty."

"And naughty stepdaughters always get a spanking, don't they?" he teased.

The words made her just as hot as his hands when he swatted her bottom again. Her answering moan was filled with whiney need. The skirts were in the way and they were keeping her from the full sensation. "Not enough, Edmund. It's...not enough."

"No, it's not. You need my firm hand on that sweet little bottom, don't you?"

"Yes," she hissed. "Yes, please."

"Say it again," he ordered.

"Please." She whispered the word against his lips, her belly fluttering with excitement when he nipped at her mouth.

He moved his attentions to her ear. "You need me to suck on your sweet tits and stroke your wet sex—"

"Yes," she moaned. Her head fell back, and for the first time ever she didn't hate herself for what she'd done that dark, dingy day when she'd been so desperate for coin she'd lost her pride.

Because now, for the first time...she was glad she wasn't a virgin.

She'd already made her choices. There was no pretending to be some innocent...not with Edmund. He knew the worst about her and he still wanted her.

He hadn't judged her. He'd understood. She'd done it to save herself and her sister. And for the first time since that horrid night, she didn't feel the curdling weight of shame.

Just like when she'd realized the freedom that came with being a scandal, right now she understood the wicked power that came with being compromised.

"Take me, Edmund," she whispered. "I want you to take me to bed."

His answer was a kiss, so sweet, and hot, and thorough, she found herself moaning low in her throat as he carried her over to the settee.

He laid her down like she was made of the most fragile glass, and when he leaned back, for a long moment he gazed down at her, taking her in from her stockinged toes to the top of her head.

She clutched the edges of the settee, resisting the urge to fidget with nerves. "What...what are you doing?"

His lips quirked up on one side and his scar glinted in the firelight as he met her gaze. "Savoring," he whispered.

She blinked in surprise, her lips parting. But before she could ask another question, his hands reached out and began to peel down her bodice and words fled from her mind.

"One day I will see all of you," he murmured, so low he

sounded as though he were in a trance. "I will see you naked on my bed, your legs spread wide for me, your sex wet and hot and eager for my cock..."

She swallowed hard, her breathing ragged as the image alone assaulted her senses, making her skin feel raw and her limbs heavy.

"One day?" she echoed, her voice strained and breathless.

The quirk of his lips morphed into a smirk as he bent forward, just as the bodice slipped over her nipples and her breasts sprang free.

He wasted no time, capturing one tight rosy bud between his lips, suckling the tip as he molded her other breast in one of his large calloused palms.

The roughness of his fingers and the delicious heat of his mouth were too much for her sensitive skin. Her head fell back with a groan, the movement giving him more access as he settled his weight on the settee beside her, leaning over her until he became her whole world.

There was nothing beyond this. He'd formed around her. She was safe here. Safe...and on fire with need.

His teeth grazed her nipple, making her hips buck, which in turn made him chuckle. "Easy, love. I've got you."

Her eyes flew open when he moved back, giving her breasts one last loving caress before moving his attention to her skirts. He made short work of piling them around her waist and tearing off her underclothes.

Her breathing was sharp, but she only felt the faintest hint of embarrassment when she found herself bare from the waist down.

And even that hint of embarrassment faded in the face of his unbridled hunger. He made no attempt to hide the lust that contorted his features and made his dark eyes seem black as pitch.

His chest heaved as his fingers bit into her thighs. He

looked up at her from beneath lowered brows, his control clearly straining. "Spread your legs."

It was a command, stern and unyielding. If she didn't do as he said, he'd do it for her.

She didn't even hesitate, eagerness to see what he'd do next outweighing reason and any fear that might have surfaced.

But this was nothing like her one other experience with that drunken lout in an alley.

This was something else entirely.

And she couldn't wait to see where it led.

For a long moment he didn't move, his gaze burned as he devoured the soft curls of her mound and the pink slit at her center as her knees fell to the sides.

"So wet for me, my love."

She bit her lip, but couldn't squelch a whimper.

"That's good," he said, his praise gruff and hard. "My girl gets wet for me and me alone, do you hear?"

Her breath caught. *My girl...*

His gaze darted up to spear her with a glare. "Do. You. Understand?"

Her lips parted with surprise. He was a man on the verge of coming undone. A far cry from the tightly controlled, regal prince she'd come to know.

He moved up over her until his lips were directly over hers, the fire in his eyes raging and wild. She gasped when he gave her sex a little slap that sent a jolt of pleasure to her core. It was a light spanking that made her sex weep and her need grow so fierce she felt desperate for some sort of release from this sweet pain. She lifted her hips for more, but he didn't give her that satisfaction.

"Answer me when I ask a question."

"Yes," she breathed. "Yes, I understand."

Pleasure glinted in his eyes at whatever he saw in her

expression. "You like that, don't you? You like when I give you commands."

She wet her lips, loathe to admit it aloud. But God yes. That tone of voice, the hard glint in his eyes…it made her heart race and her nipples harden.

"Do you like my firm hand as well, little one?"

Before she could respond, he brought his hand down again. And again the light spanking to her wet, parted folds brought with it a jolt of pleasure and pain so intense she cried out, inner muscles clenching as she brought her hips up for more.

"Greedy girl," he murmured, but the words held a note of approval that made her warm all over.

"You want more, do you?" He shifted, settling himself between her legs and spreading her thighs even wider in a way that was so lewd and so dirty, she found herself writhing in need at the sight of it.

"Yes, please." She whimpered when he positioned himself over her, bringing his head down so close to her sex, his nose grazed the curls that covered her there.

"That's it," he said, his fingers stroking her inner thighs, encouraging her to relax and open. "Beg for me."

She didn't hesitate. She had no pride, just need. "Please," she cried, arching her hips to bring her sex closer to him. For what? She did not know. "Please…more. I need more. I need…"

You.

I need you.

She couldn't bring herself to say that one word. She needed his touch. Needed his mouth. Needed him to end whatever torture this was that he'd begun.

But she couldn't bring herself to admit that she needed *him.* That felt far too terrifying to say aloud.

"Please, Edmund," she moaned.

His chuckle was a puff of warm air against the sensitive flesh of her wet sex.

She cried out, but before she could beg again, he lowered his head, burying his face between her thighs and thrusting his tongue between her folds in one long, wide lick that made her shriek with pleasure.

She felt his smile against her sex as his hands slid beneath her bottom and lifted her for better access.

"So sweet, my love," he murmured against her curls. His tongue darted out to taste her again, probing the core of her until she let out another cry. "So warm and sweet and...perfect."

She moaned, unable to tear her gaze away from the sight of this bold, insufferable, arrogant man nuzzling and licking and savoring her sex like she was his favorite feast.

"What are you...what is this..." She stopped trying to talk when his clever tongue found the hard nub at the top of her sex and flicked it.

She gasped and his smile when he glanced up was so very wicked, her heart gave a clattering thud.

"Touch your tits," he ordered, when he brought his head up and began teasing her folds with his fingers instead. Nodding toward her breasts, he added, "Don't make me tell you twice. I want to see what you like."

She deliberately hesitated, aching for another one of his punishments.

He didn't disappoint. This time he pinched that hard nub between her thighs making her cry out.

"Now touch your tits," he growled. "Fondle them. Roll your nipples between your fingers. Yes, love, just like that." He gave her sex a light spank. "Good girl."

She groaned, her head rolling from side to side as pleasure and pain became one and the same.

The pain somehow intensified the pleasure until she was

pinching her own nipples so hard she cried out, at the same time he brought his tongue back down to stroke the the seam of her folds, teasing his way down her slit until his tongue was probing her channel in a way that was exquisitely unbearable.

It was torture, plain and simple. So close to giving her what she wanted, but not nearly enough.

"What is it, love?" he taunted when she whimpered in delirious pain. "What do you need?"

"I...I...I don't know."

To her surprise, he stilled at the words, and for a moment he drew back long enough to look up at her.

There was a tenderness in his eyes that cut through the thick veil of need, straight to her heart.

"You don't, do you, love?" he murmured. He kissed the inside of her thigh. "But I do."

Her eyes widened at the promise in his voice.

He dipped his head once more and this time his insistent tongue, the stubble of his beard, and the feel of his growl against her throbbing core drove her to the brink of insanity.

Her body was flooded with fire, her skin crackled with heat, and her senses were flooded with the onslaught of pleasure.

"I can't," she whimpered. "I don't..."

"You can and you will," he growled. "Come apart for me, Savina." He slid two fingers into her wet channel, and the thick feel of him inside of her, pumping into her at the same time his mouth found that sensitive nub and he sucked and sucked and...

Savina's world was shattering. An explosion of sensations scattered her mind and sent her body to dizzying heights. Heat and pleasure rolled over her, drenching her in a wave of exhausted, delirious joy.

Her breath came in short, ragged gasps as she clawed at

his shoulders, until with one last thrust of his fingers inside her, she was lost to a tide of sheer pleasure and blissful release.

When she next opened her eyes, she saw him covering her with her skirts and adjusting her bodice.

He caught her heavy-lidded stare and gave her a small, rueful smile.

"I won't be able to avoid temptation much longer if you lie there looking like a siren."

She blinked a few times, slowly dragging herself back to her senses as she scrambled up onto her elbows.

He stopped her with a shushing sound and then situated them so he was seated on the settee and she tucked in his lap, content and comfortable as a kitten.

Indeed, Savina felt safe in his arms. Safer then she'd felt in years. He rested his chin on top of her head, and she closed her eyes, reveling in the soothing sound of his heart beneath her ear and his slow, even breathing.

For the first time since her father's death, she felt protected from the outside world. She was tucked away in a cocoon, and she could have stayed there forever if it wasn't for the persistent voice in the back of her mind that reminded her this was only temporary.

They had an attraction; they had from the start. But he'd betrayed her trust. And she had no loyalty to him. Only to Margot.

Still, her heart gave a sharp tug when he pulled away, gently setting her aside.

"Are you..." She stopped and swallowed, uncertain of how to ask. Her gaze pointedly dropped to the large, swollen bulge in his pants. "Aren't you going to, er..."

His chuckle sounded pained and he leaned down to kiss the tip of her nose. "Not tonight, love. Tonight was for you."

Her chest grew soft and warm so quickly she lost her breath. "What do you mean?"

He tipped her chin up so she was forced to meet his gaze. "I hate that you learned of a man's touch without knowing the sort of pleasure it could bring."

She tugged her chin away, her pride stinging at his mention of her sordid past, as well as the insinuation. "So this was...what? A favor? An act of charity?"

His tsking sound brought her glare back to him. She found him giving her that crooked smile, though it didn't quite reach his eyes. "You know it was no such thing. I am not a kind man, Savina. I'm selfish. I'm calculating. And I've never once let sentiment dictate my actions."

She bit her lip.

"Trust me, love." He caught her chin again, and there was that dark promise in his eyes. The fierce hunger that made her belly flutter and her heart hammer. "I will make you mine. But not until you're ready to give yourself to me."

She frowned, her mind going back to the way she'd begged him to take her to bed. Had that not been enough?

He leaned down until his lips brushed against her ear. "When I take you, Savina, I am claiming all of you. I will own you—body, mind, and heart. Do you understand, angel?"

Her lips parted but she neither shook her head nor spoke a word.

Did she understand?

No. Not at all.

He didn't seem to expect an answer. Coming to stand, he straightened his jacket. "Get some rest," he ordered as he headed for the door. When he reached it, he turned back. "Oh, and Savina?"

He waited until she turned her head to meet his gaze.

"Stay away from Benedict."

22

*M*argot was determined to escape.

She had been in the cabin for two days and was growing more restless by the second.

The first night had passed quickly. The accident and her head injury had left her exhausted.

The beast—Callan, he'd grudgingly told her when she'd pestered long enough—had fed her a simple meat stew, and once he'd left her alone, she'd passed out and stayed asleep until the sounds of birds chirping had woken her in the morning. The rain had finally stopped, no doubt leaving the earth fresh and vibrant, droplets of water glistening off the grass blades and a crisp, clean smell in the air.

But Margot couldn't experience any of it.

She was trapped in this cottage, chained by her wounded ankle and the threat of what the beast might do to her if she tried to flee.

Callan was so quiet, she did not know how to read him. If she angered him, would he explode with a roar or freeze her out with those lethal blue eyes?

Would he use his crossbow to fire an arrow through her

heart or would that cold blue gaze stare her down while he choked her to death?

But was it truly cold? Was he lethal?

He had killed a man, probaby many, yet…

Lifting her layers of skirts, she skimmed her fingers over her ankle, remembering the gentle way in which he probed it, and despite his gruff grunts and orders… the way he had clothed her in a dry shirt when he so easily could have left her freezing in her sodden dress, literally chained up on the stone cold floor.

She glanced to the door, which she had worked out must lead to his bedroom. She had heard shuffling and footsteps from the other side of the wall and imagined a simple room much like the one she sat in, with perhaps a larger bed and maybe a chair. She was trapped in the main room which also included a wooden table and served the dual purpose of being the kitchen. A pot still hung over the fire. The pot which contained the dregs of rabbit stew they'd eaten the night before. He'd prepare the meal in front of her, not saying a word as his deft hands skinned and chopped the animal, stoked the fire and served her the simple stew.

In the two days she'd been here, she'd hardly left the bed by the fire. Whenever her thoughts turned to escape, fear would follow quickly in their wake.

Callan was an unpredictable entity.

She tensed every time he looked her way or walked in to check on her. And when he came too close, her body reacted in a multitude of confusing ways.

Her heart raced, her belly fluttered, and her tongue…

Well her tongue went wild. Whether it was nerves or fear or just sheer loneliness, she couldn't seem to hold her tongue for more than a heartbeat.

Questions, usually. She peppered him with them, but to no avail. He really was the strong, silent type.

Sometimes she blurted completely unsolicited facts about herself and her interests.

Usually she got no answer, which, she supposed, she ought to take as a hint to keep her mouth shut.

Clearly he didn't enjoy her chatter. But she couldn't seem to stop. The more quiet he was, the more she felt compelled to make up for his silence.

This morning, when he'd dropped her back in her bed after a trip to the privy, she'd been half desperate to get some sort of response.

And yes, to her humiliation, Callan was forced to carry her to do her business, but it did give her a glimpse of the outside world. The door on the left took them down a short dirt path to the privy. Beyond that lay a forest of which she could only steal glances at while he carried her back and forth.

There was no obvious path to freedom that she could make out, but surely the woods would take her to a road of some kind eventually. Or maybe a brook or stream. Water. Water always led to civilization, that was common knowledge. If she could find her way through the trees to a water source, then she would have a chance.

Her eyes darted to the door again. She stared at the big metal handle, her brain ticking with calculations.

Callan came and went through that door. It had only been two days, so she did not know his routine, but he had to hunt —how else would he have returned with rabbit the night before—and he chopped wood. She had heard the thud of the ax and the crack of splintering branches. She had watched him lumber in with a pile of wood chunks, unable to tear her gaze away from his hulking body as he crouched before the fire, storing and stacking the wood beside it.

He'd left again this afternoon. Of course he did not tell her where, so she sat on the bed, curled in a ball, debating with herself if now was the time to run free. As fear ate at her stomach, her mind whirled with the obvious. She could not stay here. She must get to her sister. She must escape.

As the minutes ticked by her determination grew, stealing fear's power over her body and finally giving her the courage to act.

Gingerly, she moved off the bed, using the chair beside it to help her stand. Testing her weight on her bad ankle, she hissed, then tried again. While it gave a twinge of complaint, she could bear it.

She must.

This could be her only chance to leave. There was no other option.

Callan wouldn't answer her questions about what she was doing here, why he was keeping her or for how long. And while part of her thought he must have attacked their carriage for money, she couldn't shake the suspicion that Edmund was behind this.

Why would Callan have taken her if not to hold her for ransom?

Which meant he had to have known who she was.

Who else knew she'd be traveling that road?

Unless the attack was random, of course, but then...why harm the others and leave her alive? Why hold her captive?

None of it made any sense. But if Edmund did have some dastardly plan in place, then she had to get to Savina.

She had to warn her sister...if it wasn't already too late.

She squeezed her eyes shut, pushing aside the thought. Hopelessness never helped anyone.

All she could do was put one foot in front of the other until she found her sister. And the only thing she knew for certain was she couldn't stay here.

Even if she only made it to the next town, perhaps she could send a message or beg a stranger for help.

But as she stilled, waiting for any sign that Callan was nearby, she felt the stone walls closing in on her.

Staying here any longer felt like a death sentence.

She had already checked out the windows, but they were too small for her to fit through, so she'd have to walk straight out the front door and hope she didn't catch Callan on his way back from wherever he'd gone off to.

With swift movements, she hobbled around the table and headed to the door, which was...locked.

Drat.

She quickly rummaged through the cabin looking for something that might help her pick the lock or pry it open, and found a rusty knife on the fireplace mantle. Armed with her tool, Margot set to work.

The screws were old and tarnished, but they eventually gave way. After a little effort, she was able to yank the lock off and toss it aside. The door creaked when she wrenched it open, and she held her breath, waiting for a distant roar, charging feet or a guttural growl as he pounced on her from the shadows.

But all was still.

She inched over the threshold, barely daring to breath as she limped away from the cottage. The forest lay before her, an ominous army of pine centurions that seemed merciless in their density and stature.

It was impossible not to second-guess her decision.

The only path leading away from the cottage was the one to the privy. She turned her back to it. Freedom did not lie there. But would she find it amongst the trees?

They stretched out in every direction. There was not so much as a well-trekked trail let alone a road in sight.

She turned the other way, even hobbling around the corner of the cottage, but it was the same view no matter where she looked.

A mocking laugh punched out of her mouth. What was she expecting? That a sign might magically appear out of the forest brush?

The road to the next town is this way...

"Foolish girl," she muttered, shaking her head as despair threatened to hinder her.

No. I cannot tarry. I must do this.

Straightening her shoulders, she faced decidedly in the direction where the trees were the least dense and started to walk. "I'll just have to pick a way," she muttered to herself. "Surely every direction leads to some sort of path. Does it not?"

The forest did not answer.

And so she strained her ears for the sounds of water, limping as gently as she could over tree roots and pine needles. Weaving around trunks and bushes, she pushed branches aside and soldiered on—one foot in front of the other.

The uneven ground and the way her dress seemed to catch on every tree she passed turned the journey into an exhausting one.

She wasn't sure how long she walked, but her ankle began to throb in earnest, and even the use of a branch that she'd fashioned into a cane couldn't stop her from wincing every time she put weight on it.

But she could not give up now.

Pausing, she drew in a breath, trying to talk herself out of submitting to defeat when she heard it.

A twig cracked, the undergrowth rustling under heavy footsteps.

She flinched, barely swallowing her gasp as she swiveled to the right and tried to see which direction her attacker was coming from.

Of course he would have come after her.

Of course he'd have picked up her trail with ease.

Run, Margot! Run!

She spun back the way she'd been heading and barely made it two steps when he appeared from the trees—a bear-like apparition, puffing and snarling.

Grabbing her arm, he jerked her to a stop.

"No!" She fought him, trying to beat him away with her makeshift cane.

He grunted, scowling at her when he caught it on her next swing and wrenched it out of her hand.

Fight, Margot! Fight!

Savina's voice rang in her head and she was determined to make her sister proud, clawing and scratching at his hold on her. With a throaty growl, he turned, pulling her along behind him. He set a quick pace, but she did her best to hinder his every step.

Digging her heels into the earth, she screamed and fought, grasping at branches, dropping to her knees, so he was forced to drag her body weight.

His grunts of frustration grew with fervor and when he jerked to a stop, so he could haul her back to her feet, she did what she could to punch and kick him.

"Be still, woman," he growled.

"Never!" she cried. "Let me go! Let me leave!" Her voice pitched to a wail that silenced the birds around them.

"Be still!" he warned her once more, but she paid no mind to his orders.

She would not be his prisoner any longer.

Against her natural instincts, she continued to battle her captor, knowing it was pointless. He was too strong and her relentless struggle would only invoke his rage.

"Stop," he muttered, capturing her wrist when she tried to hit him again.

She swung out with her other fist and he caught that just

as easily, driving her backwards until she fell against a tree trunk.

"Oof." Her whimper was soft as he pulled her arms down to her sides, pinning her against the rough bark and shocking her still with a kiss she never saw coming.

Hot lips crushed against hers and her body froze, her mind going blank as the only sensation she could comprehend was that of his full mouth covering hers. His lips parted and hers followed, acting instinctively as he plundered her mouth with his tongue.

She'd never felt anything like it—this warm commanding presence, silently ordering her tongue to act. And it did, following his movements and lashing against his, tasting him, breathing in his masculine scent while a stirring she didn't recognize rippled through her.

The muscles in her stomach clenched, while a weight dropped between her legs, an aching prickle that grew and spread, curling throughout her torso until her entire body yearned for… what? She was not sure.

Her breasts felt heavy as he sucked her bottom lip into his mouth, then stroked his tongue against hers before pulling away.

His blue eyes were bright with hunger while a cold air seeped into the space between them. It was a contrast so stark from his heated kiss that it almost felt like a slap to her cheek.

She gaped at him, her eyes wide, her chest heaving as he stared down at her. His gaze grew pained as his hunger gave way to an agonized frown she did not understand.

"Be still," he muttered, roughly swiping his thumb across her wet lips before yanking her arm and throwing her over his shoulder.

She was too shocked by her body's response to him to do anything more than let herself be carried through the woods.

Her body bobbed and swayed against his back, her mind reeling as she re-lived every moment of his kiss.

It was rough and commanding... terrifying, really. Yet her body seemed to bloom and ache for more.

Her head began to swim as he marched back through the woods and it wasn't until she could see the edge of the stone cottage that she realized where she was once more.

"No," she whimpered. "Please. You can't keep me here."

He stayed silent, kicking the door open and growling in his throat as he pushed the broken lock away with his foot.

"Please don't do this," she whispered.

He paused by the bed, letting out a huff before dumping her onto the mattress as if she were a sack of grain. She landed with a soft yelp and his eyes raced over her body before crouching down and gently propping her aching ankle onto the bed.

She hissed and his hard blue gaze told her exactly what he was thinking.

Serves you right for trying to run away.

She huffed out her nose, daring to glare back at him. "How long do you mean to keep me here?"

His scowl deepened.

"Did someone tell you to take me? Is this...is this because of...who I am?"

The edge of his mouth twitched, but he did not say a word.

Her eyes began to burn as she fought her frustration, the pain in her ankle and the humiliation of her failure.

Shuffling on the bed, she glanced at the fire, then found herself thinking of that kiss again. His full mouth, his smooth—

Wait.

Her head jerked to find him and she gasped, blinking in

surprise. "Your beard." The words slipped free without thought. "I only just noticed."

His lips twitched upward ever so slightly as he ran his hand over the smooth plains of his face. His hair was still damp and she quickly figured out that he must have been bathing this morning. Bathing and… shaving.

Oh. Oh dear. He truly was handsome. The beard, it seemed, had covered a square jaw and a cleft in his chin… and was that a dimple?

She found herself gaping and he made no attempt to glance away. His eyes were soft and deep and endless.

Not lethal.

But calm like the sky after a storm.

A girl could get lost in those eyes.

They crinkled ever so slightly in the corners as he lifted his chin toward the far side of the bed. That was when she noticed the stack of books sitting on a stool beside it.

She whipped back around to look at him and she readjusted her earlier calculations. He hadn't been bathing in a stream… how silly of her to think it. He must have headed to a nearby village for a barber's shave. And to collect some books.

"For me?" She blinked, still trying to figure out this mystifying man. One minute a growling beast, the next a sweet bearer of books.

He grunted, his jaw clenching before he muttered, "You ran."

She froze, her lungs burning as she assessed him.

Was he mad? Was she to be punished?

She couldn't stand the suspense. "Are you angry with me?"

His gaze softened, even if his expression remained grim. "No." And then, just when she thought he wouldn't say another word, he added. "I'm glad."

"You're..." She frowned. Surely she'd heard him wrong. "You're glad?"

He eyed her steadily, then huffed. "I cannot leave you so easily anymore, but..." His lips twitched. "You fought like a she-devil." His eyes sparked with amusement. "It shows you have spirit." He patted his flat stomach. "A fire."

She blinked. Oh. Did she? She supposed she had *some* fire, even if it was little compared to Savina's bravery.

He took a step backward. "You need fire to survive."

She frowned. "Am I in danger?"

His gaze connected with hers, and she felt a jolt of awareness as he held her stare.

Her own words came back to her and she muttered, "Of course you're in danger, you ninny. You've been kidnapped."

She wasn't entirely sure, but she thought she saw the edge of his mouth hitch up as if to smile. But it was over so quickly she must have imagined it.

"You said..." She wet her lips, and exhaled sharply when his gaze dipped to follow the motion. "Y-you said you wouldn't hurt me."

"I never will." His gaze lifted, but it was darker now.

Her heart gave a thud at the intensity in his eyes. She swallowed hard. "But you won't let me go."

His unrelenting stare held her still. His silence was answer enough.

Tears of frustration welled within her, and she tore her gaze away. "I hate this. I hate..."

She sighed. What did he care? It wouldn't make a difference even if he understood.

He touched her leg. She'd changed back into her gown as soon as it was dry, only using his shirt to sleep in, so his hand touched her through layers of thick fabric. But even so, she felt it like a scalding burn.

In his eyes she saw a question. *What do you hate?*

She swallowed hard and met his fierce gaze. "I hate being cooped up inside. I always have. When I was little..." She hesitated, worried that she was babbling again, but he gave her a small nod, urging her to continue.

"When I was little, my father would take us to the country during the summers. I was so happy there, running wild in the meadows, picking bluebells, climbing trees, fishing in the streams and..."

He was so focused on her, for a moment she faltered. No one ever paid her this much attention. No one ever listened to her as though every word mattered more than life itself.

"And?" he prompted.

"And I hated when he brought us back to London." She smoothed her skirts, her heart aching as it always did at the memory of those happy years before her and Savina's world fell apart. "I hated it so much that my father hired a gardener to transform our town garden into a sort of..." She shook her head, at a loss for how to describe her happy haven. "A sort of nature wonderland, filled with wildflowers to pick, and thick tree branches to climb, and..."

This time when she trailed off he didn't try to prompt her. Maybe he could see that she was dangerously close to tears. She pushed aside the memory of her childhood, and turned away from his searching stare.

Her gaze fell on the stack of books. "Where...where did these come from?"

She let out a little huff when he didn't answer, and she could have sworn his eyes sparked with amusement at her show of irritation.

She reached for one of the books and held it up. A book of sonnets by Shakespeare. A smile tugged at her lips. "I do love poetry."

His answer was a grunt.

She set it in her lap and tried again. "Are these yours?"

"No. For you."

"Oh." That was all she could manage, because her belly and chest were suddenly swarming with butterflies as she realized just how much that meant.

He'd gotten these for her.

An act of kindness.

And when he'd returned to present them to her, he'd found a broken lock and an empty cottage.

Oh, but he should be furious with her.

Yet… he commended her strength.

Her eyes welled with tears, and he dropped to his knees before her with a scowl. "No crying."

She rolled her lips together and sniffled as she nodded. "No crying. I'm sorry, it's just…" She sniffed again and held up the book. "This was very kind of you. I am grateful."

He gave another grunt, and she was starting to think it was the sound he made when he was annoyed. He didn't want her thanks, that's what that growling said.

Her lips began to twitch as a laugh bubbled up in her.

"What's so funny?" While his expression was still stern, his eyes held a hint of lightness where before they'd been utterly dark.

He had the look of a man who wanted to laugh.

"It's just…" She lifted a shoulder, embarrassed now as she tried to put it in words. "I think I'm starting to understand your particular language of grunts and growls."

He was silent and she held her breath, afraid she'd angered him. Or worse, hurt his feelings.

But then he let out a huff of amusement and nodded toward the books as he rose to his feet. Once more he towered over her. "Read."

She bit her lip, reaching for another book in the stack, but when he went to leave her alone, that cloying panic came back.

She couldn't bear the thought of being alone in this room, alone with her thoughts and her fears for Savina and—"Wait."

Callan halted in the doorway to his room. He turned slowly.

She held the book up. "I could...I could read aloud." She felt as pathetic as her quaking voice sounded. Her chin wobbled. "I could read to you...if you'd like."

He stared at her in silence for so long, she began to wonder if he'd even heard her. His expression was frighteningly unreadable.

She found herself holding her breath as she clutched the book to her chest as if it could protect her from his rejection.

But eventually, he turned more fully to face her and nodded to the book. "Go on then."

She swallowed a sob of relief, and scrambled to move aside as he took a few steps toward the bed and paused. He seemed to be at odds as to where to sit and what to do, so she patted the spot beside her.

Once more he stared, but whether it was surprise or disbelief in his eyes, she couldn't say. A moment later, however, as she flipped the opening pages to find a place to start, she felt the mattress sink beside her, and no amount of steadying herself could stop her from falling against his side as the mattress sank under his much heavier weight.

For a long moment, they sat there. For her part, Margot was savoring this new sensation. Strange, but sweet. The hardness of his thigh and his arm as they pressed against her.

Memory of their heated kiss sizzled through her.

The sudden onslaught of his warmth and the spicy smell of his soap. The way his proximity...didn't *frighten* her, but it made her on edge, all the same.

She couldn't remember how to breathe properly as she

felt him shift, sliding an arm behind her so he did not slip from the bed.

It was...comfortable.

Comfort*ing*.

Even as his nearness wreaked havoc on her senses.

"Um...where was I..." She fumbled with the pages of Sir Walter Scott's "The Lady of the Lake" for a moment before risking a peek in Callan's direction. She had to tilt her head back to look up.

Fire burned in his eyes, but...it wasn't anger.

It made her heart race, but it didn't scare her. Not the way it should.

She swallowed hard, his warmth seeping through her gown and into her skin, and deeper, warming her in places she hadn't known she'd been cold.

"I guess I'll start here." Her voice was so breathless and airy, it sounded like she'd just stopped running. She wet her lips and tried. "Uh...I'll start at the beginning, shall I?"

He didn't answer but the arm that had wrapped around her tightened slightly and the hand that rested on her upper arm moved a little. A soft brush of his fingers against her skin and goosebumps broke out all over.

She held her breath, waiting to see if he'd do it again, or if he'd...

Her breath caught as heat spread through her, hot and liquid.

She wondered if he'd try to touch her somewhere else. If he'd take advantage of this proximity, of the fact that she'd invited him into the bed...

Her mouth was dry and her fingers shook as she turned the page, but for the life of her she couldn't say if she was scared or excited.

Or maybe both.

Another one of those searing kisses wouldn't go amiss.

But he didn't steal another touch.

It was with a hint of disappointment that she came to the conclusion he'd only kissed her to calm her down. He shocked her into giving up her fight and it had worked beautifully.

For a moment, it made her feel like a weak, foolish woman.

But would she have taken back that kiss had she the chance?

Not for anything.

Callan bent his head down so it was close to her ear and grunted, "Go on then. Read your book."

23

*S*avina paced the confines of her parlor.

She was going out of her mind with impatience...and worry.

She'd received a note from King telling her that he'd come by with an update at some point in the day.

She glanced at the grandfather clock.

Where was he? And what was taking his man in Bristol so long?

Truly, how hard could it be to confirm the safe arrival of a new-to-town beauty like Margot?

The sound of her housekeeper approaching had Savina spinning around quickly. "Yes?"

"There's a young gentleman here to see you, miss." The look of concern on Mrs. Baker's face did not go unnoticed.

Savina smoothed down her dress, then threaded her fingers together. "Send him in."

Mrs. Baker looked like she might argue, but she held her tongue and walked back to the foyer.

Savina had a suspicion Edmund would be hearing about her visit from King soon enough.

He'd no doubt storm in here with something to say about it.

No, he hadn't outright forbidden her to receive gentlemen callers—aside from Benedict, that was—but she didn't suppose he'd take kindly to a young brute from the rookery showing up on her doorstep.

Her chin came up as she heard King's thudding footsteps in the hallway.

Good. Let Edmund come. He hadn't returned since he'd shown her what pleasure could be found in the bedroom—or on a settee, as the case may be.

And it wasn't as though Savina had held out some girlish fantasy of being courted.

He was married, for heaven's sake. And to her stepmother.

But being ignored irked her at the best of times, and alone as she was in this townhome, with no word about what he was planning regarding Lucinda, let alone her sister's safety...

Well, she'd love to have words with Edmund right about now. So let him come in a fit of anger.

She was more than ready for a battle.

If he couldn't be bothered to update her on whether Margot was indeed in the hands of the chaperones he'd arranged for her, then he left her no option but to invite King into her home.

Her hands fisted at her sides as she heard King's voice telling the housekeeper he didn't need any tea. He sounded as out of place as he looked when he paused in the doorway.

Sporting grubby clothes, a fading bruise near his left eye, and with his permanently bent nose, she had to swallow a laugh at how out of place he looked in this clean townhome.

But she smiled with genuine delight and relief at the sight of him. "King, thank you for coming."

He wasn't one for embraces so she stayed where she was, content just to take in the sight of her tried and true friend.

"Savvy," he muttered, glancing around the parlor warily as if the doilies might strike out and pinch him.

"Come in, come in." She ushered him forward with a flick of her hand. "Please tell me you have news of my sister."

He entered, but only by a few feet, and then he stopped, his brows low and his mouth set.

Savina's belly flip flopped and bile rose up her throat. "What is it?"

Her tone was too sharp, but there was no help for it. She strode toward him, her pulse pounding. "Has your man tracked down Margot? Is she safe?"

"She never arrived, Savina." King's tone was low and grim, and he sounded decades older than his sixteen years.

Her belly sank even as her voice rose. "What?"

King exhaled sharply. "I checked with other sources before I came over here. I didn't want to alarm you if I wasn't certain..."

"What do you mean she never arrived?" Savina started to pace once more. "Did she leave the changing station?"

"Yes. She left three days ago."

Three days. Savina's insides plummeted. She'd been unaccounted for, for three days?

So much could happen in three days.

Anything could happen.

Panic tried to take hold, but she forced fear at bay. Now was the time to think, to plan, to strategize.

She forced herself to stare at the metaphorical chess board before her.

"Was she seen after the changing station?"

"Some say she was at the next inn, but no one seems to recall who she was traveling with or where they were heading."

Savina stared at the intricate pattern of the rug beneath her feet, but soon the pattern began to shift and swirl, and nausea rose up in her so quickly she had to walk again. To move. To pace away this vibrating worry gnawing on her stomach.

She should never have sent her away. They never should have parted. If anything happened to her—

Stop. Think. Emotions were useless at a time like this. She resumed pacing, and this time she stopped before the very real chess board that Edmund had sent over during her first days here after she'd revealed a penchant for the game.

Of course, she had no one to play against. But right now, being able to move the pieces, to use the pawns and the rooks to visualize all the players in this drama she and her sister had been drawn into...

"It was Lucinda," she murmured, more to herself than to King. "She had to have been behind this."

King was silent.

When Savina turned to face him, she saw his glower. "Savvy, the man who hired her carriage...the one who was supposed to ensure her arrival..."

"Edmund," she whispered. She knew where this was going. She knew precisely what King would say next, and yet she willed him not to say it.

"Could this have been his doing?"

She stared at King blankly for so long, he clearly grew concerned.

"Look, Savvy, I know you're worried. I am too. But you know how rumors fly in these small towns, and there's a rumor going 'round that there was an accident but the young lady survived."

Savina straightened. "What else are they saying?"

King gave a frustrated shake of his head. "The rest of the

stories my man heard were the sort of tall tales you'd tell a kid. Talk of beasts in the woods and all that nonsense."

Savina began to pace again, hope and fear making her heart beat a chaotic rhythm. "I have to believe she's alive." She stopped walking and turned to him. "I have to believe that I'd...I'd know if she wasn't. I have to find her—"

"I'll find her, Savvy," King vowed.

She gaped at him. "How? I mean...you and your crew might have sway in Vestry Lane, but what do you know of the world outside London?"

A muscle in his jaw ticked. "I know how to make men fear me no matter where they come from or what they do for a living. Trust me. If anyone knows where our Snow has gone, I'll find out." He smirked, and the cold cruelty in his eyes made her shiver, even though she knew it wasn't meant for her.

"You're a good friend, King," she whispered.

He shrugged off the compliment. "I look after mine, that's all. Wouldn't be much of a leader if I didn't."

"I want to come with you," she started.

King shook his head as she'd known he would.

"You know that's not smart." He nodded to the chess board. "If your enemies are here then this is where you need to be."

She bit her lip as she nodded. He had a point. If Lucinda was behind this, then the best thing she could be doing was to continue to find a way to take the woman down.

And if Edmund were somehow involved...

She turned away from King's stare with a shudder.

She couldn't believe that. Or maybe she didn't want to. But...if he was somehow involved, then she ought to stay close to him too.

Mrs. Baker interrupted them from the doorway. "You've another visitor, miss."

Savina's heart leapt with a mix of eager excitement and straight up terror. "Edmund?"

King's brow arched but he said nothing.

Mrs. Baker shook her head. "Miss Mane."

"Vivian?" Savina's shoulders sank, but she nodded with a smile. "Send her in."

To King, she added, "Vivian's father owns the gossip rags. She's been a valuable ally and…and a friend."

King was already moving toward the other door, the one leading to the back of the house. "I'll be leaving then. I've got work to do to ensure nothing goes wrong in Vestry Lane while I'm hunting for Snow."

She moved toward him as the sound of Mrs. Baker and Vivian's voices came from the hall. "Keep me abreast, King. Please. I won't be able to rest until I know she's safe and…"

And alive.

"Safe and well," she finished.

King gave another sharp nod before disappearing out the door.

Vivian entered a moment later and Savina greeted her with as much grace as she could muster.

"Is everything all right?" Vivian asked. "You look worried."

"I am, I'm afraid." Briefly she filled the other girl in.

"Oh dear!"

"It must be Lucinda." Savina had gone back to pacing as she spoke, her hands wringing as poor Vivian was forced to watch her walk to and fro.

"But did she know about Margot's travels?" Vivian asked.

Savina paused, her steps faltering. "Not that I'm aware of."

"Your stepfather made the arrangements, did he not?"

Savina's heart twisted in her chest. She had this compulsion to leap to his defense, but the answer was clear. "Yes. He made the arrangements."

Vivian said nothing. And that silence was worse than any

accusation, because Savina's mind leapt and raced to make connections.

"Why would he harm Margot?" she finally asked. "Why would he offer to help us only to hurt us?"

Vivian's expression was pained as she shook her head.

It didn't make sense. There had to be another explanation.

Savina took a deep breath, trying to separate her thoughts from the warm, fluttery emotions that seemed to steal over her whenever she thought of Edmund...or the way he'd touched her, and looked at her, and the way he made her feel.

Like she was truly wanted, and understood, and treasured. Surely she wasn't making that up entirely?

But he hardly had the same feelings for Margot. He'd never even met her sister.

Not to mention, she'd already given him the benefit of the doubt once, and he'd betrayed her trust.

Was it such a stretch to think he might be playing her for a fool again?

Her heart gave a sharp kick at the thought that he'd been lying to her about her sister. That once again he had some other agenda.

But why? Why on earth would he do such a thing? How would that help him get revenge on Lucinda for what she'd done to Savina's father, and..

She stilled as she realized the extent of her assumptions.

She'd presumed Edmund was out for vengeance because of her and Margot. That he was looking out for them for their father's sake, but...

But what did she really know about his marriage or his intentions?

Blessedly little.

Frustrated by her own torn thoughts, she spun around to face her friend. She hated the doubt she saw there. This woman didn't know Edmund. "I understand Edmund is married to Lucinda but..." She paused, those words making her stomach turn when she said them aloud.

She hadn't felt the slightest hint of guilt the other night after he'd left. She'd taken liberties with a married man, and not an ounce of shame. Lucinda didn't deserve her respect nor his loyalty.

Still, admitting that he'd *married* that woman.

That he was still married to her...

A cold prickle ran down her spine. What did Edmund do with his time? Two days and he hadn't visited once. So where was he?

Did he spend time with Lucinda?

Did he share her bed?

He'd said it was a marriage in name only, but right now, for the first time, she became overwhelmingly, horrifyingly aware of how ignorant she was when it came to Edmund and his affairs.

She'd let this attraction she felt, and the fact that he'd been her father's friend, blind her to the facts.

She'd been so eager to trust him. She'd so wanted to believe...

She was the veriest fool.

"Savina, dear, please sit. You look as though you might be ill." Vivian worried her lip.

"Nonsense, I'm just concerned about Margot, that's all."

Vivian nodded, compassion in her gaze. "Of course you are."

Savina resumed her pacing, letting her addled thoughts tumble out.

"Are you...are you worried about Prince Edmund?" Vivian spoke cautiously, her eyes darting to the floor.

"No," Savina said quickly. And oh how she wished she felt as confident as she sounded.

"They might be married, but Edmund has no loyalty to

Lucinda. He wouldn't never work to aid her agenda...whatever that might be."

Vivian nodded, but the silence that followed felt heavy. It seemed to Savina that the silence was filled with questions.

Questions...and doubts.

24

The gentlemen's club was packed today, thanks to the dreary weather.

Edmund's fingers curled into the soft leather of his armchair that was molded to his body, the teacup before him cool to the touch after all this time waiting.

Tobacco smoke filled the air around him, but he scarcely noticed. The room could have been on fire for all he knew.

His mind was far from this room, miles from this club.

He might've left Savina in her townhome days ago, but his thoughts had never strayed far.

She was his now. His in every way...even if she did not know it yet.

But the next time he saw her, the next time he touched her...

He needed her to know that he was hers as well.

And so he'd kept his distance, even though the separation felt like torture. There was so much he needed to tell her, so much to explain. But he didn't trust himself to keep his head when he was near Savina, and the less involved she was in Lucinda's devious affairs, the better.

He wasn't so dimwitted as to think that Lucinda had forgotten about her stepdaughter, but if she stayed away from Benedict and kept her attention on the games she played with Edmund, then there was a chance Savina could be spared any further harm at her stepmother's hands.

And that was all that mattered now. Savina was all there was for him.

This obsession had gotten under his skin and into his veins. He'd spent years trying to find her, and now he'd spend the rest of his life ensuring that Savina would never leave his side.

But that meant his quest to uncover Lucinda's dark secrets had never been more urgent.

He'd made some headway before discovering that Savina and her sister were still in London. Had never *left* London. He'd dropped everything in order to put his attention on saving them from the hellish life Lucinda had condemned them to.

We did not run away, surely you know this. She banished us, treated us like street rats. Threatened to kill us if we ever came back.

His hand on the table clenched into a fist.

Reason. Logic. That was how he'd win this battle. Fury would get him nowhere.

His foot tapped against the thick carpet beneath his feet.

Neither would impatience, but it had been two days since he'd seen Savina and he was crawling out of his skin with the need to know that she was safe and well.

And that no gentleman had dared to go near her.

That Benedict hadn't been to her home.

His eyes narrowed. He wouldn't put it past the boy. He'd seen how smitten he'd been. And who could blame him?

Finally, a cluster of gentlemen entered this back meeting

area, and he spotted the man he'd hired to keep tabs on Savina.

The man had been paid a handsome sum for his services, but one would never guess it by his rough-hewn clothes.

The middle-aged man with the thick beard pulled up a chair. "Good afternoon, Mr. Miller." Edmund extended his hand across the table.

The man accepted it with a hearty smile, wiping away the slick sheen of sweat from his brow with a handkerchief before taking a sip of brandy from a snifter glass that a server set before him.

"Well?" Edmund asked. "Anything to report?"

"A Miss Vivian Mane is there with her now," he started, pulling out a notepad.

Edmund sank back in his seat. Good. That was good. Vivian was a dutiful girl, and clever to boot, he'd heard. She'd be a good companion for his Savina.

"No Benedict," he confirmed.

"No, sir." The man glanced up and his hesitation spoke for him.

"What is it?"

"There was another man..." Mr. Miller hedged, shifting under Edmund's merciless glare.

"*What* other man?"

"Er, I don't know, sir." Mr. Miller made a show of flipping through his notes. "He looked like he was up to no good, I can tell you that. Dressed like a right pauper. And he had bruises like he's a brawler, if you know what I mean."

Edmund's jaw snapped shut.

Someone from her old life, then. A friend or a foe?

He pushed back from the table. "And you left her there alone with him?"

"Oh, but he left," the man hurried on. "Didn't stay long.

And you made it clear you didn't want her knowing about me..."

Nostrils flaring, Edmund struggled for calm. "In the future, her safety comes before all other concerns. Are we clear on that?"

"Yes. Yes, of course."

Edmund came to his feet. "And the other matter. Her sister."

"I've got my best man on it," he said quickly.

Edmund nodded. "Good. Now, I've got another assignment for you. Hire however many men you think necessary. Take whatever actions you require..."

The other man's eyes widened.

Edmund's heart began to pound with a furious intensity that always came before a battle.

He'd spent the better part of the last forty-eight hours doing his own investigating—into his wife.

Without Leopold's missing daughters as a distraction, he used every resource at his disposal to unbury every skeleton he suspected in his wife's dark closet.

It was his dear departed friend who'd taught him a valuable lesson once, way back in their school days. It had come in the midst of one of their long winded discussions.

Two young gentlemen of promise with nothing better to do than to play chess, discuss tactics, and wax poetic about esoteric topics like a man's character and moral ethics.

The best liars are the ones who plant their lies with a seed of truth, Leopold had said all those years ago.

And those words had rung in his ears ever since. He'd caught out many an artful liar with that knowledge...and he'd spotted that trait in Lucinda from the very start.

Oh yes, he'd known from the beginning that she was devious. And yet he'd underestimated the extent of her cruelty and her greed.

He could admit, her skill with deception had made her so much harder to defeat than he ever would have expected. From the first, she'd thrown him off track, and it had been a battle of wits ever since.

But now...

Well, now he'd taken it upon himself to dig through her mountains of lies until he could find some hidden truth that might bury her.

And he'd found it. Or at least, he was nearly certain he'd found the piece of the puzzle that would end his marriage and ruin Lucinda once and for all.

"You're to travel south," he instructed. "A small, seaside village of Hormath."

"What am I looking for there, sir?"

"Not what. Who."

The other man's brows arched. "All right. Who then?"

"A Mr. John Wilshire."

The man blinked. "And who might that be, if ye don't mind me askin'?"

A cruel smirk turned his lips up on one side. "My wife's first husband."

"But I thought..."

"That she'd been twice widowed?" Edmund smiled. "So did I."

But as he'd analyzed every lie she'd spun about Savina and Margot, he'd thought of other, similar heartbreaking tales he'd heard her tell so convincingly.

And through it all he couldn't stop thinking about Benedict.

Well...he couldn't stop thinking about Savina. And Benedict was an annoying intrusion into those meanderings.

He sent Mr. Miller off with detailed instructions on how to unearth the secrets Lucinda left behind in her home village, and he followed him out of the club shortly after, finally giving in to the need to see his luscious ward.

He'd stayed away as long as he could. But another man had been to see his brazen little angel.

Anger coursed through him. Who was this man to Savina? And what had he said to her.

Edmund had stayed away as best he could, but nothing in the world could keep him from her now.

Outside, the air was hardly any fresher than it had been inside. It smelled of smoke and sweat and horse dung, all trapped in the thick, rain-drenched mist.

In the carriage ride to her townhome, he turned over his new theory, hope warring with wariness.

If his suspicions were correct, Lucinda would have covered her tracks well.

But then again...

She was a formidable vindictive witch. But that had not always been the case. Once upon a time, she'd been a gently bred young lady with powerful connections but little dowry.

And knowing Lucinda, she'd have done whatever it took to elevate her station and her prospects.

How many times had he heard Lucinda sigh sweetly while telling her son of his poor, unfortunate father who'd died when he was just a babe?

"Such a tragedy, to lose the father of my son when I was still so young myself..."

Still young enough to marry again. Still attractive enough to lure a better husband and accrue more wealth.

It was only this time, at a small family dinner not two days' hence that he heard it and caught the lie underneath.

It wasn't a fib, necessarily, but her version of events formed a string of coincidences so perfect as to be improbable.

Possible, perhaps. But not probable.

It had been the same when it came to Savina and Margot. The tale always just believable enough, but with miniscule inconsistencies that if one were to listen carefully, one could see the truth hidden in the forest of lies.

In the first years of his marriage, he'd hoped to unravel her lies. But once she'd begun to exploit her power over him, he'd rested his hopes on unearthing those girls, so that they'd be his form of vengeance.

But now...

His insides twisted with guilt at the thought of using Savina in such a way.

The fact that he had used her at all...

That he still was...

He ran a hand over his face as the carriage rumbled to a stop. He'd fix this situation. All of it.

For Leopold. For Savina. He'd find a way to win this battle once and for all.

He leapt out of the carriage and strode up to the door, the housekeeper opening it for him on the first knock.

"Where is she?"

Mrs. Baker gestured to the parlor. "She's had visitors, my lord."

He handed over his hat and gloves. "I know."

Edmund knew something was off the moment he stepped foot in the room. "Savina."

She didn't move or turn to face him. She kept staring into the smoldering fire that did little to keep the damp chill at bay.

"Who came to see you?" He couldn't keep the anger from his voice. Perhaps it wasn't his right to be possessive. But right or wrong, he was consumed with it.

"You haven't been to see me in days and yet you begin this conversation by interrogating me about my visitors?" Her tone was teasing, but there was a flatness to her voice that made him uneasy.

He approached her slowly, not stopping until he gripped her shoulders, and then turned her to face him. "Savina," he breathed.

Her face was pale, her eyes impossibly wide.

"Have you eaten? Are you ill?"

Her lips were pale as she shook her head. To which question, he did not know.

Her gaze searched his eyes, and he was overcome with the urge to console her. To comfort her. He pulled her close and she let him, her body melting into his in a way that would never cease to amaze him.

Her body, her scent, her temper, and her wits...

To think that now, at his age, he'd found the woman who was made for him.

And she's young enough to be your daughter.

That familiar guilt rippled through him. What would Leopold think if he could see his old friend now?

"Margot is missing."

Her voice cut the silence and his brows arched in surprise, but he didn't express enough shock because her brows quickly lowered in an accusatory glare. "You knew that."

She pushed away from him, hurt evident in every line of her face.

Bloody hell.

"How did you learn of this?" he demanded.

She planted her hands on her hips, her breasts rising and falling beneath her tight bodice. "The more pressing question to my mind is—why did I not learn of this from you?"

His heart rejected the look of betrayal that pinched her pretty features. "I didn't want you to worry—"

"Not worry?" Her voice went high with disbelief. "The

only person I care about in this world is unaccounted for, and you think I should not worry?"

The only person.

His jaw ticked with anger. But there was time. One day she would declare her love for him. And until then, he'd make sure she'd scream for need of him.

He'd make her ache and yearn until she begged him to never leave her side.

The thought was an odd sort of comfort. And when he stroked her cheek and saw her eyes darken ever so slightly with awareness, his heart beat with this new desire.

To be her man. To be the only one she turned to for protection, for satisfaction...for love.

"I will find Margot," he promised.

"You will?" Her gaze searched his.

"Of course I will."

"How?" Her eyes narrowed. "What do you know?"

When he met her scrutiny with an assessing look of his own, her cheeks flushed with anger. "How am I supposed to trust you if you never trust me, Edmund?"

He felt the words like the stab of a sword. Trust had never come easily to him. Nor to any sane man who came from a family with as much wealth and power as his.

"I want to protect you," he started.

"By keeping me uninformed? How has that worked for you thus far? Because as far as I'm concerned, all it has done is left me vulnerable and weak."

Guilt flickered. She wasn't wrong. But he also couldn't have her going off with some scheme of her own and ruining the plans he'd put in place.

"Do you think...is this Lucinda's work?" Her voice wavered and right at that moment he knew he'd have murdered Lucinda if she were anywhere close just to rid this world of Savina's fear.

Hell, he should have strangled the witch with his bare hands the moment he'd learned what she'd done to Leopold's girls.

There were so many questions in Savin's eyes, and he had no answers. None that would suffice.

"I don't know," he finally murmured. "I don't see why she'd take such a risk."

Savina frowned. "Neither do I. All she cares about is father's fortune. If she were to harm anyone, wouldn't it be me? I am clearly here to regain what was ours."

He had to fight the protective surge that made him itch to lock Savina away somewhere he could protect her forever.

He forced himself to think logically, look at the situation from Lucinda's point of view. "Even if she was the one behind this attack, she'd have nothing to gain and only leverage to lose if she harmed her in any way."

That bit of reason cut through the fear in her eyes. "You're right, of course. I'm just..." She let out a loud exhale. "Edmund, I need to know that she will come back to me. If I lost her, I…"

She shook her head, her lips pressing together.

He stroked her hair back from her face. "You must know that I am on your side. I will do whatever it takes to get her back to you."

The way her gaze softened with relief made his chest swell. With pride, yes, but also purpose.

All his life he'd thought he'd known what it meant to be a leader. To be respected and to be feared. But none of that compared to the feeling of rightness in his chest at being the man she turned to in times of trouble.

It was humbling, and he wouldn't trade this role for the world.

He'd be her hero or he'd burn the world down trying.

"I will find her, Savina. Trust me."

An emotion flickered over her features. There and gone quickly but it gave enough away.

She didn't trust him. Not wholly. Not yet.

Can you blame her?

"She is the center of your world which makes her of the utmost importance to me as well."

"Truly?"

He hated the way her voice shook, and without even thinking he claimed her lips with his own, teasing a kiss out of her and invading her mouth the way he ached to claim her sweet cunny.

She tore away from him with a moan, her hand over her lips and her expression torn. "Wait, I...I don't know what to believe anymore."

He stared at her long and hard, trying to read her silence.

"Who came here earlier?" he asked again.

"Vivian."

A growl rumbled in his chest and this time when he reached for her and tugged her close, he wasn't nearly as gentle. She gave a soft 'oof' as her breasts pressed against his chest.

"Don't play me for a fool," he growled.

She pouted, and God help him he hoped she'd be a little minx so he could punish her the way they both loved.

Her eyes narrowed and darkened, and...

Fucking hell.

Satisfaction curled in his chest as he realized she wanted that too.

"Do you mean to keep secrets from me, pet?" His voice held a warning tone, and he watched in awe as her gaze darkened even further, her full lips parting.

"Why shouldn't I keep things from you when you keep secrets from me?" She pouted up at him, and the air seemed to crackle with anticipation.

"I'm your guardian, if you'll recall." He reached out and gripped her chin. He scowled down at her even as his blood heated and his muscles tightened. "You're my naughty little ward, aren't you?"

She kept quiet but her perfect tits rose and fell as her breathing quickened with excitement.

"Now you've gone and gotten yourself all worked up over matters that I will handle."

Her brows knit together, the sexual game interrupted by her very real fears. "Will you handle it, Edmund?" She leaned into him slightly until her breasts brushed against his chest and the sound of their breathing filled the air. "Will you... will you take control?"

His heart leapt even as lust destroyed every last reasonable thought. He knew what she was asking.

He knew what she needed.

Maybe even more than she did.

"I've told you time and again, love." He leaned down and tasted those sweet lips.

Lips he'd been dreaming about for days. He kissed her gently, memorizing the feel of her mouth parting beneath his, of the way her hot breath fanned across his jaw when he pulled back.

He slid a hand into her hair, holding her still so he could meet her gaze. "You are mine to protect now."

He watched the defiance and the relief. Both simmering in her eyes in equal measure.

"You've been so strong for so long, my sweet," he murmured.

Her throat worked as she swallowed.

"Now it's time for you to let me handle matters."

Her eyes grew soft with emotions that made his chest tighten and ache.

"I will find your sister and ensure her safety. And I will deal with Lucinda."

She let out a shaky breath, her shoulders sinking as she released some of the burden.

Christ, this woman was spectacular. He adored her beyond all measure.

Her gaze still locked on his, he saw the precise moment that his little minx came out to play. Her eyes glittered with mischief and darkened with hunger. "Yes…stepfather."

25

---

*H*e let out a huff of amusement. His coy little angel knew exactly how to rile him. "You had a gentleman caller."

Her lips twitched in genuine amusement and he found himself aching to hear her laughter.

"Did I?"

He growled low in his throat and was rewarded with a sweet, high-pitched giggle that stole his heart.

"Are you going to tell me who he was?"

"Are you going to tell me how you knew I had a caller?" she shot back.

He narrowed his eyes, and she did the same.

His lungs were on fire with this sudden onslaught of awareness. He dragged her closer. "Careful, pet. You're going to have to pay for your naughty ways."

She tsked, her tone taunting. "Is that a promise?"

He let her go and strode toward the door. "Mrs. Baker...Lock the door. We are not to be disturbed."

He shut the door with a loud snick behind him and

turned to see her watching him with eager anticipation. Her fingers curled into the skirts of her gown.

This…this was so much better than the fear he'd seen there earlier. If Lucinda really was behind Margot's disappearance, it was one more reason to kill the bitch.

"Now, you went against my orders and had a man come calling."

"It wasn't Benedict." Her sassy tone made his cock swell. "Your Highness."

Snagging her by the wrist he pulled her over to the armchair and then he sank down in the seat, crossing his arms and leaning back.

She wanted the imperious prince, then the imperious prince was who she'd get. "Take off your underthings, my naughty little love."

Savina looked so shocked, he thought she might argue, but she bit her lip and then slowly did as she was bid.

"Good girl." He arched a brow. "Now…Bend over my lap. Let your stepfather teach you that lesson, hmm?"

She made a high-pitched little sound as she gaped at him. He could see embarrassment and hunger written clearly in her features. "Will I have to drag you over here for your punishment, pet?" He watched her breasts heave with excitement.

Hunger would win out over embarrassment. And one day she'd come to realize there was never any need for embarrassment with him.

Not when he craved their dirty games as much as she did.

"Your punishment will only be worse if I have to take you over my lap by force."

She wet her lips and took the last few steps toward him.

Christ, she was sweet perfection. With pink cheeks she bit her lip and then with an eagerness that made his cock harden, she climbed into his lap, taking her place with her arse sticking up and only gasping with excitement when he lifted her skirts.

He groaned at the sight of her rounded cheeks, so perfect and pale. Just waiting for his touch.

The fire crackled and the only other sound was her whimpers and his labored breathing as he molded her ass cheeks with one hand, using the other to push her curls aside so he could see her biting her lip in eager anticipation.

"Do you want to be punished, my naughty girl?"

She met his gaze and lied. "No, sir."

He brought his palm down on her backside with a sharp thwack that made her hips jerk and her eyes squeeze shut as she moaned.

"No? You know I don't approve of liars, Savina."

She moaned louder as his hand came down again, but this time she spread her legs and shifted slightly so his palm came down on her wet heat.

"Oh you dirty little girl," he said with a tsk. "Are you trying to come before I say you're allowed?"

"Please," she begged.

And yes. That was what he'd craved. What he'd needed.

"Beg for more," he commanded, his voice harsh and dark.

"P-please touch me there. Spank me, Stepfather."

His cock ground into her lower belly as she wiggled her ass in invitation.

"I need it," she whimpered.

He clapped his hand down again, leaving a red mark on her bottom. He knew she needed it. She was frightened and worried, and she needed to let go. To have someone take her in hand.

He trailed a finger between her cheeks, adoring the way she blushed and wiggled.

"Let's see just how much you like for me to be in control, my naughty ward." He parted her thighs roughly, exposing her sex.

She was so vulnerable, and she was trusting him. She might not trust him entirely yet, but she trusted him with this.

He molded her thighs, trying to gain some control before he came too quick.

She made a whining noise as he teased her, trailing his fingers over her bottom, up her thighs, but leaving her wet, pink cunny untouched and exposed.

When she tried to close her thighs again, she earned herself another spank.

"Do you like being punished, Savina?"

"No," she lied again, this time giving him a flirty smile that would have won his heart if she didn't already own it.

"You can't lie to me, love," he teased as he slid a finger between her cheeks and lower, dipping his fingers into her channel, making them both groan. "So wet for me. And so bloody tight."

She lifted her hips. "More."

He cupped his hand over her pussy, teasing her nub as she wiggled her hips making the flesh of her bottom jiggle in a way that made him growl.

He knew exactly what she needed, and he gave it to her. His fingers eased inside of her as she bucked back and up, thrusting up onto his fingers.

"That's it. Take me inside you like a good girl," he growled.

She turned her head to pout up at him. "I want more."

He gave her the spanking she was asking for with his free hand, enraptured by the look of pleasure that rippled across her features as she rolled her hips in response.

He fisted a hand in her hair so she couldn't look away.

"Look at me when I fuck you with my fingers, naughty girl. And know that you are mine to command."

Her lips parted and her eyes flashed with fire.

"You are mine to tease and to pleasure. You are mine to spank and to spoil." He pumped his fingers in and out of her slick heat, their gazes locked as her eyelids grew heavy and her whole body rocked as she rode his fingers.

"Say it," he barked.

"Yes," she hissed.

He stilled his hand, his fingers curled inside of her, stroking her as he held her captive with his other hand buried in her hair. "Say it," he said again, the order so firm he felt her sweet pussy grow impossibly wetter. "Say you know that you are mine in every way."

Her breathing came in pants and her gaze was filled with emotions that made his chest feel impossibly tight. "I'm yours," she whispered. "I'm yours to pleasure and to punish."

He leaned down and ran his tongue up the curve of her ear. "Good girl."

She moaned as she bent her head, exposing more of her neck for him.

God, but she loved this play of power as much as he did.

What she needed was to lose herself. To have someone strong enough beside her to make her let it all go when it all got to be too much.

He leaned forward and licked a path from her ear to the nape of her neck, loving the way her inner muscles clamped down on his fingers as she trembled on his lap.

"Kiss me," she whispered. "Please."

Their mouths collided in a hungry kiss and he groaned in agony when she started to ride his fingers again, the bucking of her hips seductive torture as his throbbing cock bore the brunt of her wiggles.

"Careful, love." He slid his fingers out and then fucked her hard with three fingers, widening her for him. "I'm going to lose control and you're not going to like the way I fuck you if I turn into a bloody animal."

"That's what I want," she panted. "Fuck me. Make me forget. Make me yours."

Make me yours.

Yes. Fuck yes. That was exactly what he meant to do. "My naughty little girl," he growled in her ear, and then he slid his fingers out of her pussy and spanked her hard, so hard she cried out. "Maybe I should call in the servants so they can see who owns their mistress, hmm?"

She was imagining it, and his naughty minx grew even more heavy-lidded with desire.

He let out a dark chuckle as she let out a desperate moan. "You like the idea of being watched, do you? Well, that could be arranged, pet. That could definitely be arranged."

She moaned as he gave her ass another smack. "But our first time won't be in front of others, and it sure as hell won't be on the floor of your parlor, my sweet."

Her pout was adorable. "Then let me pleasure you as well this time."

He almost said no. Not out of any sort of masochistic need to refrain from taking his pleasure, but because he meant it when he'd said he had ideas for how their first time would be.

When he came with Savina, he'd be buried to the hilt inside her.

With one last spanking that made her cry out he ordered her to sit up. "Straddle my lap, princess. I want to watch those tits bounce for me when you ride my fingers."

Her eyes widened but she hurried into action.

God, but she was a treasure, just as eager for their dirty pleasure as he was.

"Like this?" She peeked up at him through her lashes as she rested one knee on either side of his thighs, her skirts bunched on his lap between them, hiding the erection that threatened to burst through his pants.

"Good girl," he grunted. "Now show me your tits."

It took some maneuvering, but soon she was sliding the material down.

"So perfect, love," he said as he palmed her lush breasts, teasing her nipples with pinches and flicks until she was rolling her hips, grinding down on his cock with abandon.

"You need more, my sweet," he said.

"Yes. I need more. I need you," she said, her voice whiny and perfect.

She needed him.

And Lord how he needed her. Always. In every way.

"Suck these fingers," he ordered, offering up the digits that were still coated with her juices. "Taste yourself and then show me exactly where you want me to put them."

Her eyes flashed with wicked mischief but she caught his hand and held his gaze as she sucked his fingers. He snagged her by the hair and pulled her in close. "You're so good at that, love. Your mouth was made for me, do you know that?"

Her breathing hitched, no doubt at the raw hunger in his voice.

"And when the time is right, and you are mine, I'm going to own that hot little mouth of yours just like I'll own your cunny."

She seemed to melt against him as she moaned, rubbing her hard nipples against his chest as her hips began to rock once more.

His little brat loved it when he talked dirty, and that was just one more sign that she'd been made just for him.

"I'm going to fuck that mouth of yours, sweetheart," he

whispered as he slid a hand up the smooth skin of her inner thigh, stopping short of touching her where she needed it.

"Whenever you make me hard with your pouting and your teasing, I'm going to order you onto your knees."

"Yes," she moaned.

"And if you ever dare to allow any man into this home, or flirt with anyone but me..."

"What will you do?" she breathed, the eager excitement in her voice making him smile.

He nipped her earlobe. "I will order you onto your hands and knees and you'll suck my cock in front of this would-be suitor. Now tell me you understand."

She leaned back, licking her lips which had curled up in a smile. "Yes, I understand, sir."

Sir. He groaned and she smiled.

She knew exactly how to play him. She knew he loved to be in command as she liked to be commanded.

Christ. He was never going to survive her.

She bucked her hips and wiggled a little until her tits jiggled right in front of his face. "Please don't stop."

He held his fingers still. "You had a command, pet. Don't tell me you forgot."

She scrambled to lift up her skirts, revealing that perfect cunny of hers and leaving him parched and speechless.

Legs parted he could see her folds glistening with moisture and smell the heady, spicy scent of her sex.

He cupped it roughly and met her heavy-lidded gaze. "Mine," he growled. "All mine. Only mine."

A long silence passed as he held her sex in his grip, his palm grinding into her hard nub as his fingers teased the edge of her entrance.

She looked nearly mad with lust, but she didn't hesitate for long. "Yours. All yours."

He drove three fingers into her so hard she screamed, and

when she fell forward he caught her, taking one of her nipples into his mouth and sucking just as hard as he fucked her with his fingers.

All too soon she was shattering and shaking.

His sweet little princess was coming apart in his arms.

26

---

*L*eft alone once more, Savina had far too much time to worry and wait.

Waiting was difficult at the best of times, but in the day after King had told her the news, it was unbearable.

King was searching for her precious sister, and Edmund's men too.

Neither man would rest until Margot was found.

But sitting here before a fire on this dull rainy day felt like the worst form of torture after a full night of lying awake in bed, replaying King's words and Edmunds actions.

Edmund had assured her before he left. He'd vowed that he'd send his best men to look into her disappearance.

She hadn't mentioned that King was already going after her as well.

He wouldn't like it. Edmund might even take steps to stop it. She could admit that she liked his commanding nature...

A memory of the way he'd ordered her to undress had the breath rushing out of her.

All right, perhaps she rather adored his commanding ways.

But when it came to Margot and her safety, she couldn't have him intervening just because he didn't like that she had male friends.

Besides, the more people looking for Margot the better. That was all anyone should be focused on right now.

Shame kindled in her belly at the thought of the pleasure she'd taken while her sister was lost.

But that was all the shame she could bring herself to feel about it. Maybe she would have been horrified if she'd been raised as a proper young lady. But Savina had seen too much.

She'd experienced too much.

She knew what it was to feel shame at a man's hands. Her stomach still turned when she thought of the way that grunting man had taken his pleasure from her. And all so she'd have enough coin for bread.

But it wasn't like that with Edmund. It was a mix of pleasure and pain; of taking and giving; of control and relief.

Relief…yes, that was it.

She picked at the embroidery of a pillow on the settee. There was a wicked satisfaction in bringing a powerful man to his knees, in seeing his tight grip on the reins of control loosen and falter as he fell victim to lust.

That part made sense to her.

She supposed she'd always loved the feeling of power.

It was the relief that came with handing over control that still surprised her. It was the way she adored pleasing him and being ordered about by him.

Why did it make her insides feel like they were softening for the first time ever?

Why did his stern commands make her turn weak and willing and…

No. Not weak.

Willing and wanted and…

And safe.

She frowned at the fire as her thoughts ran rampant.

He made her feel safe when he was in charge. Like she was fragile and delicate and the one who needed to be cared for.

Like for the first time in what felt like forever she could let it all go. The fear. The responsibilities.

The need to be strong and brave.

She swallowed hard, the realization unsettling, but undeniable.

Just as undeniable was that she knew with certainty that not just any man could bring about such a response.

It was him.

Maybe it had started because he was her father's friend, but...she trusted him. Even though he kept his secrets and played his games, she trusted him.

She'd wavered in that faith in him, but the look in his eyes when he'd sworn to find Margot, when he'd promised to handle everything...

Yes, she'd decided right then and there that she had to believe him. She needed to trust him.

The thought was alarming, and she sighed with relief when her housekeeper announced that Vivian was at the door for her again.

"Why, Vivian," Savina said, all smiles as she greeted her friend. "I did not expect to see you again so soon. But I'm so grateful for your company, I—"

Savina stopped short, belatedly noting her younger friend's nervous state. Her fair skin was paler than usual, in stark contrast to her vivid auburn hair and dark green eyes. But despite that, she looked more beautiful than ever in an emerald gown and her hair done.

"I'm leaving for the Davenports' ball soon, but I had to see you. My father doesn't know I've left..."

Fear sliced her heart. "Is it about Margot?"

Vivian shook her head. "I know nothing about Margot. I'm sorry."

Vivian still looked fearful though, and all at once Savina realized how self-absorbed she'd been. This poor dear had problems of her own to contend with.

"Are you all right, Vivian?" A surge of protectiveness rose up in her at the fearful look in her friend's eyes. "Is this about your betrothed?"

Vivian's eyes widened.

"I've been asking about him, you know," Savina continued, clutching her friend's cold hands. "And I want to help you. We must talk to your father, find a way out of this under-standing. I've heard his last wife was miserable and—"

"It's all right, Savina," Vivian interjected softly.

"But, my dear—"

"Savina, I did not come here about that," Vivian cut in, tempering the words with an apologetic smile.

There was an anxious edge to her features, though, a nervous expectancy that set Savina's nerves jangling.

"Come." She tugged the girl toward the fire as she pulled the cord for tea to be served. Once she had the young dear seated in front of the fireplace where she might warm her hands, she pulled a chair beside her.

"All right, now tell me what this is about." Savina tucked her skirts beneath her as she sat.

Her stomach sank at the wariness in the girl's kind eyes. "Is this about your father?"

The girl hesitated.

"If you wish to escape that house—"

"No, no I couldn't," Vivian said quickly.

"But my dear—"

"My mother left, you know."

Savina said nothing, waiting for Vivian to continue.

"I could have gone with her," Vivian whispered. "But I did not think it fair to abandon Father entirely."

Savina's insides twisted. Vivian reminded her so much of Margot. So kind, so sheltered, so…good.

And with no understanding of how many men would take advantage of that goodness if given half a chance.

"But I did speak to my father," Vivian continued, clearly hoping to change the topic.

"Did you tell him you are too young—"

"I talked to him about Prince Edmund."

Savina frowned. "Pardon?"

Vivian settled her hands in her lap and then resettled them. The girl was nervous, and it did nothing to calm the warning bells that began to ring in Savina's ears.

"I was worried," Vivian hurried on. "You said he'd have nothing to gain, and honestly his whole marriage to that wicked stepmother of yours seems so strange and—"

"Vivian."

The girl's lips clamped shut with a nod. "Right. Sorry."

Savina placed a hand over hers where it rested in Vivian's lap. "What did he say?"

Vivian looked pained.

"What is it, Vivian? What did you learn?"

Vivian sighed and leaned forward. "You might want to prepare yourself…"

27

---

a fire crackled in the fireplace beside the bathtub, and Margot sank down lower.

A smile teased her lips even as she told herself she should not be so content.

But while worry still nagged at her for Savina's sake, she could admit, aside from that...

She was content.

No...more than that. She felt safer and more satisfied than she'd possibly even been.

Since that day she'd tried to run away, she and Callan had fallen into a companionable routine.

So yes, she was satisfied...mostly.

Callan moved about in the other room, and her whole body responded to his proximity. Her breasts seemed to swell and that place between her thighs grew achey...

It was an all too familiar feeling these days, and it was...

Well, it was frustrating. In most ways she was utterly content, aside from her repeated demands to Callan that he find a way to tell Savina that she was safe.

The last time she'd pleaded her cause, they'd been

working together beside the fire. Now that her ankle was feeling better, she'd cajoled him into letting her help with meals and cleaning.

He'd growled about it, but when she'd pointed out that she was his prisoner, not some guest at an inn, his lips had twitched in that way she loved.

The way that made her heart do a little dance.

It was the flicker of amusement she caught when he took her out for walks in the woods—he claimed he joined her to keep her from getting lost, but they both knew he was making sure she didn't run again.

He'd listen to her chatter away about her memories of the meadows at their country home, or listen to her ramble on about the birds and their songs, and all the while she'd watch and wait for his lips to twitch upward with the hint of a smile.

Callan moved in the other room again. His bedroom.

Was he clothed? Shirtless? Oh how she dreamed of his body some days. She imagined his muscles and the way they might move, feeling his body pressed against hers... his tongue pillaging her mouth again.

Her breath came out in a shaky exhale as her fingers trailed over the top of the bath's water, then over the skin of her breasts, cresting her nipples and stomach, then moving to the mound of hair at the top of her legs.

She swallowed hard as her fingers found the aching throb between her thighs. It only ached this way when her thoughts strayed to the man in the room next door. The yearn in her belly would bloom and spread until her heartbeat was pounding where her fingers skimmed... then pressed and stroked.

And stroked again, tentatively circling and exploring her own soft folds until her skin prickled, her breathing grew shallow, and her body starting to writhe as something foreign yet enticing built within her.

She gasped and jerked, the water sloshing in the tub as this odd tension coiled and intensified.

"Margot?" Callan's voice was close. So close, he must be just on the other side of the door.

Her hand flew up and her cheeks burst into flames, as if he could see what she'd been doing.

And then...

She moaned as her head tipped back against the edge of the metal tub that Callan had filled for her.

Her mind's eye was bombarded with the image of Callan walking into the room. Of his dark, fiery gaze raking over her as she lay naked in the tub.

Her fingers ventured down again, the ache so painful now, she bit back a sob.

Come in, she could say.

She could even make an excuse about needing him to help her wash her hair.

She eyed the empty doorway, temptation warring with good sense.

He was her captor. And yes, perhaps she'd been coming to think of him as a friend, but she knew enough about men from her time in Vestry Lane to know that one did not make an offer like that lightly.

And she knew enough about Callan to know that one word, one invitation...and he would devour her.

She shivered, even though the water was still warm.

The hunger in his eyes was undeniable. Every time she caught him staring, she could feel the heat of his desire all the way to her core.

She'd taken to reading aloud in the evenings, by the glow of candlelight. And each time, he joined her in the bed, their arms brushing, their thighs pressing against each other.

Last night, she'd fallen asleep on him. When she woke, it

was to the crackle of a dying fire, and she'd been cuddled up against his chest, her arm thrown over his hard stomach, and the book strewn open beside them.

She'd started to shift, but he'd stayed perfectly still.

How long had she been sleeping on him like that?

She eyed the door now. She still didn't know.

Her fingers trailed over her breasts, lingering on her hardened nipples.

All she knew was that when she woke, she saw with her own eyes how much he wanted her.

His breeches had bulged with his erection, and rather than being frightened as she ought to have been...

She bit her lip and slid her fingers into the water again. Oh Lord, this needy ache would be the death of her.

If only she knew how to make it go away...

It was tempting to touch herself again, to stroke until that feeling built. But what if that's all it did? What if that needy pulsing between her legs didn't bring with it a release?

What if only a man could give her that satisfaction?

As curious as she was to discover the truth, she resisted temptation and curled her fingers into a fist, willing her mind away from such wanton desires.

When the water began to cool, she finished bathing and reached for one of Callan's shirts. She heard a sound from the doorway just as she'd finished slipping the soft, worn linen over her head.

She turned with a gasp and found Callan...dying.

He looked like he was dying as he stared at her. He could not hide the longing in his blue gaze.

She blushed, clutching the shirt to her breasts. But it was equal parts embarrassment and desire that had her blood heating and her heart racing.

How much had he seen?

His hands clenched the doorframe and his throat worked as his gaze locked with hers.

For a long moment they stood there like that, caught in the grip of something thick and heavy.

She wasn't certain she could draw in a breath, the air was so dense with this heated tension.

After what felt like an eternity, he turned around abruptly. "Come."

"*Come. Stay.*" She echoed his terse commands in a low voice as she followed him, but her tone held a hint of laughter. "Sometimes I really do believe you mistake me for a pet."

He stopped at the entrance to the cottage door. When he turned back, his gaze was heavy lidded as it slid over her. "You're no man's pet."

Her lips parted. "Prisoner, then."

His eyes flashed with an emotion she couldn't name. Maybe regret?

She felt an answering flare of guilt. Which was ridiculous. Obviously. She was his prisoner, and they both knew it.

The reminder rankled. It didn't fit any longer, this notion that she was merely his captive. Maybe it was the physical frustration from earlier in the bath, but she found herself frowning in irritation as she followed him out into the dark night.

The air was brisk, and with her hair still wet and her feet and legs bare, she shivered.

"You're cold." It sounded like an accusation when he growled at her.

She wrapped her arms around herself. "I'm all right. But..." She shifted, digging her toes into the wet grass as she inhaled the fresh, wonderful scent of pine. "What are we doing out here?"

He hesitated, and then... "Stars."

She blinked. Stars?

He gestured upward, and with a laugh she tipped her head back to take in the dazzling array of stars that filled the sky on this cloudless night.

He'd wanted to show her the stars. A glorious blanket of diamonds of which she'd never seen the like. She did not understand how, but they shone so much brighter in this quiet forest compared to the crowded streets of London. They were brighter. More magical. Awe-inspiring.

She stayed like that for a long moment, her head tipped back with a smile on her face. When she lifted her head, she found him staring at her. Watching her with that hunger that should terrify her.

But it didn't.

All it did was stoke this fire within and make her heart pound.

He wanted her. She'd never been more certain of anything in her life. But she was just as certain that he would never act on that desire.

Not so long as she was his prisoner.

"I need to go, Callan." Her voice was quiet in the night, but she knew he heard her. "

"It's not safe."

"Why not?" she shot back. "Because there are hooded huntsmen in the woods?"

His lips twitched but he looked away with a huff.

"You know what they say about you, don't you?"

Another huff. "Still afraid I'm going to eat you?"

His eyes glinted with amusement and she couldn't help a sheepish grin. She moved toward him. "I can't stay your prisoner forever."

He reached out and touched her cheek. His caress was so gentle and at odds with his fierce strength, it made her chest tighten in an instant.

"Can't you?" he murmured softly, and with a wry twist to his lips.

He knew the answer to that. But all the same, she looked around them. Considering...

"Meadows to run in," he murmured, echoing what she'd told him she loved so much as a child. "Trees to climb."

Her heart kicked and clamored. It was tempting. Truly. She took a deep breath of the fresh air, with this man beside her making her feel safe and cherished and...

Loved?

Her heart took a flying leap that made her breathless. No, he'd never spoken of love.

They hardly knew each other. But also...

She felt like she knew him. She didn't need to unearth the details of his past to know who he was now. It was in his touch. In the way he took care of her and looked at her and...

And she got the feeling at times that he knew her as well as anyone. Nearly as well as Savina.

The thought of her sister made her stiffen, but she had to tilt her head back to meet his gaze as Callan closed the distance between them.

"I need to go. I'm worried about my sister."

"It's not safe."

She frowned. He'd said that more than once but refused to explain what he meant.

His voice was soft. Gentle. But his words were firm. "I can't let you go."

"You can't or you won't?"

His jaw tightened, and she sighed.

"Callan, are you keeping me because you have to or because...because..." *Because you want me here with you.*

That was the question she'd never been able to answer. Was he working on someone else's orders or was he keeping her because he wanted her for himself?

271

"I want you here." His voice was so gruff it was nearly inaudible. "With me."

Her heart ached and her eyes welled with tears. At that moment, she recognized herself in him. The loneliness. And a need to be cherished.

He saw her tears and misunderstood. "You're unhappy here."

"I don't like being a prisoner," she whispered, "if that's what you mean."

His lips twitched.

"But..." She sighed. "I'm not unhappy here. With you. I like being with you." Shyness stole over her and heat crept into her cheeks at his searching stare. "But my sister. She must be so worried. And I'm worried about her. We have enemies in London..."

His brows came down and...goodness. She knew that fury wasn't meant for her but she still shuddered.

"Enemies. Who?" he growled.

She hesitated. "I don't know anything about you, yet you want me to tell you *my* whole story?"

"Yes."

She let out a huff of amusement, and his lips twitched again, the promise of a smile tugging at his mouth. But he never gave into it. He never allowed himself.

"Just once I want to see you smile." Her words slipped out unbidden. "A real smile."

He studied her in silence for so long she began to think the conversation had ended. She went back to gazing up at the stars, sighing in disappointment that yet again, just as she was starting to think they were growing closer, this wall rose up between them.

"A smile..." His voice cut into her thoughts and had her head whipping around to face him.

His gaze had a softness to it. "A smile and then you'll tell me about your enemies?"

Her lips parted in surprise and she let out a laugh. "Are you using your smile to make a bargain?"

And then it happened. Her big, burly, gruff beast smiled at her. And it was...

Everything.

Her lungs felt full to bursting as she took in the creases at the corners of his eyes, the dimple in his cheek, and the way that smile made him seem so much younger than she'd imagined.

She reached up on instinct, wanting to touch him and stroke his hair, and—

He caught her wrist, his smile fading as he tugged her close. "Tell me," he ordered, the brutish grunts back in full. "Tell me everything about these enemies of yours."

28

*V*ivian hurried to keep up with Savina as she strode up to the Davenports' townhome.

"Are you sure you want to do this?" Vivian asked. "Whatever is going on between your stepmother and her husband—"

"Has everything to do with me and my sister," Savina finished.

Your stepmother and her husband.

The words made her queasy.

When had she become such a trusting, gullible fool?

Her hands clenched into fists and she tried for a calm, even tone when she stopped to face her friend. "I must do what I set out to do. I cannot sit by any longer and trust that Edmund has my best interests at heart. And I certainly cannot trust him with my sister's fate."

Vivian nibbled on her lower lip. There were times when the girl seemed so much older than her years, but right now Savina was reminded of just how young she was.

She should likely never have told her as much as she had.

Especially not when the poor dear had problems of her own to face.

Though she seemed to be handily avoiding the topic of her fiancé and a father who must be cruel to arrange such a match.

"Listen to me, Vivian," she said softly.

Vivian's father had escorted them in his carriage, seemingly delighted as a buzzard to watch whatever carnage came about tonight with scandalous Savina's arrival at a ball to which she was not invited nor wanted.

The Davenport's were friends of Lucinda's, she'd discovered.

Nay, friends of Lucinda's and Edmund's. Because the two were married. And beyond that—according to Vivian—they were in business together. Not just the business of marriage. Oh no, it was so much more than that!

Rage simmered in her veins, but she pushed it aside to steal this moment with Vivian.

"I don't know how this all will end with me and with Lucinda—"

"Don't say that."

"It's true, my dear," Savina said with a wry smile. "I am not going in there to wave a white flag."

Vivian's eyes glinted with wary amusement. "No, I'd say you're charging into battle, if your gown is anything to go by."

Savina smiled. The gown was her favorite of all those that she'd had made this past week. The seamstress was French and had convinced her to try one daring gown of the latest fashion.

Bright red silk wrapped around her, swirling about her legs. Without a lace kerchief, her decolletage was on full display, and the skirts were constructed in such a way that her hips and bottom were equally enhanced.

She'd shocked herself, truthfully, when she'd studied her reflection. And she'd ignored a fretting Mrs. Baker when she'd left the house without a shawl to cover her.

Her hair was up, her lips and cheeks were painted red, and she knew that she looked as dangerous as she felt.

She'd said yes to the seamstress on a whim...and with Edmund's reaction in mind.

Then, she'd hoped to shock him into acting on his desire.

Tonight, she hoped to anger him into telling the truth for once.

She took a deep breath. Tonight was not about their battle for control; it had nothing to do with sexual games or whetting their appetites.

No, tonight she meant to be rid of Lucinda and Edmund both.

Either she'd get her answers, or she'd burn the last of her reputation in a blaze of righteous vengeance.

If Lucinda wanted to paint her as a scandal and a loose woman, then that was what she'd be.

"Savina, what do you mean to do?" Vivian asked, her brows furrowed in concern.

Lucinda forced another smile. "Do not fret, dear. I won't drag you into this mess with me."

"But—"

"That's what I'm trying to tell you, dearest Vivian." She clasped the other girl's gloved hand. "I do not know how this will end, or if I'll be able to stay here in London. I may need to go to Bristol myself or..." She sighed. "I don't know yet. What I do know is this. You have been a true friend to me, and if you decide you wish to back out of this marriage to—"

"Savina," Vivian interjected warily.

"If you decide to call it off, and are in need of a friend..." She spoke over her friend, smiling when Vivian sighed with acceptance. "Then you will come find me, do you understand?"

Vivian nodded, a smile on her lips. "I understand. But I have made my decision, and I am not allowing myself to look back."

Fear warred with worry as she studied the sweet girl, but Savina nodded. "Very well."

"Are you ready?" Vivian asked, looking toward the door, where music spilled out along with raucous laughter.

Ready to finally confront the woman who'd haunted her every nightmare?

Savina squared her shoulders. "I am ready."

* * *

THE BALL WAS WELL underway when Savina threaded her way through the crowd.

She was well aware of the stares and the whispers, and was thankful she'd left Vivian behind with her father.

There was no telling what lies Lucinda had been spreading about her, and she'd hate for her friend to be tainted by her acquaintance.

She didn't stop moving through the crowd until she spotted her stepmother. Dressed in dark green, with her auburn hair sparkling like a crown atop her head, the older woman really was spectacularly beautiful.

Was that why he'd married her?

Not her father. Her father she knew had been duped into believing she had the sort of maternal love that he believed the girls needed.

To be fair, she did have a maternal love...just not for them.

And that was exactly what she was counting on.

Lucinda's eyes sparked with dark humor as she watched

Savina appear, but her features remained placid as she exchanged whispered remarks with the friends gathered around her.

The friends scattered when Savina reached them. "Ah, my darling stepdaughter."

"Hullo, Mother," she replied sweetly.

The woman's flinch was minute, but Savina caught it. She'd never forget the way this woman had cringed when they'd call her by that name.

Their father wished for them to call her that, and she'd insisted, but even as a child Savina could see that she did not enjoy it.

Now, with Savina a grown woman herself, she imagined Lucinda's vanity despised it even more.

With that thought in mind, Savina batted her lashes. "Stepmother, have you seen my stepfather?" Her voice was so sweet it seemed to drip honey. "He's been so attentive to me. It's odd that he hasn't sought me out yet."

She waited on edge for Lucinda's reaction. But when Lucinda's nostrils flared, she knew she'd hit a nerve.

No matter that she'd been the one to marry the prince— and Vivian's findings made it clear they had some sort of partnership—no woman could be pleased that her powerful, handsome husband had been openly chasing after a younger woman.

It's a marriage in name only.

His voice was in her head, and for a moment, Savina's confidence wavered. Was it really or had that been another lie?

As if Lucinda could sense her shift in mood, the older woman grew coy. "Darling, it's best you learn now that men like my husband cannot be counted on."

Savina inhaled sharply.

"They always have business to attend to, you see," Lucinda

continued. "So very busy with their own agendas that they often forget about everything else."

"Is that so? That must be difficult for his wife." Savina made a sympathetic clucking noise that made Lucinda stiffen.

"On the contrary. Edmund and I are partners." Her grin was vile and it turned Savina's stomach. "In everything."

"Then you forgive him for his..." Savina paused. "Wandering attentions?"

A pink stain crept into Lucinda's cheeks but her smile never faltered. "There's nothing to forgive. Men will be men, you know."

They were both distracted by a viscount who called out a greeting as he passed.

Savina and Lucinda both smiled brightly.

"Now, this is not to say that all men are the same," Lucinda continued.

Savina's insides tensed at the smug, syrupy tone.

"Your stepfather is quite unlike any other man I know."

Savina wanted to dissolve this conversation. She didn't want to let Lucinda have whatever satisfaction she was after. But she was too curious to hear whatever Lucinda might let slip about Edmund. About their marriage.

About why he'd been lying to her from the start.

"He's so clever. Why the way he took care of your sister..."

Savina froze. Her blood turned to ice at the mention of Margot.

Lucinda looked around them, talking mildly and with a sweet smile as if she wasn't aware of the effect her words were having.

In truth, she was very clearly enjoying this moment.

"Oh yes, he's very clever. Almost...wickedly clever." Lucinda turned to her with wide eyes. "Don't you think so?"

Savina's insides trembled with this buried rage. *Tell me what you've done to my sister! Show me what you're up to!*

"Now your father, on the other hand." Lucinda shook her head with a sad sigh. "Your father was so good. So *very* good. It was a shame he didn't understand that not all of us are capable of such goodness…"

Savina struggled for calm as her pulse pounded in her ears.

But anger was what Lucinda wanted. It was why she'd mentioned Margot and her father.

She was trying to upset her.

But this time Savina was prepared. She took a deep breath, glancing around until she spotted her prey. "You're right, Lucinda. Men are so very helpless at times, are they not? So easy to manipulate. So frighteningly easy to deceive."

Lucinda's eyes narrowed slightly at Savina's sudden cheerful turn.

With a satisfied smirk, Savina turned her gaze to Benedict, who stood nearby, laughing with friends. "Oh look, there's your son now…"

Benedict looked over as if he'd heard his name, and his bland features lit with delight at the sight of Savina.

Lucinda hissed. "Don't even think of going near my son—"

"Or what?" Savina arched her brow. Only years of hiding her disgust and fear in Vestry Lane made her capable of maintaining her composure as she asked, "Will you threaten my sister's life again?"

But Lucinda was just as good, if not better. Her cold mask gave nothing away.

Their standoff lasted for several seconds. It was broken by Benedict's arrival at her side. "Savina, what a pleasure."

"Benedict, do be a dear and fetch me some punch," Lucinda started.

Savina wrapped a hand around his upper arm, making his eyes widen as his attention turned to her.

"Surely punch can wait," Savina said with a teasing pout. "I fear I am desperate for some fresh air. Would you mind…"

"Of course!" Benedict hurried her away from Lucinda, sparing only the briefest glance at his mother before turning all his attention to Savina.

"Benedict," she heard his mother call out.

"Shall we go the balcony where the other are—"

"No." Savina smiled to soften her hard tone. The balcony was where Lucinda would go. It was the direction they'd headed.

Savina tugged him toward a hallway and paused just long enough to gaze up at him. "I'd much prefer a quieter setting. Perhaps the garden?"

She saw the moment this nitwit caught on to her husky tone and demure gaze.

His own eyes darkened with clear lust that turned her stomach. The way he ogled her cleavage reminded her so much of the drunk leches in Vestry Lane, she nearly heaved the contents of her stomach.

He slid his arm around her, a hand pressing against her back. His breath stank of liquor and his hot whisper in her ear made her shudder. "I know just the place."

Benedict was surprisingly headstrong, she'd give him that. She'd thought she'd have to do some more flirting, plant some more suggestions. But all it took was a single look and he descended like a wolf.

"You're so beautiful tonight, Savina. Do you have any idea how the men are talking about you?"

She tried to smile, but her gaze went back to the town-home as he tugged her outside, toward the garden.

The further they got from the noise of the party, the more her heart clamored.

But this wasn't satisfaction or excitement, this was…

Dread.

Fear.

And it was something else.

You are mine to protect now.

Blast. Why couldn't she get Edmund's voice out of her head?

He'd lied to her. Time and again. He'd kept secrets and proven she couldn't trust him. So why…

Benedict stopped short when they were out of view of the house, hidden in the shadows of a tree.

He leered down at her, his cloying breath making her stomach clench when he whispered against her cheek. "So, this is what you were after, eh?"

When he leaned back, she stared up at him, her heart hammering.

Why did she feel like she was being disloyal?

She didn't trust Edmund. He didn't love her—

Love. What could make her think such a thing?

Of course he did not love her. No one had spoken of love.

Her thoughts were racing as quickly as her heart and when Benedict bent down and planted a sloppy, wet kiss on her lips, she nearly retched.

This was wrong.

This was all wrong.

Guilt slammed into her right alongside disgust. She pushed against his chest. "No, Benedict, wait—"

"For what? You know you want this." The lusty glee in his voice was at odds with the dopey smile he'd given her upon their first reunion. How could this sweet, clueless man suddenly be talking and acting with such authority?

It seemed like she was dealing with a completely different person.

His foul breath filled her senses when he closed the space

between them. His hands were at her waist, holding her close as his hot lips trailed across her cheek and started sucking her neck.

"Wait. Slow down." She leaned away from him, trying to escape his reckless slobbering. "Benedict…"

But he didn't seem to hear her. His hands were getting rougher, gripping her waist, his mouth working its way back to hers. His lips were harsh and demanding, his tongue nearly gagging her when he thrust it into her mouth.

She fought for air as he lifted a hand and closed it around her right breast. His squeeze was hard, unrelenting, even when she whimpered at the pain of his exploration.

"Benedict, stop," she rasped, turning her head away and trying to gain control of this situation.

Control.

Power.

How had it shifted so easily from her hands to his?

Take it back!

The thought shot through her head and just like in the alley with Mr. Capp, King's lessons kicked in and she fought back, lashing out with nails and legs.

"I said, stop!" She dug her fingers into his face while her knee gave a sharp, upward thrust.

He jerked into shock, then stumbled back with a howl. "You bitch! You… you whore!"

He screeched the insults at her, crumpled over, cradling his bruised cock while she stood there heaving against the tree trunk. She should be laughing in satisfaction but she was still reeling from the taste of his repellent tongue in her mouth and the feel of his rough fingers squeezing her breast.

If he lunged for her again, would she be strong enough to stop him?

The murderous look on his face had her fists clenching at

her sides, ready to defend herself from whatever foul deeds he was concocting.

He stumbled toward her with a growl, but the sound was lost to a roar of rage so feral, the hairs at the back of her neck prickled.

"Get away from her!" Edmund ran toward them, appearing out of the shadows.

If Savina had feared Benedict's wrathful expression, it was nothing compared to the fury on Edmund's face as he fisted Benedict's dress coat and threw him away from Savina.

The younger man stumbled and muttered curses, throwing dark glares at Savina while whispering in a savage voice, "Don't touch me, old man."

Edmund's body swiveled to block Savina from view as he faced his stepson. "Go. Get out of here before I kill you." The words came out rough and harsh, barely controlled rage tingeing each syllable.

Only a fool would not believe such a threat from such a man.

And much to Savina's surprise, it appeared Benedict was no fool in this matter.

With a dark glance in their direction, he slunk off into the night.

But Savina could not even breathe a sigh of relief.

All she could do was hold her breath as she waited for Edmund to turn and face her.

29

*E*dmund still shook with rage, and one part of him wanted to go after Benedict and beat him to a bloody pulp. But one glance over his shoulder had him spinning to face Savina, pulling her into his arms even as she stiffened and pushed him away.

After a second, she gave up the fight, and when she sank into his chest, he was horrified to feel her tears wetting his shirt. "Love, don't cry."

She smacked his chest in response. "What have you done to me?"

He frowned down at the top of her head. "What have I done? I was going to ask the same of you. You brought him out here…"

"Yes."

A shudder racked through her, and he held her tighter, resting his chin on the top of her head as he battled a possessive fury that rattled him.

Never in his life had he felt this way about anyone or anything.

When he heard Benedict's insults and saw the look on his

face as he lunged toward Savina, the emotions rising within him were more than he could contain. From murderous rage to clenching fear and something so much more—a protective possessiveness that had him running through the garden like a crazed man.

Savina's fingers curled into the fabric of his shirt and he felt her strength returning. His little hellcat was ready to do battle once more.

His lips twitched with the urge to smile even as his irritation with her flared.

"I told you to stay away from him." He'd said it mildly enough, but he was sure she understood what that cost him.

He knew without a doubt she'd done this tonight knowing full well that it would gut him.

"Why?" he asked.

She shook her head. "What have you done to me?"

Her voice was muffled and soft. She wasn't talking to him, it seemed.

His heart ached with a mix of emotions, and above them all was an overwhelming surge of love for this wicked, wonderful, maddening woman. "Come," he ordered gently. "I'm taking you home."

He expected a fight, to be honest. It was unsettling how easily she went with him, not asking questions when he avoided the crowd by going around the townhome and seeking out his carriage driver at the end of the street.

She remained frighteningly compliant, not saying a word as she climbed into the carriage.

If he hadn't come along when he had, and seen what he did, he feared for what might have happened to her. When he bumped into a worried Miss Vivian and she whispered that she'd spotted Savina and Benedict heading for the garden he'd been filled with equal measures of anger and horror. He'd strode out there ready to tell off his defiant, little minx, but then he'd spied Benedict pawing her through the shadows, and then came his insults.

Who knew what Lucinda's spawn would have gotten up to in the back garden had Edmund not gone to find them.

He shuddered to think.

Mrs. Baker fretted and hovered when they arrived back at Savina's home, but he sent her and the other servants to bed.

"I'll take it from here, Mrs. Baker." He smiled kindly, although it faded quickly when the servants didn't move fast enough.

It wasn't until the house was silent that he led Savina... not to the parlor but to the kitchen.

"What are you doing?" Savina hovered in the doorway, watching him warily. Like he was sharpening a knife rather than taking a wineglass off the shelf and searching the pantry for something to eat.

"What does it look like?" he asked, not bothering to hide his amusement.

He nodded toward the table. "Sit."

She did so slowly. "Aren't you going to yell and shout?"

"What for?"

She let out a huff of exasperation. "I defied your orders, Edmund. I went there tonight with the intent to seduce—"

"Yes," he interrupted. "So I gathered." His hands clenched into fists at what might have occurred tonight. But...his anger wasn't toward Savina.

He'd have gladly ripped Benedict's head off in that moment, but this rage wasn't even entirely toward him.

It was himself he was furious with. If he'd told her the truth from the beginning...

If he'd made saving her and Margot his only ambition...

If he'd sensed sooner that something was amiss with Leopold's widow and the conveniently misplaced daughters...

He dipped his chin with a sigh. "You did not go through with it."

She was quiet.

He reached for the bread and a knife to cut her off a piece. "You had a change of heart."

Again she was quiet. "What are you doing?"

"You look like a light breeze might knock you over." His voice was too gruff as he focused on the task at hand. "You haven't been eating enough."

"It's hard to enjoy a meal when my sister is missing, and possibly..." Her words ended with a wavering note that stabbed his heart.

"My men are looking for her, Savina. We'll find her."

"I know."

He let the silence linger this time as he finished making her a small meal. It wasn't until he placed it before her that she broke down with a sob. "What have you done to me?"

Her shoulders were slumped and her head dipped low. He hovered behind her, wanting to touch her, to soothe her...

But not certain how.

He wasn't the gentle sort, damn it. He knew how to strategize, he'd made a career out of leading men—on the battlefield and then in business.

What did he know about looking after a wounded angel?

Her voice was husky, her tone tortured. "What have you done to me that I feel this loyalty to you when all you've ever done is lie to me?"

His chest was so painfully tight he could scarcely breathe. "I'm done with lies now, Savina. Done with secrets."

She lifted her head, and he knew he'd spoken the truth when he met her glistening, pained gaze. "Is it true you're in business with her?"

His nostrils flared, his gut tightened. "Yes."

She slumped slightly as if he'd just struck her in the gut.

He sat beside her, pushing the plate and glass toward her. "Eat, love. Drink."

He waited until she reached for the thick slab of buttered bread.

"I received news of your father's death too late," he murmured.

She lifted her head, her gaze sharp. But she didn't interrupt.

He swallowed hard. Where to begin? "It's an odd fate, you know, to be born into a powerful family, with a commanding title but…" He threw his hands out. "Nothing to command."

She arched a brow, her lips twitching slightly at his rueful tone.

"I might be a prince, but I'm as far from taking the throne as you are, I'd imagine." He cringed and was rewarded with a small smile before she seemed to remember that she was angry with him.

He reached out and toyed with one of her long blonde locks, so impossibly silky between his fingers. "Eat, my love. If you want to hear the whole sordid tale, you must eat like a good girl."

She playfully pouted, but stuck a berry in her mouth.

"An injury forced me out of the military," he continued. "And truthfully, I was done with it anyhow. With no wars being waged, my highborn status made me more of a figurehead than a real part of the battle."

"Something tells me you were more than that," she murmured.

He lifted a shoulder. "I was a valued tactician," he admitted. "But the time had come for me to move on. One injury caused even my uncaring family to take notice, and suddenly I was being buffered on all sides…"

She smiled. "You must have hated that."

He returned her smile. It was a sweet moment of understanding before she retreated back to her wary cage. Shutting him out...

He drew in a deep breath. "I'll admit, I was rather...at odds."

She arched a brow. "You?"

"Mmm. Your father tried to convince me to settle down. Find a wife and start a family..." He smiled.

So did she.

"But the contented family man...that was always your father's demeanor. Not mine." He rested an elbow on the table and eyed her plate meaningfully.

With a huff she picked up the bread and shot him an arch look as she took a small bite.

"I'd done enough traveling in the Orient to have contacts, and enough money to invest in a new trading operation..."

She watched him steadily as he told her everything. All about how he'd started up a trading route with the ambitious goal of being a rival to the East India Company. About how he was traveling so much that news of her father's death didn't reach him until a full year later. How her father's last letter to him hadn't come until shortly after that.

"I knew something was not right." He frowned, trying to put it into words. "Your father mentioned you in his last letter to me. You and Margot. He was quite long winded in his correspondence, you know."

She smiled at that.

"I enjoyed it. Made me feel as though we were sitting before the fire back in our school days." He smiled at the memories. "But in passing he made mention of how his new wife wanted to alter his will."

Savina stiffened.

"Yes, your father made light of it, but by the time I received his last letter, I knew the end of his story, you see." He tapped his fingers on the table, regret spiking alongside grief. "I was suspicious enough to come here, but…I should have been more doubtful. I wish—"

He cut himself off. What use were wishes? Hindsight was a bloody bitch, and it did Savina no good now.

"So you came here and…married Lucinda." Savina's tone was just as bland as her expression, but there was no hiding the accusation in her eyes.

It was deserved, though, and he well knew it.

"Believe it or not, I married her for you and Margot as much as for my own benefit."

"But you did benefit."

He tipped his head in acknowledgment. "I confess, I knew Lucinda to be manipulative from the very moment I met her. But I could see well how your father—always more trusting than I—could have fallen for it."

"She was astute," Savina said. "Still is."

"Indeed. I saw through her from the start, but…not well enough. I did not know the full extent of her cruelty, nor the sheer magnitude of her greed."

Savina set her food down and turned to face him.

This was his last chance. That was what her somber expression told him. If he ever wanted to earn her trust and be deserving of her loyalty, this was his last chance to come clean.

"I believed her when she told me she'd sent you and Margot off to school." With a wince, he added. "Perhaps I… wanted to believe her."

Her lips pressed together but she didn't speak.

"I had no real reason to doubt her word on that at the time, and it made sense to me that she'd want you out of the way…"

"But you did not check to ensure we were safe and well."

Regret was a jagged piece of glass between each of his ribs as he admitted, "No. I took her at her word."

She met his gaze for a long moment. "Go on."

He continued, painting in brief strokes the image of what that time had been like. Only a few years ago but it seemed like an eternity now.

"She set her sights on me," he said. "I had no misconceptions about her intentions. She looked at me and saw the title." He shrugged. "And in return she offered me her connection to the crown."

Savina's eyes narrowed. "She is a distant cousin, yes?"

"Very distant." His tone was bland. "But she had enough resources and wiles to get me the licenses I needed to expand my trading routes and..." He heaved a sigh. "I told you from the start, it was a marriage of convenience."

"You did," she muttered. "But you left out the part where she holds power over your business."

A muscle in his jaw ticked. This fury was old and focused on one particular auburn-haired devil.

"I'd thought that if we married, I'd get the licenses I needed and, in addition, get closer to the woman who I suspected of wrongdoing when it came to your father."

Savina's brows knit together. "You think she was responsible for his death?"

"In the beginning, no. I merely thought she'd tampered with his will. I knew for a fact that his first priority was to you and your sister. I believed your stepmother merely fixed the will. But the more I got to know her, the more I saw the bottomless depths of her cruelty, and the twisted web of her lies."

"And...us?"

"Lucinda is a deft perjurer, but her tales shifted slightly every time she spoke of you and Margot. I grew suspicious enough to track down your father's servants. The ones Lucinda had let go upon his death."

"And?"

"And their stories corroborated my fears, so I shifted my focus to finding you and Margot."

Savina tilted her head to the side. "Where was your focus before that?"

He gave her a small, wry smile. "Allow me this one secret, if you will. I've renewed my interest in Lucinda's past...I hope to have more information soon."

After a moment, Savina gave him a regal nod of assent that made him smile.

"Thank you."

"What did the servants tell you about us?"

"Too little." He sighed. "They knew not what became of you. But several mentioned how Lucinda had an unhealthy hatred of your sister. One mentioned an incident in particular..."

"Yes," Savina said quickly. "She struck my sister once. Shouted until the whole house came to see what was the matter."

He leaned forward. "What caused it?"

She gave a helpless shake of her head. "I wasn't there, and afterward Margot was in a fit of tears. She said all she did was walk into father's sickroom unannounced."

"He died unexpectedly."

"He grew sick suddenly," Savina confirmed. "And then..."

Their gazes met and held. And after a long silence, Savina began to weep in earnest. He suspected it was years worth of grief and pain coming to the surface and so he pulled her into his arms, settled her on his lap and held her.

When the sobs began to lighten and her hiccupy breaths were interrupted by sighs, he stood, still cradling her in his arms.

"Where are we going?" she murmured against his neck.

"To bed, love." He kissed the top of her head. "I'm taking you to bed."

30

The sun was high as Margot sat beside the small pond Callan had led her to this afternoon. The breeze was a cool kiss to her cheeks as she sat beside him, holding the fishing line he'd made for her.

They had caught only two so far, but she could hardly think about eating when he was so close. So strong. Growing more handsome by the day.

Her body seemed to yearn for him with more power. Her dreams were filled with him and she woke each morning, aching for his touch.

A touch he refused to give no matter how hard she tried to hint at it.

She was never quite bold enough to outright say it, but her attempts at longing looks and coy smiles seemed to be failing her too.

How did one get a man to take her?

What 'take her' meant, she wasn't truly sure, but her body seemed to understand it and maybe she should listen to that instinct.

Callan shifted beside her, adjusting his breeches with a

small frown. He could obviously sense her stare and was making a point not to glance her way.

Her lips pursed with annoyance. He was a hard man to read, but she was learning what his looks meant. She was starting to understand the different energy that pulsed through him. She did not like this silent reticence. If anything, she preferred his anger from the night before when he'd prowled in front of the fire, looking more beast than man as he growled and muttered while she finished her tale about how she and Savina had come to be in Vestry Lane, and how they'd been found.

She likely should have been frightened of his demeanor, but those men at the inn with their tall tales of this beast... they'd been wrong.

Callan could show rage, but he was no beast. He was a man who'd suffered. A man who'd made his way in the world the only way he knew how.

He'd told her little snippets about himself over the last few days. Not much, but enough for her to glean that he was all alone in this world. That he'd been in the military, done things he couldn't speak of, and now was content to live outside society...

And outside the law.

A fact he seemed to think would frighten her.

But truly, after five years living on Vestry Lane, she understood well that there was no black and white in this world.

As she'd watched him, shaking with the effort to control his fury—a rage on her behalf—her heart went out to him. It'd given a hard tug every time his pacing brought him within touching distance of where she'd sat. And it gave a hard tug now.

Only this morning, she had murmured at the beauty of

the blue sky and without a word, he'd left the cottage, returning a while later with two hand-made fishing rods.

"Come," he'd ordered, leading her out of the house to a sunny glade and peaceful pond that had been so beautiful her eyes had watered with instant tears.

"No crying." His voice had been gruff but soft as he took her arm and led her to the edge of the pond, giving her a quick refresher on the art of fishing.

She'd smiled at him, affection blooming in her chest when he caught her gaze and flicked a hand through the air, his dimple briefly popping into place as he handed her the rod.

And so they sat in this idyllic place with the sun warming their skin and Margot's heart so full she could barely contain it.

Nerves fired through her, lighting the tips of her fingers and toes as she bit her lip and reached out a trembling hand to touch his back.

He stilled, his muscles coiling beneath her fingers as he clenched his jaw.

She could have sworn his whole body vibrated with tension and the air seemed to thicken with a new sort of weight between them.

She placed her rod aside, shifting to her knees and shuffling so close her body pressed against his side.

"Margot," he growled. "Stop." He finally turned to look her in the eyes. His gaze was dark and dangerous, but she felt no fear.

It was nerves and anticipation that made her belly tighten, and it was an awareness she'd never known before that had heat pooling between her thighs and her breasts feeling heavy and achy as she leaned into him, ignoring his command.

He looked pained with the effort to keep from touching

her. His hands were clenched around his fishing rod, and every inch of his face was taut with control.

Licking her lips, she moved in even closer until her breasts brushed against his arm. Two layers of clothing were between them, but her breath still hitched at the sweet sensation that coursed through her. Her nipples puckered and her sex grew wet.

"Margot…"

There was his warning again… and maybe a plea.

He wanted her. She suspected she'd known that in some way or another from the very start. But right now, she embraced it. A surge of power replaced her nerves and she leaned in until his scent wrapped around her, and she pressed her lips to the hot skin of his neck.

His breath came out in a hiss.

Encouraged by that, she moved again, taking the fishing rod from his hands and finding a home between his legs. She kneeled before him, resting her hands on his chest and finally satisfying her curiosity of what it felt like to trace the hard planes of his body. The fabric of his shirt was thin enough for her to feel everything and when they drifted lower, her breaths came in short puffs of eager excitement. Her hands began to tremble as she felt his stomach muscles ripple and harden beneath her touch.

The sound of their breathing drowned out the bird's song, and she was mesmerized by the spell that seemed to fall over them.

When she moved her hands even lower, he finally broke his frozen state and clamped a hand around her wrist, holding her still.

She tipped her head back up, meeting his gaze. For the first time in her entire life, she felt brave.

"Why won't you touch me?" When he didn't answer, she added, "I know you want to."

A muscle ticked in his jaw, and the fire in his eyes stole her breath. "Aren't you scared of me?"

She blinked in surprise. But she gave his question thought because it seemed important to him that she answer.

"I've always been scared of men," she whispered. "I've always been scared of most things," she amended with a rueful laugh. "But I'm not scared of you."

"Why not?"

She bit her lip. "I told you last night where I've been these past five years. So you must know, I'm not as sheltered as you might believe."

His lips twitched, and finally...finally he reached out and touched her. Just a light graze of his fingers over her cheek and jaw, but it made her tremble with need.

"You thought I was going to eat you," he muttered.

Heat surged into her cheeks as she remembered that first encounter. "Yes, well...perhaps I was frightened at first."

He smiled, and...oh.

Oh dear.

Her heart was well and truly gone.

It was his now, and the realization gave her a new surge of courage.

"Touch me," she pleaded.

The pain in his eyes pierced her heart.

"You are too good for me, Margot."

"I'm not. I—"

"You are." He paused, his gaze raking over her features and dipping down to the swell of her breasts. The dress seemed to cling and imprison her, and for the first time in her life, she wanted to rip it off and set her body free. She wanted to expose herself completely to this man.

With trembling fingers, she nudged at the bodice of her dress, slipping it off her shoulders. He stopped her before she could pull it down to her waist. His breaths were ragged as he stared at her milky skin. The hunger in his blue gaze was enough to make her wet sex start to throb.

She let out a shaky exhale.

"Your first concern when you woke in my cottage was for your servants." His husky words made her pause.

She wasn't sure how to respond.

He lifted his gaze, cradling her cheek. "You are good, Margot. You are pure."

"So are you." She covered his hand with her own, leaning into his touch.

His brows arched in disbelief, and then a flicker of anger flashed in his gaze. "I am not a good man."

She leaned away with a sigh of exasperation. "Callan, I've seen supposedly good men beat beggars. I've watched as eligible, charming young dandies use and abandon penniless women. I've seen a vicar spit on a whore he'd just lain with…" Tears filled her eyes as she willed him to understand. "And I've also seen thieves and murderers like my friend, King and his crew, be kinder and more generous than anyone in Mayfair could imagine."

"Margot—"

"I know you've done bad things. But that doesn't mean you are bad. And…and whether you think I should be or not…" She moved forward quickly, cupping his face in her hands. "I am not scared of you."

"You should be." The answer was swift and harsh.

"Well, I'm not."

He glowered at her. "I'm a killer, Margot."

She stilled, but didn't move away.

"I'm a killer and a thief. That's who I am."

She let her hands stroke the stubble of his jaw as she thought that over. Then she lifted her gaze to his. "That's what you do, not who you are."

He stared at her, long and hard. "You should be afraid of me."

"Should I?" She tilted her head to the side.

He leaned forward until his breath fanned across her lips, his fierce gaze locked on hers. "Aren't you?"

Her breath caught and her heart leapt. But not with fear.

"No," she whispered. "I know you'd ever hurt me."

With a groan, he wrapped an arm around her and pulled her close. His lips crushed hers in a kiss that was at once bruising in its hunger and so painfully tender, it brought tears to her eyes.

With a needy whimper, she welcomed his tongue into her mouth. Relief and elation stole through her as they finally repeated the kiss she'd been waiting for. She threaded her fingers into his hair, drawing him to her, even when he tried to pull away. She suckled his lips as if they were her lifeblood, drinking in every taste and sensation his tongue could offer.

He swiped at her tears with the pad of his thumb and his lips moved over hers, tasting and sucking, his tongue claiming hers.

She parted her lips for him once more, welcoming the invasion. She slid her arms down his neck and across his broad shoulders, resting all her weight against him.

He caught her easily.

"I'm a selfish bastard," he muttered.

"You're not taking anything I'm not willing to give," she whispered.

He pulled back, his gaze dark and unreadable as he studied her. "I am selfish, Margot. And I am not a good man."

She pressed her lips together, fighting the urge to protest.

With a little growl, he kissed the corner of her mouth, like he'd heard exactly what she hadn't said. And then he pinned her body against his, rolling them over so he was nestled between her legs.

He rested his weight on his elbows, gazing down at her with eyes bluer than the sky above them. "You're mine now."

Her smile was tremulous. He was trying to scare her. Giving her one last chance to back out.

But she would do no such thing.

"Yes," she whispered, her voice and body quaking with anticipation.

He lowered his hips until his stiff, frighteningly large manhood was digging into her. She could feel it through the layers of fabric and she instinctively bucked her hips, and watched in fascination as his jaw clenched and hunger darkened his eyes.

Yes. This. I want this.

Everything in her seemed to be screaming the rightness of it.

Her breathing was harsh and erratic as her hands came to his shoulders, her fingers digging into him as a crazed impatience took hold. She wanted to rip the shirt from his body, feel his hardened flesh. She wanted to gaze upon his naked form and then she wanted...

She didn't even know what she wanted from him, but she needed it desperately. "Please," she begged.

His eyes jaw clenched, his gaze so dark she couldn't help a soft gasp.

"If we do this..." he said slowly, his gaze never leaving hers. "You are mine."

She stilled, her mind working again with a jolt as she saw the grim determination in his eyes. The seriousness of what he was saying, of what she was doing...

It hit her full force, and she made herself stop to consider, because that was what he needed from her.

She swallowed hard, trying to ignore the large, throbbing shaft pressing against her lower belly as she met his gaze.

If we do this, you are mine.

The words felt good. They felt right. They settled into her chest and sent a wave of warmth sweeping over her, so intense it brought tears to her eyes.

He scowled and started to shift away but she caught him by fisting a hand in his shirt. "Not your prisoner," she clarified.

"No. Not my prisoner..." He loosened her grip on him and pressed her hand to his heart. "*Mine.*"

Her lips trembled and her throat grew painfully tight as the warmth in her chest grew unbearably sweet. "Yes," she whispered. "Yours."

He claimed her mouth with a hungry growl, and she moaned as sensations swept over her and caught her in a tidal wave of emotion.

Her answering kisses were untutored but just as hungry as his. She met him kiss for kiss, sliding her tongue out to meet his when he invaded her mouth.

He ground into her, his stiff manhood a bruising dagger that pressed into her softness.

"I can't be gentle," he muttered when he pulled back.

Insatiable need raced through her, matching his perfectly. She loved the way he needed her.

She needed to be needed, and she craved that consuming hunger she saw in his eyes, trapped behind a control he'd clamped down on himself.

"Take me," she whispered. "I want you to."

His gaze looked panicked for a second as he studied her. "I can't hurt you."

"You won't."

He huffed, shaking his head with a look that told her she

didn't understand the truth. That she was naively innocent in the art of love making.

"Show me." She felt bold in her request, despite the trembling of her voice. "I need you to show me, even if you hurt me. I have to be yours. Claim me, Callan. Claim me, now," she begged. "I want to feel how badly you need me." She buried her face in his neck, willing away the embarrassment so he could know her heart. "I need...I need you to satisfy this ache. This longing I have for you. Free me." Her voice pitched, her eyes glistening with fresh tears. "I need to know that I belong to you... that you need me and—"

He growled, shifting so he could own her mouth. His tongue was thick and hot as he devoured her, his hands finally moving to yank down her dress. He rose to his knees, fighting the fabric and quickly winning. Her breasts spilled out of their cage and his eyes lit with appreciation, but he didn't stop pulling until the dress had been torn from her body.

She lay on the grass, completely exposed to the world. To him.

Her chest heaved as the cool breeze licked her skin.

But all she could see were those blue eyes.

With a groan, he dove down and caught a nipple in his mouth, suckling her tit until she could no longer contain her cries. She panted and mewled, arching her back for more. His rough stubble against the sensitive skin of her breast seemed to send an arrow of heat straight down to her sex, and when he let that nipple go and turned his attention to her other breast, she acted on instinct, lifting her legs to wrap around him.

All that stood between them now were his breeches, which strained against his manhood.

Her fingers dove into his hair as she held him to her, her

head tossing from side to side as he sucked her nipple hard and then lapped at it with his tongue.

He toyed with her breasts, alternately sucking and licking, kissing and pinching until the mixture of pleasure and pain had her writing beneath him. She was out of control...

And she wanted the same from him.

She ran her hands down his back, pawing at his shirt until he'd yanked it over his head and tossed it aside. It landed on a bramble bush and she moaned in wild ecstasy when his bare skin met hers. Gliding her hands down the muscles of his back, she reveled in his strength, then slipped her fingers between them. The moment her hand found his hard bulge, he stilled.

"Margot," he warned.

Her breath caught as she drowned in the intensity of his stare. "I want you." She swallowed, wishing she had a better way of explaining herself. Remembering the brazen women from Vestry Lane, she blurted out the request before she could stop herself, "Fuck me. I want you to fuck me."

Were those the right words?

He went impossibly still. His gaze darkened. Her heart raced. Yes! She could see it in his eyes. The primal need, the unbridled desire. That was what she wanted. What she needed.

"Take me. Claim me. Even if it hurts, I want it," she whispered. "Make me scream, but please stop making me beg."

His hands moved to her hips, his grip so hard it bit into her skin. His breaths were ragged, his chest heaving as he stared down at the mound between her legs. Nudging her apart with his knees, he brushed his fingers over the soft curls—a feather light caress that made her whimper with desire.

"Please," she whispered.

He groaned at that, lurching forward and kissing her until she forgot how to breathe.

He was losing control and she loved it. When he pulled back to give her air, she gasped his name and said, "Fulfill my fantasy"

He stilled, his dark gaze on hers. "Fantasy?"

"Every time I took a bath and you were in the other room," she started. "I touched myself thinking about you."

A rumble sounded in his chest.

Her breathing grew shallow with excitement, the ache between her thighs unbearable as she waited for him to lose the last of his control.

"What did you imagine?" He sounded like he was choking as he held himself still over her.

His manhood throbbed where it was settled against her thigh.

"Of you," she said, her tone husky with desire. "Inside me."

His nostrils flared and his fingers convulsively clenched on her hips.

"Of you inside me and…" She thrust her hips up, rolling them so her hard nub pressed against the fabric of his breeches. She let out a whimper as the friction made her inner muscles clench.

"And what, Margot?" He caught her chin and held her still so she had to meet his gaze. "Tell me what you want me to do."

Her lips parted on a gasp. The dark hunger there…the need…

"I want you to shove your hard cock inside of me and make me scream," she breathed. "I want you to pump into me and fuck me until you come." Every word she'd overheard in the alleys, every act she'd witnessed outside the brothel…

She wanted to experience it all with this man.

She spread her legs wider in welcome, her hips jerking up as her own words made her need ratchet up even higher.

He cupped her face, the rough pad of his thumb brushing over her lower lip. Her head fell back and he slid his hand down until that impossibly large hand circled her throat, and he dipped his head to growl in her ear. "My little angel. Do you have any idea what it does to me to hear those dirty words coming from your sweet lips?"

"What does it do?"

He lowered his hips until his thick shaft was nestled between her folds, the head of his cock teasing her entrance as he nuzzled her neck. His tongue licked at her sensitive skin, and his teeth caught her earlobe and tugged.

The scent of him, the weight of him, the feel of his rough hands so firm but gentle as he held her captive beneath him...

"I'm yours," she said.

His growl drove her wild. He was so close to losing control, and it was all her doing. He might be twice her size, and an infamous beast who hunted his prey, but in that moment, she was the one with the power, and she'd never felt more brave.

She wet her lips and lifted her chest until her nipples pressed into his hot flesh. The urge to drive him to the edge, to make him lose control entirely, it made her feel wild and wanton.

More free than she'd ever been, even as he held her captive beneath him. "I want you to make me yours, Callan. Claim me as your woman." She writhed beneath him. "I want—"

His growl cut her off as he released his grip on her and shoved down his breeches. She sat up on her elbows so she could glimpse his manhood. Her lips parted as she studied the long shaft—a thick spear ready to pierce her and make her his own.

The pulse between her legs grew with intensity and when his fingers parted her folds, she let out a strangled whimper.

He nudged the head of his manhood against her slippery channel.

"So wet," he grunted. "So good."

He changed his position, lying over her so he could work himself inside her. They both gasped.

"So fucking tight," he growled.

He felt huge and he'd barely even begun to enter her. But even the discomfort felt right. She'd never known how empty she was until now. She'd never known that a part of her had been missing until him.

He was doing his best to be gentle. She could feel it in the way his muscles tensed and trembled as he nudged himself inside of her with controlled movements.

She rocked her hips up, nipping at his lower lip. "Fill me, Callan. Take me. Fuck me."

His shoulder and back muscles clenched beneath her hands as her whispers tore at his control. "Make me yours, Callan...forever."

She felt it the moment his control snapped, and triumph filled her.

With a loud roar, he drew back his hips and then drove into her with one hard shove.

Her eyes widened as pain ripped through her, and she couldn't help her sharp wail. It was both agony and ecstasy—a tearing down of the last wall that stood between them.

He stilled inside her, vibrating with a new tension as she recovered from the shock. Her breaths hit his shoulder, shaky little pants, as she dug her fingers into his back. She rocked her hips, an instinctual move that silently told him to keep going.

He thrust again and she cried out, but he swallowed the sound with his mouth, and then he was kissing her and touching her, stroking her and murmuring words of encouragement.

"So good, my Margot. So tight, so wet for me. Take your man's cock. Take it like a good girl, my love."

She spread her legs wider, softening for him, welcoming him as he kissed every inch of her neck, her shoulders, her cheeks, her breasts...

When she started to return his kisses, he moved inside her at a quicker pace, his gentle rocking growing with urgency, yet he still seemed to be holding back.

"More," she begged. "Harder. I want all you have to give me."

He gave her another hard thrust that made her breath catch. But not with pain...

This was something else. He changed their position, holding himself up on his arms, his finger coming between them, so he could find that hard nub. "Do you touch yourself here, my sweet?"

She whimpered his name.

A smile hovered over his lips as he watched her. All the while his hips rocked and his fingers worked magic. "That's it, sweetheart," he praised. "Your cunny wants this, doesn't it? It's milking my cock greedily, just like it should."

"Yes." She was whimpering and moaning, begging and pleading. She didn't even know what she was begging for but she knew he could give it to her.

Only him.

One of his hands slid beneath her and he cupped her bottom in the palm of his big hand and squeezed hard.

She gasped and her hips jerked up.

"That's it. Ride my cock, love. Grind on me and take me as deep as you can."

His words made her senseless and when his fingers flicked over that nub she found herself at the brink. She was so close to…something.

One push and she'd be over the edge. "Callan?"

"That's it, baby girl," he grunted. "Now tell me what you need."

Her breath hitched on a sob as the truth hit home. "You. I need you."

He let out a bellow as he finally lost that control. He pumped into her hard and fast, pounding into her soft wetness until her whole body felt his hardness inside her.

His teeth caught her earlobe, and he growled in her ear. "You're mine now, Margot. You are mine forever."

With one more slam of his hips, she shattered. The world came apart as pleasure splintered her body, leaving her helpless in its wake.

31

*S*avina woke when the sun was just starting to peek through the window.

Satisfaction curled through her before she could realize why. But slowly, her mind began to function and she became aware that she'd slept like the dead and was now waking in the arms of…

"Edmund." She woke with a start only to find that she was wrapped around him like ivy.

She lifted her head and found him smiling down at her as he toyed with her hair.

He was partially upright against the pillows, and judging by the shadows under his eyes, he hadn't slept at all.

"Are you…did I…" Embarrassment filled her as she shifted away from him, but he caught her to him easily, holding her close.

"Don't go," he said, the command gruff but soothing.

After a brief hesitation, she settled back onto him with a sigh, and let herself revel in the sound of his strong heartbeat as he continued to toy with her curls.

"I like you like this." His voice was a husky whisper.

She made a face against his shirt as she fidgeted with the hem of his waistcoat. "Like what?"

He stroked a hand over her head. "Real. Vulnerable. Mine." His hand paused. "Take your pick."

Real, vulnerable...

Mine.

She squeezed her eyes shut against a swell of happiness so startling she didn't know how to handle it.

But she understood what he meant. Something had passed between them last night. Between his opening up to her, and her showing him the side of herself no one but Margot ever saw...

The scared, hurt, lonely girl who she'd hidden behind sass and bravado years ago.

But last night, he'd seen her at her lowest, and he'd held her in his arms until she'd exhausted herself and fallen asleep.

She burrowed into his chest now as that sweet sensation was joined by something else that...wasn't bad. But it made her feel exposed and raw.

Vulnerable was probably the right word for it.

She felt vulnerable in the wake of him seeing so much of her. But with each stroke of his hand and with each reassuring beat of his heart beneath her cheek, she found herself settling into the feeling rather than fighting it.

And somehow, the exposed raw sensation began to feel more intimate than terrifying.

This, she supposed...this was what it meant to trust a man.

Her fingers curled into the fabric of his chest. "You think I'm yours, hmm?"

His hand stilled, but his voice was warm and laced with amusement. "Aren't you?"

Yes.

She swallowed hard. And when she finally spoke, her tone was teasing. "Well, I am your ward."

His hands stilled and he used a finger beneath her chin to tip her head up. "No. None of that."

The stern expression made her belly flutter wildly.

"None of what?"

"No games." With a twist of his lips, he added, "Much as I might love them."

She felt stripped bare under his knowing gaze. Squirming a little, she tore her chin from his grip and sat upright. "I don't know what you want me to say."

He watched her for a long moment. "This terrifies you, doesn't it?"

She looked away, out the window where the morning light seeped in.

Yes. Of course it did. He couldn't possibly know how much.

He sat upright. "Look at me, love."

She resisted for a moment but with a huff, turned to face him.

"Everyone you've ever loved has either left you or betrayed you."

The words stung and she wrapped her arms around herself. "Not Margot."

"No, not Margot. But you've had to be strong for both of you. You had to be brave and strong for both your sakes."

She frowned. "So?"

"So…I understand you're scared," he said.

She peeked up at him. "Can't you just bed me like any other man would?"

He smiled at her pout. "I will have you, love. Make no mistake. The moment I laid hands on you—no, before that. From the moment I set eyes on you, I knew that you were mine. You belong with me, and I with you."

She drew in a shaky breath but it didn't seem to fill her lungs.

He reached out and cupped her face in the palm of his hand. "But I need you to know that."

Her lips curved down. What did he want from her?

As if he could read her thoughts, he tugged her forward until she fell against his chest.

She gasped for air and found herself surrounded by Edmund. His scent, his power, his will.

She was helpless in the face of it. Energized by it, but also overwhelmed by it. He was so much more than any man she'd ever known. He was clever and insightful, ambitious and surprisingly caring...

And he wanted her.

More than that, he wanted her to drop her guard, to let him all the way in.

Could she?

The thought made her heart slam and race.

The curve of his mouth was wicked. Knowing.

"I will bed you, Savina. Have no doubt. But when I do, you will be mine in every way."

The dark promise in his words made her shiver.

"There will be no doubt who owns this body, love." He slid a hand into the bodice of her dress, cupping her breast in his firm grip. "This is mine."

"Yes," she breathed, tilting her head back so he could trail kisses down her neck.

Her skin broke out in goosebumps and her nipple hardened against his palm.

He took his hand away and she made a whining sound in protest.

"What else is mine, hmm?" He slid his hand lower, over her belly, molding her hip. He inched up the fabric of her gown and slid a hand underneath.

She was panting now, eager for his touch. So very ready to stop thinking. This sexual game she understood. And when his hand slid up her thigh, she moaned, high and breathless. "Yes, stepfather. Please touch me."

She saw his response instantly. The way his eyes darkened and his erection grew.

Her mouth watered at the sight and her fingers were frantic as she reached for the fastening. His hand came over hers.

She pouted and his chuckle was dark as he caught her lower lip between his teeth.

"You still need to punish me for the way I teased poor Benedict," she whispered when he moved away.

"Christ, you're going to be the death of me," he muttered. "I'm trying to teach you another lesson, pet. A lesson in what it means to be mine."

She knew what he meant. He wanted to talk about last night. About what they were to each other.

He wanted her to give him more than she could give.

Her body was his already and they both knew it. But that wasn't enough for her greedy prince.

She shifted so she was sitting on her heels. "What does it mean to be yours…Your Highness?"

"Savina…"

But she was already leaning forward and with a flick of her fingers had his breeches undone and his large, proud shaft in her hands.

He groaned when she tentatively wrapped her hands around it.

"Goodness, it's big." She glanced up at him from half lowered eyelashes. "Are they always this big?"

"Christ," he bit out. "You're trying to kill me, aren't you?"

She shifted back so her head could lower, but she held his gaze from beneath her eyelashes. "I'm trying to tell you that I understand that I am yours to control." She licked the tip of his cock hesitantly, encouraged when his hand slid into her hair and gripped her head tight.

"I mean to make you mine in every way, Savina. As my wife…"

The word lingered in the air and knocked her in the gut like a blow.

"As my wife, Savina. My partner." His hand in her hair forced her gaze up and she knew he had to see the fear in her eyes as he added, "You will have my name and all that I have."

Her throat was tight with emotion, her heart clamoring to believe him even as some part of her fought it.

He was asking her for everything. Her heart. Her soul. Her trust.

"I will not have you like this when you are my ward. My stepdaughter. My mistress."

Those words, at least, sparked a challenge, and that was a blessed relief compared to the confusing emotions he stirred in her.

With renewed determination, she brought her attention back to the hard shaft in her hands.

Desire she understood. This she could offer…

"Savina, listen to me…" He broke off with a groan of pleasure as she dipped her head and slid his cock between her lips. She tormented the man by experimenting with licks and sucks, savoring his every groan and taking every opportunity to explore his body as he'd done to her.

"Take off your gown, you naughty little minx."

His growl set her blood on fire, and she hurried to do as he bid.

"Take it all off, I want to see every inch of you."

Soon she was naked, kneeling before him.

He leaned back against the pillows. "Touch yourself."

Breathless, she did as he ordered, cupping her breasts, sliding a hand over her belly...

"Touch yourself where you're aching right now, my love."

My love.

The words wrapped around her and made her that much wetter. By the time she slid her fingers between her thighs, she cried out at the feel of her own wet, hot heat.

Stroking his hard shaft, he watched her. And in that moment...he was no prince. He was a bloody king.

And she knew she'd do anything he asked of her.

Will you trust him enough to give him your heart?

"Fuck yourself, princess. Slide your fingers into your cunny and show me what a naughty girl you really are."

That hard knot inside her started to come undone the moment his voice turned gruff and commanding.

Her head fell back, and her back arched. "Yes, sir," she whimpered.

She gasped at the odd sensation of her own fingers filling her hole. And when he leaned forward, his tongue darting out to part her slit while her fingers moved in and out, she could hardly stand it.

He glanced up at her, his look devious. "Is this mine, love?"

She nodded.

He pulled back. "Say it."

This time she hesitated just to see what he'd do. They both knew her body was his.

"Naughty girl, playing games," he murmured. "You want me to punish you, hmm?"

Her inner muscles clamped around her fingers as she nodded eagerly.

In this she had no shame.

No shame...and no fear.

It was everything else he wanted to give her that was terrifying.

"On your knees then, my naughty ward." He nodded to the floor. "If this is what you need to surrender, then so be it."

To surrender.

Her heart flipped.

Yes, that was exactly what he was asking of her. For her surrender. And she couldn't do that...

She couldn't give him all of her.

Could she?

Moments later, she didn't have to answer that question. Her mind went blissfully blank as she knelt beside the bed and waited for him to master her in the way she craved.

He knew exactly what she needed as he disrobed and stood before her, his hard cock thick and straight and so close it teased her parted lips.

"Open." He used his hand and took hold of her jaw, parting her mouth even wider. "Now you're going to take your guardian's cock in your mouth and you're going to let him fuck that saucy little mouth of yours until you're willing to admit that you need me by your side and in your life...not just in your bed."

Her eyes widened, but before she could protest, he did what he'd threatened. He shoved his cock into her mouth and used her hair to tilt her head back to take as much as she was able.

It was only when the head of his cock hit the back of her throat that he stopped. His gaze met hers. "Good girl."

Her pussy wept in response. Clenching and throbbing, her inner muscles spasmed as if she was about to climax herself from sucking his cock.

He slid in and out, his thrusts growing harder as he gave her sharp commands. "Touch your tits...that's right, show your master how you like to be fondled…did I say you could touch your pussy, little brat?"

She moaned as his thrusts grew more urgent, his hands in her hair more brutal.

When he pulled out of her mouth, she nearly sobbed as she begged for more.

"You want me inside you?"

She nodded, her lips chafed and her body pulsating with need. And…she'd never felt so alive.

He studied her, his jaw tight, and his eyes dark.

She could have sworn he saw all of her. Every sin, every flaw, every shameful deed.

"You are perfect, Savina," he hissed. "You are perfect, and you are mine."

Her knees were starting to ache, her whole body trembled…but his gaze held her there.

"Say it," he ordered.

She shook, a tremble starting in her belly and spreading out to her core.

He reached down and scooped her into his arms. "Not ready yet, hmm? I suppose you need another lesson to get that blasted clever mind of yours out of the way so you can be free."

His words made no sense to her, but it was still an odd sort of relief when he pointed to the bed frame. "Bend over, Savina. You'll admit your mine yet. And not just your body…"

She hurried over to the bed frame and bent over it, her bare bottom in the air.

He came behind her, his hard shaft brushing against her bottom as he gripped her hips. "I'll give my future wife a spanking, love. But I'm not going to give you my cock until you say it. Understood?"

She bit her lip. The need was already more than she could

bear. The empty ache inside her was so painful her thighs trembled with it. But he was right. She needed that relief...

Now more than ever. With all that he was asking from her...

She turned her head to look over her shoulder at the man who'd broken through her walls and stolen her heart. "Teach me a lesson, Stepfather."

His nostrils flared. "Stubborn little brat," he grunted. And then he swung his hand back and let it land with a smack that made her cry out in relief.

The sting was sweet and brought about the sharp focus she'd come to crave. It blurred everything else in its wake and made her entire world come down to the sensations.

Her skin tingled with it, and she was achingly aware of the chill that made her nipples hard and the warmth of Edmund's big hand as he smoothed it over her arse cheek, soothing the stinging flesh.

"Ready to admit you love me?" His tone held a challenge that stirred her and made her hips arch, eager for more.

He gave it, another smack that made the flesh of her bottom jiggle and the soft place between her thighs grow ever more sensitive.

His hard shaft settled between her arse cheeks and he stroked it once, twice.

His breathing was as ragged as hers with this tension.

They both needed relief. She wiggled her bottom in invitation and earned herself another spanking.

"Yes," she hissed. "I need that. I want that."

"Why?"

His voice was close to her ear as he leaned over her, pressing his chest to her back as he reached around to cup her breasts, grinding his cock between her thighs as they both moaned.

"Why?" he said again. This time he pinched her nipples hard. "Answer your husband when he asks you a question."

"You're not my husband."

"I will be."

Said so simply, it made her knees go weak. He caught her about the waist, holding her in place.

He was crushing her to the bed now, and with his knee he spread her legs further as he situated his cock against her entrance. It was a cruel tease, so close but not penetrating.

"Why do you want a spanking, love?" He spoke as though he already knew the answer.

"Because I love it."

"You love when I take control. Yes, I know. But it's more. Why do you want me to punish you when I could be making love to you?"

She stiffened beneath him and his hand moved lower, covering her belly in a way that felt somehow more intimate than when he'd cupped her tits.

This was soothing more than sexual, and it made her throat tighten.

He nuzzled her neck, burying his lips in her hair. "I'm working on a plan, Savina. And when I'm through, I'll be able to make you my wife."

"You can't," she whispered.

"Why not?"

She shifted and he let her go. She spun around in his arms. "I'm a whore."

"You're my wife."

Her eyes welled with humiliating tears. "I'm not. I'm your stepdaughter. I'm your mistress. And I'm no virgin."

His kiss was hard and merciless. "You are all of those things and more." He crushed her to him. "And that's why I love you."

She gasped as he kissed her, and then moaned into his mouth as it slanted over hers.

"You are brave and strong, and you're so dirty in bed that I feel as though you must have been made just for me," he breathed into her ear. "You did bad things, yes. And I've done far worse. Don't you see that's why we are meant to be?"

She choked on a sob and his next hungry kiss swallowed it.

He gave her bottom a light spanking that made her squeak. "Get on the bed and spread your legs wide for your husband."

It was the commanding tone that she couldn't refuse, and really…she didn't want to refuse. She was tired of fighting it.

On her back, her legs spread wide, he loomed over her. "I'm going to fuck you, my beautiful bride. But first…"

He knelt over her, his hand clamping over her sex, his fingers teasing her slick channel. "First you're going to tell me that you're mine."

Her lips quivered, her heart leapt.

Fear threatened to rise up. But he seemed to see that and his grip on her sex grew harsh. "Say it."

Her eyes welled with tears, but she fought past the choking sensation and her gaze met his as she whispered, "I'm yours, Edmund. And I…I love you."

The tenderness in his eyes nearly undid her, and the last of that hard knot disappeared as his grip on her pussy turned to soothing, tantalizing strokes and he leaned down to kiss her gently. "Good girl."

He spread her legs wider and grazed his nose against hers. "Now. Let's see how hard my wife likes to be fucked."

A grin split her face and she laughed, breathless with relief. It felt like a dozen years of defensive walls had come tumbling down, and she opened her arms as well as her legs.

"Yes, please…husband."

She hadn't thought he could get any harder, but calling him husband had done the trick.

She wrapped her arms around his waist and moaned when he slid his thick bulge inside her. "Show me how to take my husband's cock."

He groaned in her ear and then kissed her hard as they rocked together, finding a rhythm that set them both on fire.

She'd never experienced anything like it, this wanton need so easily satisfied by his brutal thursting. She welcomed it, her fingers digging into his arse cheeks as he pounded her. His appreciative grunts filled her head, a delicious smile cresting her lips as his speed and urgency grew with fervor.

"Yes," she begged him, her sex milking his shaft as his body began to vibrate.

A low, guttural moan grew in his throat, spilling out of him as his thrusts turned reckless and uncontrolled. Gliding her hands up his taut back, she held him close as he arched, his chest and neck muscles straining. Ecstasy stole over his face as he pumped her again, her name coming off his lips in a strangled cry as he released his seed inside her.

32

The next day Margot was sore, yes. But she certainly wasn't an invalid.

Memories of Callan taking her innocence in the glade sizzled through her. She couldn't fight her smile as she thought of the aftermath. He lay over her, his body a delicious weight atop her as he recovered. He'd gazed down at her, gently touching her face, then whispering, "Are you ready?"

"For what?" She'd been perplexed, but his tender smile had eased her nerves as he gently took her hand and led her into the pond.

The cold water shocked her skin but cleaned away the evidence of her lost innocence. His hands were careful as he washed between her thighs, cupping her sex and kissing her deeply.

As her body adjusted to the cold water, the heat between them rose to a fervor. His shaft grew hard and greedy before they could leave the pond and she was once more begging. He gave into her pleas with barely a protest, lifting her against him in the water.

Her legs wrapped around his muscly torso as he pressed her back against a rock and drove into her for a second time that day. Her cries of pleasure echoed in the forest as her wet, god-like beast took her in the pond with an animalistic growl that made her heart soar.

And here she was again, in the water, although the tub was not nearly as erotic as their pond.

"You know you don't have to bathe me, Callan," she murmured. "I'm not a child."

He made a grunting sound, no doubt in amusement because her protest was somewhat ruined by the fact that her head was rolling to the side against the edge of the tub and her words had come out slurred and slow.

In her defense, she hadn't gotten much sleep. Callan had been rather...insatiable.

Between bouts of lovemaking they'd snuggled and talked about everything and nothing.

Well...she'd done most of the talking. But he wouldn't stop asking her questions, his curiosity about her and her history seemingly endless.

She'd gotten some stories out of him, though. He didn't want to frighten her with tales from his time in the war, but he did tell her about his childhood in a small village, and how he'd learned to hunt and fish and fend for himself.

He kept telling her she had to sleep, to get her rest. But Margot had discovered any number of ways to change his mind.

Truly, he was easy to convince. A light touch, a kiss to his chest... and he was ready to bed her again without much prompting at all. But much to her delight, Margot had discovered early this morning that all she had to do was whisper that she couldn't wait to have his babies, and...well...

It seemed Callan liked that image very much indeed.

She was tempted to try it again right now, but her dratted eyelids kept trying to shut, and not even the feel of his hands sliding over her with the soap could rouse her...much.

She was starting to drift off when the cold air woke her and she found herself snuggled against Callan's chest as he carried her to bed...

To *his* bed.

She started to protest but his voice was a low soothing rumble in his chest. "Sleep." He set her gently on top of the covers "You need sleep."

The last thing she remembered was the feel of his lips and the stubble of his jaw as he pressed a kiss to her forehead.

She woke some time later, disoriented but cozy.

Callan had piled blankets on her, no doubt because she'd been naked and wet when he'd set her in here. But now she was dry, and warm, and...

Completely confused as to what time it was.

Or where Callan was for that matter.

The chirping of birds outside the window told her it was still day and she sat up, oddly sad to find herself alone.

True, he was probably doing Callan things. Finding them food or boiling their water. Or splitting logs...

Still, she was greedy for more of him. And not just in that way. Though...a blush crept into her cheeks as she recalled the night before, and just how much she'd enjoyed having him.

All of him.

The thought had her hopping out of bed. She paused long enough to snag one of his shirts and throw it on. She headed out of his room, but paused when she heard something utterly unfamiliar in this cottage...

Voices.

A warning pang shot through her, even though she knew it was silly. But still...

One of the male voices she didn't recognize, and while she knew Callan's, she'd never heard him sound like this. Like…

Like he was trying not to be heard.

Instinct had her moving softly, quietly. It wasn't like she was trying to eavesdrop. She was just…being cautious.

But the closer she drew, the more her heart hammered.

Which was so ridiculous.

She inched toward the crack in the door, and stopped just short of being seen.

"I told you, I handled it." Callan's voice was so low she barely heard it.

"Yeah, well, her majesty wants proof." The other man's tone was sharp and filled with dry humor. "You want to get paid? Show me where you buried the body."

"You doubt my word, it's your body they'll be looking for."

Margot shivered and pressed her back against the wall. Her heart rattled as her hands grew clammy.

"Who told you how to find me?"

She flinched on the other man's behalf. There was something dangerous in Callan's tone, even though he didn't raise his voice or make a threat. It was underneath his words, a cold, hard sharpness that made Margot's belly quiver with fear.

The other man didn't seem to hear it, though.

"Pete told me."

There was a silence that Margot hated. It made her legs shake along with her belly.

Who was this man?

What business did he have with Callan?

Whatever it was, she knew better than to show herself.

"I don't believe you," Callan growled. "He wouldn't give my location away."

The words dropped into Margot's belly like rocks. Her chest felt too tight as her fingers clenched the edges of Callan's shirt.

"Can't trust anyone in this world, now can we? Not when a shiny piece of gold is being offered. Even friends can be turned for the right amount of money." The man's taunting tone made Margot wince.

Did he not know that Callan was dangerous? Could he not hear the trouble he was in?

"Give me proof the girl's dead and we won't have no trouble." The man stated it so simply, as if they were discussing a Sunday picnic and not some girl's death.

Margot's heart stuttered in her chest.

Some girl…

Wait…

"What other information did you get from Pete?" Callan's voice was low and…easy. Almost conversational.

Margot struggled to draw in an even breath. There was something so wrong about the way he was talking, about what this man was saying…

It was all wrong, and yet…

Her stomach heaved.

"Pete?" The visitor moved, and Margot realized he was inside their cottage.

Well, Callan's cottage. But at some point she'd come to think of it as hers as well.

"I wouldn't worry 'bout Pete. Like I said, Pete had no problem giving me directions to this place." The man's tone turned to one of playful mockery. "Maybe he doesn't like you as much as you thought, eh?"

Callan's voice was as cold as ice. "Or maybe he likes you even less."

The sound that followed wasn't human. It was a guttural

noise, a whimpering choke, a gushing of blood. It was a sound she recognized...

It was the sound of death.

Margot's stomach heaved and she bent over, gripping her mouth with a quivering hand.

She wasn't aware she'd made a noise, but then came a thudding of feet and Callan was standing in front of her, glowering down with a steely blue glare.

It took her several seconds to catch her breath and be able to speak. "The girl..." She swallowed hard, her gaze falling to his blood-covered hands. "The girl you were supposed to kill..." She lifted her gaze to meet his. "It's me. You're supposed to kill *me*."

33

*I*t was night by the time Savina roused herself from her satisfied haze.

She turned to find Edmund hurriedly donning his clothes.

"Going somewhere?" she murmured sleepily.

He turned, and the crooked smile that softened his features made her heart feel like it was melting in her chest.

She swallowed hard against the surge of emotion as he came over to the side of the bed and brushed a lock of hair out of her face. "Mrs. Baker came to the door while you were sleeping. I have a visitor."

She frowned, her mind still sluggish. "You? Here?" She straightened. "Is it about Margot?"

He shook his head, his expression grim. "I'm afraid not. It's the man I hired to look into a certain matter in Lucinda's past."

She narrowed her eyes, but mostly in teasing. "Are you being intentionally vague?"

His smile grew and his eyes danced with a happiness

she'd never seen before. A contentedness that made her feel warm all the way through. He leaned down and kissed the top of her head. "Get dressed and you can hear what he has to say for yourself."

Savina flew out of bed and hurried into her gown. Even so, she came into the meeting between Edmund and his man too late. Edmund held up a piece of paper and turned to her with a look of such triumph she couldn't help but return his smile.

"Mr. Miller here may very well have found the answer to our problems." He grabbed Savina by the shoulders and gave her a hard kiss, regardless of the other man's presence. "I must go, darling. Immediately. If his information proves accurate…"

Mr. Miller cleared his throat and made some excuse to give them privacy. Neither she nor Edmund paid him any mind.

"What information? What do you mean?" Savina asked.

He leaned forward until his forehead rested against hers, and Savina's heart thudded wildly at this new intimacy between them, new and precious and…

Well, still a little terrifying.

"Do you trust me?" he asked, his voice low and gruff.

"I…" She closed her mouth, opened it, and then shut it. He drew in a deep breath, and was just about to pull away with a resigned sigh when she finally found her voice. "Yes. I do trust you."

He stilled, his gaze on her as he pulled back slightly. Whatever he saw in her expression had his gaze heating to molten lava right before her eyes. "Then I must go."

She frowned. "What?"

"I have to follow where this leads." He held up the parchment again.

She rested her hands on his chest. "Edmund, trust goes both ways, you know…" She arched a brow meaningfully and his head fell with a rueful laugh.

"You're right, my love." He kissed the tip of her nose. "You are right. Keeping my plans to myself will be a difficult habit to break, so bear with me, hmm?"

She laughed and held her hand out. He gave it to her readily but the name and address meant nothing to her. "Should I know who this gentleman is?"

"If my guess is correct, it's Lucinda's first husband."

"Benedict's father? But he's—"

"Dead?" Edmund supplied drily. "Yes, that's what she's led everyone to believe. But just as I grew suspicious about the way her story changed regarding you and Margot's absence, and the way I found her stories a little too convenient…the same was true for her tragic tales about her first husband's early demise."

"But…" Savina frowned, trying to recall the story of her first husband. But she'd been too young to care back then. "You think…you think he did not die….?"

"I think for a clever, ambitious woman like Lucinda, faking the death certificate of a man of no consequence who lived a quiet, hermit-like life in the middle of a godforsaken countryside—"

"Yes," Savina breathed, nodding as her mind caught up with what this would mean.

"If he never died, then…"

"Then her marriage to your father was never legal," he supplied. "And her marriage to me…"

"Is null and void," Savina finished.

They shared a long look, and Savina tried to keep hope in its place.

She failed. Hope blossomed and grew until her hands

shook as she reached for him. He pulled her into his arms and held her tight.

"I told you, I will make you my wife." He pulled back to add, "And do not think for one moment that I've forgotten about your sister. I still have men scouring the forest for any signs of her."

Savina hesitated, but then she admitted, "So do I."

He arched one brow, and she waited for his irritation, but it never came. He kissed her forehead. "Of course you do, darling. Of course you do."

"You should go." She gave him a nudge toward the door. "If this man truly exists then you must get to him before Lucinda finds out that you know."

"Yes, you're right." He was already hurrying toward the front door, and Mr. Miller preceded him out. He turned to pull her into his arms and kiss her soundly. "I will be back, love. I promise you, I will be back for you. Nothing could keep me away."

Her heart fluttered at the intensity in his gaze. He knew... he knew how much she needed to hear that. Especially now after she'd lain her heart open to this man and admitted that she loved him.

She gripped his lapels and forced a smile. "You'd better be back, and soon."

With a low growl he kissed her hungrily, not stopping until they were forced to come up for air. Then he took his leave, and Savina shut the door behind him with a sigh.

It was so late the servants were still in their quarters, and Savina felt a wave of loneliness.

But he'd be back. He'd promised.

A hard knock on the door had her straightening, a laugh on her lips as she turned to open it. Edmund. He'd be back for one more kiss—

She swung the door open, but…it wasn't Edmund.

"What are you doing here?"

Her visitor's smile was as broad and charming as ever, not faltering until he struck her with the back of his hand and her vision turned to black.

She made the gesture again as though she had forgotten.

"What are you doing here?"

He rolled onto his back, his elbows slumming from the ... him ... he reached for ... with the flick of his hand and he waited for a reaction.

34

allan towered over Margot, his scowl deep and fierce. "You're frightened."

Margot eased her grip on the edge of his shirt and forced herself to straighten. All the while she met his gaze as she turned over his words.

Was she frightened?

She bit her lip and then said, "Not of you."

The tension in him seemed to ebb. "You should be."

She lifted a shoulder. Perhaps she should. Unless she was mistaken, he'd just murdered a man.

In their kitchen.

"You were supposed to kill me," she said.

His grunt was a yes.

She swallowed hard, her mind back on that fateful day when he'd descended on their carriage like the horrible beast he was made out to be.

A tremor of fear surfaced at the memory, and he saw it.

He took a step forward, the glower back, creasing his brow.

She forced her mind to the present. He hadn't hurt her then, and he'd never hurt her since.

"You didn't kill me." The moment the words came out, she wished she could call them back.

What a silly thing to say. But her mind was still hazy with the scent of blood and death coming from the other room.

"No. I did not," he murmured.

She let out a little huff of exasperation. Pushing away from the wall, she moved toward him until she was so close she could feel the warmth that radiated from him. Even now, everything in her wanted to seek comfort in his arms.

He eyed her warily, not moving.

So as not to frighten me. She knew it like she knew her own name. He was worried that she'd be scared of his touch.

Something in her chest seemed to snap in two, and she closed the distance between them, wrapping her arms around his waist, and closing her eyes to savor the sound of his strong heartbeat as his arms closed around her tightly, his face buried in her hair.

"You didn't kill me," she said again. "Why?"

There were other questions to ask. Obviously. But this seemed the most pressing.

His large hand moved over her, his palm so big it seemed to cover her entire lower back as he pressed her in close. "Couldn't," he rasped. "I took one look at you and…I couldn't."

She swallowed hard, her eyes welling with tears at how close she'd come to losing her life. Savina wouldn't have recovered and…

"Savina!" She pulled back with a gasp. "Is Savina in danger?"

He frowned down at her. And that was her answer. He didn't know.

"Who…who hired you?"

But she knew. Of course she knew.

"Your stepmother."

A trembling took over her entire body, starting from low in her belly and spreading outward. "But...w-why?"

Callan huffed, part anger and part frustration. Then he scooped her into his arms and sat her on his bed. "Stay," he ordered.

She pulled her knees up and nodded.

He left and she heard him working in the other room. *Cleaning up his mess...*

The thought brought with it a hysterical giggle and she clamped a hand over her mouth.

This wasn't humorous. Not in the least. She squeezed her eyes shut and focused on her breathing and the sound of birds outside her window. Anything other than the rustle of her lover cleaning up the dead body...

The man he'd killed. For her.

Reason told her that much. The man who'd come to their door had been checking up on him to ensure she was dead.

That was how badly Lucinda wanted her out of the picture.

But why?

And Savina...

She squeezed her eyes shut tighter as fear for her sister bombarded her.

When Callan entered at last, not even sparing her a glance as he gathered sparse belongings and threw them into a sack.

She scrambled to her feet. "Callan, my sister—"

"I will protect her. And you." He paused in the midst of his packing. "We must go."

She nodded, her heart in her throat as she let Callan help her back into her gown.

He hastened her out of the cabin, with all of the necessary supplies, his gaze alert as he took in their surroundings.

But the woods were still as they set out. Even so, Callan moved them quietly and cautiously. Margot was starting to wonder if he was being paranoid, but that was when it happened.

A twig snapped in the distance. Callan halted. He turned slowly, taking in the trees and brush.

The first man to attack seemed to come out of nowhere, and Margot screamed as the figure lunged for Callan.

Callan caught the man with a swing of his fist before they hit the ground, and tumbled across the damp earth. They flew into a furious tussle as more dark figures rushed toward them, seemingly from every direction.

Margot screamed and braced for impact, but not one of them was heading for her. Their attention was fixed on Callan.

And that was when Margot began to actually look at their faces. The one wrestling Callan on the ground looked familiar. Her breath caught as she recalled hugging this man who the others called Beast.

Two beasts. Her lips parted in shock as she watched hers battle the one she'd left behind in Vestry Lane. But it was the sight of another familiar figure rushing toward them that jolted her out of her surprise. "King? King!"

Everyone seemed to take notice of her at once, and King came to a sudden stop to turn and face her. His eyes grew round with recognition, a small smile lighting the corners of his face before he rounded back on Callan, a rageful glare transforming his features as he lifted his knife with a growl.

"King, no! Stop!"

35

*S*avina came to slowly, but the room around her seemed to tumble and swirl every time she opened her eyes.

She squeezed them shut, willing away nausea as she propped herself up on her elbows first and then shifted into a sitting position.

Once her head stopped spinning, she opened her eyes again, and this time...

Her stomach heaved.

She was in a cellar, it seemed. Someplace dark and dank, with stone walls and a dirt floor and...

Chains.

They rattled when she moved her limbs, and panic tore through her as they clanked against the cold stones.

She had chains on her hands and feet!

Horror seized her in its iron grasp.

What has happened to me?

She scrambled backwards until her shoulder hit the stone wall with a thud. Desperation flared as she tugged at the chains, the harsh metal digging into her delicate skin. Fingering the keyholes, her breathing grew short and erratic.

"I wouldn't waste my time if I were you." Benedict's voice reached her from the shadows and she sat upright with a start.

He ambled toward her with that blasted smile of his, so charming and sweet and...

False.

So utterly false. How had she not noticed that before?

He was yet another person again. How was it so?

How could one man transform from clueless dolt, to groping pervert to suave, deceitful, cold-hearted woman beater in such a short space of time?

He was a man of many faces and she hated herself for not seeing through him sooner.

"Where am I?" she bit out. "What have you done to Margot?"

Because surely this two-faced snipe must be involved in her sister's disappearance as well. It was with heart-sickening realization that she saw Benedict was capable of anything.

Just like his mother.

Her stomach pitched.

Edmund. Had he gotten to Edmund too?

She swallowed the question. Hopefully her prince was well away from here, on his way to expose Lucinda for the conniving fraud she'd always been.

"What a darling sister you are." He smirked. "Concerned with Margot's welfare when you yourself are...well, *here*." He laughed, as if this was a splendid joke.

The chains bit into her as she jerked and growled in frustration. "Where is Margot?"

"She's been taken care of." His smile fell and the meaning behind his words became clear.

Her heart plummeted, ice swimming through her veins.

She stopped fighting her bonds and stilled, barely able to choke out her denial. "No, you're wrong. You're wrong!"

He ignored her shouts, which made her agony that much worse.

She wanted him to argue, to engage. To do or say anything that would make him wrong.

Margot couldn't be gone. She'd know if anything had happened to her.

Wouldn't she?

Benedict crouched down before her, studying her like she was some specimen at a museum. Pinching her chin, he moved her head from side to side with a callous smile. She jerked away, freeing herself from his touch.

He let out a mirthless laugh. "It's unfortunate, really. If I recall, Margot was a good little girl." His lips twisted into a sneer. "Not a bloody whore like you."

Savina's lips trembled as she pulled them into a venomous scowl. He reached for her again and she tried to pull away but there was nowhere for her to go as he caught her jaw in a hard grip. "Such a tease, aren't you, Savina?" His finger trailed down the smooth line of neck, cresting the top of her heaving breasts. She wrestled against his touch, the chains rattling with complaint. "You use that body of yours to drive a man to distraction, and then have the nerve to push me away?"

She narrowed her eyes. "You're not man enough to have me."

He spat in her face, laughing when she winced at the grotesque blob of saliva that landed on her cheek. He let her go and stood, towering over her with arms folded. "It's history now, isn't it? You'll get what you deserve, mark my words."

"What have you done?" Savina's voice was low and savage. "What did you do with my sister?"

"Oh, it wasn't me, dear stepsister." He smiled, clearly enjoying himself as he rocked back on his heels. "Mother hires help for that sort of thing. You know the type, surely. The sort of mindless, cruel monsters you lived amongst in the rookery."

Her heart stuttered as she wiped his spit of her face with trembling fingers. They'd sent someone to kill dear, sweet Margot?

That was why she never arrived in Bristol.

Her stomach turned, bile rising in her throat.

The rest of his words were slower to register. And then he was talking again, strutting before her like a proud, ridiculous peacock. "Oh yes, Margot was easy to handle. You were the troublesome one, Savina." He wagged a finger like he was chastising a child. "Unfortunately, we didn't see you coming until it was too late." He smiled. "Couldn't very well slit your throat in the middle of a ball, now could we?"

She gaped up at this madman. How had she ever thought he was just a mild mannered pawn in his mother's games?

"I still think we ought to send you back to that whore-house in Vestry Lane." He leaned down, close enough that she could smell his sour breath. "I could pay Madame Bernadette good money to keep you…occupied by the foulest of men. Truly depraved souls."

Her stomach turned at the mere thought of Madame Bernadette's and the poor, unfortunate young women who'd been stuck there to pay off their father's debts by catering to the clients with the sickest perversions.

"You…you knew…" She stopped when he started to laugh.

"Did I know where you were all these years? Of course I did." He tilted his head to the side, his eyes glinting with pleasure. "You thought I didn't?"

She fought the urge to shout, the urge to cry…

None of that would do her any good right now. She needed to find a way out.

"Where am I?"

He straightened, his smile falling at the perfectly ordinary question. "Don't you recognize your own home? Your *old* home, I mean. It hasn't been yours for some time now, has it?"

Her heart faltered as her jaw fell open. She was…home?

She looked around her and…yes. She could see it now. She hadn't spent much time down here as a child, but now that she knew, she could practically hear Margot's laughter as they played a game of hide and seek behind the wine barrels and empty crates from the kitchen.

Margot…

She swallowed hard. Blast it all, she would not cry in front of this man.

He was watching her closely. Almost eagerly. Oh yes, he wanted her to break down.

He wanted to destroy her—shatter her soul into a million tiny pieces.

Well, he would get no satisfaction.

Her chin came up. *Never.*

"Edmund will find me. And he'll make you pay for this."

Benedict sneered. "Nice try, sister. But Edmund is off chasing a dead man." He rose to his feet.

Lucinda's voice came from the far end of the cellar. "He'll be a dead man himself soon, if he's not careful." She strode toward Savina with a cheerful smile, her hands clasped together like she was coming to welcome her to tea. "My darling husband has his uses, but I'm afraid he's beginning to be more trouble than he's worth."

Savina's heart tripped and fell. No. *No, no, no!*

Lucinda tilted her head to the side. "Did you really think my husband could fool me? I have eyes and ears everywhere,

347

my dear." She turned her head slightly to give Savina a knowing smirk. "You have been a naughty girl, haven't you?"

Savina glared up at her. "Why are you doing this? What have my sister and I ever done to you?"

"You?" Lucinda arched her brows in feigned surprise. "Why you've done nothing, dearest. Other than amuse me with your slattern ways." Her smile faltered a bit and anger flared in her eyes. "Little strumpet. It will serve you right to wind up back in the whorehouse."

Savina lunged forward, but the chains caught her, and all she managed to do was scrape her wrists as Lucinda and Benedict laughed.

"Why did you harm Margot?" she grit out between clenched teeth. The ache in her chest was unbearable, but she would not let them see her cry.

Still...

She needed answers. Margot was the gentlest of souls. Lucinda's hatred of her had never made sense.

Lucinda pursed her lips, seemingly thinking over whether she'd answer. Apparently her enjoyment of her position of power won out. "Haven't you guessed? Your sister saw too much. She wandered where she shouldn't have and has had to pay a price for that."

"What...what do you mean?"

"Your father was a dear, but he was far too devoted to you girls," she said simply. "He had to go."

"You...you..."

"Moved him along. Yes, darling. Do try and keep up."

Savina's vision swam as shock and horror welled inside her, making her shake with helpless fury. "He was sick—"

"Because I made him so." Lucinda's voice bristled with impatience. "And here I thought you were the smart one."

"But Margot—"

"Margot." Lucinda's voice held a world of derision in that

one simple word. "Sweet, kind, angelic Margot." Her tone was scathing now. "Your father doted on her, didn't he? And he never said no to the simpleton. She never knew her place."

"She was good—"

"Oh yes, well mannered, for certain. Far more pleasant than you. But she had no notion of privacy. She was always running into rooms where she didn't belong. Like your father's bedroom when he and I were…negotiating."

Savina squinted in confusion.

"I needed him to change the will, didn't I?" Lucinda's eyes were wide with feigned innocence. "Anyway, your sister saw things she shouldn't have."

"She didn't know what she saw."

"Of course she didn't. But that doesn't mean she wouldn't have said the wrong thing to the wrong person…like Edmund, for example."

Savina jolted upright at the mention of his name.

Edmund. *Edmund, where are you?*

"I knew I'd made the right decision sending you girls away the moment Edmund arrived on my doorstep asking all sorts of inconvenient questions."

"He never believed your answers," she whispered.

"No, I never assumed he did. But he had so little to go on, it hardly mattered. And being partners in business and in our home gave me the distinct advantage of being able to keep track of his findings."

"Yet, he still managed to find us."

Lucinda's frown was sudden and terrifying. Her eyes glinted with malice. "Benedict was right. I should have just killed you back then."

Benedict's lips twisted in a small smile when Savina glanced at him.

"But…" Lucinda heaved a sigh. "I'm too softhearted, I suppose. I couldn't bring myself to kill two little girls."

"So you left us to die in a gutter." Savina's voice was bathed in contempt and she did nothing to hide her baleful sneer.

Lucinda lifted a shoulder. "At least you had a fighting chance."

Her insides flashed with rage. "You wretched bitch! I'll kill you for—"

Benedict's fist collided with her jaw, cutting off her savage curse and leaving Savina bent over, blood dripping from her mouth as her vision went black.

"We should take her to the whorehouse now," Benedict snapped. "Or get rid of her once and for all."

"Not yet, dearest." Lucinda's feet came into view as she hovered over Savina's crumpled form. "She may prove useful if Edward becomes a problem. He seems to have grown attached to his little whore of a stepdaughter."

Benedict sighed.

"Soon, dearest," Lucinda cooed, her tone soothing and maternal. "She'll be out of our lives soon."

Lucinda aimed her next words at Savina, her tone turning ice cold. "Just like her sister." Lucinda crouched down, and it wasn't until too late that Savina noticed the wet cloth in Lucinda's hand. "But in the meantime, you and I have a ball to prepare for, Benedict. And you..." Her smile was too sweet as she lifted the damp cloth to cover Savina's mouth before she could scream. "We can't have you making any noise while preparations are underway, now can we?"

That was the last Savina heard before drifting off into a deep, dark stupor.

36

*E*dmund had a feeling something was wrong from the moment he left Savina behind.

He'd left Town in a hurry, and that haste bothered him with each mile he put between him and his future wife.

He'd hired a messenger to ride ahead of them, to get there as swiftly as possible while he'd gathered some men and made the arrangements to bring her former husband back with him. To ensure the man was there and that he knew they were coming. So perhaps he needn't be in such a hurry.

Perhaps he should turn back and try again when Savina was safe at his side.

"I've left her alone," he muttered when he and Mr. Miller changed horses.

The messenger would have been there already. If Lucinda's first husband was in fact still alive, he'd be waiting for Edward's arrival.

He stood there too long, deliberating. His eagerness to prove Lucinda a lying snake battling with this paranoia when it came to Savina's safety.

And it likely was just paranoia. She was likely safe and content in her townhome even now.

"She'll be all right," Mr. Miller said with a hand on his shoulder.

Edmund looked over with a start. He'd forgotten he'd spoken his concerns aloud.

Mr. Miller patted his shoulder in an off-puttingly familiar way. "Won't take long to get to this town and back, I'd suppose."

"You'd suppose" Edmund repeated.

He turned to face the cheerful-looking man. "Does that mean you do not know?"

Mr. Miller blinked. "What's that?"

Edmund turned to face him head on. "Mr. Miller, I was under the assumption that you'd sought out this gentleman I've been seeking. To do so, surely you must have traveled to the village yourself."

"Oh, er…" A bead of sweat broke out on Mr. Miller's forehead as he gave his head a shake. "Got the tip from someone else…" At Edmund's glower, he added. "Someone who should know. I trust the bloke."

Edmund opened his mouth to unleash a barrage of questions. But before he could utter a one of them, he heard shouts from outside the inn where they'd been waiting.

"What is it?"

A stable boy pointed down the road. "There's been an attack, sir. It's not safe to travel this road. Oh sir, you mustn't—"

But Edmund had found his horse and was hoisting himself up into the saddle, that same ominous feeling he'd been battling all day growing with intensity.

He gave his horse a kick, spurring him into a gallop until he caught sight of his messenger, who'd stopped to assist with a carriage accident.

Edmund pulled his horse to a stop. "What happened?"

A man who appeared to be the driver sat on the side of the road, pale and visibly shaken.

As Edmund dismounted, he smelled it.

The scent of death.

The messenger was a young boy and he looked like he might be ill.

"What are you doing here?" Edmund said, pushing the boy away from whatever unpleasantness lay inside the carriage. "You were supposed to go to—"

"I was there already, Your Highness," the boy interrupted. He pointed to the small carriage that was stopped at an awkward angle in the middle of the road. "The man...the one you sent me to fetch..."

Edmund's insides froze, and his gut twisted. "That's him."

The boy swallowed convulsively. "He looked terrified when I told him I was there on your behalf. He wouldn't listen to me when I said you'd be along shortly. He insisted on heading out straight away. Said he needed protection. Said he'd been threatened, and..."

Edmund scrubbed a hand over his face, trying and failing to block out the cloying scent. "What happened?"

"An attack, sir. Must've been a highwayman or some such thing. I'd ridden ahead so I didn't see. It was only when I realized he wasn't still following behind that I turned back and..."

"I see." Edmund was already heading back to his horse. His heart was clattering in his chest, an overwhelming sense of dread making him nauseous.

Lucinda had known he was coming.

Which meant...

He started to run, not stopping until he was on his horse and racing back toward London.

Please let her be safe.

353

For a man who'd never prayed once in his life, it was all he could do now as he sped toward the city.

Straight to the woman he loved.

37

*S*avina lost all concept of time.

She'd wake for a little, disoriented and queasy. Then much as she fought to stay awake, she'd find herself slipping into darkness again.

This time when she woke, it was only her painfully empty stomach that gave her any sense of how many hours had ticked by.

Her mouth was dry as sand and she groaned in pain as she moved her aching limbs on the cellar floor.

She had a vague recollection of seeing Benedict again. Of being dosed with whatever foul poison they were using to keep her quiet.

Between the drug, hunger, and thirst, she was almost eager to slide into oblivion again.

Only the thought of what would become of her if she did had her fighting to keep her eyes open.

Worry also kept her mind working as it tortured her with possibilities about what had become of Margot and Edmund.

Tears stung the back of her eyes and she drew in a shaky

breath as she struggled to sit upright. She'd only just righted herself when…she froze.

Her gaze darted to her left, into the deep, dark shadows that stretched beneath the stairs.

Had she heard something?

There it was again. Something soft and rustling and…

Rats, no doubt. With a convulse swallow, she peered into the shadows, getting ready to defend herself from the rodents. They'd nibble her skin and make her sick. Those filthy, vile creatures. Her mind reeled as she tried to comprehend the epic fall her life had taken.

Her breath quickened as she fought off the despair, then gave a jolt of surprise when the door above her screeched open and Benedict pounded down the steps.

As he came into view, she rose to her knees. Last time she'd been too weak, but now…

Well, now she was still weak, but at least she was fully awake. She'd use her chains to strangle him. She'd use her nails to scrape and claw.

Blast it all. She'd do whatever it took to be free of this place.

He had the keys to her chains on him. He'd taunted her with them during one of his visits, rattling them in front of her groggy eyes, laughing when she tried to whisper her foul insults, her words coming out slurred and incomparable.

"Ah, you're awake." His smile was oily and made her stomach revolt. "How lovely. I was beginning to think I wouldn't be able to have any fun with you before…well…" He stopped in front of her. "Before you're disposed of."

She bared her teeth in a snarl as she lunged to her feet. The chains rattled, tugging at her limbs like devil's talons.

Benedict snickered as she lurched at him, smacking her aside easily. She fell to the ground, landing on her arm with a painful thud while her ears began to ring.

"I'm so glad you're getting some spirit back, stepsister," he taunted as his hands came to the fastening of his breeches. "This will be so much more fun if you fight back."

She made a savage sound in the back of her throat as she tried to lift a foot to kick his groin.

But the shackles around her ankles were too heavy, and all she ended up accomplishing was grazing his shin with her toes...and making him cackle with glee.

"Oh, this is a pathetic sight." He crouched beside her. "I do hope you'll put up more of a fight than that when I fuck you." He stroked her cheek, which still ached from where he'd hit her earlier...

Or was it the day before?

She jerked her head back out of his reach and he laughed.

"Or maybe you'll be a crier." He pulled his shaft out and bile rose up her throat.

"Is this the only way you can get a woman to touch your ugly body, Benedict?" she spat. "I bet it is. I bet the only way you can get hard is if you're hitting a girl, am I right?"

"Shut your mouth." He backhanded her away, but this time she managed a laugh as she spit out blood.

"I know men like you, Benny. I know you better than you know yourself. You're a weak coward, unable to be a true man, and so you take it out on those who are even weaker—"

He grabbed her by her hair and dragged her upright until his cock was right in her face.

"You disgust me," she snarled. If he tried to force himself into her mouth, she would sink her teeth into him, bite down until he howled like a stuck pig. "You poor sniveling excuse of a man."

His face contorted with rage as he shoved her back. Her shoulder hit the wall, the chains letting out a dull clunk as he grabbed her ankle, dragging her across the harsh stones until she was on her back. She kicked and flailed, but the chains hindered her, giving him the upper hand as he tugged at her skirts, forcing her legs apart. "You filthy whore."

Fear clutched her as she tried to wriggle free, but he gripped her thighs, his fingers digging into her flesh as he wrenched her legs open.

Swallowing down her whimper, she fought for calm, control, begging her brain not to give into the fear that was threatening to freeze her.

She winced, as Benedict's foul fingers tore the fabric of her undergarments, then pinched the soft flesh of her upper thigh. No amount of bathing could ever get his stench off if he took her now.

She could not let this happen.

Swiping at his face, she tried to scratch him away, but he captured her wrist, forcing her arm back as he other hand went for her unprotected cunny.

His vile lips curled into a triumphant smirk. "Now I don't want you to enjoy this. I want—"

He stopped so suddenly, for a moment Savina flinched, waiting for a blow. But then his grip slackened.

His glare turned hollow as blood leaked out of his mouth.

Savina drew in a breath, ready to shriek in horror at the mask of death looming over her when…all at once, Benedict crumpled, and she found herself staring at a knife in the back of his neck, before looking up to see a man she knew like a real brother.

Well, a boy, really.

"K-king?"

"Let's get you out of here, Savvy." Her old friend knelt next to Benedict, a murderous look on his face as he pulled Savina's skirts back down, restoring her dignity.

"In his jacket pocket," she managed through frozen teeth, nudging Benedict off her ankle. She was still trying to keep up with what was happening, but at least some part of her mind was still functioning. "The keys for the chains are in his pocket."

King gave a grunt as he callously pushed Benedict over, treating the dead man like a sack of grain.

The heavy chains rattled against the wall when King worked the locks, freeing her aching wrists from their bonds.

Her eyes welled with tears at last when they hit the stone with a resounding clank. "King, they said Margot—"

"Is safe." He paused, looking at her, his gaze so serious and so certain that she started to weep.

"She's safe? You're certain?"

"I saw her myself. They did hire someone to kill her, but...well...I'll let her tell you that story."

She wasn't sure, but she thought she saw a flicker of amusement in his eyes.

"We have to hurry." He took her hand and stood. "We have to get you and Margot out of town before—"

"No." Her legs wobbled as he helped her to her feet, but her voice was firm. "Take Margot to safety, but I'm not going anywhere until I know Edmund is all right."

He frowned as he studied her, reading her features. But a noise at the top of the steps interrupted whatever he was going to say.

"Come on." He tightened his grip on her hand, pulling her away from the stairs. "There's a back entrance we can get to from here."

38

*J*f it wasn't for Callan's strong, steadying presence beside her, Margot surely would've gone mad by now.

As it was, she paced the edge of the small garden behind her childhood home.

Callan and King hadn't wanted her to come this far, but hidden in the shadows, and with Callan at her side—she was safe, and they all knew it.

It was Savina they were worried about.

A quick visit to her home and to a panicking housekeeper had ratcheted up her fears until it was unbearable. This waiting would be the death of her.

"She was just…gone," the housekeeper had blubbered, her hands twisting. "I sent word to Prince Edmund but he'd left the city, and I'd hoped she'd return on her own, but…"

The woman had wept, and Margot had found herself consoling the lady as she herself struggled to keep her composure.

Panic threatened, worse than any fears she'd had on her own behalf. And blinding her to all else.

She didn't even fear running into Lucinda or her men.

Callan was with her. He'd keep her safe.

She'd wanted him to go in with King to see if he could help find Savina, but both he and King had agreed that Callan would only cause suspicion.

They'd watched servants and workers heading in and out all day in preparation for a ball, and unlike Callan, King wouldn't be recognized. And with his average size, he wouldn't stand out.

And so here they were.

Waiting.

Callan caught her by the waist the next time she passed him, and she let him drag her close, burrowing into his chest and gripping his shirt as a shuddering breath left her.

"I cannot bear it a second longer, Callan."

"I know, love." He stroked her hair and held her tight.

She pressed her cheek to his chest to hear the steady, reassuring beat of his heart.

He was the only thing holding her together, and had been ever since they'd run into King and his crew in the woods.

They'd joined forces with the men Edmund had sent to find her, and by the time they got back to London, Margot had felt like she was traveling with her own personal army.

But any comfort that had brought her vanished when they'd arrived at Savina's doorstep to find that she'd been missing for nearly two full days.

But King would find her.

She had to believe that.

He had every man in his network searching for her, questioning every servant and urchin in her neighborhood, and finally they'd gotten word that someone had seen her being carried into a carriage in the early morning with a young gentleman. The description soon led them all to the same conclusion.

Benedict.

And so now she was here. Back at her childhood home. The place that had once held so many wonderful memories, and now...

Her gaze took in the trees that her father had planted for her, the vines that now covered every inch of a trellis. "I hate it here," she whispered. "There's nothing left of my father anymore. Only cruelty and evil."

"We'll be gone just as soon as we find your sister," Callan promised.

She nodded, holding onto his certainty.

King would find her.

And he'd find her alive.

There was no other scenario Margot could entertain.

Her fingers clenched the fabric of his shirt. She had to be alive. She just had to.

She felt Callan stiffen first, then she heard it. Twigs snapping and leaves crunching...

She spun around and a choked sob escaped when she saw King...and Savina. Margot rushed to her side.

King seemed to be holding her upright, and her face was bruised and bloody but when Margot reached her, Savina lurched forward with a sob of her own and soon the two were clutching each other, weeping as they held each other upright.

"You're alive," Savina whimpered.

She said it so many times and with such overwhelming emotion, Margot squeezed her eyes shut, feeling the pain of whatever her sister had suffered.

"She told me you were dead." Savina pushed back just enough to eye Margot as if she couldn't quite believe she was there. "But you're all right."

Margot nodded. "I'm fine. But you..."

Now it was Margot's turn to study her sister, and what she saw made her heart ache. "What has she done to you?"

Savina's jaw clenched and her gaze hardened. "Nothing she won't pay for."

Callan made a quiet huffing noise behind her and Margot smiled. He approved of that sentiment, no doubt.

"Come, we must get you home," Margot said. "Callan, will you help her?"

King was already peering through the hedges and checking out who might stand in their way.

Savina's eyes widened slightly when she noticed Callan hovering just behind Margot.

"Savina, this is Callan, he's my...um...he's, well..." She trailed off with a blush that she hoped wasn't apparent in the dark.

Callan settled a hand on her shoulder. "I'm hers."

Margot couldn't help but smile at that. Yes, that worked. To Savina, she said, "Callan will help get you back to—"

"No." Savina shook her head, and then wobbled dangerously. Callan caught her by her elbow.

"Come, we'll get you food and drink," he said softly.

Savina squeezed her eyes shut as if she could persevere through sheer will.

"Savina, don't be stubborn. I know you want vengeance, but—"

"I need to know what's happened to Edmund." She nodded toward King. "His men say Edmund left town and hasn't returned, and—"

"Edmund," Margot repeated. "The Prussian prince?"

Savina's breathing grew shallow and her eyes welled with tears. "He's more than that to me, Margot. He's...he's..." She glanced up at Callan and then back to Margot. "He's everything."

364

Margot's throat grew tight at the emotions in her sister's eyes. "We'll find him then."

"We will," King said as he came over to join them. "I swear we'll find him, Savvy. But not now. Not when you're so weak."

Savina's chin set and her brows drew down. Margot knew that stubborn look well. Savina wouldn't go anywhere without finding out what Lucinda knew about Edmund.

Margot moved closer and clutched her shoulders, forcing Savina to meet her gaze. "Savina, you and I are both in danger if we stay here any longer."

"That's right," King said, clearly catching on. "Margot is in danger here. You said so yourself that Lucinda will stop at nothing to get rid of Margot."

Savina nodded, her expression torn. "That's true." To Margot she added softly, "I know why now, Snow. It's because...she murdered our father. And...apparently you saw something you shouldn't have when you barged in on them—"

"I did? But I didn't know...I..." Guilt swamped Margot unexpectedly. Silly, to be sure, but she couldn't fight it. "So all this time, it was my fault—"

"No." Savina cupped her face between her palms as Callan settled a hand against her lower back. "No, dearest, none of this was your fault. It's Lucinda's fault, all of it. And she will pay."

Callan growled his agreement.

"But not now," Margot whispered with a look to King.

"She's right. We've got to regroup. Come up with a plan. You're no good to Edmund like this."

Savina finally nodded. "Very well. We'll get Margot to safety, and then we will find out what that bitch has done to my Edmund."

39

*S*avina was out of her mind with worry.

Only the thought of Margot's life at risk convinced her to go back to her home, with Margot, Callan, and King at her side.

King sent his newest recruit, that overgrown boy he called Beast, to keep an eye on Lucinda's home for any sign of Edmund.

"I wonder how long until Lucinda discovers Benedict's body," Savina mused as she let Mrs. Baker fuss over her, pouring her more tea and nudging food under her nose.

Savina took a bite of bread, forcing it down as her body rebelled.

But King and Margot were right. She needed her strength if she was going to face Lucinda and find out where Edmund was.

With all Lucinda and Benedict had said in the cellar…

Savina forced the food down with a hard swallow.

Lucinda had known where Edmund was heading. She'd been ahead of them this whole time.

King entered the kitchen and Savina's head came up. Her

heart sank when he shook his head. He'd been checking in with his crew regularly for any sign of Edmund at his home or on the road into town.

Either he'd already come back and wasn't at home or he was still on his way to see Lucinda's first husband.

"Have some more tea," Margot urged.

Savina reached for her cup with a sigh. "Between you and Mrs. Baker, I feel outright henpecked."

Margot smiled, and not for the first time since Savina first caught sight of her sister, she noticed the change in her. She looked healthy and well, and…

She caught Margot exchanging a look with that giant friend of hers, a smile on her lips.

She looked happy. Content.

Savina's heart lightened at the sight of Margot's happiness. She'd yet to hear the whole story of how Margot's would-be assassin—yes, that confession came as quite the shock—became her…well, she supposed Callan was now Margot's would-be husband if those heated glances and shared smiles were anything to go by.

And Savina was glad. More than anyone, Margot deserved that sort of happiness. She'd always wanted a loyal husband with a handful of children running around. If Callan could give her that, then Savina would be forever grateful to him.

Margot would have her happy future, even if their past was anything but.

Her stomach twisted into knots as she considered her own future. With Edmund missing, it seemed impossibly bleak.

She wasn't certain at what point he'd become so integral to her happiness, but she could no longer imagine a life without him at her side.

He understood her in a way no one ever had. He gave her

safety and confidence and freedom in a way she suspected no one else ever could.

He was her other half. She was meant for him.

And by God, if Lucinda had harmed him in any way...

She shot to her feet. "I'm going back there."

"I'm going too," Margot said.

Callan glared at her, and Savina did too.

"I don't think that's wise, Snow," King warned. "You're the one she's after."

Callan wrapped an arm around her. "I need you to stay safe. I will go." He shared a look with Margot that Savina couldn't read. "I'll finish this."

Margot bit her lip, but then she nodded. "Do it. None of us will be safe otherwise."

"I'm coming with you," King clipped.

Savina turned to her friend. "Please, stay with Margot. I need to know that she's safe, and there's no one else I'd trust with her life."

King and Margot both seemed to be fighting the urge to protest, but in the end, King nodded. "Yeah. All right." He turned to Callan. "I'll send some of my boys to have your back."

Callan nodded, and Savina and King both turned away to give Margot and Callan privacy as they said goodbye with a kiss.

"How will you get in?" King asked Savina. "Same way we left?"

She shook her head, her mind busy working. She'd been so angry with Edmund for the way he'd brought her into society, but his reasoning was sound.

"I'm more at risk if no one knows I'm there," she said. "The best thing I can do is walk in through the front door."

"You won't get in looking like that," Margot said from behind her.

"Come with me then," Mrs. Baker said, wiping her hands. "I'll get one of the maids and we'll do what we can to hide your bruises and fix your hair."

Savina hated the idea of wasting any time, but she supposed they were right. She wouldn't get past the front door looking like this...or without an invitation.

She turned to King as she followed Mrs. Baker to the stairs. "King, have one of your boys send a message to Miss Vivian Mane..."

* * *

Savina waited just down the street from her childhood home. Carriages lined the street, and laughter and music could be heard coming from the ball.

She fidgeted with her cloak, grateful that Callan was hiding just around the corner. He was out of sight, but she was well aware of his presence.

Neither of them had been pleased to leave Margot's side, but they had to trust that King and his crew could look after her.

She'd never be safe until Lucinda was out of the picture.

Savina peered into the dark and let out a sigh of relief when she spotted Vivian heading toward her, walking so fast it was nearly a run as she glanced back over her shoulder.

When she spotted Savina, she threw her arms around her. "Oh, I'm so happy to see you. I've been so worried! Mrs. Baker came to see me when she couldn't find you and... where have you been?"

Savina patted her friend's back. "I'm all right now, and that's what matters."

Vivien pulled back and her eyes narrowed on Savina's face. "Are you...are those bruises?"

Savina tried to smile but it hurt too badly so she just

pulled her friend back in for another embrace. "I promise I will explain everything after all is said and done, but for now, I really must go into the ball. I must find Edmund and—"

"But Edmund is here," Vivian interrupted.

Savina blinked at her. Some part of her wondered if she was still dreaming. "He's...here?"

Vivian nodded so eagerly, her headpiece tilted and she was forced to right it. "He's here, now. I only saw him at a distance but everyone is whispering about the state he was in. I heard Lady Arbor say he was most distressingly dirty and was riled like a bull ready to charge!"

"He's here..." Savina started toward the townhome.

"Savina, wait. Here." Vivian handed her an invitation.

"Thank you, dear. And I promise, I will explain everything just as soon as I can."

Vivian waved her off. "Go, go. I wish you luck, Savina."

"Thank you, my friend!"

40

*E*dmund shook with rage.

This fury was overwhelming, made all the worse by the helplessness that came with it.

"Where is she?" he roared.

But Lucinda merely smiled from where she leaned against his desk in the study. "My, my. I never thought I'd see the day that the high and mighty prince lost his wits over a no-good little whore—"

He caught Lucinda by the throat, and the bitch had the nerve to laugh.

"You're not a killer, Edmund," she taunted.

"You have no idea what I've done," he growled. "Or what I will do to find the woman I love."

He tightened his grip until her eyes went wide and her hands came to his wrist.

He leaned in close, letting her see the all-consuming insanity that came with spending hours riding through the night, not knowing what was happening to the woman who was his heart.

"If you hurt her, I swear to God—"

"I'll tell you," she whispered.

The party continued unawares outside these walls, the music swelling as people laughed and danced, oblivious to the anger raging through Edmund's soul.

He loosened his grip, taking a small step back while she soothed her neck with trembling fingers.

"Let me call for Benedict," she said. "He'll take you to her—"

"I wouldn't bother."

Edmund's heart stopped at the sound of her voice behind him. Hope and joy and disbelief ripped through him as he spun with an elated smile that quickly disintegrated.

Savina.

His Savina.

Hovering in the doorway, a vision in her ballgown, her hair piled high and...she'd been wounded. He could tell by the haunted look in her eyes, the puffy shape of her cheek.

"Ah, my incessant stepdaughter," Lucinda sneered.

"You're hurt." He strode toward her, reaching Savina in a few short strides, and crushing her in his arms the moment he was close.

That was when he realized she was trembling.

His love was trembling.

"I thought you were gone," she whispered.

The agony in her voice ripped his chest to shreds and he clutched her close as if he could make her a part of himself if he held on tightly enough. "I thought I'd lost you too."

"Well," Lucinda drew the word out behind them. "I see you've managed to escape death once again. You're like an insect that refuses to be crushed."

Savina stiffened in his arms, and Edmund turned to see that Lucinda had a pistol trained on them.

"It would be admirable," Lucinda continued. "If it wasn't such a nuisance."

Edmund shifted so he was in front of Savina, but she fought him, struggling to be seen.

"Lucinda, I wouldn't do that if I were you," Savina warned.

"And why not?" The woman smirked, the gloating look in her eyes enough to make Edmund's blood boil all over again.

"Because I know where your son is. And let me assure you that it is not at the ball. And that vile leech will not come running when you call for him."

The room went deathly still as Lucinda's smile faded and her gaze hardened on Savina.

Edmund shifted, trying to get between them, but Savina's voice held a note of confidence and her gaze when she looked up at him said clearly, *Trust me.*

"Where is he?" Lucinda snapped.

Savina edged out from behind Edmund, her smile small and coy. "Come with me and I'll show you."

"What did you do to him?" Genuine fear flickered behind her malevolent glare.

Edmund glanced at Savina. He could ask the same. Savina had a smug air about her as she headed toward the office's back door which led to the kitchen and servants' quarters.

"Surely you noticed he was missing," Savina said. She seemed oblivious to the gun that was still pointed at her.

But then again, she knew she held the power just now.

"He's out," Lucinda clipped. She seemed to be trying to convince herself. "He'll be back…"

Savina paused at the top of the cellar steps. "Are you sure about that?"

Lucinda's eyes narrowed and then she was racing down the stone steps, Savina right behind her and Edmund in the rear.

They'd only just reached the bottom when Edmund heard Lucinda's blood-curdling scream. "Benedict! No!"

Savina sighed and Edmund stared in horrified fascination as Lucinda threw herself over the corpse of her son.

The smell was putrid, and the air dank and thick.

The pistol was forgotten at her side and Edmund lunged for it. He caught it and aimed it at Lucinda, who was staggering to her feet.

"You," the woman hissed. She was staring at Savina with murder in her eyes. "You did this."

"I wish I had," Savina said. "But no. It wasn't me."

Lucinda took a step toward Savina, her eyes wild with rage. "I will kill you for this. I will kill you!" With a feral cry, she lunged for Savina, her sharp nails scraping at her step-daughter's throat.

Savina stepped back, raising her arms to defend herself as Edmund aimed to shoot. But before he could, an arrow whizzed past him and struck Lucinda directly in the heart.

She let out a horrified whimper, staring in wide-eyed shock as she crumpled to the floor.

The room fell silent.

Savina's soft pants were the only thing to disrupt the eerie stillness, until Edmund spun, trying to spot this new danger. He raised his pistol in warning, but Savina rushed to his side, placing a hand on his arm and lowering the weapon. "He's on our side," she assured him.

And then, from out of the shadows, came a towering brute of a man. For someone so broad and tall, he moved quietly in the cellar, coming to stand beside them, looking down at the woman he'd killed.

"Thank you, Callan," Savina whispered. To Edmund, she explained, "This was the man Lucinda sent to kill Margot…"

In a few sentences, Savina filled him in on what he'd missed. Including how Benedict had come to die, and how Margot was safe with King.

"Go," Callan said when she was through and Edmund had her tucked safely in his arms. "I'll take care of the bodies."

Edmund frowned. "I can't let you—"

"You'll be the first person they suspect," Callan said simply. "Go. Be seen." His gaze flickered to Savina and back to him. "Both of you."

After a moment, Edmund nodded. "You're right. Thank you for your help."

"For Margot," he said simply.

Edmund felt a smile tug at his lips. That much he could understand. For the first time in his life, he fully grasped what it meant to love another more than himself. "Still, we owe you."

Savina tugged on his arm. "Come, let us be seen and make some excuse about their absence."

Edmund nodded, already leading them toward the cellar steps. "You're right. This night isn't over yet."

41

$\mathcal{T}$he rest of the night was torture.

Savina managed to get a message out through one of King's crew to Margot and King, letting them know that the nightmare was over.

For the most part.

"Dear, you really ought to have stayed home to rest after such an accident." The viscountess addressing her was fussing over the worst bruise, which no amount of powder had been able to conceal.

"I tried to tell her that," Vivian cut in, mercifully ending the lecture. "But Savina was so very eager to attend her stepmother's ball."

The viscountess tutted and muttered something about impatience and young people, but she eventually walked away.

"Thank you," Savina breathed.

Vivian smiled. "My pleasure. I take it now is not the time for you to tell me all that I've missed...?" She arched a brow, her smile mischievous.

Savina laughed. "My dear, I'm afraid you'd faint if I told

you all. But I will tell you this. My sister is safe now. We both are."

Vivian's smile grew. "That's all I need to know. Does that mean she'll be joining you here in London for the remainder of the Season?"

Savina hesitated, her gaze seeking out Edmund, who seemed to tower above the crowd around him. Tall, gallant, and the epitome of poise even after all they'd been through. They hadn't had time to discuss what they'd do next...but they couldn't stay here.

"We cannot stay," she said slowly.

Vivian sighed. "I was afraid you'd say that."

Savina reached for her friend's hands, all her worry for the girl returning. "Come with us."

"What?" Vivian blinked in surprise.

"I mean it. I know you're loyal to your father, but this match is wretched. No girl your age should be forced to marry a man like that—"

"Savina," Vivian interrupted gently. "I love that you worry about me, but I assure you...I've made my decision and I am quite resolved to see it through."

Savina eyed her friend, looking for any hint of weakness, but it seemed Vivian might be just as stubborn as she was. With a sigh, she kissed the girl's cheek. "I'll stay in touch. And if you ever need me..."

Vivian squeezed her hands. "Thank you. Just knowing I have a friend out there in the world is a comfort to me."

Vivian's attention was caught by her father, who stood with her ancient, lecherous old fiancé. Her smile faltered but then she turned to Savina with her chin held high. "I must go. But I do hope I'll see you again one day."

Savina nodded, her throat tight. "I hope so too, my dear."

She watched the other girl go, and knew Edmund was at her side before he even spoke a word. "Are you all right?"

Savina turned to face him, drawing in a deep breath and saying yet another prayer of gratitude that he was safe and well, by her side.

And Margot too was finally out of harm's way.

"Just tired, that's all."

He made a sound of agreement. "I'll have you in bed soon, my love."

Her lips twitched as that wicked impulse flared. Her tone went high and breathy. "Promise, stepfather?"

His eyes glinted with hunger. "I very nearly lost you, my love. Just as soon as we're somewhere safe, I won't be letting you out of my sight...or my bed, for that matter."

She grinned, wishing she could lean into him now. She ached to be back in his arms, in his bed...

But they still had work to do and plans to make.

For what felt like an eternity now, Savina and Edmund had been spreading lies wherever they went at this dreadful ball. They made excuses for the hostess's absence, and Edmund spun a tall tale about Benedict's desire to leave for the country earlier than intended.

They were counting on the fact that gossip would spread, and their stories would stick, which would buy them time to leave the country before the bodies were discovered.

And they had to be discovered if Savina and Margot stood any chance of inheriting what was rightfully theirs.

Savina suspected neither of them cared much about the money or property that was owed them anymore. As Edmund pointed out when they'd had a moment to talk privately...he had enough to provide for all of them until this latest scandal died down.

It was the principle of the matter, though. One day she might have a child...

Margot definitely wanted children. And the future generations deserved to know where they came from and where they belonged.

"I can hardly wait to be on our way," she said as they both nodded and smiled at a passing couple.

"Where?" He lifted her gloved hand and led her onto the dance floor. "Where would you like to go next? The world is yours for the taking, my love. Name the place and that shall be our next home."

She smiled up at him. "Wherever you are, that is my home."

The affection in his eyes was very nearly her undoing. After all she'd been through, in the cellar and ever since...

To think, it was the sight of unabashed love and tenderness in her lover's eyes that nearly made her crumple.

His arms tightened around her. "Not much longer now, my love."

"I know, it's just..." She swallowed down the urge to weep. But these tears were ones of relief, of anticipation...

They were tears of joy over all that was to come.

"What is it?" he asked.

"I can see a future now, Edmund. I never could before. I'd never been able to see beyond surviving the next day, the next night. But here, with you...the future is there before me and it's beautiful."

His arms tightened and his gaze grew dark. "Some part of me knew that I was madly in love with you the very first moment we met. But when I thought you were in danger..." His jaw worked and his eyes grew fiery with emotion. "When I thought I might lose you..."

She bit her lip. God, how she wished she could go up on her toes and kiss him, reassure him she wasn't going anywhere.

He tugged her closer despite the crowd around them. And then he dipped his head to whisper in her ear. "It was all too clear to me that you're more than the love of my life, Savina. You are my life. You are everything to me." He brushed his lips over her temple. "I cannot live without you."

Her lungs hitched and her heart raced because...she understood completely. She felt the same. "I love you, Edmund," she whispered. "As soon as we're out of this nightmare of a ball, I plan to show you just how much."

"I have a better idea."

She pulled back to see his eyes burning bright with desire, along with the same overwhelming need that was in her heart.

Her limbs went heavy and heat coiled in her belly. "Oh yes, please," she breathed.

His lips twitched at the corners. "Please, hmm? You've learned your manners. What a good girl."

She batted her lashes. "I'd like to show you just how good and obedient I can be."

He leaned down and whispered in her ear. "The garden. Now."

Her hands shook with eagerness as she held onto Edmund's arm and let him steer them toward the back veranda.

"I'm afraid my stepdaughter needs some fresh air," Edmund murmured when someone tried to stop them.

He was guiding her with such force she knew without a doubt he needed it just as badly as she did. Release. Satisfaction. And above all, the reassurance that the other was there, safe and well and no longer in danger.

The air was brisk, which was good. It meant all the other couples had found a place indoors for their rendezvous.

Edmund eyed the garden, his gaze falling on the cluster of trees where Savina had found Margot waiting for her only earlier that day.

So much had changed since then. Relief nearly swallowed

her whole again and she found herself leaning against Edmund.

He brushed his lips over the top of her head. "I'm going to make sure you're safe and out of sight. You go back there and get ready for me."

Her blood was already pounding, her sex already growing wet...

"How shall I do that...Your Highness?"

His eyes flashed.

God, how she loved their games. Loved even more that he knew exactly what she desired.

He knew when she needed to be held, understood when she needed him to physically take control, and at moments like these...

He seemed to know exactly how to make her hot and ready.

Leaning down to whisper in her ear, he said, "Take off your underthings, get your tits out for me, and when I find you, you'd better be stroking your pussy..."

"Or what?" she asked, her voice so breathless she could barely be heard.

"Or you'll get a spanking, princess."

She shivered in the night air, anticipation building with each heartbeat. "Don't be long."

"Get your tight little cunny ready for me." He gave her arse a little slap that made her laugh. And then she was heading toward the trees, eager to do his bidding.

By the time he reached her, she'd done exactly as he'd asked. Her hand was lost in the sea of skirts and she arched her back, giving him a better view of her breasts.

Her gown was hanging off her shoulders, her undergarments tossed to the side.

She looked like a slattern. Like a wanton woman.

And maybe she was. She arched her neck as he leaned

over her, his growl of approval rippling over her sensitive skin.

Maybe she was wanton and dirty and naughty...

But only for this man.

And that was exactly how he wanted her.

"Touch me," she begged.

"Are you wet for me?" He had that commanding tone, the one that made her inner muscles clench, needy and ready for his thick cock.

She nodded, her fingers gliding through her wet folds, her breath coming in pants.

"Show me," he said.

She pulled her hand from between her thighs and showed it to him. His eyes half shut he slid her fingers into his mouth and sucked off her juices with a groan of approval. "You taste like heaven," he said when he removed her fingers from his mouth. Still holding her wrist in his tight grip he slid her hand down to cup his hard manhood.

Now it was her turn to groan, because...Good God, he was so hard and so thick. So ready for her.

"Do you feel what you do to me?"

She nodded.

"Say it."

"Yes, sir."

"And are you going to take that cock all the way inside you?" He slid a hand into the back of her hair and tugged so her head was bent back even further as he sucked and nipped at the sensitive skin of her neck.

"Y-yes," she whispered.

"Are you going to take your pounding like a good girl and then beg for more?"

"Oh, yes, yes..." Her hips started to rock as her aching sex throbbed with need for him. "Please..."

He licked her lower lip and then sucked it into his mouth. "Take what you want then, my naughty little ward."

She wasted no time unfastening his breeches, her breaths coming in short pants as he nudged her up against the tree trunk until her back was pressed against the bark and his knees were spreading her thighs.

He lifted her, and when he pinned her body against the rough trunk, her breasts crushed into this chest and his thick shaft pressed against her soft flesh...

She cried out at the perfection and his mouth was there to devour her cries.

The head of his cock probed her entrance, teasing her mercilessly as her hips rocked and jerked, trying to take more of him.

He chuckled darkly. "My needy little princess. Tell me what you want..."

"You. Inside me."

"And?"

She stilled, he was so close and the waiting was agony. She pressed her breasts against him, rubbing against him everywhere she could, the friction a sweet relief. But she needed more...

He caught her chin roughly and forced her gaze to meet his.

"Tell me what you need."

"You," she said simply.

She saw the satisfaction, the happiness, the sheer humbling unconditional love in his eyes. His voice was gruff with emotion. "Good girl." His kiss was achingly gentle, but then...

He shoved his cock into her, hard and deep.

Anything but gentle. He was claiming her. Spearing her and taking her and...

Like always, he knew exactly what she needed.

The sudden thick invasion made her vision go dark and her thoughts scatter.

"I'll always take care of my naughty little ward," his breath was hot against her ear. "I'll always give you what you need."

"Yes," she moaned, her eyes shutting as sensations flooded her. His hand cupped her breast, molding her flesh as he rocked his hips furiously.

"You're mine to take," he growled, nipping at her ear. "And I am yours to command."

A sob caught in her throat as the tension inside her built right alongside this swell of emotion. "Yes, Edmund. Yes, I'm yours."

"And I belong to you," he finished. "And tonight and every night you're going to take all the love I have to give you until I plant a baby in that belly of yours. Understand?"

Tears welled in her eyes at the image of her and Edmund…and their family. Their future.

"Yes, Edmund. Fill me up. I need it. I need you…"

He gave another hard thrust, his thick shaft filling her so completely she cried out. She was close. So close…

"Say it," he commanded, his voice alone driving her to the brink.

And she knew exactly what he needed to hear. What she needed to say.

"I love you."

The words set him off, and he pounded into her until she was shaking in his arms, coming apart at the seams.

She exploded in his arms and he came apart right after, but they stayed there and held each other tight for a long time after, murmuring words of love, promises for the future…

And sacred vows they would never break.

42

*M*argot wasn't sure she'd heard Callan right. "You...you want me to go?"

Callan's stare was intense and unreadable.

Only hours before she'd flown into his arms when he'd finally returned to Savina's home. He'd caught her by the waist and held her close.

He didn't need to tell her what he'd done. She'd heard it all from Savina and Edmund.

And he'd done it for her. All of it. She shared the blood on his hands, and somehow that only seemed to solidify their inexplicable bond.

Edmund had called him away after they'd eaten and bathed, and now here he was...telling her to go.

"I...but I thought..." She fought against the wave of hurt.

She hadn't had much time to plan for her future, of course. She'd been merely trying to survive, and waiting to hear if her sister and lover had made it...

But she did know that somewhere in her mind an image had formed.

A dream, perhaps.

A dream of living with Callan in his stone cottage, surrounded by little ones and…and…

And now he was urging her to get on the ship and travel to the continent with Savina and Edmund?

She didn't want to leave Savina, this much was true. But she'd thought Callan would want her to stay. Her lower lip trembled, which made him frown.

"You want me to leave?" she said again.

"He's a prince." Callan's brows drew down. "He can give you a good life. And you want to be with your sister."

"Yes, but…" Drat. She didn't want to cry, but she didn't want to say goodbye either.

She'd thought…she'd thought this was something more.

For her it was, but maybe for him…

"If I go, what will you do?" she asked.

His brows hitched slightly as if that surprised him. "Follow."

She blinked a few times, afraid to hope. But also… "You'd follow *me*?"

He touched her cheek so gently it made her chest tighten and her belly flutter. "I told you, Margot. You are mine now. But…" His gaze flickered over her features like he was trying to read her every thought. "But you are not my prisoner. I won't hold you back."

She drew in a shaky breath as relief and happiness rose up at a dizzying speed.

His brows drew down. "But I won't let you go either."

It seemed to be a warning. As if maybe she'd protest.

She broke the silence with a loud, tinkling laugh that she couldn't help. When his brows knit together in confusion she went up on tiptoe and grabbed his head to pull him down so she could rain kisses all over his face until he let out a low chuckle that made her grin.

She loved all his growls and grunts, but she decided here and now that he needed to laugh more often.

And she'd happily spend the rest of her life making sure he did just that.

She dropped down onto her heels. "Callan, I don't want you to let me go. I want to stay with you."

His chest rose and fell as he nodded. "Okay."

She grinned. "Okay."

And just like that, it was settled.

He wrapped his hands around her waist and lifted her until her face was even with his. He rested his forehead against hers. "You're my family now. You know that."

Her heart nearly burst. This man hadn't had a family since he was a child, and she knew exactly how much that meant to him.

"And you're mine," she whispered.

He kissed her lips gently, and only pulled back far enough to look in her eyes. "Marry me?"

She burst out in another laugh, this one bubbling up out of sheer happiness. "Yes. Definitely yes. Absolutely yes."

He chuckled again as he crushed her to his chest and kissed her thoroughly.

* * *

LESS THAN TWENTY-FOUR HOURS LATER, they were on their way. The four of them embarking on their next adventure.

Or, they would be soon enough. They hadn't boarded the ship bound for France yet, but they were at the docks, surrounded by King and his crew who seemed to think it was their duty to protect them until they left the country.

"I can't believe you arranged all of this so quickly," Margot eyed the ship. Her heart fluttered with excitement at the prospect of the wide open sea, and whatever lay beyond.

She and Savina had spent hours talking about where they'd like to go. Edmund and Callan had left it to them.

They planned to start on the continent, but Margot had heard enough tales of the wide open prairies of America, and Savina was curious about New York City, and...

She suspected that was where they'd end up eventually.

There'd be no rush to return to London for any of them, but least of all Edmund and Savina, who'd be leaving speculation and scandal in their wake.

While Savina and Margot had discussed their future travels, Edmund and Callan had talked at length about security.

Well...Edmund had talked at length. But Callan had listened with an intensity that Margot adored.

Edmund had seemed to understand without being told that Callan was loath to take charity, even if Edmund did owe him their lives. And so a deal had been struck. Callan would be the head of security for this royal party, and it was a task Callan took seriously.

Even now, he and Edmund were trying to convince King to leave Vestry Lane behind and join them in far more luxurious settings.

"We are indebted to you, King," the prince said. "Come with us. Join Callan's team...we'll make sure you're paid handsomely."

King was shaking his head before Edmund even finished.

"I appreciate the offer, but I can't take it." His tone was determined.

Margot sidled up next to him, and Savina linked arms with him on his other side. "King, we adore you for being the very best friend two helpless girls in a rookery could ask for," Savina started.

"But," Margot continued. "If you think we're going to just leave you behind to face life in that rookery with Madame Bernadette and the like..."

Savina scowled. "You can think again."

Edmund and Callan exchanged a knowing look.

"You ought to know better than to argue with my Savina," Edmund said mildly.

"Margot too," Callan added. "She's small but determined."

This made even King chuckle, but he shook his head. "I was helping friends, that's all."

Margot nudged him gently. "But you've got other friends in Vestry Lane. Ones who rely on you…"

"Not to mention the helpless young girls and husbandless mothers who could use your protection."

Edmund stepped in, arms crossed. "How much?"

King arched a brow. "Pardon?"

"How much to stake a claim in Vestry Lane?" Edmund said.

Savina brightened. "How much to drive Madame Bernadette and her like out of that alley?"

"How much to make it safe for your crew?" Margot added.

King's eyes narrowed as he gave it some thought. He threw out a number with a bravado that made Margot swallow a smile.

Savina too looked like she might laugh aloud. No doubt King thought he was asking too much. To him, it was a fortune.

But Edmund considered the number and then said. "Double it. That's the amount I'll have my man of business deliver to you."

King's eyes widened.

"Do me a favor," Savina said. "Keep helping the helpless."

"Like you helped us." Margot smiled. She gave his cheek a kiss and Savina did the same.

"Good luck, Savvy," he rasped, obviously still in shock. He turned to Margot, "Godspeed, Snow."

And with that, he and his crew took off when the ship began to board.

Savina linked arms with Margot as their men followed closely behind, ever alert to any danger that might have followed.

"We've done it, Snow," Savina said softly. "We've left the rookery, and all the horrid memories behind."

"Father would be pleased," Margot murmured. "Even if we're not living the lives he expected for us."

Savina grinned. "I have to believe that he wanted us to find love above all else…"

Savina and Margot glanced back at the same time and then they turned to one another with matching smiles of sheer, giddy joy.

"And we have done that," Margot said with a giggle.

Savina laughed. "Yes, we certainly have."

Made in United States
Troutdale, OR
10/09/2023

13544048R00246